DRAGONS IN OUR MIDST
STORY WORLD READING ORDER

To the keepers of the light.

When we set flame to a candle, we bring light to the world.

When we build stone upon stone, we erect the temple of God.

But when candle and stone are removed from the foundation,

The light is captured, imprisoned, destroyed.

How great is the darkness!

Let us never forget our first love,

And our light will spread across the world.

Other Books by Bryan Davis

The Candlestone

Bryan Davis

The Candlestone
Volume 2 in the Dragons in our Midst series

Copyright © 2004 by Bryan Davis
Published by Scrub Jay Journeys
P.O. Box 512
Middleton, TN 38052

www.scrubjayjourneys.com
email: info@scrubjayjourneys.com
Author website - www.daviscrossing.com

Print Edition ISBN 13: 978-1-946253-96-5
Kindle Edition: 978-1-946253-94-1
ePub Edition: 978-1-946253-95-8
Twelfth Printing - July 2018

DRAGONS IN OUR MIDST, ORACLES OF FIRE, and CHILDREN OF THE BARD are registered trademarks of Bryan Davis.

Cover designed by Bright Boy Design, Inc., Chattanooga, Tennessee

Printed in the United States of America

Merlin's Prophecy

When hybrid meets the fallen seed
The virgin seedling flies;
An orphaned waif shall call to me
When blossom meets the skies.

The child of doubt will find his rest
And meet his virgin bride;
A dragon shorn will live again
Rejecting Eden's pride.

A slayer comes and with his host
He fights the last of thee;
But faith alone shall win the war
The test of those set free.

A king shall rise of Arthur's mold,
The prophet's book in hand;
He takes the sword from mountain stone
To rescue captive bands.

cave

omega
entrance

weapons
cache

boy's dorm

girl's dorm

bonnie
(diver)

lab table with beakers

lab table with flasks

flexible tubes

flexible tubes

pedestal for candlestone

wall safe

panel

derrick
(anchor)

restore

panel

master control

ashley's seat

photoreceptor
collector

drop ceiling area

open cavern area

alpha
entrance

The
Underground
Labratory

The Art of War

With sword and stone, the holy knight,
Darkness as his bane,
Will gather warriors in the light
Cast in heaven's flame

Out of the blackness a growling voice rumbled. "She will come." The rough words reverberated, bouncing off shrouded walls that echoed dying replies.

A solitary man listened in the dark room, lit only by flickers of soft light coming from his hand, a dozen fireflies in a jar. They danced with hopeless wings in stale air, waiting for death to arrive, their distress signals serving to guide the man as he paced the stone floor. "And what makes you so sure she'll come?" he said, his voice tiny and squeaking by comparison. "She won't trust me. Why should she?"

The rumbling voice responded. "You don't understand her; you never did. She listens to a call that rises beyond your senses. She has faith." The growl changed to a deep sigh. "But, alas! What would you know about faith?"

"More than you think." He held up the jar and watched the dimming flashes. "I do know this; it was by her faith that you're in this predicament. I hear she was quite handy with that sword."

The growl deepened, its bass tones making the ground tremble. "If you really think she knew I would end up in this prison, then you're a bigger fool than I thought." After a few seconds, the echoes died away again, and the voice became soft and melancholy. "You have no worries. She will come. She is driven by forces you cannot possibly understand."

When the last flicker of light blinked out, the man opened the jar's lid. With a quick shake, he dumped the dead fireflies onto the floor. "Very well." His voice stretched into a foreboding snarl. "We shall see."

2

    •   •   •   •   •   •

Swish! The gleaming sword swiped by Billy's face, its razor point slashing the air and its deadly edge humming a threatening tune in his ear. He jumped back, his cheeks turning red hot. Another mistake like that and this fight would be over in a hurry. He planted his feet on the tile floor and raised his sword, careful to keep it from stabbing the low ceiling.

Eyeing his opponent warily, he slowly counted to ten. He had to keep his cool. He would never win if his brain was fried. Besides, the sword weighed a ton. He had to conserve energy. Drops of sweat pooled on his brow and streamed down, stinging his eyes and blurring the light from the ceiling fan. Its whirling blades blew a cooling breeze through his hair, a welcome relief in the spacious but stuffy rec room.

His opponent charged, his sword raised to strike. Billy dodged, swiping at the attacking weapon from the side as it passed. The clank of metal on metal rattled his brain. His opponent twirled and set his feet, bending his knees to brace himself. With his sword held out in defense, he waited.

Billy puffed a loud, weary sigh as he readied his sword for an attack of his own. Heavy, sweat-drenched clothes clung to his body, and the weight of the hefty blade dragged his tired arms downward. He dared not let it fall.

His opponent, a tall, lanky man of considerable years, was quick and agile at the start of the battle but now slower and deliberate. He had spunk, though, a real kick-start in his old engine, and that last charge proved his stellar swordsmanship.

Billy lifted his sword and pointed it at his mentor, recalling what he had taught. *A knight opposes his enemy face to face. A stab in the back is the way of the coward; a pre-emptive strike of death is a strike of fear. If you must fight, attack your enemy head on. That is the way of valor.*

Billy took a deep breath, charged, and swung his sword. His opponent met the blow, and the swords clashed once again. This time Billy pushed downward, then back up in full circle, wrenching his opponent's sword from his grasp and flinging it away. He dashed to where the ringing blade fell and stamped both feet on its polished steel. He lifted his own sword and with a pretend scowl dared his opponent to approach.

"Way to go, Billy!" Walter shouted.

Bonnie joined in. "Yay, Billy! You were awesome!"

A surge of heat prickled Billy's face as he drew in a deep, satisfying breath while nodding toward his friends. "Thanks."

Walter clapped Billy on the back and helped him remove his helmet. "I told you you'd win if you used my helmet. Hambone licked it for good luck."

Billy accepted a towel from Bonnie and wiped his forehead, pushing his damp hair to the side. Bonnie pressed her thumbs behind the front straps of her ever-present backpack, as locks of her straight blonde-streaked hair draped her navy polo shirt.

Her blue eyes sparkled, greeting Billy with silent messages of congratulations.

A hearty voice boomed from nearby. "Well done, William!" The British accent made its owner easy to identify, his teacher, his mentor, his friend, and now, his conquered opponent, Professor Hamilton. The professor approached with deliberate, stiff steps, and his tall form cast a shadow across Billy's face, his own face veiled by a helmet and face guard. "William? Are you all right?"

Billy wanted to say, "I'm fine," but his muscles ached, a good, satisfying ache. He lifted his wet shirt, peeling it away from his shoulder. "I'm sore, but I'll be all right." He laid the sword on the floor and pulled off his protective gloves. "Do you think I'm ready? I mean, we've still never fought all out. And we're not really using the same equipment those guys had on the mountain, you know, the authentic battle armor and stuff."

"No, we're not." The professor picked up his vanquished sword and slid it into a scabbard on his back. "We battled *all out*, as you say, with foam swords early in your training. Just now we did restrain our thrusts with our metal replicas, but it was still a strenuous workout. Yet, until we can combine the weight of authentic swords and armor with the passion of unrestrained zeal, we'll not be sure you're ready."

"Right. That's why I want to train with the real stuff."

The professor unfastened the scabbard and tossed it onto a nearby sofa. "Unfortunately, I have no true armored helmets, and my fencing guards are inadequate for mortal combat. I'm afraid it's not safe to attempt an unrestrained match."

Billy ran his thumb along the edge of his blade, leaving a shallow slice in his skin. "Is it *safe* if we don't prepare for real?"

The professor slid off his headgear, a modified Washington Redskins helmet, his white matted hair pulling up with it,

4

creating a frenzy of wet strands. "Your point is well taken, William, but we would have to find a better sparring partner for you. Your potential opponent will not likely be a creaking old man such as myself." He ran his hand through his tangled hair and examined the logo on his helmet. "And I'll have to find suitable armor. The authentic helmets I've seen don't have an American Indian on the side."

Walter took Billy's sword and rubbed the etchings on the blade. "This looks like a picture of two dragons fighting, but what do the other marks mean?"

The professor stroked the blade with his index finger. "There's quite a story behind these runes." He gave a tired sigh and gestured with his head toward the hallway. "Walter, I trust that your father won't mind if we build a fire and sit in the den while I tell the story. Although our swordplay generated considerable body heat, we will cool off quickly. But first, I must visit the water clo—I mean, the restroom, and clean up a bit."

Billy tugged at his plastered shirt again. "And I have to change these sweaty clothes."

Walter ran ahead. "I'll start the fire!"

❖　　❖　　❖　　❖　　❖　　❖

Bonnie joined Walter in the den. Kneeling, he held a lit match next to a rolled-up newspaper that had been stuffed under a pile of logs in the fireplace. The end of the paper flared, but the flame soon died away.

Bonnie adjusted a strap on her backpack and peeked over his shoulder. She had been wondering what he had seen on the mountain after he kept the dragon slayer from following her that day back in November. Now was her chance to probe him for the truth. Had he discovered her dragon wings? She gently cleared her throat. "I was just thinking, Walter. When I was watching Billy fight just now, it reminded me of when you hit Devin with the tree limb."

Walter tore a second match from a matchbook. "Yeah? It wasn't much. It's not so brave to bash someone's head when he's not looking." He struck the match and set the end of the paper on fire again.

Bonnie watched the struggling flame and shifted her weight to her heels. "I was wondering, though, about how you showed up in the field to help us, right when we ran into the search party. Did you follow us down the slope?"

Walter struck a third match and held it against the newspaper, waiting for it to catch. He shrugged. "I saw your tracks in the snow. It wasn't hard."

Bonnie crouched next to the hearth. "What I mean is, did you see us on the way down? Or did you just follow the tracks?"

"Ouch!" Walter shook his hand and sucked his scorched finger. "I was super pumped after whacking Devin, so everything's sort of jumbled in my memory. I don't remember all the details." He rose, still sucking his finger. "What difference does it make?"

Bonnie straightened and folded her hands behind her. "When you met us at the bottom of the trail, did you see anything peculiar? I mean, it seems like you're Johnny-on-the-spot all the time, so—"

"So you're wondering if I *spotted* anything?" Walter dried his finger on his jeans and flashed a grin. "Maybe I'm like an angel. Maybe God puts me in the right place at the right time."

Bonnie smiled in return, reading Walter's playful tone. "You think so?"

"Why not?" He pointed toward his back. "Except I don't have any wings. That would be cool." He stuffed the empty matchbook into his pocket and rushed toward the doorway. "I think Dad bought some starter logs. I'll go get them and another matchbook." He almost slammed into Billy as he dashed from the room, deftly spinning around his friend. "Back in a minute. Gotta get something to start the fire."

* * * * * *

Billy, now wearing a fresh long-sleeved shirt and his favorite cargo pants, spied the blackened matches at the front of the fireplace, then winked at Bonnie while nodding toward the door. Crouching at the hearth, he leaned toward the logs and waited for Bonnie to block the room's entrance. She stepped into the doorway, using her body as a shield to hide Billy's deepest secret, the dragon trait handed down to him by his father. Walter was a great friend, but Billy didn't want to let him know about his dragon heritage, at least not yet.

Billy took in a deep breath and blew a stream of fire at the pile of oak, spreading it evenly across the wood. Within seconds, the logs ignited, shooting flames and smoke into the flue above.

7

"Knock, knock."

Bonnie spun. "Walter!"

"Mind if I come in?"

Billy jerked himself to his feet, and Bonnie jumped away from the door. Walter sauntered in with a bag of paraffin kindling and set it next to the hearth. He nodded toward the blazing logs and smiled. "Nice job. You got better matches than I do?"

Bonnie set a hand over her mouth, apparently holding back a snicker, and Billy folded his arms across his chest. "I guess you could say that."

The professor entered, his face washed and his hair plastered and parted down the middle. He carried the sword at his side and sat in an easy chair next to the fire. His face beamed. "William, I must reiterate my pride in your effort. You were outstanding with the sword."

"Yeah," Walter said. "You rocked!"

Billy bowed his head, his cheeks warming. "Thanks again."

The professor's eyes narrowed at Walter. "Rocked?"

"Yeah … rocked. You know; he was awesome. He really kicked … uh … gluteus maximus."

"Is that similar to being the cat's pajamas?" the professor asked.

"The cat's pajamas?" Walter said. "What's that?"

"It's an American idiom. It refers to someone who is well liked because of his accomplishments. I see, however, that it has passed out of common usage." The professor gestured for his three students to gather around. "Shall we discuss the sword?"

He placed the blade on his lap and pointed at the etched writing. "Some of these lines are inscriptions in an ancient dialect." He touched the blade. "This one says, roughly speaking, 'May the Lady's purity never depart from the one found worthy to draw the sword.'"

"The lady?" Bonnie said. "Who's the lady?"

"The Lady of the Lake. The legends say that she gave Excalibur to King Arthur."

Bonnie rubbed her finger along the raised pattern on the wooden hilt. "Can a lady be strong enough to battle with a sword like this?"

"I think a sturdy woman could wield it." The professor handed it to her. "Give it a try."

Bonnie grasped the hilt with both hands and held the blade up, her feet spread as if bracing for an attack. She waved the sword through a series of pretend maneuvers while the professor's eyes followed the blade's swings and parries. "You seem to have no trouble carrying it," he said.

Bonnie returned the sword to the professor's lap. "I guess it's not as heavy as I thought it would be."

The professor slid the sword back into its scabbard. "It's probably not as heavy as the real Excalibur, but its mass is substantial."

"It seemed heavy to me," Billy said.

"As it should, William. You worked with it for nearly an hour today, nonstop. But I perceive that Miss Silver is considerably stronger than her frame would suggest."

Bonnie's face flushed. "I'm sorry, Billy. I didn't mean to say—"

He waved a hand. "It's all right. I know what you meant."

Walter picked up the scabbard and examined its ornate designs, an embossed angelic creature with knights on each side bending a knee in respect. "Do you think those Arthur stories are true, Professor?"

A dreamy expression floated across Professor Hamilton's face, the dancing fire reflecting in his eyes. "Arthur is the stuff of legends, the search for the Holy Grail, the splendor of Camelot. It's hard to decide what is factual among the myriad tales." His scholarly air returned as he took the scabbard from Walter. "It seems that each new storyteller tried to outdo the previous one, not really caring whether or not his tale was true. Legends are, after all, not meant to be historical fact. For example, I certainly doubt the existence of a goddess in a lake, but I have no doubts that Arthur once wielded the great and mysterious Excalibur."

He ran a finger along the scabbard again, pausing on one of the worshipful knights. "This is a replica handed down through many generations. Its shape and details are based on legends and descriptions in journals. Many tried to copy Excalibur's image, but no one could reproduce its power."

Bonnie's eyebrows rose. "It had power?"

The professor wrapped his fingers around the hilt and drew the blade out a few inches. "Power incomprehensible.

9

Whosoever held the sword in battle could not be defeated, as long as the wielder was pure of heart. And the offensive powers in the hands of the holy were a terrible sight to behold."

Bonnie put her hands behind her back and shifted her weight toward her toes. "Does the real Excalibur still exist?"

The professor glanced from Billy to Walter to Bonnie, as if searching for something in each set of eyes. "I have no doubt about it, Miss Silver. I have hunted for it throughout the world, following many rumors and obscure tales. Finding it would make my life complete. You could say that it's something of a Holy Grail for me."

"What about the sword that guy took from Whittier's office?" Walter asked. "Didn't it have some kind of marks on it?"

The professor slid the sword into the scabbard. "Your memory is accurate, Walter. That sword had many similar characteristics, but I couldn't be sure of its identity. I would like to pursue that lead at the appropriate time." His gaze fell on Billy and Bonnie and lingered. "And I suspect that there are some people I know who might be able to enlighten me concerning its whereabouts."

Billy twisted his shoe on the carpet as if he were squishing a cockroach. How could the professor guess what was going on? He wasn't there when Bonnie battled the slayer in the mountain forest, and no one told him that Bonnie dropped the sword while flying away from the battle scene.

"In any case," the professor continued, "my sword is adequate for William's training. While this replica is valuable and one might think that we would not want to risk breaking it, its symbolism is paramount for his development. His skill in swordplay will become necessary before long. And there is no concern for the replica's safety. It is practically indestructible."

Billy, now warm and dry, stepped away from the dying fire. "When are you going to explain all that to me, I mean, the stuff I'm training for?"

"In due time, William. I'm just putting the pieces together myself." The professor rose to his feet and strolled around the room, holding the sword casually across his shoulder. "Since you were expected to be out of commission for quite a while, I sent our mystery book to a friend of mine, an expert in antiquities. He has completed his analysis and will return the book in time for class Monday. I assume that when we decipher it we will learn a great deal."

Billy folded his arms across his chest and rubbed his aching biceps. Thinking about that book and how it had come into their hands made him feel sore all over. During his ordeal on the mountain with the powerful dragon slayer, Billy sat against the trunk of a tree, his hands and feet bound. The slayer opened a book and claimed that reading from it would summon a dragon, whom the slayer wished to kill. The poem sounded sort of like English, but Billy couldn't understand it. Yet, Clefspeare, Billy's father in dragon form, showed up before the poem ended, making it unclear whether the words actually summoned him or he had sensed his son was in danger and flew to the rescue.

11

The professor stopped his pacing and gazed at the fireplace, sighing before turning toward his students again. "William, I hope you and Miss Silver will carefully consider telling me what you know." He fingered the designs on the replica's scabbard. "I have discerned that you're confused and frightened, and I understand completely. I believe I would be as well. Both of you were severely wounded, yet you have mended at a miraculous rate. These are among the many perplexing mysteries to be solved." He straightened, holding his head high. "I hope you will decide that you can trust me with your secrets.

To be quite frank, I think I have earned your trust." A smile appeared on his wrinkled face, though a hint of sadness crept into his eyes. "Good night, students." He turned and stepped quickly out of the room. Seconds later, the front door clicked open, then closed with a muffled clap.

Billy flopped into the easy chair and slapped his hands on the chair's arms. Bonnie sank onto the sofa with a sigh, her brow knitting into deep furrows. Walter sat on the other end of the sofa, his feet propped on the coffee table, one shoe on top of the other. He picked at his fingernails, then retied his shoes, his gaze wandering toward Billy and Bonnie every few seconds. He finally jumped up. "I'd better make sure Hambone's warm." With a graceful bound, he dashed from the room.

Billy set a hand to his ear. "Was Hambone whining?"

She smiled and shook her head. "Not a whine or a woof."

A sparkling gleam shone in Bonnie's eyes, though only the fading light from outside and a few dying embers in the fireplace illuminated the room. Billy sighed. "Either Walter has mind-to-mind connection with that dog or he knows more than we think."

"Uh-huh, I think he knows something."

"You do? Why?"

"Just some things he said to me today. And you know the professor's going to put all the pieces together before long."

"Yep. He'll figure it out sooner or later." Billy walked to the den's small window. As he looked out, his thoughts traveled to the distant horizon, hills stretching into tree-covered mountains. He pictured the leaf-strewn battle scene and the dark, breezy cave. Bonnie joined him. Together they gazed at the deepening winter—thick gray clouds, cold, leafy breezes bending naked trees, tiny snowflakes threatening to bring millions of their friends later that night.

Bonnie's phantom reflection appeared in the window, smiling and peaceful. Billy kept his eye on the transparent image and pushed his hands into his pockets. "I think I'd better talk to Dad. I've only seen him once since I got hurt, and I was still pretty bad off then. I didn't ask him about a bunch of stuff that doesn't make any sense."

She turned away from the window and leaned against the sill, bending forward to leave room for her backpack. "A bunch of stuff? Like what?"

Billy turned with her. "Like, what's the deal with the sword you used on the mountain? And what happened to the slayer and that crazy candlestone? Stuff like that. And if I'm going to tell the professor everything, my father should give his permission, don't you think? I mean, I know the professor's going to ask lots of questions, so I'd better have a few more answers ready." Billy set a hand on his stomach. His lips forming a circle, he created a perfect ring of smoke and pushed it into the air. "Besides," he added as the ring expanded, "I've been practicing fire breathing. I want to show my dad how I'm doing."

13

Bonnie put her hand through the ring, scattering the remaining smoke. "Are you going to ask your mom to fly with you back to the mountain?"

"Uh-huh. Tomorrow, if we can. We have a primitive airstrip up there now, so it's easy to get in and out."

"Is it all right if I come with you?"

"That would be great, but isn't tomorrow the big day, you know, the thirty-day deadline?"

Bonnie set a hand on her hip. "Right. I almost forgot. Mr. Foley wants to finish the adoption paperwork as soon as possible. The judge said he would sign it for us even though tomorrow's Sunday."

"Mr. Foley? Aren't you going to start calling him 'Dad'? That's what Walter calls him, except when he's acting crazy and calls him 'Pop.'"

She turned toward the window again and hitched up her backpack, her stare on the winter scene outside. "Not yet. That's going to be hard to get used to. I called my real father Daddy for so long. That is, until he betrayed me."

Billy turned with her once more. Tears welled in her eyes, and her pain drilled a hole in his heart. How could anyone, especially a father, give an awesome girl like Bonnie over to a dragon slayer? And now she was on the verge of being adopted by Walter's parents, two really cool adults who still had no clue about her dragon heritage. Although Walter's father knew about Bonnie's wings, he hadn't asked her to explain. He told her to take her time and tell her story when she was ready. Her silence wouldn't slow the adoption. If her real father didn't make contact in time, the judge would declare abandonment and let the adoption go through.

Billy tapped on the window pane. "I know what you mean. I'm going to a cave in the mountains tomorrow, and I'll be calling a huge dragon Dad." He set a hand on Bonnie's shoulder and pointed, as if he were showing her something in the distance. "Can you see it? I'll be going, 'Dad! Dad!' And then I'll hear a roar, and a huge rush of flame will come flying out of the cave. And then I'll go, 'Dad! There you are!'"

Billy and Bonnie laughed together. When their eyes met, her smiling countenance melted into a sincere, searching gaze. Billy drew his hand away and cleared his throat. "Anyway, since it's your big day, I think you'd better stick around here. I should be back the same day or early the next."

They walked to the sofa and sat. Bonnie placed her hands in her lap, nervously rubbing her thumbs together. "But what if we do hear from my real father? I don't know what I'd do without you here to talk to, I mean, if he wants me back and stops the adoption."

Billy glanced out the window toward the mailbox at the street. "There's no mail tomorrow, so the only way he could contact you would be by phone, right?"

"I guess so. Why?"

Billy kept his stare on the street. "I don't know. Maybe you should come with me after all. Maybe it doesn't make much difference whether you're here or not. I mean, even if your father called, Mr. Foley would be the one to talk to him." He turned back to Bonnie and sighed. "But I'm not sure if Mom'll have time to go or what the weather's supposed to be like tomorrow. And since they started rebuilding our house, she's always busy with that."

"When will she be back?"

He glanced at a clock on the wall, an old cuckoo with dangling, weighted cones and a stopped pendulum. "It'll be a while. She spent all day training a new pilot to carry skydivers, so she has to catch up on paperwork. She was pretty worried about the training. Dad used to do that kind of stuff."

Bonnie rose and stepped toward the window again. Billy joined her and pushed the sash up, letting in a cold, fresh breeze. Walter was playing fetch with Hambone in the leaf-covered grass. The old hound wore a thick doggy sweater, so he probably didn't mind a little romp on this blustery January day. The dog's owner, Arlo Hatfield, a hunter who lived in the mountains, never dressed his tracking hounds in anything so spiffy. Hambone yipped and raced through the leaves, grabbed a ragged ball, and rushed it back to Walter.

Billy leaned out the window. "Hey, Walter. Give the old dog a break."

Walter and Hambone stopped. The hound sat on his haunches with his long tongue hanging out. "He's posing for you," Walter shouted back. "He knows you're doing a portrait of him."

Bonnie shivered and rubbed her hands over her arms. "You're doing a portrait?"

Billy slid the window closed. "Yeah. You want to see it?"

"Sure."

Billy led Bonnie to a small utility room that Walter's father had converted into a serviceable art studio. He stepped to the far corner where he kept his easel, dodging several rolled-up posters and an empty frame. Gandalf, Billy's cat, lay curled on top of the stool under the heating vent. Apparently, he had no plans to move. Billy lifted the cover of the sketchpad, revealing his drawing.

Bonnie let out a chuckle. "That's Hambone, all right. Those big sad eyes and long ears are perfect."

"Thanks. Do you think Mr. Hatfield will like it?"

"He has to. It's beautiful. With all those shades of gray it looks almost like a black and white photo. It's so real."

Billy reached into the deep, side pocket of his cargo pants where he always kept paper and something to draw with. He withdrew a pencil and signed the bottom of the portrait, including his trademark—two letter B's, the first one reversed, sitting back to back with the second. "Well, it's the least I could do. He didn't have to lend me his favorite dog."

"Are you going to give him the drawing when you visit your dad?"

"If I can. Mr. Hatfield doesn't have a phone, so I can't call him to see if he's home."

Walter ambled in, holding a pretend phone and talking in a high-pitched hillbilly twang. "Hallow? Do yew have a number fer Arlo Hatfield? The city? Nowheresville. You know, rait over dere next ta Boondocks? Yeah, I got a drawin' fer him. He caint read, so I drawed a pitcher fer him."

Billy roared with laughter. Bonnie held her fingers over her lips and turned crimson. Following her lead, Billy tried to stifle his own laugh, letting out a muffled snort.

Walter continued, exaggerating the accent even more. "Naw, he don't have no phone. Why in tarnation wood I want to go and tawk to that critter on the phone? Yew caint send no pickshures over the phone. What kine of fool do yew take me fer?"

Billy snatched the pretend phone from Walter and held it to his ear. "I'm sorry, ma'am. He's a bit loony. We're sending him back to the electric shock room now."

Bonnie folded her hands in front and feigned a snobbish air, her eyes closed and her nose raised. Her lips trembled between a frown and a smile. "Well, while you two, ahem, gentlemen decide who's the more loony, I shall be in my room writing my English essay. I suggest that you do the same. Evening is at hand, and it is due on Monday." She walked out, maintaining her stern librarian frown, but soon burst out laughing and hurried down the hall.

17

*   *   *   *   *   *

Bonnie flipped on her desk lamp. With Billy's mother out late, the Foley household had opted for an a la carte dinner. Bonnie had brought in a chicken sandwich and salad from the kitchen and set them on her desk blotter along with a tall glass of water. Although it was time to relax, she kept her wings hidden in her backpack, choosing to endure the discomfort rather than risk someone popping in on her while she perched on her chair like a freakish bat.

After kicking off her shoes and socks and changing into a comfortable set of sweat clothes, she sat at the desk and chose a felt-tipped pen from her collection of markers in the middle drawer, pausing a moment as she read the calendar hanging on the wall in front of her. She leaned forward and carefully drew a dark "X" on the current date, the second Saturday in January. The box for Sunday was already filled with a happy face surrounded by pink and yellow flower stickers. At the bottom of the box a caption read, "Adoption Day!"

Bonnie deposited the felt pen in the drawer and pulled out a three-ring binder stuffed with pages. The first hundred or so were filled with flowing script—her journals, a number of writing assignments, and a sizable collection of stories and poetry. Although Billy and Walter shared a computer to write their assignments, Bonnie preferred the feel of setting pen to paper and letting her words pour out from mind to hand.

Her script revealed her moods—the weightiness of the day exposed in dark, heavy strokes, or happiness riding the page on sweeping loops and roller-coaster m's. The blank pages summoned her eloquence more than any word processor ever could. And clacking on keys just wasn't the same. Computers produced too many distracting beeps and pop-up windows to get any thoughtful work done. No, this way was much better, the soothing slide of her lovely silver Papermate on the crisp, white sheet.

Tonight, as she wrote her essay entitled, "Counting the Cost," her uneven script meandered, frequently slipping below the rule line. Dark ink blotches told of her weariness, and her supper remained barely touched. Through bleary eyes she stared out the window at the thickening fog. The clear, breezy evening had given way, and a cooling blanket of rich mountain air had seeped into the valley in thick soupy layers. The short days of winter had brought once again an early sunset, and mist shrouded the last remnant of twilight. Darkness had fallen, and even the porch lights were swallowed by the engulfing gloom.

With her eyelids drooping like heavy curtains, she jerked her head up. Then, a call came from somewhere, her name whispered in a long, dying echo. It was soft, yet urgent, as though someone had rung the dinner bell to signal suppertime while she played in a field far away, or the wind had picked up the

18

call and carried the syllables to her ears, lengthened and distorted, but still distinct and familiar—Mama's voice.

Bonnie looked around. No one else was in the room.

She had heard that voice several times over the last few
weeks and had assumed her mind was playing tricks on her.
She missed her mother so badly that part of her brain thought
she was still around, in the next room making the bed, or in
the kitchen cooking dinner, or in the rocking chair ready to
read her a story. Although the voice sounded sort of like her
mother's, it wasn't exactly the same. Somehow it carried the
chill of a haunted house.

With no hope of staying awake at her desk, Bonnie got up
and slid her window open. The breezeless air outside allowed
the mist to seep into her room in wet creeping fingers, moist-
ening her face with humid coolness and sending shivers across
her arms. A faint trace of wood smoke tinged the air, a sure
sign that the mountains had lent their freshness to the valley.

Maybe going outside would shake off the sleepiness.
Although darkness had fallen, it was a little early to go for a fly.
She usually waited until late at night when everyone was asleep,
but the fog would surely keep her hidden.

She climbed out the window and onto the roof, a trick she
had perfected over the last few weeks. Since her second-floor
bedroom was the only one that faced the rear of the house, it
was perfectly placed for her covert escape.

Bonnie took a deep breath of the wet, cool air, and, after
glancing around to verify her privacy, she unzipped her backpack, then let it dangle until her nimble wings pushed it off.
Once freed, her dragon wings unfurled and spread behind her,
the span extending more than twice her body's length.

She sat just above the eaves, pulling her knees up and admir-
ing her surroundings, how the upper branches of the trees
drank from the gray, hovering mist, how the birds flitted so

19

differently in a night fog, with rapid wing beats and without chirp or song.

As darkness wrapped her body, she threaded memorized verses through her mind. Tonight, as on many nights, she chose a passage from a psalm of David, having set it to a tune during one of her many rooftop visits. She took in a breath and sang.

Whither shall I go from thy spirit? Or whither shall I flee from thy presence?

If I ascend up into heaven, thou art there: If I make my bed in hell, behold, thou art there.

If I take the wings of the morning, and dwell in the uttermost parts of the sea;

Even there shall thy hand lead me, and thy right hand shall hold me.

If I say, Surely the darkness shall cover me; even the night shall be light about me.

Yea, the darkness hideth not from thee; but the night shineth as the day:

The darkness and the light are both alike to thee.

With a long, satisfied sigh, Bonnie rose to her feet and climbed to the apex of the roof. Her flying experience told her that fog layers are often shallow. She hoped to be able to cruise above them, finding light in the moon and stars. With a flap and jump, she took off. Propelling herself nearly straight up, she catapulted into the mist, her hair and face dampening as she flew. She pushed onward, beating her wings against the cool air and watching for a break in the fog, but the wet vapor persisted, thinner as she flew upward, but still too murky to fly safely.

Not wanting to get too high and fearing she wouldn't be able to find her way home, she leveled off and began flying in a small circle. The sensation felt like swimming rather than flying as streams of water soaked her hair and dripped into her eyes.

Blinking at the droplets, she peered down for any hint of light. After a few seconds, she spotted a light below, small, but bright enough to pierce the fog. She extended her wings fully and glided toward the steady beam. As she approached, the glow took shape, a neighbor's halogen yard lamp. She would have to act quickly, land on the run, stuff her wings into her sweatshirt, and sprint about one block home. She folded in her wings and went into a freefall, planning to unfurl them again just in time to parachute to a soft landing.

When she came within fifty feet of the light, it moved. It wasn't a yard lamp at all; it was the glow of a car's headlights. She couldn't abort her landing. She was falling too rapidly.

Bonnie spread her wings and pulled against the air, flexing her canopies in the dark gray mist. She drew one wing in and swerved, zipping in front of the moving car's windshield and angling toward the curb.

The car's brakes squealed. Her legs already running, her bare feet hit a sidewalk, but she couldn't keep her balance. She toppled forward, banged her head on the ground, and rolled into the roadside grass.

A door slammed. Footsteps pounded on pavement. She sat up and looked around at the thick fog, too stunned and dizzy to do anything else. Feeling stark naked with her wings exposed and no hope of hiding them in time, she stayed perfectly quiet and waited, hoping the fog would mask her presence.

21

Then, from the dark shadows of a hundred nightmares, a tall specter strolled out of the soupy mist and stood in front of her.

Bonnie gulped. "Daddy?"

Counting the Cost

Bonnie jumped up to run, but her father caught her wrist and pulled her back, grabbing her other arm to hold her in place. His hands felt like iron clamps, and the pain of his clenching fingers stiffened her body.

"Settle down," he said. His voice was forceful but not coarse. "I'm not going to hurt you."

"Right," Bonnie grunted. "Tell that to my mother." She kicked him in the shin as hard as she could, stinging her bare toes. He let out an angry yelp and shoved her backwards, making her fall heavily on her bottom. With a flap of her wings, she rose and leaped into the sky. He grabbed her ankle and jerked her to the ground, this time throwing her onto her back and pressing her hands against the cold grass.

Bonnie exhaled. She was beaten. Her father had always been athletic, with strong, toned muscles and an agile body, and now he seemed more powerful than ever. Her unusual genetics made her stronger than a lot of grown men, but she was no match for him, and with her wings crumpled between her back and the ground, she had no hope of escape. Struggling to breathe under his crushing weight, she growled, "If you don't let me go, I'll scream."

He slapped a hand over her mouth. "I don't want to hurt you. Just listen to me." She shook her head violently, let out a muffled scream, then tried to bite his hand.

Hot anger burned in his gray eyes. Sweat beaded along his brow, making his short red bangs stick to his forehead. He pushed against her cheeks with his fingers, squeezing them against her teeth while making a shushing noise, his face so close she could smell his coffee breath. "If you'll just be quiet and listen, I'll let you up. Don't be stubborn. There's a lot you don't know, and I have news about your mother."

Pain jolting her into compliance, Bonnie let herself go limp. Her father slowly released the pressure on her face and smiled. "I thought that would cool your jets. Are you going to be quiet and listen?"

Bonnie nodded and tried to calm down, but she couldn't slow her gasping breaths.

"Good." He rose and helped her to her feet.

While brushing herself off, she glared at him, trying her best to show distrust and anger at his rough treatment.

"Your mother hid your tracks well," he said. "I was still trying to find you in the foster system when the ad showed up."

Bonnie took a deep breath and folded her arms in front, trying to hold back her tears, but she couldn't keep her voice from shaking. "Mr. Foley and I thought an ad was the best way. We hoped you wouldn't see it. The state said we had to make an effort to notify you."

He let out an agreeable laugh. "Your plan almost worked. I didn't see the ad, at least for a while. Someone told me I should be checking the papers for an abandonment summons, so I went back and found it, about two weeks ago now."

"Two weeks? Why didn't you call?"

"I had a lot to prepare. And I wanted to show up in person and surprise you."

"Yeah, right," she said, squinting and setting her hands on her hips. "I'll bet you did." She wanted to stay on the defensive, to be tough and uncooperative, but his comment about her mother burned in her mind. She had to ask, but she crossed her arms again and looked away, feigning disinterest. "So what's the news about my mother?" She glanced back to catch her father's expression.

He stared at his feet. Now he seemed hesitant, unsure of what to say. When he lifted his gaze, his expression turned soft, his brow rising and his eyes wandering. "I assume you think she's dead."

Bonnie's heart thumped. She could barely breathe. She almost choked on her response. "Of … of course, she's dead. I saw her die." His penetrating eyes and her exposed wings made her feel like a naked lab rat. He had always had that effect on her, staring at her as though his gaze could pierce her soul.

"You're not a doctor, Bonnie. You only thought she was dead. When I found her, she was near death. Her vitals were almost imperceptible. But she was alive. Badly wounded, to be sure, but alive. And she's alive now."

Bonnie sucked in a breath. Now she knew she would cry. "I don't believe you!" She trembled, her voice cracking. "If she were alive, she would have found me. She knew how."

"I'm sure she would have, but she's been in a coma. We have pretty high hopes, though. You know how strong she is, and being an anthrozil, she has more strength than normal humans."

Bonnie narrowed her eyes. "Anthrozil?" The slayer had used that term before, and now her father's mention of it provided

25

evidence that they had worked together. If she played dumb, maybe she could learn more. "What's an anthrozil?"

"It's a name I came up with for what you are. The DNA seems to indicate that somehow you're fully human and fully dragon. You have the complete code for both species. *Anthro* is a common prefix for man, and I got *zil* from Godzilla, the movie dinosaur. Anyway, your mother still has some of the toughness of the dragon species in her, so she managed to survive."

Bonnie's defenses began melting. She wanted to believe her mother was alive. She wanted to go back to a normal home with a real dad who wouldn't treat her like a science experiment. But it just couldn't be. She couldn't trust this man, this awful monster she had learned to despise.

For months and months she had blamed him for her mother's death. Wasn't he the one who had used them like guinea pigs? Hadn't he led the murderers to their home? Couldn't this be another trick to bring her back into his lab and possibly into the clutches of the dragon slayers?

"I understand your hesitation." He held out his hand. "But your mother calls for you, even from her coma. Maybe if you answer, it will help her wake up."

Bonnie's hands trembled. There *was* a voice! She had heard it so many times. Her legs grew weak. Tears, hot and wet, joined the cold misty dew on her cheeks. "I ... I don't know what to think." She swallowed down a sob. "I don't know what to believe."

Her father sighed. "I know you don't trust me, and I don't blame you. I was suspicious of Devin, that is, Dr. Whittier, when he started asking questions about your mother, but I never let him see you or even told him about you."

Bonnie wiped her tears with her knuckles. "How long did you know Devin?"

26

"For quite a while. He was interested in DNA research and proved to be very knowledgeable. That's why I let him team up with me. Since dragon DNA is remarkably similar to human DNA, the research was complicated. I thought our combined expertise would help me pursue my goals, so I told him about my anthrozil theory. When he first learned that I was using dragon blood, he demanded to know where I was getting it. I refused to tell, of course, but when his demands became increasingly violent, I let some information slip. That's when he found your mother." He lowered his head and shifted his weight uneasily. "I'm just glad my mistake wasn't fatal."

He extended his hand again, his fingers trembling. "Come back with me," he said, tears forming in his eyes. "Maybe together we can right this wrong. I couldn't do it by myself. Maybe you can call her back from the dead."

Bonnie stared at his hand, the hand she had feared for so long. Now it reached for her to take it in hers, to be led away from a life she loved and into the unknown. How could she trust a man who jabbed her with needles and drew her blood time after time, breaking promises never to do it again? Yet, how could she not go? If there was any way his story could be true, that her mother really was still alive and she could possibly help her, she had to do it. Wasn't it worth the risk?

She lifted her arm and began to reach out. The rough tussle had forced her sleeve up toward her shoulder, staining her arm with grass and dirt. As she raised her bare forearm into the glow of a nearby streetlight, tiny white scars appeared, the remnants of dozens of needle marks.

He reached farther to take her hand, but she drew it away, stepping backwards in the same motion.

"No," she said softly.

"But—"

Bonnie stepped back again and strengthened her voice. "No. No, I can't." She turned and shot into the air, her wings exploding into flight.

He shouted behind her, his voice muffled and distorted in the fog. "I'll come back in the morning. Think about it. You might be your mother's only hope."

Bonnie found the roof and landed softly near her backpack. She put it on, struggling with it as she panted heavily in the midst of sobbing spasms. When she pulled the last strap tight, she climbed into her bedroom and wiped her face with the dinner napkin.

After stifling her crying, she looked around the room. What could she do? Who could help her now? This was her legal father wanting to take her home. She wasn't sixteen yet. She had no right to declare emancipation.

Haunting memories of emotional tortures streamed back in flashing visions and vivid detail—the look in her mother's eyes and the deep gash in her abdomen, a replay of her last words gurgling in blood, and the weeks of lonely journeys from home to home in search of someone who would take in a scared orphan who was hiding a terrible secret.

"Don't let ... let them find you," her mother had said as she lay dying. "There's another dragon ... I'm sending you to find him. Don't come back here unless I call for you." With a last burst of strength, she cried, "Now run, dear child! You know where to go!" She sighed a last breath and made no other sound.

And Bonnie ran, ignoring the tears, the horrible pain, never looking back, never stopping. In the last few weeks, with the Foleys opening up their home to her, she felt like she had finally stopped running, but the pursuing demons had now caught up, and they cast their dark shadows on her very door.

Bonnie repeated the words to herself. *Don't come back here unless I call for you.* And now her mother had called, or at least that's what her father said. And she had heard her call, a voice crying deep within her soul that she thought was just her brain cracking up.

Now the phantom sound became an irresistible pull, a loving voice begging her to believe. But why should she believe? Her father had lied so many times before, pretending to be a loving husband and father while fostering an alliance with a demon. Yet, what if his claims were true this time? She had to help her. What choice did she have? She couldn't abandon her own mother.

Darkness seeped into her soul, the same loneliness she had suffered in the foster homes. The decision was too awful to make, and who could possibly be wise enough to help her? Nobody on earth could ever understand all her feelings.

A poster on the wall drew her eye, the same poster that had helped her so many times in the past, a drawing of an angelic girl praying on her knees at her bedside. The little girl's eyes focused upward, and the caption said, "Trust in the Lord with all thine heart; and lean not unto thine own understanding. In all thy ways acknowledge him, and he shall direct thy paths."

Falling on her knees, she folded her hands on her bed, allowing herself to weep out loud, her backpack securely hiding her wings. She cried out silently to God, her words cascading from her mind and her feelings pouring out in heart-rending sobs.

My cup of wisdom is poured out, my Father, empty and dry. My heart aches. My very bones feel crushed by this burden, a shadow falling on my soul like Sheol's dark loneliness.

As she prayed, she strove for eloquence, not because God honored pretty words. They were just natural for her. Although

29

they probably sounded pompous to others, God wouldn't mind if she cried out in her own way.

Soon, warmth flowed, the soothing blanket of God's love wrapping around her chilled soul. She had already been through worse struggles. She could get through this, too. Even as her aches were being assuaged with a spiritual balm, she cried on, the release bringing cleansing satisfaction, the joy of being held in her heavenly father's arms.

* * * * * *

With his easel turned away from the studio door, Billy sat on a stool, using a pencil to fine-tune a facial detail on his sketch paper. Every once in a while, he glanced at the closed door, wary of a surprise visitor. This was his secret project, one that poured out a mystery in his heart. He sighed and shook his head, pressing an eraser on a lower part of the portrait and rubbing out a line. *I can't remember exactly what the blade looked like.*

He pushed the stool back, and, blowing his heated breath on his cold hands, he surveyed the entire picture. Bonnie stood in a flowing white robe, her wings fully expanded. In her outstretched arms she held a glowing sword, the blade resting in her palms as though she were presenting it to whoever was studying the portrait. Her blazing eyes seemed to beg that the sword be taken and used by her valiant knight.

Billy took in the details. What was it about Bonnie that was so different? Was it power that blossomed in her spirit? Was it peace? Yes, she practically gushed peace. Even with all the problems she faced, she seemed to walk in a garden of serenity.

He sighed. If only he could walk the same path, to find peace even as he struggled over the loss of his father. At least if his father were truly dead, he could cherish fond memories. Instead, his shadow lurked in the shape of a winged monster,

30

and its haunting presence never let him rest. Every time he thought about his dad, something boiled in his belly, a deep-seated anger that sometimes took control of his mind, making him feel abandoned, alone. If there was a God, why did he take his dad away?

A gentle knock sounded at the door. Billy flipped the page to his drawing of Hambone. "Come in."

Walter's nose appeared first, protruding through the opening. The hinges creaked in the otherwise quiet house as the rest of his face came into view.

Billy set the point of his pencil on the page and added a bit of shading to Hambone's ear. "What's up, Walter? Is it my turn on the computer?"

"No." Walter gestured with his finger. "Just follow me."

Billy tiptoed behind Walter down the hall. When they reached Bonnie's bedroom door, Walter whispered. "Listen."

Billy pressed his ear against the door. Within a few seconds, the distinctive sounds of mournful sobs came through.

"Did you go in and talk to her?" Billy asked. "Do you know why she's crying?"

Walter shook his head. "You know the rules about her bedroom. No trespassing for us y-chromosome types."

A new voice entered the hallway. "Is something wrong?"

Billy swiveled his head. "Mom," he said, keeping his voice low. "When did you get home?"

"Just now." She set a plate of food on the hall table—a thick sandwich, several raw baby carrots, and an apple. "Is Bonnie all right?"

"She's crying. Is it all right if I check on her?"

Mom's brow furrowed as she took a step closer. "Sure."

Billy tapped on the door with a knuckle. "Bonnie? You okay?"

The crying stopped, but no one answered.

Billy turned the knob and pushed the door slightly, allowing his mouth to penetrate the opening. "Bonnie? … Um … It's Billy. Walter and my mom are with me."

A faint reply floated into the hall. "It's okay. You can come in."

Billy opened the door and stepped inside. Bonnie knelt with her hands on the bed, her eyes closed. The sight was wondrous. In her praying posture, Bonnie was an angel, beautiful in form and radiant in appearance. He imagined her hidden wings spread out to shield her body, protecting her from whatever tortured her mind.

With Mom and Walter following, Billy edged toward Bonnie's bed and stood at her side. Mom knelt and gently rubbed her neck. "Bonnie," she said tenderly. "What's wrong?"

Bonnie lifted her head, her wet eyes red. "I … I was outside, and he was there."

"Who was there?" Billy asked.

"My father."

"Your real father?"

She nodded and started crying again. "He … he wants me to go back to Missoula with him."

"To Missoula? But what about—" Billy wanted to kick the bed, but he just tapped it with his toe. He glanced at Walter, wondering how far he could question Bonnie without giving away their secrets.

Walter slid his hands into his pockets and stepped toward the hall. "I'm going to get a cold, wet cloth for her."

"And a dry towel," Mom said.

Walter nodded and hustled out of the room.

Billy whispered. "He's going to make you go?"

Bonnie rose and sat on the bed, her head bowed. "I don't think so. At least, he didn't say that. But I think I need to go with him."

"What? Why?"

She looked at him. "He said my mother's not dead."

Mom sat next to her. "Not dead? Didn't you see her die?"

"I thought she was dead when I left her, but my father says I was wrong. She's in a coma, and he said she calls for me."

Billy let out a huff. "And the sound of your voice might snap her out of it, right?"

She looked at him. "How did you know?"

"Sounds like an old movie I saw."

"And did it work?"

"Well … yeah." Billy paced the floor, gesturing with his hands. "But this isn't some corny old movie. It's real life. And how can you trust him, anyway? Didn't he rat on you and your mom to a dragon slayer?" Billy pinched his chin, still pacing. Something wasn't making sense, and he couldn't put his finger on it.

Bonnie's stare followed him. "That's exactly what I asked myself. That's what I've been asking God. How can I trust a man like him?"

He stopped in front of Bonnie's poster of a praying girl. "Well, asking God and all that is great, but maybe you should ask your father for proof."

"Proof? Like what?"

He waved a hand toward the poster. "Like a picture of your mom in the hospital bed. Or we could call the hospital and ask about her condition. If she's really dead, there'll be a death certificate somewhere. I'm sure Walter's dad can dig that up."

Mom rose and stood next to Billy. "He's right, Bonnie. I'm sure we can get to the bottom of this."

Bonnie's eyes sparkled with new life. "Can you believe it? When he held out his hand to me, I almost took it. I almost left with him then and there."

Billy's cheeks burned, compassion flowing. His muscles flexed as if ready to go to battle, and he tried to think of some way to communicate his feelings to Bonnie, some way to strengthen her, too. "You can believe this," he said, extending a hand toward her, "you can always trust me. This hand will never lead you astray."

Bonnie took his hand and pulled herself to her feet. Her fingers caressed his ring, the ring that held the rubellite stone his father had given him, and her matching ring clicked against his. "I will never forget those words," she said softly. "I do trust you."

Walter walked back into the room, a white facecloth in one hand and a towel in the other. After Bonnie used them to wash her tear-streaked cheeks, she took a deep breath, and her face regained its usual glow. "We'd better get some rest," she said. "We have a lot of detective work to do tomorrow."

34

* * * * * *

Mr. Foley strolled into the dining room carrying a cup of coffee and a yellow legal pad. Walter and his mom sat on one side of the table, and Billy's mother sat between Billy and Bonnie on the other side. They were still dressed in church clothes, having arrived home to a scant brunch that Mr. Foley had prepared while they were gone. The leftovers lay scattered around the table—half of a cold piece of toast on a serving plate, shallow pools of milk at the bottoms of cereal bowls, and orange pulp clinging to the rims of several drinking glasses.

Mr. Foley took a seat at the head of the table, grabbed a pen from his pocket, and scratched a note on his pad. "Okay, I made a bunch of calls. There is an Irene Conner listed in the hospital database in Missoula, and the most recent report says she's in a coma." He sipped his coffee and drummed his fingers on the table. "I pulled all the strings I had, but we couldn't come up with a death certificate. That's not conclusive, though. I couldn't raise much activity so early on a Sunday morning."

He looked at Bonnie, his face turning dark and sad. "In any case, your father showed up. We can't declare abandonment. He'll have to relinquish his rights voluntarily."

Billy grabbed his spoon and tossed it into his bowl. "Fat chance of that."

"That only means we can't legally adopt you," Mr. Foley said, "at least not yet. It doesn't mean you have to go with him. We can fight for a charge of child endangerment, but that would be hard to prove, since all he did was draw blood. It's fair to assume he was qualified to do it, and we have no idea what he was doing with your blood."

Bonnie kept her gaze fixed on the table. She nodded with tight lips and a firm chin. "Don't I have to take the chance?" She looked up, tears glistening in her eyes. "If there's any chance at all, don't I have to take it?" She extended her arm, pointing westward, her voice trembling. "Didn't Billy risk his life for me up there on that mountain when the only proof he had was a lock of hair? Shouldn't I do the same for my own mother?" She sniffed and covered her face.

Billy rose, his fists tight. "What I did is history. And I was wrong. You weren't on the mountain. That doesn't mean I wouldn't do it again. I would. But Devin fooled us, and he has so many cronies, he could be fooling us again. Should we just waltz right into another trap without checking it out first? I say we demand a video, or at least a picture of Bonnie's mom in the hospital." He sat again and set his chin on his fists.

"That shouldn't be hard to arrange," Mom said as she draped her arm over Bonnie's shoulders. "Surely someone can e-mail us a digital photo."

"Right," Walter said. "I'm with Billy. I wouldn't trust this guy as far as my mother could throw him."

Mrs. Foley's forehead wrinkled. "As far as I could throw him? Why me?"

"I've seen you throw." Walter shrugged. "Sorry, Mom, but you throw like a sick duck."

"A sick duck?"

"Yeah. Remember when you threw the baseball and it hit the window?"

"Yes. So?"

"Well, you barely quacked it."

A shower of boos and balled-up napkins rained on Walter, but the doorbell interrupted the jeers. Bonnie jerked her head toward Billy. Her eyes gave away her fear.

Mr. Foley rose from his seat and answered the door in the foyer. His voice drifted back to the dining room. "Yes, Dr. Conner. I'm Carl Foley. Come in. We've been expecting you."

"Thank you. Call me Matt. Bonnie told you I'm a doctor?"

"Yes, a research professor in pharmacy at the University of Montana, newly appointed dean, if I'm not mistaken. I must admit that I have checked up on you."

The two joined the others at the table. Dr. Conner tugged on his shirt cuff, then dug his hand into his pocket. "That's perfectly understandable."

"Yes," Mr. Foley continued, "and Bonnie told me she talked with you briefly last night when she was out for a walk."

Dr. Conner glanced at Bonnie and smiled. "A walk?"

Bonnie turned crimson and shifted her backpack higher.

Billy edged between Bonnie and her father. "Mr. Foley, didn't she say she went out for some fresh air?"

"Right," Mr. Foley replied. "What's the confusion?"

Dr. Conner pulled on his cuffs again and straightened his watch. "None at all. It's just that she was kind of zipping along when I saw her. I wouldn't have called it walking."

Billy eyed the two men. They both knew about Bonnie's wings, but neither wanted to mention them, probably out of concern that not everyone present knew the secret.

Mr. Foley cleared his throat. "Dr. Conner, Bonnie and I have discussed this, and considering the circumstances, I think you would agree that some sort of positive proof of your claims is reasonable. After all, technically you are not the legal custodian. She's in the foster system now."

Dr. Conner's lips pursed, and his tone hardened. "You're requiring proof to allow me to take my own daughter home? Don't give me that nonsense about the foster system. She was made a ward of the state without my consent and without a court order."

Mr. Foley squared his shoulders. "If you want a legal fight, Dr. Conner, I assure you I can deliver one. If, however, you can prove that Bonnie's mother is still alive, I'll have no legal grounds for keeping her here."

Dr. Conner resumed a congenial air. "Considering the circumstances, I can agree to that. Have you called the hospital?"

"Yes. Your wife is listed in the database, but I couldn't verify whether or not she is a patient there right now. We were wondering if someone at the hospital could send us a photo of her."

Dr. Conner raised a finger. "No need to bother anyone for that. I have a picture on my laptop. I'll get it." Without waiting for a response, he hurried outside.

Billy fingered the handle on his spoon and flipped it out of the bowl. He mentally followed Dr. Conner's progress to the car and back. Did Bonnie's dad really have a photo of her mom? Could it be a fake? If he could produce a photo, how would they be able to tell a real one from a phony? After several more seconds of uneasy silence, Billy spoke up. "It has to be a recent photo. We don't want anything from months ago."

"Right," Mr. Foley said, again drumming his fingers. "It has to—"

Dr. Conner reentered, unzipping a leather case. "I took a picture yesterday morning before I left for the airport. I thought Bonnie might want to see it." He placed the computer on the table and turned it on. After he tapped the keyboard for a few seconds, a photo replaced the screen's desktop, an image of a woman covered by blankets up to the chin of her calm, pale face. A feeding tube protruded from her nose, and various medical supplies and equipment surrounded her bed. A photo of Bonnie sat on a table next to a vase of wildflowers.

Bonnie drew closer to the screen. She covered her mouth with a hand. "It's her," she said, her voice tortured but still under control. "It's my mother."

Mr. Foley tapped the base of the laptop. "May I use the computer for a moment?"

Dr. Conner turned the screen his way. "Be my guest."

Mr. Foley pecked a few keys. He let out a low, "Hmmm" before rotating the computer back toward Dr. Conner. "The file is time stamped yesterday morning."

Dr. Conner nodded. "I understand your mistrust." He pulled a disk from the laptop case and inserted it in the drive. "I'm making a copy for you. You can check it all you want. You'll see that it's authentic. My wife is very sick, and all I want to do is help her and get my daughter back." He popped the disk out and handed it to Mr. Foley.

Billy clenched his fists. He wanted to argue, but his supply of reasons was hurtling off a cliff like a bunch of lemmings.

Dr. Conner rose from his seat, packed up his laptop, and pulled the strap over his shoulder. "Bonnie. I know you don't trust me yet, but when you see your mother, I'm sure you'll feel better about everything."

Bonnie's wet, red eyes darted all around. Billy swallowed hard, trying to push down the swelling knot growing inside.

As if reading the fervent distrust in the room, Dr. Conner added, "My flight is a private charter, but I don't have permission to invite anyone. Otherwise you would be welcome to join us." He set a business card on the table. "This is my address. Please come and see us anytime. Just give me a call." He extended a hand toward his daughter. "Bonnie, we shouldn't delay. We have to drive to the Charleston airport. Remember, your mother is calling you. Will you come?"

Bonnie looked at Billy, but he had no idea what to say. His mind was shouting, *Danger! Don't go!* But he couldn't tell if it was his dragon danger signals working or his tremendous distrust of this man who would take away his friend.

Bonnie turned to her father and nodded. "I'll go."

She took his hand, and the two walked toward the door. She looked back, and Billy read a message of courage in her face. Tears streamed, but her countenance remained stoic, her chin firm. The unspoken message said, "No good-byes. I'll be back." Then she silently mouthed words that Billy read easily—"Trust me."

Dr. Conner paused at the door. "I'll purchase her immediate needs and send for her belongings. Thank you for taking such good care of her."

When the door shut, Billy jumped from his seat and ran to the front window in the living room. Dr. Conner and Bonnie slid into the car. Before the motor started, she held up her fist, displaying her rubellite ring. A few seconds later, the car disappeared around a corner.

Billy plodded back to the dining room. Every eye stared at him as his tangled emotions swirled in a dizzying array of hate, love, anger, and compassion. He balled his fists, his rage growing to overwhelm all other feelings. He just had to let it out, somehow blow off steam without blasting fire.

He started with a whisper. "I can't believe this." His voice then grew with every word, spelling out his anger in face-contorting passion. "I just let a monster take her back to her nightmares! She told me how scared she was of him, and I didn't do anything about it!"

His mother and Walter joined him. She rubbed his back, and Walter smacked his fist into his hand. "We'll get that creep," he said, his face aglow in crimson. "My dad will figure out what he's really up to."

Mr. Foley gripped Billy's shoulder. "We may have quite a battle on our hands. We have to keep our heads on straight. It won't help for you to lose your temper." He pulled the disk from his pocket and turned toward Walter. "Call the professor. I'll need help examining the photo."

"On it." Walter hurried for the phone.

Billy took a deep breath and let it out slowly. "Could you ask him to bring the sword again, Walter? I want to take a picture of it."

"And get some more practice, maybe?" Walter asked as he punched in the phone number. "If he brings the other sword, I can spar with you."

Mom massaged Billy's neck, pressing her strong fingers into his taut muscles. "That's a good idea. It'll do you good to practice and get your aggressions out. After listening to that fraud, I'd like to get a few hacks in myself."

"Practice didn't help us keep Bonnie here, Mom. I mean, I've been training like crazy, you know, to battle like a knight when the time comes. But now this guy just waltzes in the door and waltzes right back out, taking Bonnie to who knows where, and we just let them go." He leaned close and whispered, careful to keep his sizzling breath away from her ear. "I was so mad, I could've turned him into a giant French fry right in front of everyone."

"I know what you mean," she whispered back. "And I'd have supplied a gallon of ketchup. But I don't want you getting put away for murder."

"No way. Who'd ever believe it? We could've just called it a case of spontaneous combustion."

    ❋   ❋   ❋   ❋   ❋   ❋

Billy leaned around Mr. Foley and blinked at the image before him. The hospital photo filled the computer screen, a large flat panel display sitting prominently on Mr. Foley's mahogany desk. Something was off, but Billy couldn't quite put his finger on it.

Walter burst into the office. "The great guru of graphical gawking has arrived," he announced as Professor Hamilton followed him inside.

Billy shoved Walter's chest. "How long did it take to dream that one up?"

Walter grinned and shoved him back. "About two seconds. It beats the cat's pajamas has arrived, doesn't it?"

"Just barely."

Professor Hamilton handed each boy a sword. "Shall we get our aggressions out in a profitable manner, gentlemen?"

Billy grabbed the Excalibur replica and opened the double French doors that led to the rec room. As soon as Walter was ready, Billy lunged, and their swords clanked together. He positioned himself near the office entrance, hoping to watch Mr. Foley and battle Walter at the same time.

Mr. Foley extended a printed photo of Bonnie's mom to the professor. "Use this for comparison. It's older, but it should be a close match. I e-mailed the hospital image to a friend of mine, Fred Hollings. He's a real techno-geek who's trying to start a computer company in the industrial park. He might be

41

able to tell if the computer pic's authentic or not, but he's out of town right now."

The professor studied the image on the computer screen for several minutes, zooming in on numerous details and rubbing his chin thoughtfully. He alternated between the photo display and the Internet browser, poring over dozens of web pages.

Billy's mother and Mrs. Foley entered the rec room, whispering to each other while they watched their sons practice. Finally, Professor Hamilton cleared his throat. Billy stopped his sword in mid-swing and let it droop at his side.

"It is my opinion," the professor said, as everyone crowded into the office, "that the image is indeed a genuine digital photograph of Miss Silver's mother. The facial features in the image are too close a match to the other photo to be counterfeit. Such a fake would be extraordinarily difficult to manufacture."

42

Billy hiked the sword up to his shoulder. "So Bonnie's mom really is in a hospital in Missoula? Dr. Conner was telling the truth?"

"Oh, no. I didn't say that at all. I'm quite sure he was lying."

"Lying?" Mr. Foley repeated. "What do you mean?"

"He told the truth about this being a photo of his wife." The professor pointed at the computer screen. "He lied about the date. This photo was taken at least four months ago."

The Dragon's Lair

B illy dropped his sword. "Four months ago, Professor? How do you know?"

"Yeah," Walter said. "That wouldn't be long after Bonnie came to West Virginia."

"The flowers in the vase give away the season." The professor pointed at the screen again. "They are glacier lilies, which usually bloom from March through July, perhaps as late as August, but certainly not in January. It's not likely that a local florist cultivates such wildflowers in the dead of winter, so I deduced the approximate date by logic."

Billy's mom tapped her head with her finger. "You just happened to know so much about glacier lilies, Professor?"

The professor waved a hand. "Oh, no. I have only recently learned about your West Virginia varieties, and I'm not at all familiar with those from Montana. I am, however, quite proficient at horticulture in general. The British wildflowers are exquisite, and I enjoyed them immensely in my home fields. I merely noticed the lovely flowers in the photo and searched the Internet for a match. With my current knowledge, finding the species was not difficult." The professor pushed the eject button and handed the diskette to Mr. Foley. "It's a simple matter to alter the date and time stamp on a computer file. Dr. Conner took an older file and renewed it on his computer, apparently with this kind of deception in mind."

Billy smacked his fist into his palm. "So he *is* a liar! I knew it!"

"Yes, William. And I think a man who would deceive us would not have Miss Silver's best interests in mind."

Mom picked up the sword and extended the hilt toward Billy. "Let's get packed and make a flight plan. We're going to Montana."

Billy grabbed the sword and pumped his fist. "Now you're talking!"

"How many passengers can you fit?" Walter asked. "I'll squeeze into a suitcase if I have to."

Billy pushed Walter's arm. "As if I'd leave you behind."

Walter raised his eyebrows toward his father, and his cheeks sagged like a young basset's. "Can I go, Dad?"

Mr. Foley whispered to his wife, then tapped the professor on the back. "I'd feel better, Prof, if you'd go along. They might need you to help figure out what's going on."

Professor Hamilton stood between the two boys and pretended to bump their heads together. "Of course. With all of my students in Montana, I would have no one to teach here."

Mom laid a hand on Mrs. Foley's shoulder. "We have room for everyone."

"I'll go wherever my husband goes," she replied, giving his hand a squeeze.

Mr. Foley stroked his wife's hand lovingly. "I have a trial tomorrow, but I can make calls from here and do a little more detective work. If the trial ends before you get back, we'll hop a flight to Missoula. I don't expect it to last more than a day, but you never know."

While Mom discussed the flight arrangements with the Foleys and shared her strategy for packing, Billy looked at the professor, drawn by his steely gray eyes, as if caught in a gravitational pull. The professor broke his silence with a whisper. "Will you trust me?"

Billy lowered his head and stared at his gym shoes. "I … I do trust you," he said, looking up again, "but some of the secrets aren't mine to reveal."

"Yes, of course. I assumed Miss Silver plays a major role."

"Not just her. She'd trust me to tell you if I thought it was right."

Mom's voice grew louder, as if she wanted Billy to hear. "Our first stop will be in the mountains. I need to look for something in the wreckage."

Billy smiled. That meant she planned to visit Dad as well. The thought brought warmth to his cheeks along with a bit of fear. The sight of the massive dragon was enough to scare anyone. "I'll tell you what, Prof. I can explain a few things as soon as we take off, but we're going to stop and ask someone's advice up on the mountain where we battled Devin. If he says it's okay, then I'll tell you everything." He extended a hand. "Deal?"

Professor Hamilton shook his hand firmly. "I will gladly accept that deal, William." His head tilted. "Who is your friend? I heard the story of the hunter. Are you going to ask his advice?"

Billy laughed. "You mean Arlo Hatfield? No, but I'd like to see him again. I drew a picture of Hambone for him."

Mom extended a bag of cheese puffs toward Billy. "Then bring it along. I'm sure we can arrange to have it delivered."

45

She offered the bag to the professor. "So, when can you be ready?"

The professor smiled and waved a hand at the bag. "I shall return in less than an hour, Madam." He pulled his watch from his pocket and wound it. "And, William, I have the mystery book once again. Its properties are quite astounding. I suspect that we will be informing each other about many things before this day ends."

⁂

With Billy in the co-pilot's seat and his mother flying the plane, the professor and Walter leaned forward in their two-seat passenger bench. The sound of the buzzing props nearly drowned Billy's voice. "I can't tell you everything yet, but basically, Bonnie's the one who took care of the slayer. She used his sword, and from her description, it looked a lot like your replica of Excalibur. Anyway, she said a really bright beam of light surged out of it, almost like a light saber from Star Wars, and when she pointed it at the slayer, he vanished in a flash of sparks that kind of swirled around and disappeared, like water going down a drain."

"Just like flushing a toilet, huh?" Walter swirled his finger in tightening circles as he lowered it toward the cabin floor.

Billy slapped at Walter's arm. "No, genius, not like a toilet. Anyway, that strange stone I told you about, the candlestone, was there on the ground. We think that had something to do with it. What do you think, Professor?"

The professor pulled a pair of old-fashioned spectacles from his shirt pocket and slipped them on. "I'm certain the candlestone is involved, William."

"Really? How?"

The teacher opened a satchel at his side. "Now is a good time to show you the book." He withdrew a leather-bound volume. The cover was about the size of an eight-by-ten photo, with raised runic characters that looked like a bunch of lines and dashes—nothing like the lettering in the ancient King Arthur lore the professor had used at school. The book held a modest collection of parchment, making the volume about the thickness of a notebook computer. The professor opened the delicate binding to the first page and held it on his lap. "There is mention of the candlestone in this book, and it's a clue to what the verse means."

"The verse?"

"Yes, there are verses, strange and cryptic. The initial three pages are intelligible. The first one claims the author was Merlin."

Walter shifted closer. "Merlin? That's so cool! What did he write?"

"I suspect that it's a journal of sorts, somewhat like a modern diary, but, as you might expect from Merlin, it contains a great deal of mystery."

Billy leaned around his seat to get a better view of the strange diary. The ragged yellowed parchment held odd-looking characters, none of which looked like English letters.

"The first page," the professor continued, running his finger under the lines as he translated, "merely states, 'the musings of Merlin, a servant of Our Lord, the Christ, a collection of prophecy, poetry, and pedantry.' The next page adds our dash of mystery. It says, roughly speaking, 'As you read, reflect. Although blank to the evil eye, the page will be painted in the vision of the wise, and in the language of his time shall my words come hither. Do not despise prophetic utterances, for they expose and condemn an oath falsely divined. Beware, however, lest you reveal a page before its predecessor is complete. It is the patient soul who finds the desire of his heart.'

47

"And page three contains poetry of an ancient sort in an old variety of English. It starts with a title, 'To Call a Friend, If a Dragon's Friend You Be,' and an explanatory note, 'Those who call must beware. One who summons lightning from heaven to strike his foes may find his enemies picking through his own charred bones.'

"The actual body of the poem follows." He drew a folded sheet of paper from his shirt pocket and spread it over the book. "I took the liberty of writing a translation, and I added a simple rhyme and meter pattern that the author seemed to design for this poem. I took some liberties to do so, but I think the translation is accurate."

Come thou bane of devil's mount;
Secure thy fortune in thy breast.
Diamonds, pearls, and emeralds count
And rubied crowns upon thy crest.

Fly to me O ancient sage,
Who gathers light to draw his breath,
Proving why the heathen rage
Against thy life, to seek thy death.

Darkness hates thy light-filled soul;
'Tis truth it shrouds with darkest ink.
Take thy place, thy dragon's role;
From wisdom's lake O give me drink.

Shall I use yon candlestone,
Absorbing light to steal thy fire?
If I shouldst lie beneath its trone,
Excalibur builds my funeral pyre.

God, my lord, do send my plea
To dragons' ears both far and nigh.

48

Send me help I ask on knee;
Transluminate me lest I die.

Walter leaned back and propped his head against the window. "Wow! Now that's a cool poem!" After a few seconds his face puckered, and he lifted his head again. "What does it mean?"

"I'm still working on it, Walter. Clearly it's a summons, a prayer to call a dragon, and with the properties of Excalibur and the candlestone becoming clearer, the meaning of the poem is taking shape. I have not decided, however, what *transluminate* means."

"What's on the next page, Professor?" Billy asked.

"Remarkably enough, the remaining pages, I'd say fifty or so, are completely blank. It seems we have many pieces missing in our puzzle. And that brings me to my most burning question, William. You haven't told me what became of the sword or the stone."

"Oh, yeah. Well, Bonnie couldn't lug the sword all the way back down the hill—"

"I suppose not," the professor said, "especially with her knee making her unable to walk."

"Yeah, right. Her knee. And she threw the candlestone into the woods."

"If she threw it, then it wasn't too heavy to carry, I would guess."

"Well, uh, no, that is—"

The professor folded his spectacles and slid them back into his pocket. "I understand, William. Clarity is elusive when you are honor bound to hide the details. I assume you will tell me more once you have permission from your friend, correct?"

"I want to tell you, Professor, but I really have to wait."

"Of course you do. It's clear that the story has many holes that beg for filling. I have deduced that the sword and the candlestone are the keys to the entire mystery, though I do not yet see the purpose of the stone. The sword, however, must be the true Excalibur. It had the power to transform matter into light energy when wielded by one who has a heart made pure by God and—" The professor halted, his mouth dropping open.

"What's up, Professor?" Billy asked.

The professor smacked his forehead with his palm. "Transluminate! Of course!" He retrieved his spectacles and tapped his finger on the page. "Trans means change, and luminate refers to light. The poem uses the word transluminate to describe Excalibur's method of transforming matter into light. I should have thought of that immediately."

Walter let out a snort. "It's okay, Prof. What did it take you? A whole minute?"

The professor laughed and laid his palms on top of the diary. "You are kind, Walter to ... how do you say it? Cut me some slack? In any case, it seems that the mystery is beginning to coalesce, and the clues point to Excalibur. If you could show me the approximate place of its disposal, William, I should like to search for it while you visit your friend."

"I can only guess and point out the area from the sky. It's probably within walking distance of where we're going to land though."

"Very well. While you are consulting your friend, I shall have a look around."

* * * * * *

After landing on a crude airstrip atop a grassy mountain, Billy and his mother secured Merlin II and joined their two passengers near a wing. Professor Hamilton studied his hand-held GPS while Walter looked on. A chilly alpine breeze blew against their heavy jackets. The northwesterly winds bent the brown, snow-speckled grass, signaling a renewal of winter's icy spell.

"I anticipate," the professor said, pointing down the eastern slope, "that our search should begin about one and one-third kilometers in that direction." He tucked the GPS under his arm, zipped his black leather jacket, and stretched a taupe beret over his wild hair. "Does that sound correct, William?"

"I think so." Billy fastened the next to last button on his lined Washington Redskins jacket. The bottom button was missing, lost in his backyard after he tackled his father during a Thanksgiving Day football romp. He pulled a baseball cap out of his jacket pocket and pressed it over his head. "Bonnie could tell you better than I could. I'm just not sure."

"Very well. It should take about fifteen minutes to get to our starting point, and we'll search for about thirty minutes. Then we'll meet you back here in, shall we say, one hour?"

"One hour sounds good," Mom said. "At least one of us will be here. The other might stay with our friend."

"The mystery dude?" Walter asked. "Will we get to meet him?"

Mom smiled. "If you do, don't call him the mystery dude.'

The professor checked his GPS coordinates as the breeze blew tufts of thick white hair protruding from his cap. "Shall we go, Walter? We must step lively."

Walter and the professor marched down the hillside, the professor relaying coordinate data. His voice faded as their forms shrank in the distance.

When they had traveled out of earshot, Billy turned to his mom. "I guess we'd better get going." He picked up a cardboard tube that held his drawing of Hambone. "Dad already knows we're here."

"You can sense that?"

Billy stepped toward a slope that descended at a right angle to the one the professor had chosen. "Sort of. He probably heard Merlin's prop anyway." They left the grassy area and entered a sparse forest. As they walked, the growth thickened. Leafless branches above made stick-figure shadows on the carpet of brown, crackling leaves. Bright sunshine poured through, enough to take the edge off the dry chill and sharpen the landscape.

"I guess we don't have to worry about any ambushes around here," Billy said. "There's no place to hide, and with all the crunching leaves you could hear someone coming from a mile away."

Mom stepped on a knee-high stone and vaulted over. "No slayers lurking, that's for sure." She patted a side pocket on her windbreaker. "But if one does show up, he'll find out you're not the only one packing heat."

As they plunged deeper into the forest, the towering trees gathered into dense columns of massive, wooden sentinels. The two hikers maneuvered through the twisting maze, shuffling through a familiar path and talking in soft whispers, giving each other reminders of where to turn as they approached rocks and trees they had marked on their previous visit. After winding their way through the heaviest wall of trees they had yet encountered, the oaken soldiers gave way, opening into a tiny glade surrounded by a wall of stone on one side and a fence of winter-stripped oaks on the other.

A halo of thick branches stretched above to create an ornate ceiling of knobby fingers overarching the flat, leaf-strewn ground. The sanctuary's rock boundary towered almost to the tops of the trees and bent over to create an arch. Where the arch met the trees, the sun was squelched, and the shadows painted a black curtain on the mossy stone wall, the shadowy entrance to the cave.

They walked straight toward the granite blockade and passed through the dark curtain. "It's not as cold in here," Billy said, his voice resonating in the damp recesses of the yawning tunnel.

Mom pulled a flashlight from her belt clip and flicked it on. The stream of light shot into the depths of the cave. Swirls of mist dashed through the beam in currents of newly awakened air, and a low rumble rode the air from deep within.

"I hear him," Billy said. "He's here."

"I do, too."

As they ventured farther in, a glow from somewhere in the midst of the cave brightened. The rumbling grew, like the churning of ocean breakers. They turned a corner and beheld the sight they had journeyed to find. Shrouded in a dome of sparkling light sat a massive winged dragon.

53

4

EXCALIBUR

Walter stopped beside the professor. "Is this the spot?"

Professor Hamilton eyed the GPS. "I believe so. It matches the coordinates I calculated, but it's all based on a guess I made while we were in the air."

Walter kicked at a pile of dead leaves and surveyed the bare trees that stood like sleeping wooden skeletons on the gentle incline. "Okay. What now?"

The professor marched across the slope, sniffing the brisk air as though a scent might give him a clue. "We just have to look around."

"If the sword is here, won't it be covered by leaves?" Walter picked up a rotting maple leaf and tossed it into the wind.

"Good point. Be sure to shuffle as you walk."

The two searchers dragged their feet across acres of uneven terrain, kicking up dozens of small logs, stubbing their toes on hidden rocks, and dampening their shoes in concealed snow-melt puddles. In spite of their logical, crisscross search pattern through the layers of countless leaves, they knew they could be shuffling right past their quarry, perhaps missing the sword by mere inches.

After about twenty minutes, the professor pulled his pocket watch from his trousers. "We're running short on time, Walter. We'll start heading back. Perhaps we can return with a metal detector on another day." He pointed up a rocky slope. "We'll hike over that rise and cover an area we haven't seen yet. It's a roundabout way of getting back to the plane, but we should make it on time."

"Suits me, Prof." Walter followed his teacher over the protruding crags, struggling at times to scale the larger boulders that the professor chose to climb rather than go around. The older man scrambled along with amazing agility.

He stopped near the top of the hill and set a hand over his eyes to block out the glittering sun. He stiffened. "Walter, did you see that?"

Walter shielded his eyes and stared in the same direction. "See what?"

"That glimmer." He pointed downslope toward a group of protruding rocks that interrupted the treescape about a hundred or so yards away. "Over there."

Walter caught a glimpse of a bright reflection, like the sun's rays bouncing off a car mirror. "Yep. Got it marked."

The professor marched straight toward the rocks. Walter bolted down the hill and led the way. Just before reaching their target, they stopped and stared. A gleaming sword quivered in the wind, its blade wedged deep within a large stone.

The professor gasped. "Excalibur!"

＊　　＊　　＊　　＊　　＊　　＊

Bonnie blew on the car window's glass and wiped it clean with her sleeve. The view of her old hometown brought a stream of poetic memories. The mountains that bordered Missoula were always tall and majestic, but this time of year they had settled into their long winter's nap, undressing their trees in the usual way, shaking off leafy garments in the early autumn winds, waiting to be covered in frosty white raiment. There was little snow on the bare limbs today, though a thick blanket dressed the base of the trunks, like silver skirts on pencil-thin supermodels. The road from the airport to the university was clear and dry, but dark clouds loomed in the mountains. A sporadic ensemble of flakes danced across the hood as the Ford Explorer roared onto the campus road.

The hill that towered over the University of Montana carried a huge, block letter *M* prominently emblazoned in the frosted grass near the top. On warm, sunny days, dozens of students and faculty members climbed the hill, negotiating the steep inclines on a path that switched back and forth across the hillside's broad face. Today, with snow threatening, the trails remained empty except for a dusting of frozen white and a lone bird flitting around the gigantic letter.

Throughout the trip, Bonnie answered only the most necessary questions. Since the private chartered flight had required no security check, her wings remained safely tucked in her backpack, so she didn't have to dream up any ways to dodge a search. She and her father were the only passengers in the small jet, and the lack of conversation made the flight seem interminable.

Now, after parking near the Skaggs Building, which housed the Department of Pharmaceutical Sciences, Bonnie knew she would have to break her silence. She had hoped to go straight to the hospital, but for some reason her father had to stop by his office.

"I have to pick up something here," he said as he got out of the Explorer, his smile oddly boyish. "And there's someone I want you to meet. She'll be traveling with us."

57

Bonnie pulled her coat on over her backpack and climbed out, her curiosity piqued by her father's expression. She followed him toward his office across a snow-patched, grassy field on a narrow footpath, worn to the dirt over the years by hundreds of tromping feet.

They rounded the corner of the building, past two enormous white panels that looked like oversized garage doors. The boxy structure loomed over them, its bricks showing off patterns of red, black, and gray, a vivid contrast to the tiny flecks of white falling from the darkening sky. Square, borderless windows hid the interior with dark, reflective glass, making it look like a secret headquarters for a government agency or a prison for dangerous spies. With gloomy gray clouds silently hovering, the building seemed morose and lonely, not an exciting institution of higher learning.

After taking an elevator to the third floor, they crossed the carpeted hall to the entrance of an office suite numbered 340, not the same workplace Bonnie remembered. Her dad's smaller, cramped office used to be on another floor. This suite held the office of the dean, and a nameplate carried her father's name.

"When did you get the promotion?" she asked.

He turned the knob and pushed the door open. "A few months ago. The president likes my work."

A young female greeted them from behind the waist-high receptionist's desk. "Good afternoon, Dr. Conner." With a big smile she extended her hand over the desk. "And you must be Bonnie. I'm Ashley Stalworth. Pleased to meet you. Your father's told me all about you."

Bonnie took her hand and shook it firmly, trying to return her genuine smile. "Hi, Ashley." Bonnie looked her over. She seemed too young to be a college student, maybe seventeen at the most.

"Ashley is supposed to be a junior in high school," Bonnie's father explained, "but the school's science department couldn't challenge her, so they sent her here. She's a true genius, and she's helping me with my research."

Ashley put her hands behind her back and blushed. Bonnie caught her glancing at the lump under her coat, her hidden backpack. *He told Ashley all about me? I hope not everything.*

Bonnie's father picked up a briefcase from the floor in front of the desk. "Do you have everything packed?"

Ashley held up a large wooden case with squared corners. "The latest results are in your briefcase, and the samples are in here."

"Then let's hit the road."

Bonnie's mind raced with questions. What was the research? How had her father become so familiar with a high school girl? But the most important question burst through her thoughts and came out verbally. "Aren't we going to the hospital to see my mother?"

He hurried out the door. "No. I'll explain on the way."

Ashley locked the office door, using a set of keys that hung from her belt loop. Down the hall, Bonnie's father had already punched the elevator call button and now stood inside the waiting car. Walking quickly, Ashley lugged the briefcase and held out her free hand, gesturing for Bonnie to join her.

For some reason, Bonnie wanted to grasp this friendly girl's hand, a little sister kind of feeling she had never had before, but she declined with a brief nod and a smile. There were too many weird things going on, too many unanswered questions to allow herself such familiarity.

Ashley didn't seem to mind. She just marched into the elevator, and Bonnie followed. After the slow car lowered the silent trio to the first floor, they clopped along the shiny terrazzo floor toward the exit doors. Once outside, Ashley dutifully strode behind her professor across the field to the parking lot.

Bonnie stayed close, eyeing every detail through the thickening snow flurries. Ashley wore designer jeans, modestly cut, fairly loose fitting and riding high on her slender waist. With her coat slung over her shoulder, her long-sleeved blouse was exposed, feminine but not fancy, tucked in and accentuating her fit body. She was obviously athletic, with toned muscles tightening the sleeve on the arm that lugged the heavy case. The stiffening breeze threw its weight against their bodies, blowing Ashley's shoulder-length brown hair around her face.

Bonnie shivered. *She must have logs burning in her belly. I'm freezing with a coat on!*

When they arrived at the Explorer, Ashley set her case down and opened the front passenger door for Bonnie.

Bonnie tapped her knuckles on the back window. "Why don't we sit together?"

Ashley smiled. "Great! We have a long drive ahead of us. Maybe we can get to know each other."

Bonnie pulled off her coat and slid into the back. By the time she was seated, her father had already started the motor. "A long drive?" she said. "What's going on?"

He backed the SUV out of the parking space. "We're not going to the hospital. We're going to a lab that I built up near Flathead Lake a couple of hours away. Because of your mother's deteriorating condition, the doctors gave up hope and recommended that we remove her feeding tube and let her die. But I couldn't give up. I had her moved to my lab quite some time ago, and I've been taking care of her myself."

"Some time ago? But what about the picture? I thought you took that yesterday."

"Actually, I took it a few weeks after you left Montana. I faked the date to get you to come home. If I had explained everything, I would have had to reveal some secrets I wasn't ready to reveal."

Bonnie scowled, a feeling of dread creeping along her skin. "You mean, you lied?"

He stared straight ahead, waiting for a traffic light to change, silent, as if trying to think of a good answer.

Bonnie looked at him in the rearview mirror. Those cold, calculating eyes revealed another lie brewing. He would speak it soon.

Nausea churned her stomach. She turned her head to watch the worsening weather. Large, wet flakes fell all around, sticking easily to the grass but melting as they tumbled to the warmer pavement.

When the light changed, he cleared his throat. "A lie is sometimes necessary to save a life, Bonnie. And that's what I'm trying to do, save your mother's life. When we get to the lab, I'll explain everything, and I think you will be very pleased at what you see."

61

Bonnie dug her fingers into the armrest. Sure, lying to save a life is one thing, but lying to your own daughter to send her back to her nightmares is another. She rubbed her hand up and down her sleeve. The thought of a laboratory gave her the shivers—needles puncturing her skin again and again, each drawing yet another tube of blood. Her arm itched and her head pounded, but she would face a ten-foot-long needle and give a gallon of blood if it meant helping her mother.

The strange haunting call grew louder. It had to be her mother calling. What else could it be? And now she was probably only a couple of hours away from seeing her again, face-to-face. Only two hours. They would seem like an eternity.

* * * * * *

"Professor, it's stuck, like someone stabbed the stone."

"Indeed, it is, Walter." The professor walked around the head-high boulder, rubbing his gloved fingers along its granite-like faces. "Extraordinary. It sliced the rock like it was a rotting mushroom, and there's not a hint of rust on the blade even after weeks of exposure."

"And the markings look like the ones on your replica. It's Excalibur, all right." Walter climbed onto the boulder and grabbed the hilt. "Hey, Professor, want to see if I'm the rightful king of England?"

"Pull all you wish, Walter. The legends speak of a sword in a stone, though most say it was not Excalibur. I expect, however, that we're seeing history repeat itself, and Excalibur might well reveal the rightful heir."

At first Walter tugged lightly on the sword, then with all his might. When it didn't budge, he gave up, gasping for breath. "I guess ... I guess I don't qualify."

The professor waved a hand for him to come down. "I have no doubt that you have strength, Walter, but an heir to the throne you are not."

"Then the sword's stuck there? How are we going to get it out?"

"I have a theory, but—" A ringing sound interrupted. The professor reached for the phone at his hip. "Charles Hamilton speaking. ... Yes, Carl. I'm with your son on a mountain. We're still in West Virginia. ... No, of course not. You may call me anytime. ... Yes, that is important news. I'm not sure what it means for our journey, but we will soon find out. I will try to call you tonight to let you know our progress. If you discover anything further, please let us know right away." He pressed a button on the phone and held it at his side.

"What's up, Prof?"

The professor returned the phone to his belt, his hands moving slowly as he snapped it in place. "Your father got through to his sources. They found a death certificate for Miss Silver's mother."

"So Bonnie's mother really is dead?"

"I'm afraid so. Although it pains me to say it, we must leave the sword behind for now. We should hurry back to the airplane to meet the others. I think this news corroborates my earlier fears. Miss Silver is in serious trouble."

*   *   *   *   *   *

The dragon peered at his visitors, his red-centered eyes wide and gleaming. As Billy and his mother crept closer, the massive beast rose to his feet and stretched, scattering his brilliant regeneracy dome into thousands of sparkling glitters rolling across the floor, fizzling and fading away. For a moment, darkness filled the cave, but a flash of streaming fire hurtled from the dragon and splashed onto one of the walls. The flame ignited the rag-covered top of a torch that hung in a metal stand, brightening the cave.

Fresh from his regeneracy sleep, the dragon appeared vigorous and well rested. His two enormous outstretched wings flapped, shifting him toward them, and his regal face seemed to smile.

Mom edged forward. "Jared, it's so good to see you again." She reached out and clumsily touched his closest flank.

"Marilyn, dearest one," the dragon replied, "I am enraptured to see you again. But, please, call me Clefspeare, for I am no longer a man. Jared, your husband, has died."

Mom lowered her head and covered her mouth with a fist.

Billy winced. Those words had to hurt. He stepped forward, shuffling his boots in the loose dirt. "Uh, Dad."

The dragon swung his neck around and drew his head near. His hot breath flowed across Billy's hair. "I will allow you to call me Dad," Clefspeare replied, "though I prefer my dragon name. You need to reckon with the fact that your true father is gone. Jared's son lives on, though Jared is no more."

Tears welled in Billy's eyes. He clenched his teeth and balled his hand into a fist. His mission was too important. He had to keep his composure. "We have some news, and we need your advice."

"I will help if I can."

Billy told Bonnie's story in as much detail as he thought necessary. He also explained the presence of the professor and Walter on the mountain and their desire to know what was going on.

"So ... Dad. What do you think we should do? Should we let the professor and Walter in on everything?"

Clefspeare heaved a deep sigh. Sparks flew from his nostrils, settling on the cave floor and dying on the cold ground. "You may bring your friends to me. While you are away, I shall consider what I will reveal. But do not prepare them. I know Walter, but I have never met your professor. How a person reacts to a shocking discovery helps me evaluate his character."

"Sure. It's your call." Billy reached for his mother's hand. "C'mon. Let's go get them."

"No," Clefspeare said, his gentle but firm command echoing throughout the cave. He cast his gaze on Mom. "Let your son fetch his friends. We need this time to talk." She nodded, her head still low.

Clutching the flashlight, Billy hustled out of the cave, retraced his steps to the plane, and bounced on his toes as the cold breeze bit his tightening cheeks. After a few minutes, the professor and Walter appeared on the slope, huffing as they strode up the steep incline.

"It's okay," Billy called. "My friend said you can come and talk to him."

The professor halted and let out a long stream of white vapor. "Very good. I also have two news items for you. We found the sword, and it is Excalibur."

"That's awesome! Where is it?"

Walter posed as though he were trying to pull a sword from the ground. "It's stuck in a rock. Caught like a twenty dollar bill in a politician's hand."

"And you can't get it out?"

Walter shook his head. "Not a chance, unless you know someone who's kin to a king."

Billy squinted. "Kin to a king? What're you talking about?"

"We shall address that issue later," the professor said. "The other news item is more pressing. Walter's father called. It seems that Miss Silver's mother really is dead. They were able to find a certificate of demise a short time ago."

A boiling sensation erupted in Billy's stomach, and icy chills spread across his skin. His teeth chattered as he stalked down the slope. "Come on," he called with a wave of his hand. "Let's get this show on the road."

Walter followed, but the professor paused. "Shall I retrieve Merlin's Diary from the airplane? Will your friend know anything about it?"

"He might," Billy called back. "It's worth a try."

Professor Hamilton climbed the slope back to the airplane and returned with the book tucked under his arm, then the three marched down and hustled the rest of the way.

When they arrived at the cave, Billy pointed out the shadowy entrance. "It's right here where the stone turns dark."

"A cave?" Walter said. "Who's your friend? Fred Flintstone?"

"This is not the time for jesting, Walter," the professor said. "I believe we are just beginning to probe a series of mind-bending mysteries, and I can feel the excitement of adventure racing through my bones. Let us conduct ourselves as men now and not as boys. I perceive that we shall need all of our cunning and strength." He straightened his beret. "Lead on, William."

65

With the professor and Walter close behind, Billy entered the tunnel, a cold shiver running up his back. This wasn't a game; it was life and death. A bad decision could keep them from finding Bonnie before it was too late.

They rounded the bend. The moment of truth had arrived. The great secret would be out—his dragon nature revealed. How would the professor take it? Would Walter understand?

His mother met him at the opening to the inner chamber and walked with him, her head low. Light from the torch illuminated his fellow travelers' faces, the dancing flame reflecting in their narrowing pupils. The professor's mouth gaped, but Walter stood calmly, a huge smile growing on his face.

The dragon's pointed ears perked up and rotated in all directions as though they were satellite dishes searching for a distant signal. He bowed low, a formal, stately bow of submission. After clearing his throat to speak, Clefspeare trembled as though shaken by awestruck wonder.

"Master Merlin! You have returned at last!"

5

THROUGH THE VEIL

The drive to Flathead Lake cut through a long, mountain-bordered valley. Dark clouds hovered over the peaks to the right, while bursts of dancing flurries pelted the windshield. The gorgeous scenery and friendly conversation with Ashley drew Bonnie into a pleasant state of distraction. Her worries about her mother faded to a mere nagging feeling in the back of her mind. "So what do your parents think about your research projects?" Bonnie asked. "Do they mind you being gone a lot?"

Ashley hesitated, and her shoulders sank with her lowering voice. "My parents died when I was a toddler."

A lump grew in Bonnie's throat. "Oh … I'm so sorry." She reached out a hand. Ashley took it, intertwining her fingers with Bonnie's.

Bonnie resisted an urge to draw away. Ashley's affectionate response was more intimate than expected, but it felt good, the melancholy touch of a sad friend who needed closeness. She ran a thumb along Ashley's hand. "Do you mind telling me how it happened?"

Ashley shook her head while staring at the clasp of hands in her lap. "I'd tell you if I knew." She turned to Bonnie, her smile slowly reemerging. "You see, my grandfather adopted me. He's the only father I can remember. I even call him Daddy. He's a widower, so all we have is each other." She returned her gaze to her lap and sighed. "I must have asked him a hundred times what happened, but he kept telling me it was too awful to talk about. I looked through old newspapers at the library, but I couldn't find anything about accidents or fires or anyone who knew more about the story, so I finally decided to try to forget about it."

Bonnie's own sad stories returned to mind, the loss of her mother and how she suspected her father of contributing to her death. She whispered, "Do you remember your parents at all?"

Ashley freed her hand and pushed back her hair, though it needed no grooming. "Sometimes I think I remember them, images now and then, but it's not much, so I can't say I miss them." Ashley's smile made a complete comeback, and a refreshed glow shone in her eyes. "Daddy's been the best father a girl could ask for. He's gentle and sweet, and he loves to sit and talk about anything that's on my mind, except, of course, my parents."

Bonnie smiled with Ashley but kept her voice low. "He sounds wonderful. Do you have to spend much time away from him when you do your research?"

"No. He's the main reason I'm involved in the project. When I started, he was getting old and feeble, so I made sure he stayed where I could be with him if he needed me. We both live in the lab complex now. I get to see him every night."

"He lives in the lab? So the lab is a motel, too? When are you going to tell me what's going on there?"

Ashley gave her a coy smile and leaned back in her seat. "You'll find out soon."

Ashley's refusal to explain brought Bonnie's nagging thoughts to the forefront again. Not knowing what was going on or where they were heading was maddening. She sighed and settled back in her seat, letting the awesome landscape consume her thoughts again. To her left, Flathead Lake stretched for miles and miles, a magnificent blue expanse of silky smooth water, a tree-lined mirror for the heavens. She vaguely remembered riding on a boat there once when she was little, but after her wings started growing, she didn't get to go to the lake again or to most other public places.

To her right, a series of dirt and gravel driveways led to precarious heights in the foothills and mountains, each a mystery. Who lived at the ends of those paths? Were they lonely way up there where the snow-filled clouds shrouded their homes? Did they store up months of supplies and hibernate for the winter, ready to emerge when the sunny days of spring melted their fortresses of ice? Images of hiking in snow-covered forests seeped in, visions from her childhood. Her short legs scampered over deep drifts, and a strong hand held her up from one side. That was a long time ago … back when she looked normal.

With haunting memories and mysteries abounding, Bonnie felt trapped, riding in a vehicle driven by a man who might really be a monster. Her stomach churned like a bubbling vat

69

of curdled milk. She was so far from home, even the Montana home she used to know.

"I … I think I'm getting sick," she said.

Her father tightened his grip on the steering wheel and slowed down. "Do we have to pull over now, or can you last till we get there? It's less than thirty minutes."

Bonnie pointed at a store ahead, a Conoco station with a homemade sign on the front—Barbara's Market. "Can we stop there? I'd better run to the bathroom."

"Okay. I'll gas up while we're here. Do you need any money for anything?"

"No." Bonnie patted her jeans pocket. "I still have what you gave me at the airport."

With snow falling in thicker streams, Ashley and Bonnie hurried toward the shop, not bothering to pull on their coats for the short walk. The fresh breeze and quick march had already relieved Bonnie's nausea, and her brain kicked into gear. All these delays weren't making any sense. She had to let someone know where she was and how to find her.

After brushing lingering flakes from her shoulders, she hurried toward the restroom at the back of the store while surveying the colorful assortment of convenience grocery items, tourist souvenirs, and grab-and-go fast foods. She stopped at a carousel of postcards and scanned the bank of cards nearest her.

Ashley grasped the card rack. "I thought you were sick."

"Uh, I am. I mean … I was." Bonnie pushed her thumbs behind her backpack straps and hitched it higher. "I'm feeling better. I guess I just needed to move around. I think if I wash my face I'll be fine."

"Okay. I'm getting a drink. Want anything?"

Bonnie shook her head. "I'm fine. Thanks." When Ashley turned, Bonnie grabbed a postcard and stuffed it into her back pocket before heading to the restroom. Once inside, she splashed cold water on her face and dried off with a paper towel. She then pulled the postcard from her pocket and a pen from her backpack. One side of the card had a photo of Flathead Lake, and the other side carried the name of the store imprinted near the bottom. It was perfect. She sat, wrote a note, and addressed the card.

With the postcard still in hand, she slowly opened the restroom door, but it flew open on its own, revealing an elderly woman. Bonnie jumped back, holding a hand over her chest and pressing the postcard against her shirt.

"I'm sorry, dear," the woman said, smiling. "I didn't mean to frighten you."

Bonnie took a deep breath to quiet her pounding heart. "That's okay. I thought you were someone else."

The woman stepped into the restroom and gestured toward the card in Bonnie's hand. "Careful. You don't want to bend that pretty card." She turned the water on and picked up a bar of soap. "Is it for friends back home?"

"Uh … yes. It's for close friends. I'm visiting from West Virginia."

The woman gave her a knowing nod, her short gray hair bobbing around her perky eyes. "We get lots of folks from the East. Not as many this time of year, but we do get them."

"We? Do you live around here?"

"For sixty-five years," she replied with a proud smile. "I run this store."

Bonnie fished in her front pocket and withdrew a wrinkled five dollar bill. "Please, ma'am, I'm in a big hurry." She smoothed out the bill and extended it, trying to keep her hand from shaking. "Will this cover the cost of the card and postage, and would you mail it for me? I need it to get there as soon as possible."

The woman looked at Bonnie's hand for a moment, then caught it in her own, closing Bonnie's fingers around her money. She whispered, "Is everything all right? Are you in trouble?"

Bonnie let her hand relax. "I'm okay. I'm with my father, but I haven't seen him in a long time. I'm just … kind of nervous."

The woman nodded. "Oh. Nervous. I see."

Bonnie drew back and handed the card to her, then presented the five-dollar bill again, this time without shaking.

The woman waved her hand. "Oh, don't worry about it. I'll be glad to mail it for you." She eyed Bonnie carefully once more. "I'll send it the fastest way possible."

"That's great. I can't thank you enough."

"Just tell your friends back home to come out for a visit."

Bonnie headed for the exit and turned back. "That card might just do the trick."

* * * * * *

Professor Hamilton stiffened, his stare fixed on the giant creature bowing before him.

Billy grinned. The professor had said he expected strange events, but seeing a real dragon, and a prostrate one, no less, obviously caught him off guard.

The professor clasped his hands together and cleared his throat. "Merlin? Why do you call me Merlin?"

The dragon peered through his partially closed eyes. "Master, I have not seen your face in over a thousand years, but your image was etched into my mind as surely as the commandments were chiseled into tablets of stone by the finger of God. I remain your humble servant, Clefspeare."

"Clearly this is a case of mistaken identity, Mr. Clefspeare. My name is Charles Hamilton. I am a homeschool teacher, former professor at Oxford University, and specialist in Arthurian history and legends. Although I am very familiar with the history and myths surrounding Merlin, I assure you that I am not he."

Clefspeare rose to his former sitting position and extended his neck. "Remarkable," the dragon kept repeating as he moved his head to take in the teacher's image from various angles. "Then it has happened. It must have happened."

The professor kept his body stiff, though he moved his eyes to follow the dragon's glowing face as it glided all around. "Sir, having a dragon such as yourself examining me with such fervor is quite unnerving. I shall be glad to answer whatever questions you wish to ask, but I must request that you proceed before I leap right out of my shoes."

Billy slapped a hand over his mouth while his mother stifled a laugh. "Yeah, Dad," Billy said, speaking between his fingers. "What's up?" He glanced at Walter. He was smiling, almost laughing, like he was enjoying a funny movie.

Professor Hamilton turned his head toward Billy, squinted, and mouthed, "Dad?"

"Yes," Clefspeare said. "I am Billy's father, in a manner of speaking. Forgive me for my emotional outburst. I was a human for over a dozen centuries, and seeing your face brought a flood of fond memories from times long ago. Though you did not know this before today, you are the image of Merlin, the great prophet, and, not only that, you carry his journal.

The leather cover bears his scent to this day. But we will discuss your resemblance and how you came by the book in a moment. We have urgent business in Montana."

The professor set the book on the ground and pulled a copy of the hospital photo from his coat's inner pocket. "Yes, the matter of Bonnie Silver." He displayed the photo for Clefspeare. "I assume that William has apprised you of all that he knows, but there have been new developments. Walter's father has discovered a death certificate for Bonnie's mother, so her father's pretext was false. This makes his character that much more doubtful, even sinister, I would say."

Clefspeare gazed at the photo for several seconds before responding. "You have spoken well. These developments are distressing. In order for me to help you, however, it is imperative that you understand my history. Being a man of sound intellect and training, I assume you want to know everything about how a dragon could be Billy's father."

"Yes, and any extraneous details that might help me combine your knowledge with my own to solve other puzzles we have unearthed."

"Such as?"

The professor returned the photo to its place and retrieved Merlin's Diary from the ground. "Such as this book. Its mystery is great. I have pondered its meager contents for hours, yet I have solved very little. We have also found Excalibur, but we don't yet have it in our possession. It's embedded in a stone quite nearby, and I'm afraid King Arthur is no longer available to extract it."

"I will help you understand the book soon enough," Clefspeare replied. "Perhaps when I tell my story, you will figure it out for yourself as well as the mystery of Excalibur's power. I advise all of you to have a seat. It is a long tale, and although Bonnie's fate depends on swift action, I assure you that understanding this story will help you in rescuing her."

The dragon waited for his audience to sit comfortably, then raised his head high. First, with a puff of dense smoke, he blew out the torch, and blackness descended on the cave. Then, with a soothing, hypnotic tone, he spoke in a quiet voice, and the words reverberated in gentle echoes. "Do not be distracted by thoughts of the day or your cares for loved ones. Cast your eyes deep into the darkness and see the images of antiquity. Let your thoughts walk through the winding cave. Let your minds wander into the past.

"I am Clefspeare, your guide into forgotten days, the age of knights and kings. Follow my light and see the ghosts of the past come to life before your eyes." The dragon blew a ferocious stream of white-hot flame against the cave wall, filling the entire cavern with intense heat and light. Then, in a second, the blaze disappeared. Yet, the wall held a glowing imprint of the flame's violent massage. Fiery characters emerged, first a man wearing a crown, then a man and a woman in front of him, each on bended knee. They seemed to move, animated somehow by the crackling, pulsating cinders. As his listeners watched in silence, Clefspeare gave the characters voice.

"Clefspeare, I dub you Jared, son of Arthur." The king tapped the bowing man's shoulder lightly with a gleaming sword. "By this decree, I name you my son, though truly you are closer than any of my natural offspring." He turned and tapped the lady's shoulder, touching her long flowing blonde hair that draped her sparkling white gown. "And you, dear Hartanna, I dub Irene, for your very presence brings peace to my soul. You are now my daughter, a treasured princess, who I hope will always find peace within the walls of my palace."

King Arthur lifted Excalibur from Irene's shoulder, then handed the blade to an old man who stood uneasily at his side. The sword maintained its faint white glow, strong enough to illuminate the wrinkled hands of the older man, yet it seemed no more than the brightest candle among the dozens that lined the inner court of the king's palace. When the older man slid the sword into its sheath, the ornate scabbard swallowed the glow, allowing the candlelight to spread throughout the room.

The two men stood on a raised platform, not as high as a stage, but high enough to display the honor and authority of anyone who would sit on the throne at its center. Arthur lifted a scroll from a table at his side. "For your protection, I have entered your names as Reginald Bannister and Tabitha Silver in the official records as my adopted son and daughter. Hide your identities well, for if your enemies discover them, you will be chased by bloodthirsty hounds for centuries to come. I suggest choosing different surnames for yourselves for the time being, though you may return to Bannister and Silver to protect your inheritance when a safer time comes."

Jared lifted his eyes toward the king and slowly rose. "Sire, I humbly accept your gracious bestowal of your good name. May I always bring the name of Arthur honor and a good heritage."

Irene stood at Jared's side. "I, too, am honored, Your Majesty." She rubbed her hand across her bare forearm. Her skin seemed to radiate silvery white. "Having shorn my scales, and with them the dignity of a dragoness, I feel clothed once again with the integrity, nobility, and heritage that your deeds have inspired. May I wear this livery well."

King Arthur's solemn face broke into a proud, fatherly smile. "Well spoken, my friends. I trust that I will be able to live up to my duty and keep you safe in your new skin. Have the other dragons taken the necessary steps to secure their safety?"

Jared glanced at Irene, then refocused on the king. "The ladies have taken new names and blended into life in the nearby villages, as you instructed. We do not know, however, what has become of Irene's brother, Valcor."

The king's brow lifted. "The other male dragon?"

"Yes. With Gartrand's death, he and I are the only remaining males. He disappeared soon after our transformation."

Arthur stroked his short, graying beard. "Hmmm. Perhaps his secrecy is for the best."

Irene nodded. "That is what we thought as well. Devin will never be able to learn his whereabouts from us, even through torture."

"True. And speaking of Devin, now that our ceremony is complete, we must make haste." He turned to the man at his side. "Merlin, is there any new word?"

The older man raised a long staff and set its end on the platform floor. He placed Excalibur on his chair and cleared his throat. "No, Sire. My counsel stands. Devin's traitorous band could attack at any moment. I have arranged for your knights to secretly assemble at Blood Hollow. I suggest that you leave through your escape route at once to convene with them. Gawain will meet you at the tunnel exit and escort you to the other knights."

Arthur strapped on his armor and weapons, then took his sword from Merlin's seat.

Merlin grasped Arthur's wrist. "But you must leave Excalibur."

Arthur pulled away from Merlin's grip. He lifted Excalibur, extending his arms to display the sheathed sword in his palms. "Go into battle without the sword?" He strapped the scabbard to the belt around his waist. "I should say not!"

Merlin held out his hands. "I have more need of it. Devin's tiny army is counting on surprise to win. When you arrive, your forces will crush him like a shoe on a cockroach. Should you come late, Excalibur is my only hope for survival."

Arthur placed his hand on Excalibur's hilt and hesitated, while outside the door the distant sound of clanking steps shattered the evening's quiet meeting.

"There is no more time," Merlin said, his hands shaking. "Trust me. Leave Excalibur and fly to Blood Hollow. Gawain will have a sword for you."

Arthur unfastened the sword from his belt, scabbard and all, and handed it to Merlin. He then scrambled to a door at the corner of a nearby wall and shut it behind him. The secret door disappeared from sight when its edge met the perfectly matched wall.

Jared hurriedly put his arms through the sleeves of a purple robe, not Arthur's formal council robe, but one that the king often wore during evening meetings. "Should I wear the crown?"

Merlin helped him straighten the sleeves. "No. Your hair is a close enough match, so the robe should be sufficient. Just keep your back to the door. I expect Devin to enter at any moment." He turned to Irene. "You may face the door, kneeling before our faux king. Can you make yourself cry?"

Irene shook her head. "Not without provocation. I have not yet learned all the ways of women."

"Then try to look sad, as though entreating the king for someone's life."

Within seconds, a servant came to the inner doorway of the court. "Sir Devin to see His Majesty."

"Let him approach," Merlin said. "I will speak to him."

When the servant departed, Jared spun toward the back of the room. Irene dropped to her knees and extended her folded hands toward him, twisting her face in counterfeit pain. Merlin stepped to the entryway to intercept the quickly marching Devin. "His Majesty has a guest, Sir Devin. May I give him a message for you?"

Devin looked over Merlin's shoulder at Irene and squinted. "Is the lady ill? She seems to be having intestinal distress."

"Not sickness. Her entreaty is a private matter. We will be in prayer for her for the next half hour, and then I shall escort His Majesty to his chamber if he wishes to go."

Merlin noted a hint of a smile in Devin's otherwise stoic expression. Devin bowed and spoke in his most formal and reverent voice. "Please give His Majesty my blessings, and I will spend the entire half hour on my knees as well." Devin gave Merlin a polite nod. "Good evening to you, Master Merlin." The knight left the court with the same quick march that brought him in.

When the door closed, Jared turned around. "Do you think it worked?"

"I think so. A man who is not trustworthy rarely trusts anyone, yet, I believe that our ruse has convinced him that King Arthur is in this room."

Irene rose and approached Merlin. "Then how soon will he attack?"

"He believes he has a half hour, so I would guess we have only half again of that before he strikes." Merlin knelt on the platform, and Jared and Irene joined him. "We should pray, as I told Devin we would, but not for the lady's entreaty, rather for the king's quick return with his men."

After a few moments of silence, Merlin stood and pulled Excalibur from its sheath. The sword blazed. Jared jumped to his feet, his heart pounding at the sight of its brilliant, unearthly glow. Irene's eyes widened to take in the beauty. It shone much more brightly than when its gentle flat side dubbed them Arthur's adopted heirs. Now it looked ready to sever the heads of a thousand hardened soldiers.

As Merlin waved the blade slowly, a blinding beam of light shot from its tip and burned a hole through the ceiling. "It will cut boulders and oaks for any warrior that wields it," he said, "but its greatest power is reserved for the hands of the holy."

Merlin tilted his head upward as though talking to someone suspended in the air. "I am now certain that the king will not arrive in time. I will have to use Excalibur to extinguish the enemy, and in the process, I will conduct my greatest experiment."

"Experiment?" Jared asked.

Merlin cast his gaze on Jared and Irene. "Excalibur does not merely cut," he continued, "it transforms. It changes matter into light energy. It transluminates. If I wield it to kill, its radiance will shatter a man's bones into shards of flashing luminescence, and his remains will be absorbed into a candle's breath or crushed by the ignorance of a dark shadow. And his soul? If it is not somehow trapped on the earth, it will be sent straight to the judgment seat of God."

Jared stared, enraptured by the old man's explanation, while Irene stood equally transfixed, frozen in fear on the cold stone floor.

"Jared, you and Irene must enter the tunnel door for safety. When Excalibur's power fills the room, all who remain will be transluminated, perhaps even you, though you now wear the king's name. Since I bear the sword, I think I will not die, but since I am not of Arthur's lineage, I am still vulnerable. I believe I will be changed."

"Changed?" Irene asked. "Changed into what?"

"As with the rest, my body will likely become light energy, though I think I will survive. Whether I will live on in spirit or not, I cannot say. Perhaps I will come back in another form, as another person, restored to physical matter."

"Reincarnation?" Jared asked. "As the heretics teach?"

"Not at all like reincarnation, Jared, but I am impressed. You have learned your theology well in such a short time, though you may need to learn to express it with a bit more grace. I'm hoping my adventure will be as Jesus taught when speaking of John the Baptist, 'et si vultis recipere ipse est Helias qui venturus est.'"

"I ... I do not understand."

"Neither did his disciples, even when it was spoken in their own tongue, for they did not have ears to hear. You, on the other hand, have not yet learned Latin. It means, 'And if you care to accept it, he himself is Elijah, who was to come.'" Merlin picked up an old book that rested next to his chair and showed Jared and Irene the back of the title page. "Can you read this?"

They looked over Merlin's shoulder. "Yes," Jared said, "The words are quite clear."

Irene nodded. "I do not understand the riddle I see, but I am able to read the text."

Merlin turned the page. "And now?"

Jared smiled. "Is this some kind of jest, Master? The page is blank."

Merlin put a hand over Jared's eyes. "It is as though a veil is covering your eyes." He lifted his hand and waved it over the page. "And now, Jared, son of Arthur, can you read it?"

Jared stared at the book's crisp, clean page. This time, dark script slowly appeared, beautiful handwriting, phrases cut into poetic lines. For some reason, however, he could not bring them completely into focus. "I see the writing, but it seems to float, as though I am seeing it through a thick dark glass. I cannot read it."

"Before this day is over," Merlin said, "the words on this page will become clear." He placed the book in Jared's hands and picked up Excalibur. "This is my perpetual diary. Guard it with your life. In some ways it is more dangerous than the great sword, but only a wise man will glean from its counsel. To understand its wisdom requires the brightest of lights and the greatest of the abiding gifts."

The clanking of soldiers' weapons and marching footsteps approached. Merlin pushed Jared and Irene toward the corner door. "Go! Go!"

They hurried to obey. Jared knew he had no place in this matter. Having become a human only a few weeks before, he understood neither his standing nor his responsibility in the domain of men. After seeing Irene to a safe place in the low inner hallway, he shut the door almost completely. He left a crack, just enough to watch the events unfold, but not enough, he hoped, to allow Excalibur's lethal radiance into the secret chamber.

Two armed men broke down the door and stretched loaded bowstrings back to their ears. Merlin stood tall, holding the great sword in both hands, its point straight up. The men stopped, mesmerized by the brilliant glow, while six others poured through the door. Each halted as they beheld the sword.

Jared searched the faces but couldn't locate Devin. Would he come later to try to assume the throne? *The slimy worm. Letting his lackeys take the brunt while he prances on daisies out in the garden.*

When a band of twelve or so had arrived, Merlin waved the sword in a great circle. The treacherous soldiers seemed rooted to the stone floor, their legs trembling like saplings in a storm's fury. A single beam from Excalibur's tip multiplied into hundreds and flashed in all directions until they joined into a massive wave of light.

The luminescent surge washed through the court, and particles of sparkling light buzzed through the traitors like starving locusts. Their bodies melted away, and only swirls of twinkling effervescence remained. Shields and armor clattered to the floor to mark where men had stood.

Just before Excalibur's beam flashed into his corner, Jared slammed the door shut. He could almost feel the rush of light crash against his escape hatch. Maybe its probing fingers would find no cracks, no breach to seep through to grab another victim.

Jared pressed his hands against his body—his solid, intact body. Irene sat against the opposite wall, holding her arms around her knees. A single, wall-mounted lantern reflected in her wide eyes. Jared pressed his ear against the thick door but could hear nothing.

He waited, nervous and uncertain. The light had flashed around the room as if driven by wrath—possessing an intellect, a mind of fury. Never before had he felt such terror. As a dragon he had feared nothing, but now, without scales or lethal breath, he was helpless, trained only in the rudiments of combat.

Still carrying the book, he pushed the door open, mentally shushing its barely audible squeaks. With one eye he peeked into the courtroom, trying to adjust to its candlelight. Gradually, the shadows dispelled. The room was barren. Only dark lumps of armor lay scattered over the white stone floor, like black toadstools polluting a pristine field.

Jared gestured toward the wall lantern and whispered to Irene. "You had better douse that light so you will stay hidden."

Irene nodded and stood to blow out the flame.

"Will you be frightened?"

"I was a dragon," she replied, a sad smile gracing her lips. "I am accustomed to dark places."

Jared stepped out into the field of metallic debris. He walked to the throne's platform and placed the diary on Merlin's chair. Littered beside the throne lay the remains of the first traitor, a swirl of sparks rising like glittering smoke. Jared picked up a shield and an empty mail shirt. The undergarments were gone but the armor remained. What did it all mean?

Rapid footsteps carried from the hall into the room, growing louder by the second. Jared looked back at the secret door.

Irene peeked through the gap. He signaled for her to hide. She ducked inside, leaving the door partially open.

Jared rushed to a curtain behind the throne and twisted the silky fabric around his body. Through the veil he could see Devin march into the room. His shoes clacked and echoed in the strangely quiet chamber, then stopped dead still.

The armored knight stalked from the doorway to the center of the chamber, picking up mail shirts and letting them clatter back to the floor. He pivoted toward the throne and stared as if he could see Jared wrapped in the purple fabric. With a lunge, he leaped onto the platform, then stood with his hands on his hips. Jared's heart thumped so hard he could feel it pulsing in his throat. Should he fight? Should he run?

Devin leaned over. When he straightened, he held a sword in his hand—Excalibur. Its residual glow shone brightly, piercing the veil. Devin, the lone remaining traitor, the self-styled knight, tightened his grip around the hilt. The sword's light vanished.

Devin sheathed the sword and turned away. The evil knight's footsteps clopped, and his laughter echoed as he left the room. "Palin, bring the stone," he shouted, his voice fading in the distance.

Chills covered Jared's skin, goose bumps that chided him, each calling him a milksop for hiding like a thumb-sucking toddler behind his mother's skirt. A boiling factory of rage and embarrassment sent pulses of blood toward his eyes, turning his face hot. When he was a dragon, he would have sent a tsunami of white-hot fire roaring out of his mouth and nostrils to personally escort "Sir" Devin into a dragon's version of hell. *Welcome to my inferno you sniveling caitiff!* Yet, Jared had become the sniveler, and cold sweat replaced the fiery blasts. *Do all humans feel this way? Why do I feel so small and sick?*

Jared snatched a mail shirt from the ground and slung it across the room, his gaze following it as it slid to a stop in front of Merlin's chair, his empty chair.

The book!

He scrambled over the armor and frantically searched around the chair, the throne, and then back to the chair. The book was gone!

Jared fumed. It must have been Devin. He was the only person in the room, the only one who could have stolen Merlin's diary.

He grabbed a sword from the floor and screamed, "Devin, you son of a leprous jackal! You recreant thief, plucking treasures from dead men's bones! Come back here and fight like a man!"

Devin appeared at the door, his shoulders squared and his jaw firmly set around a vicious smile. A gleaming gem swayed in front of his chest, dangling at the end of a gold necklace and absorbing swirls of sparkling light. It seemed to carry his malevolence as it drew in light as easily as the evil knight drew breath.

Jared stiffened, not knowing whether to fight or run. He had learned some swordplay, but he had little hope of matching blades with a knight, even a self-proclaimed one. His mind battled his body, and he cursed his petrifying fear.

If I run from this serpent, I will be the worst of infidels. It is time to be a man. He held his ground, raising his sword in a defensive posture. Devin laughed derisively and set the diary on the floor. He lifted the gleaming Excalibur with both hands, marched to Jared, and knocked his sword away with one swing.

"No time to kill you properly," Devin said. "The king's army is closing in on the castle, so I came back here to search for an escape." He looked past Jared toward the secret door, still ajar. "I cannot allow you to tell the king of my whereabouts. I shall have to dispose of you without giving you a fair fight."

Devin raised the sword again. Jared leaped forward, tackled the evil knight, and wrestled him to the floor. As they fell, Jared felt Excalibur's sting, the edge of the blade catching his neck and slicing deeply. Jared rolled on the floor in agony. Blood spurted like a scarlet geyser.

After grabbing the diary, Devin hustled through the escape door, closing it behind him while Jared lay writhing and pressing his palm against the hemorrhaging artery. The last thing Jared remembered was a dozen gauntleted hands lifting him. Then everything went black.

87

"Jared survived," Clefspeare continued as the cinders on the wall faded, "but he was not the same man. He vowed never to hide from danger again nor fear any weapons of this earth." Clefspeare relit the torch with a fiery snort, and everyone in his audience rubbed their eyes to adjust to the light. "He learned the ways of men and lived as one for over a thousand years, only to be returned to the draconic state you see before you now. Irene watched the cowardly Devin rush right past her, and she ran to help her adopted brother. She carried him to the physician with the help of the king's knights who arrived only moments later. She, like Jared, married a normal human over a thousand years later, and she gave birth to a daughter, whom they christened—"

"Bonnie," the professor finished.

"Yes. Bonnie. And she, like my son, has dragon traits. Billy has fiery breath with protective scales in his mouth, while Bonnie has dragon wings and can fly."

"Wings hidden in her backpack," the professor said. "Who could have guessed?" He stared at Billy, as though seeing him for the first time. "Are there any others? Any other dragon children?"

"That is a mystery. In order to maintain secrecy, the remaining dragons rarely communicated with one another. I knew that Irene had a daughter, and I had heard rumors of other children. The slayers have been obsessed with finding any that might exist, and they know such children might not always be easy to identify. There are characteristics of dragons that are not unique to our species. Humans have a portion of them, so these may be magnified when one parent is also a dragon. We are great storytellers, so their gift could be profound eloquence. You might also see unusual strength or deep wisdom. It's hard to say what these unions might create."

Walter jumped to his feet. "C'mon," he said, pulling Billy up and slapping him on the back. "Show us some fire breathing!"

"Walter, be polite," the professor said, "Young William might find such a display embarrassing. After all, his talent is not exactly commonplace."

Billy scratched the cave floor with the toe of a shoe. "No. It's all right. I'll show you guys." His concealed a smile. Actually, the professor was half right. There was some embarrassment, but he also wanted to show off for his dad.

He turned toward an empty part of the cave and stepped into the shadows. After taking a deep breath, he opened his mouth in a wide circle. With his chest muscles taut, he began exhaling slowly. A narrow stream of yellow flowed out. It grew rapidly, brightening until it became a blazing river of flames, stretching out over a dozen feet before vaporizing into a column of gray smoke. Billy continued blowing the fiery jet for ten seconds before finally letting it die. He closed his mouth and slapped a hand over his chest. "Whew!" A ring of smoke passed through his lips and wafted into the darkness.

"Cool as ice!" Walter shouted.

"Bravo!" the professor added, clapping. "William, that was amazing!"

"Thanks." Billy looked at his mother. She smiled with tight lips but said nothing.

Clefspeare sighed, letting a few sparks fly into the cave's flowing air columns. "Yes, Billy, you have developed your gift quite well. I am proud and impressed." The dragon shuffled closer to the professor. "Now I believe you know all of the basic facts, Professor Hamilton, and Billy can fill you in on the details, but there are mysteries remaining to be solved."

"Indeed." Professor Hamilton opened Merlin's diary to the blank page. "Now we have two of the mysterious treasures restored to us, and it's clear that the slayers never discovered how to make these pages reveal their secrets."

Clefspeare's scaly brow furrowed. "Yet they have used Excalibur in a way I do not yet understand. It gave this son of Devin youthfulness and vigor, though he could not use it to transluminate his victims."

"Then we must make sure they don't get it back," the professor said. "I thought perhaps your son might be able to draw the sword out of the stone."

Billy's heart thumped. "Me?"

The professor placed a hand on Billy's shoulder. "I had suspected that William is in the royal lineage, and your story bears that out. It was an adoption, to be sure, but it was legal and fully binding."

Clefspeare growled, his eyes shining like a ruby laser. "You are right. The sword must be kept out of evil hands." His eyes then slowly dimmed, and his voice mellowed. "I believe the evil rock Master Merlin called the candlestone could be housing Devin's light energy, his mortal essence, within its prism walls. After I recovered my strength, I searched for the cursed thing for days, but I could not find it. I can only guess that his dark henchman returned to collect his remains. If Palin and Dr. Conner are in the slayer's service, they might have formed an alliance to restore their master. How they would use Bonnie is a mystery, but they are already using her love to deceive her. There is no greater motivation than love and no greater evil than treachery."

Clefspeare lowered his head to Billy's eye level. "Your professor could be right about the sword and the stone. Remember Merlin's prophecy.

A king shall rise of Arthur's mold,
The prophet's book in hand;
He takes the sword from mountain stone
To rescue captive bands.

Billy nodded. "Yeah. I remember."

"Try to pull it out, but if you cannot, you may use Merlin's prayer to call me. I will help you if I can."

A lump swelled in Billy's throat. The revelations were coming way too quickly. Royal lineage? Pull out a sword? Who were they trying to kid? "I'll do my best. Anything for Bonnie."

Professor Hamilton gasped. With the diary lying open in his hands, he stared at the pages, his mouth agape.

Walter rushed to his side. "I can read it. It's even got normal words, not that old English stuff or funny looking letters."

"Yes," the professor said, breathless. "The veil is lifted. I know we're in a hurry, but I must read this to everyone immediately."

The Chamber of Light

Heavy snow pelted the windshield as Bonnie's father drove deeper and deeper into a dense mountain forest. The Explorer bumped along on a narrow, snow-covered hiking path and swerved around sharp, slippery bends. Nail-biting drop-offs fell away on one side, and steep slopes rose on the other. The tires slipped through the deepening snow, all four churning to avoid a sideways slide over a precipice.

Bonnie kept one hand in her lap, the other fastened to the armrest as she watched the deteriorating conditions through the frosting window. She was accustomed to heights, but her wings would be of no help should the SUV plunge into one of the gorges. Though she tried to hide her nervousness, she gripped the armrest more tightly with every swerve.

Ashley's eyes stayed focused on the tree-lined path ahead rather than on the rocky cliffs below. Her folded hands seemed relaxed, her thumbs merely caressing each other during the jolting bounces, probably accustomed to the route after many visits to this secret place. Too accustomed.

Bonnie's cheeks warmed. But why? Why the strong reaction to Ashley's familiarity with her father's new life? Was it jealousy that he had found a replacement daughter of sorts? Or was it distrust that her new friend could be allied with this man whom her bad memories had painted as a demon over the past several months?

The SUV slowed to a crawl at the crest of a hill in a more open part of the forest. It turned left onto a side path, a narrow clearing pockmarked with icy potholes. Each divot surrendered its snowy covering as the SUV bucked and bounced through them and finally stopped. Bonnie peeked through the window. No buildings were anywhere, only a scattering of poorly dressed trees standing around in the snow.

Her father got out, opened the rear door for Ashley, and motioned for Bonnie to slide over and get out on the same side. Bonnie glanced to see if anything barred the door on her side, but nothing was there.

Bonnie slipped on her oversized coat and stepped out into the wintry Montana storm. Cold wind blasted her face, and her shoes sank in the snow. While she labored to pull her feet from the wet drift, her father retrieved the cases from the cargo space, handed the larger one to Ashley, and marched farther up the crude driveway. Ashley extended her free hand toward Bonnie and pulled her out to more solid ground. Snow seeped into Bonnie's socks, chilling her feet. Maybe the hike wouldn't be a long one.

With snow pelting their heads and wind blowing icy flakes into miniature white tornadoes, they trudged to a head-high mound of rocks pressed into the mountainside's steep upslope.

A wooden door no more than five feet high had been crudely wedged into the rocks, and lumpy mortar filled the gaps between the frame and stone. A large letter A had been carved in the door at waist level exposing fresh wood grain not yet weathered by Montana's cruel winter.

Bonnie rubbed her gloved hand on the marred wood. "What's the A for?"

Ashley set her load down and stretched a rubber coil that held a key chain to her belt loop. "It's a capital alpha, a Greek letter. We had another entrance that we called Omega, but it's closed now." Using a long silver key, she unlocked the door and pushed it open on its creaking hinges. "Are you ready for a big surprise? It won't be long now."

Ashley's genuine smile promised a good surprise, so Bonnie kept her hopes up. Maybe her mother really was around somewhere. Maybe this entrance led to the lab Ashley talked about, even though it looked more like the opening to an ancient mountaintop outhouse.

Her father reached in and plucked a flashlight that dangled from a hook on the inside wall. He flicked it on and ducked through the entrance. "Follow me," he said before descending a stairway leading into darkness.

Ashley picked up her case and motioned with her head for Bonnie to follow. They bent under the door's upper frame and walked out of the bitter cold and into quiet stillness. "Should I close the door?" Bonnie asked softly. Even her quiet voice sounded like a trumpet in the narrow stairwell.

"Yes," Ashley whispered.

Bonnie pushed the door until the latch clicked in place. As they followed her father, the waving flashlight beam bobbed down the corridor. Their footsteps clopped and echoed, making their furtive march sound like a small army stomping down the stairs.

"Stay close," Ashley said, raising her voice. "It's pretty far, and it gets steep in places, but it levels out in a few minutes."

Bonnie counted the stairs but lost track after nearly two hundred as she had to concentrate on the uneven planks. As Ashley had said, the descent eventually leveled out, the stairwell smoothing into a narrow tunnel they had to negotiate single file. Loud drips echoed from somewhere ahead as if big water drops plunged into static pools and played a rhythmic harmony to their crunching steps. The floor felt like crumbling asphalt, but at least it was dry.

They marched on in silence. The darkness of the corridor seemed to seep into Bonnie's mind. How difficult would it be to climb back to the surface when they returned … if they returned? A feeling of dread crawled across her body, like roaches skittering across a dirty kitchen floor. Something was wrong, desperately wrong.

* * * * * *

Professor Hamilton squinted at the page, speaking slowly as he read.

The veil once pierced is split for good
By truth's sharp sword it's torn;
Take care that all can bear it well
That all may be reborn.

Without the sword the war is lost;
Excalibur's edge must fight,
Yet not with foes of shield and sword
But those who veil the light.

Bring here the sword of Camelot
To read of wisdom's page;
Without its words, instruction blurs

He pulled the book close to his eyes.

"What's up, Prof?" Walter asked. "What's the next line?"

The professor reached for the corner of the page. "Perhaps the next page will tell—"

"No!" Billy shouted, leaping toward him. "Remember the warning!"

"Yes, William." The professor set a hand on his chest and took a deep breath. "This page must be completed first. Thank you for the reminder."

Billy stood at his side and looked at the mysterious script. "It sounds like we have to get Excalibur if we're going to read the rest of it."

Billy's mother clenched a fist. "Then let's get moving. There's no telling what Bonnie might be going through while we just stand around here." She grabbed Billy's arm. "Let's yank that sword and head west. I know a pharmacy professor who's in for a big surprise when we show up. We'll give him some medicine he'll never forget."

Billy grinned. "Mom, I love it when you're ready to bash a few heads together."

"Yeah, Mrs. B," Walter said. "Let's go kick some gluteus maximus!"

*　　*　　*　　*　　*　　*

Ashley turned a knob and pushed a door open. Bonnie followed her inside, stepping out of the cool corridor and into a balmy cavern. The room was dark except for a bright crack of light streaming from under a door far to her left and her father's flashlight beam meandering up the wall.

"Hit the lights, Ashley."

Ashley's hand appeared in the beam as she reached for a series of switches on the wall. Then, in concert with four clicks, rows of ceiling lights flashed to life. Incandescent flood lamps and banks of fluorescent panels illuminated an enormous underground chamber.

Bonnie's eyes took a few seconds to adjust. A circular laboratory about a hundred feet in diameter had been erected in the center of the cavern and elevated on a low platform. A network of tangled cables snaked underneath like thick black spaghetti.

The lab was a technological maze, a dizzying collection of instrument panels and glass enclosures. Everything was oriented around a point at the center where a flat marble pedestal stood, sort of a stunted ionic column about four feet high and maybe a foot in diameter.

Three instrument panels formed an arc around an inner circle, each spaced evenly about twenty feet from the center. The panels were a techno-geek's dream come true—at least a dozen rows of dials, sliding bars, diodes, and who-knows-whatsits covering the black acrylic front.

Three tall glass cylinders, like life-sized china doll display cases, stood between the panels and the center pedestal. The panel nearest the door, covered with twice as many buttons and meters as the other two, faced the cylinder on the opposite side.

A drop ceiling, suspended by supports unseen, hovered over the raised lab area, housing a bank of spotlights aimed at the equipment below.

Ashley lifted her brow, probably hoping for a gasp of wonder or at least a statement of appreciation. Bonnie searched for something nice to say, but she hadn't come here to be impressed by a technological assemblage of gadgets from the Bat Cave. She wanted to find her mother, and all this gawking at gadgetry wasn't getting her anywhere.

Bonnie took a step forward and nodded. "This is … amazing. Um … What is it?"

Ashley shed her coat and hung it on a wall hook. "It's our lab. It's the most advanced mechanical photosynthetic lab in the world."

"Photosynthetic? You mean like what plants do to make food?"

"Very close. Plants change light energy into food. We're trying to create physical matter from light energy in a very different way."

Bonnie glanced to the side at her father. He stood at a table by the wall unloading and examining the cases they had brought. She took another step toward the platform. "How does photosynthesis have anything to do with pharmacy? I didn't know my father was into stuff like this."

"He's not, or at least he wasn't. That's why he needs me." Ashley scooted toward the array of instruments and gestured for Bonnie to follow. "This research combines physics with chemistry, and it will take a while to explain, but it's the most exciting project I could ever imagine. We've come a long, long way in a very short time."

Ashley sat at the panel with the most buttons. "This is the master panel," she said, flipping a switch. "It controls that glass cylinder in front of me." A low hum sounded from the seven-foot-high cylinder at the opposite side of the circle. A bright light flashed on from its smoothly curved cap, making it look like a futuristic transporter tube. The bass drone reverberated throughout the cavern, and gentle vibrations radiated from the floor and into Bonnie's legs.

Ashley touched a slider bar on the panel. "If I were to move this up, the beam inside the dome would activate, becoming more and more agitated the higher I slid it."

As the quivering floor sent a buzzing sensation into Bonnie's teeth, her pulse quickened, and sweat moistened her forehead. She took off her outer coat and laid it on a chair. "What does the beam do?"

Ashley flicked off the cylinder's light, and the tremors faded along with the drone. She walked back to Bonnie and spoke softly, almost in a whisper. "It mimics Excalibur's beam, the light energy you used to transluminate Devin."

Bonnie bit her lip hard. Excalibur's beam? Transluminate Devin? How could Ashley know about Excalibur and Devin? And what did she mean by transluminate?

Ashley clutched Bonnie's arm and drew her close. "I know about you," she whispered. With a quick glance at Bonnie's back, she added, "And your wings."

Bonnie let out a low gasp and stepped back, but Ashley held on. "Don't worry. Your father knows that I know about you, but I've learned a lot more than he thinks I know."

Ashley set a hand on Bonnie's pack. "Shall I help you take this off so you can get more comfortable? I really want to see your wings, and, besides, everyone here knows about them."

Bonnie shifted her weight from foot to foot, and her ears turned warm. Ever since she was little, her wings had been a secret, even an embarrassment, worse than an ugly zit or a bad haircut. But Ashley seemed gentle and sincere, so when she reached over and loosened the straps on the backpack, Bonnie stayed put, not resisting in spite of an urge to run.

"You said *everyone*," Bonnie said as Ashley slid a strap down her shoulder. "Is there anyone else here besides you and your grandfather and my father?"

"Actually ... yes. But I'd better let Dr. Conner tell you about them."

"Them? More than one?"

Ashley pulled the backpack away, letting it fall to the floor. Bonnie unfurled her wings and stretched them straight back and then out.

Ashley's eyes bulged. "Wow! I knew they had to be big to carry your body weight, but ... Wow!"

Bonnie's cheeks grew hot. Ashley's gawking made her feel more freakish than ever. She bowed her head, hoping the color in her face wouldn't give away her thoughts.

Ashley cleared her throat, then leaned close and whispered, "I think I know how you feel. It's not as obvious in me, but I'm different, too."

She spread her arms toward the center of the lab. "Look around, Bonnie. I designed all of this, and I helped build it. My brain is a freak. It works so fast, it's like a supercomputer on nuclear steroids. The kids at school think I can even read their minds. I can analyze and deduce so well, I'm usually saying what they're thinking as soon as they realize they're thinking it themselves. That's no way to make friends. Do you think any of the girls want to be around me, believing I can read their minds? No way. And the guys? Forget it. When I come around, I've seen them put their hands over their ears."

She clapped her hands over her ears. "What are they thinking? That their thoughts leak out? Of course it's ridiculous, but it doesn't change anything." As she lowered her hands, her voice dropped again, catching in her throat. "I … I've heard them call me … mutant … and alien. … I know how it feels. And sometimes … it makes me wonder. Maybe they're right. … Maybe I am a mutant."

Dr. Conner joined the girls, one hand in his pocket, the other carrying a spiral notebook. "I see you two are becoming acquainted."

Bonnie read the familiar expression on his face, a smiling glow that had fooled her for years. With her wings exposed, everything seemed out in the open—vivid, clarified, transparent. Now she saw in his smile the pearly whites of a polished hypocrite, a charlatan scientist. His act was wearing thin. It was time for him to deliver. She crossed her arms over her chest and tapped her foot on the floor. "Can I see my mother now?"

"Very soon," he replied. "I promise."

"Is she here?"

"Yes. I'll explain in a moment." He handed the notebook to Ashley. "The samples are excellent. I think the photoreceptors are working. I see no reason why we can't begin in the morning, but let's set up a communication session for tonight."

Ashley's smile stretched across her face. "Great! I'm going to check on Daddy first. I'll be back." She grasped Bonnie's wrist and gave it a squeeze before jogging toward a far corner of the lab.

Dr. Conner picked up the backpack from the chair, lifting and lowering it a couple of times. "Is something in here?"

"Just my journal. I can't fit much else when my wings are in there."

He laid the pack on the chair with her coat and buried both hands in his pockets. "I've heard about your dangerous adventures, and you've been very brave. I'm asking you to be brave once again, because only you can rescue your mother. That's why I brought you here."

It was a practiced speech, like many she had heard through the years. His eyes gave away a hint of insecurity, like he was covering hidden fears, conveying urgency and dread. But his speech, and so many other things, weren't adding up. What did he really know about her adventures?

Scenes from her battle with Devin flashed through her mind, the slayer's gleaming sword heavy in her trembling hands and his hateful eyes glowing with vengeance. The memories pumped adrenalin through her body, and her heart raced. She fought against the overwhelming thoughts and her father's powerful sway over her, but she couldn't keep her lips from trembling. Yes, he might be lying, and, yes, it might all be a sham, but, at least for now, she had to go along with him to learn the truth. She swallowed, barely able to speak. "What do I have to do?"

103

❋ ❋ ❋ ❋ ❋ ❋

The professor hurried through a path of thick leaves and scattered stones. "It's just over this rise."

Billy jogged after him, Walter at his side and his mother tracking close behind. When they came to a clearing, the professor stopped and pointed as he tried to catch his breath. "There it is. Exactly as we left it."

Billy and Walter halted next to the professor and looked in that direction. The sword stood upright, its blade embedded in a boulder.

Mom caught up, breathless. "What are we waiting for? Let's do it."

The foursome ran to the foot of the stone. "C'mon, son," Mom said, making a cup with her interlocking fingers. "I'll give you a boost."

Billy stripped off his gloves and handed them to her. "Thanks, but I can make it." He leaped to the first ledge and grappled the top of the stone. Two seconds later he stood next to the sword, ready to grasp its hilt, but he paused and leaned down. "The prophecy says I have to hold the diary."

The professor stretched his lanky body and handed up the diary. Billy straightened, holding the book in his left hand. With his right, he grasped Excalibur's hilt and took a deep breath.

He tensed his muscles. As he tightened his grip, heat radiated from the sword. Steam rose from the crack in the rock, and the sword moved easily, like a spoon in thick pudding. He pulled it out effortlessly and stared at the blade. The newly exposed portion glowed hot. His arm trembled under the sword's weight, but he managed to raise the blade high above his head.

Walter pumped a fist. "Yes!"

Mom gave Walter a high five, and the professor copied their actions, clumsily giving high fives to each of them.

Walter clambered up the stone, slapped Billy on the back, and relieved him of the book. After two catlike leaps, Walter landed on the ground and handed the diary to the professor.

"Bring Excalibur down, William," the professor said as he opened the book. "We must make haste."

Walter peered at the ragged parchment. "I can't see any new lines, Prof."

Billy joined them, gripping Excalibur with both hands. The professor eyed the book closely. "William, hold it nearer. I can see something."

As though summoned by the sword itself, new words appeared on the page, matching the calligraphic script of the lines above. The tantalizing letters grew clear and bold.

After gesturing for the others to stand back, the professor cleared his throat. "I shall begin reading with the first line of the previously unfinished quatrain."

> Bring here the sword of Camelot
> To read of wisdom's page;
> Without its words, instruction blurs
> For all who hear the sage.
>
> The candlestone conceals a trap
> Where Satan's minions dwell;
> In darkness she will seek her joy
> And find the gates of hell.
>
> A sword, a knight, a fiery son,
> Transluminated heir,
> Shall enter into darkest realm
> To battle in its lair.
>
> Beware, O knight, of easy prey
> Who stand with back yet turned.
> For cowards strike a blinded foe
> And die for what they've burned.

He lifted the book closer as though he were trying to read microscopic print. "That's all I can see. The metric beat and rhyme scheme are complete, and the script nearly fills the page. Perhaps that's all there is."

Billy held the sword close to the book again. "Then we should be allowed to check the next page. Let's see if something shows up."

"Very well." The professor turned the page.

"It's blank," Walter said. "Blank as my brain during a math test and empty as my stomach is now."

The professor closed the book and tucked it under his arm. "Obviously the diary has nothing more to reveal at this time. Let's hurry back to the plane and decipher this new conundrum." He placed a hand on his stomach. "Perhaps we'll be able to think more clearly once we have taken a meal."

Mom returned the gloves to Billy. "Then let's get airborne. There isn't anything left to do here. Jared—I mean, Clefspeare said he'd deliver your drawing to Arlo's porch, and we have the sword."

"Right. Let's go." Billy pulled the gloves on and heaved the weighty sword to his shoulder, holding the hilt with both hands in front. As he trudged through the forest, the final stanza of the poem smoldered in his mind. "Prof, the last part of that poem, the part about cowards striking a blinded foe. What do you make of it?"

The professor kept his stride, his white hair bouncing under his beret. "I thought you might find its lesson familiar, William. I've said something similar a number of times. A knight opposes his enemy face-to-face. A stab in the back is the way of the coward. If you must fight, attack your enemy head-on. That is the way of valor."

"I remember. But what if he wants to kill you? Shouldn't you take him out before he takes you out?"

"Yeah," Walter said. "What's wrong with a surprise attack on the bad guys? They deserve it, don't they?"

The professor halted and faced his students. "If God commands a surprise attack, then so be it; he has done that before. But a brave warrior assumes that his Lord will protect him as he charges with confidence into battle. He will even call out to his enemy to stand face-to-face." The professor's furrows deepened. "Considering the words of this prophecy, we can assume that God has ordained that we carry out no surprise attacks. Do you understand?"

Walter nodded. "Sure, Prof. I get it."

Billy kept his eyes focused on his mother as she stood next to a large oak tree ahead, waiting for them to catch up. "Yeah, I think so."

As they quick-marched through the forest, the professor's warning blistered Billy's mind. *No surprise attacks.* He twisted his neck and eyed Excalibur's blade. He held in his hands the ultimate weapon, one that could vanquish the dragon slayers and rescue Bonnie. The poem was clear enough. Bonnie was in trouble—something about Satan's minions and the gates of hell. But what could he do? He had practiced long and hard, and he felt the urge to zoom to Montana and do a little transluminating on Devin's cronies, or at least whack their ugly heads off. Was he brave enough to do it face-to-face?

As he tightened his grip on the sword's hilt, courage flowed, but something was wrong. The blade's surface held the strange etchings he had expected, and it was as heavy as a bundle of crowbars, but it lacked luster. In fact, it was dull, nothing like the glow the stories mentioned and no beam shooting out like when Bonnie held it. Sure, he pulled it out of the stone, which was cool, but why wasn't it working now?

He tried slipping off his gloves again and holding it with his bare hands, but that didn't change anything. Had anyone else noticed?

As he hiked onward, the sword's weight pressed on his shoulder, pinching his skin even through his jacket. If the sword was such a burden when carried like this, how could he possibly wield it in battle? He boosted the blade higher and kept moving while listening to the leaves crunching under their hurried steps. He couldn't help but feel they were all rushing headlong toward a whirlpool, and he didn't even have a paddle.

•   •   •   •   •   •

Bonnie sat on one of the swivel chairs. Her father stooped and set a hand gently on her knee. "This is all very difficult to explain," he said softly, "so I want you to pay close attention."

She studied his expression, his eyes sincere and his soft lips poised in a half smile, quite different from his lying face. The words that followed would probably be true.

He cleared his throat before continuing. "You might not have guessed what happened to Devin. Excalibur transformed him into light energy, and the candlestone absorbed his fractured particles. Devin's cohort, Palin, saw your battle from a distance but couldn't get there in time to help. After you threw away the stone, he knew he couldn't battle both you and a dragon without it. Even though you flew away, Clefspeare was recovering, so Palin waited for him to leave. He searched for hours but never found Excalibur. He wondered later if you flew away with it, but I told him it was much too heavy. You'd never be able to fly with that much weight.

"Anyway, he found the candlestone and he brought it to me, thinking I could help him resurrect Devin and reconstitute him. He knew Devin and I had worked together, studying dragons and their ability to use light energy to extend their lives. I was the only person who might be able to help.

"You see, back then we had Excalibur in our possession and learned quite a bit about how it works. When Devin took off on one of his rabid dragon hunts, I insisted on keeping the sword with me, because our analysis of its power wasn't finished, but I promised to send it to him if he needed it. Later, he convinced me that he could capture a dragon for our research if he had his sword. That's how it came back into his hands. Apparently it's lost forever."

Bonnie nodded. Although she didn't know exactly where the sword was, she could probably find the area where she dropped it. Considering her father's treacherous past, it was best to keep that information to herself, at least for now.

He gestured for her to stay put and walked to a safe embedded in the wall. With a flick of his wrist, he spun its dial a couple of times, then opened its door. He pulled out a lockbox, sliding the small metal case with great care, and brought it to Bonnie. When he opened the lid a crack, she rose from the chair and peered inside.

A gem rested at the bottom, the candlestone she had taken from Devin. Even with this minute exposure, it seemed that a darkening cloud enshrouded the box, the loss of light starting at the edge of the lid. A hint of queasiness bubbled within her, a minor version of the sensation she experienced on the mountain when the slayer first showed her the stone, the bane of every living dragon.

He snapped the box shut. "Palin's claim that the stone had captured Devin intrigued me, so I told him I would look into it. Of course, I had no intention of bringing that monster

Devin back to physical form. I wanted to create a test to see if he was somehow really within those crystal walls. That's where Ashley came in. In our efforts to mimic a dragon's ability to capture light energy, she had already helped me build miniature synthetic photoreceptors that could attach to human tissue. With her knowledge of physics and physiology, I thought she could come up with a way to figure out what's going on in there."

He motioned toward Ashley's equipment. "When you see how all of this works, you'll be amazed."

Bonnie pointed at the box. "So is he in there? Inside the candlestone?"

"Yes, and he's fully alive."

"What does that have to do with Mama and me?"

He stepped back to the safe and slid the box inside. "When Palin brought the candlestone to me, your mother's health was rapidly deteriorating. I was desperately trying to bring my photoreceptor research far enough along to help her, but there wasn't enough time." He closed the safe's door and spun the dial. "I decided to take a drastic step. I transformed your mother into light energy and allowed the candlestone to absorb her, keeping her safe for the time being, hoping that someday I could restore her when my research provided a way to keep her from dying."

Bonnie's throat caught. "And now you've found a way?"

He nodded. "Indeed I have."

The words shot through her brain like machine-gun fire. It was just too much to take in. Her mother was in a wall safe? Impossible. Yet this lab and all its equipment lay before her, futuristic machines that made a Star Trek studio look like a toddler's collection of Lego models. And there was the candlestone, definitely the same gem that sucked the slayer into its grasp like a light-slurping straw. Her father couldn't possibly have gone through all this trouble just to trick her. "What do I have to do? How will you bring Mama back? How did you transform her in the first place?"

He pointed toward a dark corner. "Ashley's coming back. I'll have her explain everything else to you. She'll take you to the girls' dorm so you can get ready."

"The girls' dorm?" Bonnie surveyed the vast chamber. "Are there other girls here?"

"Yes, there are a few others. Ashley will introduce you and answer any questions you have."

"I'm here." Ashley walked slowly to them, her head low. "Something's wrong with Daddy." She lifted her eyes, tension obvious in tight lines on her forehead. "He says he's fatigued and dizzy. He looked pale, so I put him to bed."

"Probably just a virus." Dr. Conner gave Bonnie a gentle push toward Ashley. "Why don't you introduce Bonnie to the girls while I check on him?"

Ashley nodded, her brow still furrowed. She smiled at Bonnie, but her lips quivered. "Did he tell you where your mother is?"

"Yes, but it sounds too crazy to be true."

Ashley guided her toward a door at the opposite side of the chamber. "Crazy is right, but we'll sort it all out for you. For now, let's get you settled in, and you can meet your dorm mates. They're quite an unusual crew, but you're pretty unusual yourself, so prepare for some gawking."

111

7

Speaking to the Dead

With no firefly light to guide him this time, Dr. Conner inched his way through the blackness, his arm extended as he groped for the inner gate. After finding the iron bars, he ran his fingers across several of them until he came upon the latch. He pecked at the metal door with a key, missing the hole a few times before finally unlocking the deadbolt.

The air felt wetter than usual. A musty odor filled the cavern, and the damp bars slipped in his hands as he pushed the gate to the side. The metal frame squealed through its top and bottom runners, echoing in tiny chaotic squeaks, like a swarm of bats awakened to go on their nightly rounds.

He paused, listening. Unnatural breathing, labored and intimidating, drifted through the darkness. Within seconds, a gruff voice replaced the low rasps.

"Is she here?"

Dr. Conner trembled and cleared his throat, trying not to sound mousy. "Bonnie has come. As you predicted." He walked through the gate and into a cave, his shoes tapping on the stone floor.

The deep voice rumbled. "And is she going to do it?"

"We're preparing her." Dr. Conner stepped farther into the cave and stared into the black void. "But she doesn't know yet what's involved. If she's unwilling, I'll have to take drastic steps."

A loud sigh filtered through the darkness. "She is willing. She will give you no trouble."

Dr. Conner edged closer. "What if I told her that she might not survive?"

"She would not give it a second thought. Apparently you have not yet understood what drives her."

Dr. Conner squeezed his keys in his fist, feeling them bite into his skin. "Yeah, yeah, I've heard it before. I don't know what love is, so I'll never understand Bonnie." He felt a pebble under his shoe, kicked it away, and listened to its tumbling clicks die out in the depths of the cave. "Well, it might be very interesting to put her to the test. Self-preservation instincts are stronger than love. That's why I have my doubts."

"No, that's why you're a fool." The final word bounced off the walls—fool, fool, fool—denouncing Dr. Conner like a wraith from a haunting nightmare. The voice paused until the last echo faded, then continued slowly. "Irene's daughter understands love. Her mother's life is more important to her than her own, though she has no idea that Irene is no more. Perhaps by watching her, you will learn what motivates your enemies."

"I didn't come here to be lectured." Dr. Conner released his grip on the keys and let them dangle from a finger. "My firefly colony is dead, so you'll get nothing but candles until summer comes. Remember, you're still alive because I find you useful, so you should show me a little more respect. You know my real reason for bringing Bonnie here, and it wasn't to rescue you."

The voice rumbled to life once more. "Perhaps not, you simplistic fool. But don't be surprised if your plans fail. Love could very well turn on you and set all of your captives free."

Dr. Conner let out a huff, pivoted on his heel, and inched away, his arm again extended. His fingers sifted through his keys until they clasped a diode light attached to the ring. He pushed its button, sending a thin beam toward the exit. Finding the open gate, he followed the light, but it bent and scattered, as if trying to reverse its course. He released the button, killing the beam, and hustled to the exit. With the squealing of metal on metal and a final clank, he slid the gate closed and firmly set the lock.

115

*   *   *   *   *   *

The purring sound of a propeller filled the plane's cabin, a whispered lullaby in Billy's ears, but there was no time to sleep. Too many puzzles remained unsolved. He turned in his co-pilot's chair and huddled with Walter and Professor Hamilton. The professor, seated behind Billy with Merlin's diary propped open on his lap, kept a bent finger on a line of text while Walter looked on from the other side of the aisle.

Failing daylight illuminating the text, they stared at the mysterious words, reading them aloud between bites of cold meat sandwiches and crackers.

"It's gotta be Bonnie," Billy said. "She's looking for her mom, and she's going to find trouble instead."

The professor nodded. "Agreed, William. And it appears that the candlestone is involved in the deception. 'The candlestone conceals a trap where Satan's minions dwell.' What do you make of that?"

Billy set a foot against the side of Mom's pilot seat. "Well, if Dad was right, and Devin is inside the candlestone, then he could be Satan's minion. And remember, Dad said Devin walked in with it around his neck after his knights got blitzed by Excalibur, so maybe there are more bad guys in there."

The professor raised his index finger. "Therefore, the plural *minions*."

"Right. But I can't see how they could hurt Bonnie from in there."

Mom grabbed his foot and dropped it to the cabin floor. "Well, we know the candlestone makes you and Bonnie feel weak. I guess it could be used as a weapon."

Walter lifted a cracker to his mouth. "How could a little crystal hold someone inside? It doesn't make sense."

The professor opened his sandwich and inspected the meat inside. "Walter, there are many realities in life that don't make sense to our limited understanding. They seem warped, out of line with what we know. As truth is revealed, however, what was once absurd is able to untwist as our minds grasp what we witness. This poem, for example, seems to describe what someone has seen with his own eyes, so we shouldn't take his witness lightly. But you are right, in one sense. We should not simply accept what seems absurd without corroboration."

He took a bite of his sandwich, waiting to swallow before he continued. "Let's follow this logically from the beginning, step-by-step. William, do you remember how you described what happened to the slayer after Excalibur transluminated him?"

116

Billy made a circular motion with his finger. "Bonnie said there was a flash of sparks, and they swirled around, like water going down a drain."

The professor tilted his head upward. "Yes, yes, a drain. That is the word you used, and it reminds me of something." He flipped to the previous page in the book. "Here it is, in the prayer to summon a dragon."

Shall I use yon candlestone,
Absorbing light to steal thy fire?
If I shouldst lie beneath its trone,
Excalibur builds my funeral pyre.

"Apparently," the professor went on, "the one who wrote this prayer considers the candlestone as a dangerous weapon of last resort. 'Shall I use it?' he asks himself. We know the candlestone absorbs light, and we know Excalibur changes a person into light. So, when he says, 'Excalibur builds my funeral pyre,' he could mean that he's risking getting caught in the absorption if the sword is used in combination with the stone."

Walter swallowed his last bit of cracker and wiped his lips on his sleeve. "I don't get it, Prof. What do you mean?"

"Let's put it this way, Walter. Using Excalibur and the candlestone in combination is like battling someone in a space ship and you punch a hole in a wall to create a vacuum. Your enemies are instantly killed, but you manage to put on a space suit just in time. You're alive but trapped forever to float in space, never able to return home."

"But you'd run out of air," Walter said with a sly grin. "You'd die before long."

"Yes, Walter. I realize that. The illustration does break down, yet the parallels are there."

"Yeah, Walter," Billy said. "Give him a break. He just means that the candlestone could be a safe place if you're changed into light by Excalibur. Punching a hole is like using Excalibur, and the space suit is like the candlestone."

"Exactly, William. Look at the poem again. The poet chose an interesting word, *trone*. There are a number of meanings for the word, but the one that sparked my memory of this passage is William's use of the word *drain*. A trone is a drain. The poet might be taking literary license, but perhaps he sees light as draining into the candlestone, and Devin at this moment is lying under it. This poem, therefore, is an eyewitness account of an event similar to what Mr. Clefspeare theorized. Devin is literally a victim of a luminescent whirlpool."

Walter's eyes brightened. "That's like a nightmare I used to have. When I was little, I dreamed about getting sucked down the bathtub drain." He brushed cracker crumbs from his hands. "But what's that got to do with Bonnie?"

Billy let the facts run through his mind. If Devin really was in the candlestone, and Dr. Conner lied to Bonnie to get her to go with him, could that mean they needed her to release Devin? It sounded too crazy to be true, but nothing else made any sense. "I think I know," he said, his heart rate accelerating. He half-closed his eyes and leaned back in his seat.

Walter tapped Billy on his head with his knuckles. "Then let's have it, Sherlock. What's the deal?"

Mom chimed in. "What is it, Billy?"

"Yes, William. We are all in great anticipation."

Billy chewed on his lower lip. Why had he spoken up? The more he thought about the idea, the crazier it sounded, but now he had to spill it. "They're going to change Bonnie into light energy and send her into the candlestone to get Devin out."

Walter reached over and felt Billy's brow. "No fever." He closed Billy's eyes with his fingers, but Billy slapped his arm away. "He must be hallucinating if he thinks Bonnie's going to try to rescue the slayer."

The professor laughed. "You're correct, Walter. Such an act would be counter to her character, but on the other hand, William's theory has merit. Remember, Bonnie doesn't know that her mother is really dead, so we can't be sure how an unscrupulous man could manipulate her with lies. Perhaps she might be persuaded by deceit to enter the stone, or even by force or threats."

"Maybe." Walter chewed another cracker. "But we have Excalibur. How can Bonnie change into light energy without it? And even if she does, how can she bring anyone out of that thing? Won't she and Devin still be sparks of light if they do come out? I think it would just suck them right back in again."

119

"Very perceptive questions, Walter. There are still missing pieces to this puzzle."

Billy sat up. "But will we be too late? How long till we get there?"

Mom pointed at the map on the plane's GPS screen. "We'll have to stop for fuel, but we're not carrying any cargo. I think we can make it in about eight more hours, depending on the weather."

"Eight hours." Billy looked at his watch. "What's the time zone in Missoula?"

She studied the map again. "I think it's mountain time."

The professor closed the diary and pulled a gold chain from his pocket. An old-fashioned watch dangled at the end. "Yes,

Marilyn. The Pacific zone begins at the western border of Montana." He flipped open the cover and checked the time. "Our watches are two hours ahead of those in the Treasure State."

Walter eyed the watch. "The Treasure State, Prof?"

"Yes, the nickname refers to the importance of mining there."

Billy set his watch back two hours. "Then we'll get there at about midnight, Treasure State time, and we'll start some digging of our own."

"Midnight sounds about right," Mom said. "You and I can take turns napping and flying, and Walter and the professor can try to sleep. Maybe we can find a motel and get a few more hours before Dr. Conner's office opens in the morning."

Billy leaned back again. "Sounds like a plan. We'll be his first appointment, if he's there."

Mom pointed at the console where she kept Dr. Conner's business card. "It's at the university, but we don't know if he has office hours or classes in the morning."

"Don't worry. We'll find him." Billy set a hand in front of his mouth and blew gently on his fingers. "I think it's time I had a heated discussion with him."

Walter's brow lifted. "Hey, speaking of heated, think we can get a pepperoni pizza when we stop for gas?" He pointed at Billy with his thumb. "With old lava breath here, we can keep it hot the rest of the way to Montana."

"Sure. Some hot food would be great." Billy looked at the professor. "What do you think?"

He nodded. "I enjoy pizza. But could we get one with mushrooms? If I were to eat pepperoni, I don't think you would enjoy my company in this enclosed cabin."

*   *   *   *   *   *

Ashley unlocked a door on the far side of the chamber, opened it, and walked through. When Bonnie followed, Ashley locked the door behind them.

Following Ashely again, Bonnie walked along a clean, linoleum-floored hallway, drawing in her wings to keep their outer edges from scraping against the rough plaster walls.

Three equally spaced, wooden doors lined both sides of the long, well-lit corridor. A small cardboard sign hung on each door, probably the girls' names. The dull white walls were clean but unadorned with decorations of any kind, and a faint scent of ammonia hung in the air. Bonnie scanned the corridor for the source of the odor and spotted a mop and bucket in a corner at the end.

Ashley halted, smiling. "I'm going to call the other girls to come and meet you now." In a singsong voice she shouted, "Come on out! Bonnie's here!"

Several loud thumps sounded from within the rooms. Two doors flew open on opposite sides of the hall, revealing four running girls of different shapes and sizes. With big smiles and wide eyes, they all stopped well away from Bonnie, staring at her with gaping mouths. The tallest girl, a green-eyed redhead, edged forward. The others followed, their expressions alternating between fear and delight. The redhead cautiously reached for one of the wings. When Bonnie opened them more fully, the girl jerked her hand back.

"It's okay," Bonnie said softly. "You can touch it."

The girl, about twelve years old, smiled and caressed the wing with her fingers. Her hands were pasty white, matching her pale face and neck, a stark alabaster background for her myriad freckles. The other girls joined her, giggling and whispering oohs and aahs as they touched the wings.

"What are your names?" Bonnie asked.

The redhead spoke up. "I'm Karen." With a finger she tapped the tallest of the other girls on her blonde head. "This is Stacey. She's eleven." Karen moved her hand to a shorter dark-skinned girl. "This is Rebecca, but we call her Beck. She's nine." Karen then pointed at a petite Asian girl. "And Monique is four, but we call her Pebbles."

"Pebbles?" Bonnie said.

Karen grinned and cracked her chewing gum. "Yeah. When Doc found her, she was so hungry she was trying to eat pebbles."

"Doc? Who's Doc?"

"Your father," Ashley said.

Bonnie nodded. "Oh … okay." Devin had mentioned a "Doc" back in West Virginia, proving the partnership her father admitted having with the slayer, but how close were their ties? Maybe her dad didn't really trust Devin and was simply picking his brain for research, just like he had said. Or, maybe not.

Bonnie concealed a sigh. These girls were precious, but the delay pinched her patience. They needed to get on with it—to find the truth … and her mother. She took a deep breath and caught Karen's eye. "And do you have a nickname?"

Stacey piped up. "We call her Red."

Karen bopped Stacey on the head with her fist. "My name's Karen, you silly goose."

Bonnie grinned. "And how old are you, Karen?"

"Thirteen," she replied, shrugging. "But I can't prove it."

"No birth certificate," Ashley said. "You see, your father took these girls in. They were either street kids, abandoned children, or runaways. Nobody wanted them." She set a hand on Karen's shoulder. "Her mother left her out in a snowstorm when she was just a toddler, and she's been in the foster system ever since. Six months ago she ran away from an abusive home and wound up wandering the university campus looking for a job. A lady at Human Resources called your father to tell him about her, so he took her in.

"Doc found Stacey in an alley with a man who … well, let's just say he didn't have her best interests in mind. I'll bet that guy won't be bothering any little girls again after Doc got through with him. Anyway, Stacey refused to tell Doc where she came from, so he just kept her.

"Beck came over the border from Baja California. Both her parents died in the desert. A California family hid her for a while and then sent her to some friends here in Montana. That family dumped Beck into the foster system, and your father heard about her. They were going to ship her back to Mexico. Doc has a friend in the foster system who let him keep her until they, as he put it, 'can look into the matter.'"

Ashley patted Monique's head. "And little Pebbles is a long story. We think she's Korean, and it looks like she was smuggled into a port on the Washington coast, probably for a black market adoption. Your father was surf fishing with a friend, and she was wandering on the beach trying to find something to eat. There was no one else around. The poor little girl was trying to bite into pebbles and pieces of driftwood."

Bonnie gazed into Monique's wide brown eyes. "That's amazing. How does he just find these girls? That seems too weird."

"Pebbles was first," Ashley said. "After taking her in, he actually started looking for orphans. Once a month he went into bad parts of town at night looking for runaways. And he

123

asks his friends to call him if someone needs a home. He feels he can help them, and at the same time they can help him with his research."

Bonnie took Monique's hand and held it close to her side. "Well, it's awesome that they have a home now, but how can they help him?"

"Explanations are coming." Ashley waved toward the dorm rooms. "Go on back now, girls. You'll get to talk to Bonnie more in a little while."

Karen shook Bonnie's hand. "I hope to see you later."

"Same here." Bonnie eyed Karen's arm as she drew back. Were those needle marks? A sense of dread returned, stronger than ever.

Karen paused at the doorway to her room, stared at Bonnie for a second, then ducked inside.

Ashley unlocked the first door on the left. "This is your room. The other girls live two to a room so they don't get lonely. I'll be staying here with you, if that's all right."

Hoping to keep her voice from shaking, Bonnie cleared her throat. "Sure. I guess so." She read the homemade cardboard sign on the door—Alberta Einstein.

Ashley guided her inside. "You look tired. Why don't you rest up? The bathroom is the last door down the hall on the left, and there's a shower there, too." She set her hands on her hips. "Does the room look okay? Check it out."

Bonnie scanned the dorm room. Two beds on opposite walls displayed colorful, quilted bedspreads and lacey dust ruffles. Soft, light blue carpet covered the floor, matching the hint of azure in the off-white walls.

A poster of Albert Einstein hung on one wall, and a drawing of the cavern laboratory had been taped next to it. The most prominent feature, however, was a strange painting, the portrait of an old man—old, that is, from the neck up. His face was worn and haggard, but his body exuded youthful muscles, bulging through a track athlete's uniform. He was planting his feet at the start of a race, ready to sprint from the block. A caption read, "Daddy's Dream: A Sagacious Mind in a Robust Body," and the painting was signed by Ashley.

Bonnie opened the closet on her side of the room. A burst of colors greeted her eyes, a dazzling assortment of beautiful dresses and stylish slacks hung from the clothes rod, and boots, shoes, and sweaters lay in cubbyholes beneath. "Are these for me?"

"Uh-huh. I had to guess your size from an old photo. I hope they fit."

Bonnie pulled out a dress and held it up. She draped one of the long turquoise sleeves down her arm and smiled. "It looks perfect."

"Then I guessed right. I'll help you alter them for your wings later." Ashley stood in the doorway and pushed her hand through her hair. "For now, you should get some rest. I'm going to set up a communication session for tonight, and you'll want to be wide awake for that."

Bonnie put the dress back in the closet. "Communication session? With who?"

"I'll explain exactly how it works when we do it, but I've built a way to communicate with the life forces inside the candlestone." Ashley set a hand on Bonnie's shoulder. "It might be hard to believe, but within a few hours you'll be talking with your mother."

8

Voices in the Dark

D r. Conner spun the dial on the wall safe, then steadily guided it through its combination stops. After he reached the final number and turned the handle, something unusual clicked. He spun toward the sound. Ashley stepped out of the dorm's hallway and locked the door behind her.

Dr. Conner pivoted back to the safe, slid the candlestone's protective box from within, and gingerly walked it to the marble pedestal at the center of the chamber and set the box on top.

Ashley strode to his side and lifted the lid a crack. She peered at the candlestone for a moment before closing the box. "How's Daddy doing?"

"I'm sure it's just a virus. I gave him something to help him rest. He's sleeping now." Dr. Conner walked the few steps back to the main control panel, sat at its swivel chair, and flipped a switch. A device that looked like a futuristic ray gun rose slowly from the floor near the pedestal. When the gun's barrel reached the level of the candlestone's box, the movement stopped. "Is Bonnie asleep?"

Ashley joined him at the controls. "If she's not, she will be soon. She looked real tired, so I told her to get some rest." She pointed at a line of numbers on a flat-panel monitor. "If you're going to shoot it now, you'll have to set the distortion allowance to seventy-five."

Dr. Conner turned one of the dozens of knobs while watching the monitor. "What did she say about the girls?"

Ashley bent close and read a stream of data that began flashing on the screen. "Not much. They were excited to see her, and she was friendly, even when they crowded around and wanted to touch her wings."

Dr. Conner rotated a dial, clicking it from zero to eight. A thin beam shot from the gun, painting a tiny crimson circle on one side of the candlestone's leaden box. "It would be better if she doesn't talk to them privately. Do you understand?"

Ashley sighed. "Yes. I understand."

Dr. Conner looked over the controls. "Which voiceprint is in memory right now?"

Ashley pointed at a switch. "Devin's. His is channel A. Bonnie's mom is channel B."

"He's communicating on alpha frequency, right?"

Ashley pushed her hair back with one hand and tapped a digital display with the other. "Uh-huh. That's where he's supposed to be. But I noticed lately that he's not always there, like he might be experimenting with other frequencies."

Dr. Conner jerked his head around and glared at Ashley. "Nonsense. You must have been misreading it."

Ashley let her hair fall haphazardly and blew it out of her way with an angry huff. "Misreading it? Me? You're the one who didn't know which frequency to use just now."

Dr. Conner turned his attention back to the controls and adjusted a dial. "I was just double-checking. And you should tell me when you notice something unusual in the stone, especially frequency drift. I don't want you speculating. You know what happens when your head gets in the clouds."

Ashley stepped back from the panel and set her fists on her hips. "In the clouds? What are you talking about?"

Dr. Conner rose and pushed a hand into his pocket as he let out a sigh. "I'm sorry. I shouldn't have said that. I should know better." He laughed and added, "Before you came here I didn't know squat about physics. How did you say it that day you got so mad at me?"

Ashley pressed her lips together. "You don't know a tachion beam from a tackle box."

"Right. Back then I was just a research panhandler begging for a government grant. Yesterday I turned down two geezers who practically threw their money at me."

Ashley met Dr. Conner's gaze. "Well, using dragon blood was your vision."

"Then we're a good team, and I'll try not to forget it." He fished in his pocket for his keys and extended the key chain toward her. "As my teammate, would you please go up to the Explorer and get my spiral notebook? I left it on the front passenger's seat."

Ashley grinned, and her eyes sparkled. "Sure, Doc." She hurried toward the Alpha exit door. "But I have my own set of keys, remember?"

"And would you hit the lights on your way out? Switch them from manual to panel control."

"Sure." Ashley swiped at the light switches and closed the door behind her. Darkness flooded the chamber, and her footsteps faded in the corridor.

The scarlet laser beam knifed through the blackness while a faint glow from the control panel diodes cast a ghostly light. Dr. Conner followed the beam to the pedestal. Ashley would be gone for a while. Although the hike through the tunnel was easy, the hundreds of upward steps that followed would slow even the best athlete.

He opened the box, took out the candlestone, and set it on the flat marble surface directly in the laser's path. The candlestone absorbed the red beam like a thirsty sponge. Its surface glowed pink, then stark red as the light poured through every crystalline particle. After a few seconds, it became engorged with ruby light and spurted bright cherry sparks, like blood pumping from a beating heart.

The stone's exit facet leaned against a nickel-sized grid attached to the end of a curved glass pipe that protruded from the top of the pedestal. The drops of discharged light collected in the grid and sped through an optic tube that ran across the tile and into a floor-standing computer near the control panel.

Dr. Conner returned to his seat at the controls and raised a black shield at the back of the panel, deflecting the glowing lights from the candlestone. With the flip of a switch, large floor speakers on each side of him began spewing static. As he adjusted a series of slider bars, the various sounds harmonized, coming together like altos and sopranos in a haunting electrostatic opera. With another click of a switch, the sound changed abruptly, and a deep, throaty voice replaced the operatic buzz.

"—delays are annoying me. Can you hear me now?"

Dr. Conner snatched a microphone from the top of the control panel. "Yes, yes. I hear you. Can you hear me?" As the doctor spoke, each word etched a fluctuating pattern of red on the candlestone's surface.

"Yes, Doctor. It's about time you provided an update."

Dr. Conner wiped beads of sweat from his forehead. "Of course. That's why I'm contacting you now." He swallowed hard before continuing. "Bonnie's here. She's anxious to see her mother. I don't think she suspects anything. I plan to set up contact at nine tonight. Are you still able to mark time?"

"Yes. What time is it now?"

Dr. Conner pressed a button on his watch, lighting up its analog face. "Exactly two minutes after six in the evening."

"I've got it. Are your daughter's friends going to be any trouble?"

"Palin called. Our colleague in West Virginia says that they're on their way—the Bannister boy, his mother, another male teenager, and an old man. If they go to the address on the card, my greeting party will take care of them."

"The man is likely a teacher I know, Charles Hamilton. He is brilliant and cunning, but he is, as you say, an old man. Bannister, on the other hand, might be more trouble than you've bargained for. His breath can kill you with one puff."

"I've heard," Dr. Conner replied, trying not to sound agitated. "But don't worry. Palin will be there."

"Good. He'll know what to do. We've battled dragons with more fire than that mongrel could ever blow."

Dr. Conner pushed a hand into his pocket and felt for his keys. "Are you planning to kill him?"

131

"What I decide is of no consequence to you, Doctor. Remember our deal. I'll spare the girl and leave her with you, but I get the boy, no questions asked. Understood?"

Dr. Conner gulped as quietly as he could. "Understood. But I'm keeping the DNA markings encoded, just to make sure you keep your end of the deal."

"I understand completely. There's no honor among liars, is there Doctor? But you have nothing to worry about. Your daughter cannot fulfill the prophecy without the boy, so I can leave her in your protective custody."

Silence descended in the dark lab, and the red light ceased its flickering dance on the wall of the candlestone. Dr. Conner glanced at the Alpha exit door, then at the door leading to the girls' dorm.

The sparks exiting the candlestone flashed to life once more. "Tell Palin to kill the others and bring the mongrel to me."

* * * * * *

Bonnie opened the door to her dorm room and peered out through the crack. No one was in the hall. She stepped into the hall, careful to set her shoes quietly on the floor and tiptoe to Karen's room on the opposite side of the corridor. The label on her door said in multicolored strokes of wide ink, "Red and Pebbles." Bonnie turned the knob and pushed the door open. She whispered through the gap, "Mind if I come in?"

Something rustled, then thumped. The door flew open, and Karen's bright, welcoming eyes appeared. She grabbed Bonnie's hand and pulled her inside before she had time to contract her wings. They bumped painfully against the frame as she entered.

Karen peeked out the door before closing it behind her and bouncing back into the room. "Sit," she said, pointing at one of the beds. "Pebbles won't mind."

Bonnie perched on the edge of the bed and watched the sleeping Asian girl. "Evening nap?"

"Yep. She has nightmares, so she catches a catnap once in a while." Karen plopped on her own bed and bounced lightly, as if in time with music only she could hear. "So why'd you come to see me?"

Bonnie caught Karen's gaze straying toward her wings but pretended not to notice. "I just wanted to get to know you better and find out what's going on here. You don't get to see an underground laboratory complete with a girls' dorm very often."

Karen laughed. "No. I guess this isn't the traditional American home, is it?"

"No, not exactly traditional." Bonnie nodded toward the door. "Are you allowed to go outside? What about school? What do you do all day?"

Karen shifted her gaze toward the ceiling. "We don't go outside much," she said, regaining eye contact with Bonnie, "at least not lately. There used to be an easier way out than that long tunnel and those awful stairs. It's a little door that leads to a cave and then another tunnel. They called it the Omega exit, but I never found out why. It comes out at about the same level we're at, sort of like in a valley. There's a real cool place to play there, a creek and a grassy field, but I never went out much after the wildflowers sprouted. I'm real allergic to bee stings." She let out a sigh. "Anyway, I suppose it's covered by snow this time of year, and Doc says there's a monster in the

133

cave now, so we can't go through there anymore to get to the valley."

"A monster?" Bonnie tried not to sound too doubtful. "Do you believe him?"

Karen nodded, her eyes bulging. "I've heard it growl. We all have. I imagine it's too dark in there to see it, but it's there all right. I thought at first that it might be a grizzly bear, but it doesn't sound like any bear I've ever heard. It's more like a Mercedes diesel engine without a muffler."

Bonnie dragged her teeth across her bottom lip. A monster? Was it a ruse to keep them in line? With all the equipment her father had, it would be easy to fool the girls into thinking something weird was in that cave. "What do you do here all day if you can't go outside?"

Karen tapped a stack of books on her nightstand. "When Ashley's here, she teaches us for a couple of hours a day and gives us assignments, and sometimes Doc calls one of us out to the lab to help him."

Bonnie clenched her hands in her lap. This was the perfect opening. "Help him? What do you do?"

Karen hesitated, her smile fading. "Well," she said, glancing toward Pebbles as she squirmed under her bed sheet, "I ... I'm not sure what I can tell you."

Bonnie rose, tiptoed to Karen's bed, and sat next to her, taking Karen's hand in hers. "You might as well tell me everything. I think we're in this together now."

Karen sniffed, and a tear trickled down her cheek. "Okay. I guess it's all right." She nodded toward the hall. "We—that is, Beck and Stacey and me—we're part of Doc's experiment. He's trying to figure out a way to get people to live longer."

"Oh? What does he do?"

Karen ran her index finger along the needle marks on her arm, her voice cracking. "Well, he used to take our blood and then put it back in after he did something to it. He said he's trying to make our blood work better."

Bonnie ran a finger along Karen's tiny scars. "Used to take it? What does he do now?"

Karen's voice strengthened. "It changed all of a sudden. I guess you've seen the lab out there. It was a lot different a few weeks ago. A couple of guys came in, and they worked with Ashley to build those glass things and all those instruments. That's about the same time they wouldn't let us use the tunnel anymore. Anyway, now we do some really weird and scary stuff."

Karen clutched Bonnie's hand tightly, rubbing her knuckles with her thumb. "It doesn't hurt or anything, but it's real scary. He doesn't explain what's going on, except a little at a time."

Bonnie laid her other hand on top of Karen's. "Go ahead and tell me. Maybe I can figure out what's going on."

Karen pursed her lips. When she continued, her voice trembled again. "Well, I stand in one of those glass things, and Derrick—he's a seventeen-year-old over in the guys' dorm—he stands in another. Then Ashley turns on Derrick's glass, and he disappears, and all I can see is a bunch of jumping light where he used to be."

She took a deep breath and closed her eyes. "Then, I see the light from his glass thing coming toward mine through something like a transparent vacuum cleaner hose, and then Ashley turns my glass thing on. All of a sudden, I see everything differently, but it's not like seeing at all. I can't really describe it. You sort of feel it, but you understand everything around you just like you're seeing it, only stronger. Anyway, Derrick's light reaches through the tube and grabs hold of me, and I can hear him say, 'Hang on!' Then I'm sucked through a chute, flying down real fast like a big dip on a roller coaster. And it gets real dark, darker than anywhere I've ever been, sort of like floating in the middle of the universe, with nothing to sit or walk on. I feel like a ghost, but I can't see anything, except the last few times they did it, I could see flashes of light, like night lightning far away."

Karen opened her eyes and relaxed her grip on Bonnie's hand. "It only lasts a little while, at least I think it's only a little while, and then I get sucked right back into my glass thing. I can open my eyes, and everything's back to normal, except—" She stopped and covered her mouth, letting out a laugh as her cheeks reddened.

Bonnie laughed with her. "Except for what?"

"Well, the first time, when it was over, I ended up wearing just my underwear. But it was all right. I had on long johns, 'cause I get cold in that lab." She held up her hand, displaying a thin gold ring. "And this ring was on the floor next to my clothes. So was an ankle bracelet I used to wear. Every time after that, though, they gave me a long white robe to put on, sort of like a church choir robe, and I didn't end up in my underwear anymore."

"And what happened to Derrick?"

Karen pulled her hand from Bonnie's lap and gave a wave of dismissal. "Oh, he was fine. I don't remember what happened to his clothes 'cause I was worried about my own."

"Do Beck and Stacey ever do anything?"

"Yes, they take my place sometimes, but it's usually me, 'cause I'm older, I guess. It's always Derrick in the other one, though."

Bonnie set a finger to her chin and spoke slowly. "I saw three glass domes out there. Did they ever use the third one?"

Karen shook her head. "They never told us what it's for."

Bonnie took a deep breath and blew it out in short puffs. "I can't figure out what's going on, at least not yet, but I'm going to have a look around tonight. Want to come with me?"

Karen shook her head. "Ashley always checks on us and locks the hall door when she goes to bed. She's almost like a jail warden. But she and Doc are good to us. We have good food and TV and computers and lots of nice clothes."

"Hmmm." Bonnie looked around the room. Each girl had a computer system, and there was an assortment of dolls, board games, and stereo equipment either pushed against the walls or stored neatly on various shelves. Karen also had a collection of model cars on her side of the room, along with a short stack of automobile magazines.

"You like cars?" Bonnie asked.

Karen blushed again and folded her hands in her lap. "Yeah. I like to read about them, and I have some videos. I want to be a mechanic someday, maybe even in a pit crew for NASCAR races."

Bonnie scanned the room once more, finding an encyclopedia set, an antique music box, and a huge collection of computer games. She let out a low whistle. "All this stuff makes me wonder where they get the money to finance this operation."

"I asked that a long time ago. There's lots of old rich guys who want to live forever. It's easy to get money."

"Don't they have to prove that what they're doing works?"

Karen's eyes widened like glowing emeralds. "Oh, they have proof, all right. Ashley's grandfather lives in the boys' dorm, and he got healthier every day. He was in a coma for a while,

137

but the last time I saw him he was walking around. His muscles were getting stronger all the time."

"*Were* getting stronger?"

"Well, he sort of leveled out, I guess. I don't think he's getting any worse, though."

Bonnie tapped her foot on the braided rug. "I wonder if Ashley would let me see him. Maybe he would give me more information."

Karen shrugged. "Who knows? Ashley's real nice, but she keeps a lot of secrets. She likes to say, 'Too much information can make your brain choke.'"

Bonnie laughed and rose from the bed. She helped Karen to her feet and wrapped her arms around her new friend. "Yes, Ashley is secretive, but I'll bet I can find the keys and get us out tonight. We need to learn what's really going on around here." She pulled away and looked into Karen's bright eyes. "Are you with me?"

Karen's head drooped. She drew her hands into fists, making her knuckles crack. "I … I guess so."

Bonnie hugged her again, this time wrapping her with arms and wings. "Don't let your heart be troubled, Karen. Someone is watching, and he's on our side."

9

THE TRANSLUMINARY TRIANGLE

Bonnie spent the remainder of the evening in her room with only a desk lamp illuminating the area near her bed. She rested on her pillow with her eyes closed, sometimes dozing, sometimes praying. Normally she would have taken the time to jot some of her thoughts down in her journal, but the old notebook still lay where she left it, out on one of the lab chairs. She wanted it back. She had spent too many hours recording her amazing adventures, her lonely wanderings, and her heart-felt prayers to have them exposed to an unauthorized reader or accidentally thrown away.

One of her prayers had been that someday her writing might help someone, maybe even change someone's life. Her own story had been one of heart-rending loss changed into great gain—sorrowful valleys that had transformed into exhilarating heights of love and joy. Maybe other troubled souls could be encouraged while in the valleys of their own lives.

Bonnie awoke from one of her short naps and found a dinner tray on the table next to her bed, visible in the glow of a nearby nightlight. A sub sandwich perched on a stoneware plate next to a pile of rippled potato chips. The sandwich was stuffed with turkey, a dark green lettuce leaf, and sliced black olives. Her stomach growled its approval. As she squeezed the roll, honey mustard oozed out the sides and dripped onto her plate. After taking a bite, she let out a satisfied sigh. It was so good! How could Ashley know what she liked on a sandwich?

Next to her plate, a ripe Anjou pear held down a folded note. Bonnie pulled it out, flicked on the night table's lamp, and silently read the handwritten words. *I hope you enjoy your meal. We normally eat together in the kitchen, but I didn't want to wake you. I'll come by later this evening. By the way, I found your backpack and journal. I put them and your coat in your closet next to your shoes.*

Bonnie smiled. Maybe Ashley really could read minds. She took another big bite just as the door swung open.

"Wake up, Bonnie," Ashley called with a cheery voice as she walked in and flicked on the ceiling light. "Oh, you're already awake. How do you like your supper?"

Bonnie set the sandwich on the plate, chewing, then licking the drips of mustard. She laughed, her mouth half full. "It's perfect. Thank you."

"Do you want to finish it, or can it wait? It's time to talk to your mother."

Bonnie pushed the tray to the side and grabbed her shoes from the closet, chewing and swallowing quickly. "Does she know I'm here? Will she be surprised?"

Ashley withdrew a pair of dark brown hiking boots from Bonnie's closet. "Here," she said, setting the boots at Bonnie's feet. "Your shoes still look wet."

"They are." Crouching, Bonnie pushed her foot into one of the boots. It fit perfectly.

Ashley watched as Bonnie looped the laces through the hooks. "We told your mother you were coming, but we haven't contacted her since you got here." She rocked from her toes to her heels, carrying some kind of clothing over her left arm. "It's all set up, though. We're just waiting for you."

Bonnie leaped up and headed for the door. "Let's go, then."

The two stepped quickly through the hall and out into the lab, Ashley pausing only to relock the hall door. The ceiling lights in the chamber were dim, but Bonnie could see well enough to make her way toward the center where the candlestone sat on the pedestal, glowing crimson at the end of a laser's steady beam. As she approached, nausea churned. She walked more slowly toward the control panel, trying to fight off the sickness.

"Bonnie, wait." Ashley caught up and handed her a white robe. "Here. Put this on over your clothes."

Bonnie took the robe and put it on while Ashley adjusted her wings underneath the material. When everything was smoothed out, Ashley pulled the robe's hood up over Bonnie's head. "Good," Ashley said. "It's big enough to cover everything."

Bonnie untwisted the long sleeves that wrapped her arms, remembering what Karen had said about wearing a robe. "Is this some kind of protection?"

"Yes. It prevents light absorption. I don't think it will be perfect, but it should keep you from getting too sick."

"You knew about that? How?"

"It stands to reason." Ashley fussed with Bonnie's robe, smoothing a bunched place on one side. "But don't worry about that now. It's showtime."

Ashley led the way toward the control panel where Bonnie's father sat peering at the various displays and lights on the board. Bonnie kept close behind, using Ashley as sort of a shield. Talking to her father again wouldn't be easy.

Static filled the area with an irritating hum. Ashley cupped her hands around her mouth and shouted, "Bonnie's here. Are you going to talk first?"

Dr. Conner kept his stare fixed on the monitor as he picked up a microphone and spread a hood over the control panel. "Yes. I'll do the introductions." He turned a dial. The lights dimmed further until they went out completely. He licked his lips before pressing a button on the microphone's throat. The static fell silent. He spoke slowly while Bonnie stepped closer, staring at the flaming red candlestone as it greedily drank from the glowing scarlet laser beam, spilling and spitting the energy out in red sparks on the other side.

"Irene? Irene, are you there?" He released the button and adjusted a knob on the panel, apparently trying to remove the returning static. "Beta frequency is not as stable," he said, turning to Ashley.

She reached to the panel and pushed a slider bar. "Try raising the distortion allowance. That's worked before. I think beta's a little off from what we guessed when we first calibrated the settings."

As the rasping noise died away, they waited. Sweat trickled down Bonnie's back, though her hands were like ice.

The speakers crackled back to life. A female voice poured forth in a sweet, melodic alto. "I'm here. Is Bonnie out there?"

Bonnie gasped. Mama's voice. She took a quick step forward and shouted, "Here I am! I'm right here!"

Her father extended the microphone. "She can't hear you without this."

Bonnie grasped its throat with both hands. Pushing the talk button with her thumb, she lifted the microphone slowly and spoke. "Mama? It's Bonnie." She released the button and waited a few seconds, nervously licking her lips.

The voice boomed again from the speakers. "Bonnie, my darling! Is it really you?"

Bonnie's tears flowed. She replied, laughing and crying at the same time. "Yes ... yes, Mama, it's me." She wiped hot wet streams from her cheeks, and her voice broke into a mournful lament. "Mama, I've missed you so much!"

A few more seconds passed before a soft, comforting voice replied. "I've missed you, too, sweetheart. But don't despair, we'll be back together soon."

"But how, Mama? How?" Bonnie looked at her father, then at Ashley, searching their eyes for an answer.

The voice from the speakers became softer, more urgent. "Bonnie, I need you to come in here, inside the candlestone. I'll attach my light energy to yours, and you can draw me out."

With cold fingers of fear creeping all over her body, Bonnie could barely speak. Her voice cracked. "I ... I'll do anything to help you, but I don't know how to get in there."

The loudspeaker coughed and spat a round of rough static, and the voice disintegrated into buzzing chaos. Bonnie could barely make out the words. "Don't worry, honey. They'll teach you—"

143

The voice died. Dr. Conner twisted dials on the panel, but his adjustments were to no avail.

The microphone trembled as Bonnie pushed the talk button again. "Mama? Are you there?"

Ashley touched Bonnie's shoulder and turned on a small lamp attached to the control panel. "It takes a lot of energy for your mother to communicate. She has to decipher our energy input and then create a light energy answer for our computer to decode."

She took the microphone and set it on the control panel. "The computer then uses her digitized voiceprint to make the output sound like her voice. It doesn't take long for her to get too tired to continue." She brushed a new tear from Bonnie's cheek. "Remember, she was already mortally wounded when your father transluminated her, and her life force is still weak. But don't worry. She'll be fine. And if you're willing, you can help us get her out in the morning."

Dr. Conner switched off the laser, and the gun descended toward the floor. "That's the big *if.* If you're willing. It's dangerous. We've succeeded in sending people into the candlestone, but only for a couple of minutes, max. They're not able to stay long, because they don't have the same makeup as you do. They have no natural light receptors, so they go into the stone out of the proper phase. We believe that you can go in and attach yourself to your mother and pull her out."

Bonnie gazed at the tiny stone, imagining a miniature universe within its crystalline cage. "How can I do that? Once I'm in there, won't it trap me like it did Mama and the slayer?"

Ashley flipped a switch on the panel's side. The static died away, and silence filled the room. "We have what we call an energy anchor, a boy named Derrick that we've trained to attach himself to the person going into the candlestone. He has a perfect record in being able to hang on to our diver."

"Diver?"

Ashley motioned with her hand, making it look like a person diving into the water. "That's what we call whoever's going into the stone."

Bonnie nodded. "Okay, but how do they get changed back to normal?"

Ashley turned up the ceiling lights and gestured for Bonnie to come to the center of the room. While Dr. Conner put the candlestone away, Ashley pointed at the glass cylinder opposite the main panel. "This one we call the diver's dome." She touched a slender flexible hose joining that cylinder to one that sat to the left of the master board. "It's hooked to what we call the anchor dome by this special tube. Each dome transluminates the person inside, and the anchor stretches his light energy through this tube and attaches himself to the diver's energy."

Bonnie imagined a stream of light leaping from one cylinder to the other, passing through what looked like thirty feet of vacuum cleaner hose, and popping out at the other cylinder. The second cylinder stood a third of the way around the perimeter of the circle. Someone would have to stretch out pretty far to get it done.

"As you can see," Ashley continued, pointing again at the first dome, "the diver's dome has an outlet hole and a plain glass tube that ends near the candlestone. When I open the tube, the candlestone draws the diver's light into itself while the anchor hangs on. The anchor remains here in the lab, because most of his energy is held in the special tube between the domes where he can attach to crystalline spurs that mimic the candlestone's absorption properties, except that they don't permanently entrap his energy."

Ashley held out her two fists and pumped them like she was pulling on a chin-up bar. "These spurs act sort of like friction grips for photons, something that Derrick can hang on to, anchoring him in place. After a while, as the candlestone keeps pulling, the anchor's attachment point gets stretched out, and he begins to lose contact with the diver. That's when we shift everything into reverse."

Bonnie set her hand on the hose. It felt like dimpled glass, wrinkled and semi-transparent. "Reverse? You mean you bring the diver back?"

"Right. I created synthetic photoreceptors, just like the natural ones your mother has in her blood and you have in yours. They change light energy into matter. That's why dragons live so long. They're constantly regenerating. I figured out how it all works by analyzing Excalibur's beam. I was able to capture the beam's profile, even though we were only able to turn the beam on in short bursts. I discovered that Excalibur's effects can be reversed by slowing the newly created tachions and reversing their space-and-time framework, in effect, making them anti-tachions. As their hyperlight speed slows toward the mass-energy asymptote, the photoreceptors cause the energy to begin a reassimilation process, using light-encoded cell structure information, data that should still exist in your mother's energy matrix."

Bonnie tried to replay Ashley's explanation in her mind, but the technical terms flew right by. As soon as her brain grabbed one of the hundred-letter words, another zipped through. It was like trying to grab a handful of fog. "I have no clue what you're talking about," she said, "but I heard one word that bothers me."

"One word? What word was that?"

"You said, *should*, that her information *should* still exist. How do you know it'll work?"

Ashley ran a finger across the dome's glass surface. "It worked for Derrick and the girls." She pressed a button at the base. With a low hum, the glass began rising. "We first transluminated rats and then larger animals before we considered using humans." She sat on the dome's base and rested her chin in her hands. "The animals didn't go into the candlestone, though, until we started training Derrick to be an anchor. We lost a few animals until he learned how to hold on, but now he's a real pro. He held to a chimp that we sent into the stone, and it was a complete success. The chimp came back with all of her faculties and memories in place. After several perfect trials, we decided to send in Karen. We needed someone who could tell us what it was like inside before we could analyze what it would take to draw your mother out."

"And what happened?"

"It worked fine. Karen is perfectly normal with no aftereffects, except for being a bit embarrassed. We didn't figure it out at first, because Derrick always wore cotton, but it seems that the translumination affects only certain organic substances. Karen was wearing something synthetic and came back dressed only in her cotton underwear."

Bonnie nodded. Hearing corroboration of Karen's story meant that Ashley was telling the truth. Maybe she wasn't hiding anything after all. "So why is it dangerous? It sounds like everything's working great."

147

"So far." Ashley rose from the dome base and heaved a deep sigh. "There's one part of the procedure that's never been tried. Although Karen was able to perceive another entity in the candlestone, she was never able to make contact with it." Ashley reached for one of Bonnie's wings and held the outside edge. "We believe that with your dragon-like genetics, you would probably transluminate into a similar photo-dimension, a sort of light energy frequency that matches your mother's, and you'll be able to find her. But once you attach to her, we don't know if you'll be able to pull her out or if you'll be drawn completely in and cut off from the outside world. It just hasn't been tested."

Bonnie peeked at her father. He was studying meter readings on the panel and scribbling notes in a spiral journal. "Where will my mother show up when I bring her out?"

Ashley released Bonnie's wing and smiled. "*When* you bring her out? I like your attitude." She led Bonnie to the third glass cylinder. "This is the recovery tube. We sometimes call it the restoration dome. When Derrick pulls you out, you'll be attached to your mother in your dome. We told her that she's supposed to go through another crystalline pipeline on the opposite side of Derrick's, passing through a series of photo analyzers that will read her encoded light structure.

"You see, her encoding might be shifted or out of phase because it's been so long since she was transluminated. She went inside in an agitated state, but after a while, her light energy settled down. It's like a reflection in a pond that gets disturbed by throwing in a rock. Eventually, the water settles, and you can see the image again. All the parts of the messed-up image are the same as the clear image, except that they're scrambled. So, if slowing your mother's tachions doesn't create an auto-assimilation, I'll have to use the computer to rephase her structure."

Bonnie pressed her palms against her temples. "You're making my brain explode."

Ashley pulled Bonnie's hands down and smiled. "It sounds worse than it is. I tested it with a rabbit by messing up her encoding and shifting her frequency phasing. Then, I passed her light through the analyzer. No problem. She came out a perfectly healthy bunny." She tapped on the cylinder's glass with her knuckles. "In short, a few seconds after you show up in your dome, you'll see your mother in this restoration dome. We don't know for sure what kind of condition she'll be in, but we're convinced that since we can communicate with her, she will be out of the coma, maybe even perfectly well. It could be that you'll be in each other's arms less than a minute later."

Bonnie's heart thumped. Could it really be true? Could all of this really work? Would she finally see her long-lost mother?

"We're waiting for morning," Ashley continued, "so Derrick will be wide awake and strong. Anchoring is a grueling job, and he gets exhausted after just a few minutes. But that's okay, because we don't want to go longer than a few minutes anyway. The light energy begins getting out of phase in about two hundred and fifty seconds. We have to be sure to throw it into reverse before we hit that time mark."

Bonnie set her hands on her temples again, closed her eyes, and began praying silently for her mother, Derrick, and herself.

Ashley's tone softened. "Did I give you a headache?"

Bonnie smiled but kept her eyes closed. "No. I'm just praying." When she finished her prayer, she opened her eyes and took Ashley's hand in hers. "I'll do it."

149

Ashley grinned from ear to ear and began talking in rapid-fire fashion as she led Bonnie back to the dorm. "That's
awesome! You need to get plenty of rest, and we'll make sure
the robe fits you better so it won't drag the floor of the dome.
But don't worry. It won't really matter anyway. It all gets
changed into light. And translumination doesn't hurt at all.
At least that's what they tell us. Derrick's done it about twen-
ty-five times, and Karen's done it about a dozen or so."

As they entered the hall, Bonnie laughed. Ashley halted and
blinked at her. "What's so funny?"

Bonnie pulled a wing to the front and pinched the edge.
"You act like you think I might be scared."

Ashley's dark eyebrows arched downward. "Aren't you?"

Bonnie shook her head. "I'm excited, but I'm not scared.
Not really."

150

Ashley fussed with her keys as she unlocked their dorm
room. "You must have a lot more faith than I do. I don't think
I'd be so calm."

"Why? You're the one who's been propping me up, telling
me why it's all going to work."

Ashley pushed the door open but blocked Bonnie from
entering. "It's not the technology." She looked down the hall,
then lowered her voice to a whisper. "Have you forgotten?
Devin's in the candlestone, too."

Bonnie's throat grew a lump the size of a golf ball. In all the
joy and excitement of hearing her mother's voice, she really
had forgotten about the dragon slayer. "But ... but he's on a
different phase or something, isn't he?"

Ashley motioned with her head for Bonnie to come inside.
After closing the door quietly, Ashley sat on the bed under the
Einstein poster and patted the space next to her. When Bonnie

joined her, she leaned close and whispered, "Devin has always communicated with us on the alpha frequency, and your mother's always been on the beta. I think you'll go in with your mother's phase, and he probably won't even know you're there. But there's one problem. Sometimes I search for him in his phase, and I can't find him. I think he's up to something. I don't trust him."

10

Love Lifts the Veil

Ashley had been asleep for more than an hour when Bonnie decided to make her move. The dorm room was nearly dark, but enough light came from under the door to allow her to find her way around.

Bonnie slid out of bed and held up her nightgown to keep the skirt from sweeping the floor. Since she and Ashley had cut holes in the back earlier that evening, her wings protruded, exposed but motionless and quiet.

She tiptoed across the room to a wall hook where the keys dangled. She lifted the keys, crept to the closet, and grabbed her jeans and gym shoes. Then she skulked to the door and opened it part way. The hinge squeaked. Bonnie spun toward Ashley. She lay motionless in bed, breathing steadily.

Folding her wings tightly, Bonnie squeezed through the gap and left the door unlatched. After pulling on her jeans under her gown, she crossed the hall to Karen's door and gave it a couple of light taps. Two seconds later, it flew open, and Karen appeared.

"You ready?" Bonnie whispered.

"Ready." Karen showed no signs of sleepiness, her eyes shining brightly.

Bonnie bent down and slipped her shoes over the socks she'd worn to bed. She tied the laces hurriedly, then headed for the hall exit, winding up the lower part of her gown and tucking it inside her jeans as she walked. She stopped at the door and searched through the keys while Karen looked on. "It was one of the brown ones," Bonnie muttered, "but there's a bunch of them."

Karen pointed at a key with a rounded end. "I think it's that one."

Bonnie tried Karen's choice, and the lock turned smoothly. She cracked the door open and peeked out into the dim laboratory chamber. The lamp of the main control panel gleamed, but there was no sound, no movement. Bonnie opened the door fully and entered, waiting for Karen to follow before silently closing the door.

Bonnie hopped up to the lab platform and headed straight for the main control panel where her father's spiral-bound notebook lay. She picked it up, placed it under the lamp, and studied the last few pages.

A strange array of numbers and letters filled most of the entries—characters that were hard to read, made with dark hasty strokes scratched across the page without regard for the lines. Each number had a letter next to it, a cryptic message that seemed indecipherable.

Bonnie flipped back to earlier pages, scanning them for words she could understand. Finally, near the front of the notebook, she found a narrative penciled in more careful script. She read silently while Karen looked on.

Seeing that dragon's blood is the only real agent that can actually regenerate tissue, it has become clear through many trials that our triangle will be successful in reversing Excalibur's transluminating process only if we supply the tachion engine with the receptors from the blood itself. The receptors seem impossible to synthetically produce, at least for this application. The lab rats were expendable. We can't risk trying it on humans until we have successfully restored at least a rat, and, ideally, a higher order mammal upon which we can test memory restoration. Ashley believes that her synthetic receptors will eventually work. Time will tell if she is correct.

At the end of the entry, a series of numbers and labels followed, again impossible to decipher. Bonnie flipped the pages forward, looking for more text. After about a dozen pages of cryptic data, she found a series of block letters. They didn't make real words, but they were separated into word-like letter strings. It started, "QRL AFXN NXC" and continued with similarly jumbled chains.

Karen whispered, "Does that stuff make any sense to you?"

"Maybe. Something about this looks very familiar." Bonnie thought back to a time when she and her father traded coded messages, a game that allowed them to write to each other about anything related to her dragon characteristics without anyone else understanding, even if someone happened to read one of their notes. It had been more than a year since the last time she decrypted his code, and he might have come up with a new system, but it might be worth a try. She tore out a blank sheet from the back of the notebook and found a pen on the control board.

After a few minutes of work, she came up with a translation and whispered it to Karen. "Her idea has failed, but replacing the synthetic receptors with real ones in the presence of the candlestone has made the process work until now. I will have to let her know eventually, but as long as her grandfather improves, she won't ask questions, and our investors will be happy. I can't explain it to her yet. I also cannot tell her why the blood has been so readily available." Bonnie looked up from the page. "Does that mean anything to you?"

Karen scratched her thick mane of red hair. "Well, they've mentioned putting receptors in my blood to see if they would work. I got the idea that it didn't take for me, but I think it did take for Ashley's grandfather. At least it did until recently."

Bonnie closed the notebook and waved it toward Karen. "Well, I'm not sure how old this entry is, but it was something my dad obviously didn't want Ashley to read."

Karen lifted her brow and smiled. "So Ashley's not the only one who's keeping secrets, huh?"

"Apparently not." Bonnie surveyed the cavernous room, looking for something that might spark an idea—a new object, maybe another notebook, anything. Above, fluorescent light fixtures had been set in drop-ceiling panels. How high might the true ceiling be? Even if she were to walk to the cavern's wall and look up, it would be too dark to see the real ceiling with only a single desk lamp for light.

She scanned across the chamber to a door in the far corner and pointed toward it. "Is that the door to the monster's cave?"

Karen nodded. "Yep. That's the one."

Bonnie laid the notebook where she found it and skulked toward the cave, but Karen stayed put.

Bonnie glanced over her shoulder. "What's wrong?"

"Nothing." Karen scrambled off the platform but slowed as she drew closer.

When Bonnie reached the door, she noticed an odd shadow on the exterior. She ran her hand over the surface and felt the outline of a horseshoe-shaped symbol scratched into the wood. "An omega, right?"

Karen tiptoed to the door. "Yeah. That's what Ashley told me. An upper case omega."

Bonnie pulled out the set of keys and tried several in the lock, but they all failed. She turned to Karen. "Have you ever seen Ashley open this door?"

She shook her head. "Only Doc."

"Hmmm. The things that Ashley doesn't know are piling up." She set her ear close to the door and listened.

"Hear anything?" Karen asked.

"Shhh." A faint murmur emanated, altering its pitch and roughness. "It sounds like sawing wood, and then it changes to more like a train rumbling, and then back to sawing again. It's like an old man snoring and wheezing."

"Sometimes it's louder," Karen said, "more like growling or even moaning. If it's not a monster, I don't want to guess what else it could be."

Bonnie stepped back from the door and frowned. "Monster, schmonster, Karen. He's just trying to scare you."

"Scare me? Why would he want to do that?"

"To keep you girls in line, maybe?"

Karen squared her shoulders. "No way. We don't give him any trouble."

157

Bonnie gestured toward the boys' dorm hall. "Derrick, then?"

"Not a chance. He's real quiet and shy."

"Does Ashley ever say anything about the growling?"

Karen looked down for a moment before shaking her head. "Not that I can remember. If it's fake, she just seems to play along."

"Interesting." Bonnie pushed on the door with her shoulder while turning the knob, but it didn't budge. A siren wailed, faint and distant. She stepped back, nearly stumbling. "Is that an alarm?"

Karen's eyes darted. "You must have tripped something. Sounds like it's coming from the boys' area."

A sudden bump and click sounded nearby. The door to the boys' dorm swung open. Bonnie led Karen into a dark corner and whispered, "Let's wait here. Don't make a sound."

"Is somebody out there?" a man called.

"It's your father," Karen hissed.

"Shhh." Bonnie crouched, pulling Karen down with her. Her father walked toward the chamber's main light switches, one hand in his bathrobe pocket and the other reaching for the wall. Just as the fluorescent panels flashed on, Bonnie grabbed Karen around the waist and held a hand over her mouth, then leaped into the air. She flew around and above the drop ceiling toward the upper reaches of the cavern, lugging Karen like a sack of wiggling cats.

After finding a stable rafter, she perched there with Karen and looked down through the wide gap between the edge of the ceiling and the cavern wall. Below, her father checked behind panels and opened storage closets.

Karen's deep gasps sent rushing air blowing across Bonnie's palm. Bonnie whispered into her ear, "Don't worry. I've done stuff like this before. Now relax and be quiet." She slowly released her grasp.

Karen whispered coarsely, "That was so cool. Are you going to fly down, too?"

"Shhh!" Bonnie clutched a vertical beam with one hand and Karen's shirt with the other. She took slow, shallow breaths of the warm, stale air, barely making a sound. Beads of sweat trickled from her brow and cheeks. The rocky ceiling trapped the heat and exhaust from the laboratory equipment, and it seemed that no vents brought fresh air into the chamber, at least at this level.

After a few minutes of checking around, her father tested the door that had tripped the alarm and found it securely locked. With a shrug, he flicked off the lights and disappeared behind the boys' hallway door.

159

Bonnie whispered, "Let's wait another minute. I want to make sure he's not coming back." The seconds seemed like hours. Their perspiration dripped, falling like hot raindrops to the nearly invisible floor below. When Karen's shirt grew damp, Bonnie released the beam and clutched Karen with both arms. "Okay. Hold your breath."

She leaped from the rafter, throwing her wings into a full canopy and flapping to catch and hold the motionless air. The girls dropped to the floor, Bonnie trying to hit the concrete surface running.

Karen's feet tripped over themselves, and the two landed in a crumpled heap, rolling and grunting as their momentum carried them forward.

Bonnie jumped up and helped Karen to her feet. "Are you okay?"

Karen nodded, rubbing her elbow. "Yeah. Just a scrape."

"Good." Bonnie tilted her head and listened, ready to fly again if necessary, but all was quiet. It seemed that no one had heard their spill.

Bonnie took Karen's hand. "Let's get back to our rooms. I don't think we'll learn much more tonight." They crossed the cavern, passing through the main lab, and reentered the girls' hall. Bonnie relocked the door and whispered to Karen as she led her back to her room. "I've figured out a few things but not everything. I need to talk to Ashley in the morning, then maybe it'll get clearer." Bonnie pushed Karen's door open and set a hand on her shoulder. "Try to get some sleep. I'll see you at breakfast."

Karen smiled, stretching the tracks of dusty sweat smearing her cheeks. "Okay." She turned to go into her room. At the last second she spun back, stood on tiptoes, and kissed Bonnie on the cheek. As a tear formed in Karen's eye, she whispered, "Thanks. For everything." With that, she tiptoed in and closed the door.

Bonnie touched her cheek. Thanks for what? What had she done for Karen?

She pulled the skirt of her nightgown out, slipped her shoes and jeans off, then wadded them into a bundle. She looked at Karen's door. Did she think they were sneaking around for her benefit, trying to figure out what they were doing to her, maybe find a way for her to get out? Probably. She was trapped in this place like a human guinea pig in a bizarre experiment, living a nightmare, an imprisoned orphan in an underground cage.

Bonnie knew what it felt like—loneliness, hopelessness, despair. All this time, she had been thinking about finding her mother and not much else. Sure, the girls were important, but that wasn't why she was skulking around for clues.

As she pictured Karen's grimy face and sad, teary eyes, her own tears welled. In her mental image, shackles appeared on Karen's wrists and neck, and Ashley held a leash, smiling while leading Karen to the diver's dome.

Bonnie balled her hands into fists. Heat spiked in her face until she thought steam might spew out her ears. She threw open her door. Light from the hall poured into the room. Ashley sat up, bleary eyed and blinking. "What's going on?"

Bonnie stalked in, closing her wings to get through and then opening them again in the middle of the room. She flung the keys and the wad of clothes on her bed and planted her fists on her hips, not knowing where to begin.

Ashley stared at her. "Are you okay? Are you sleepwalking or something?"

Bonnie pointed toward the hallway, passion erupting in her voice. "They're human beings! Not stupid lab rats!"

Ashley jumped up, marched to the door, and closed it with an authoritative click. "Shhh!" she warned while turning the light on. "Do you want to wake the girls?"

Bonnie kept pointing, her arm now shaking. "As if you really cared about them. Can't you see you're using them? They're people! I noticed no one ever mentioning *you* volunteering to get transluminated!"

Ashley walked slowly toward her bed. Her voice stayed calm, her tone condescending as she raised her eyebrows. "I have to run the equipment, Bonnie. It would be suicide for a diver if something went wrong and I wasn't available to fix it."

Still fuming, Bonnie grabbed Ashley's arms and turned them over to expose the undersides. "But it's okay to use other people for pincushions, I see, and keep your own skin from getting gouged."

Ashley shook Bonnie's hands loose and pulled her arms back. "It's the same deal, Bonnie. If something bad happened to me, who would continue the research? No one else knows how the photoreceptors work."

Bonnie furrowed her brow. "Are you sure they really do work?"

Ashley's eyes seemed to darken. "Of course I'm sure. My grandfather is living proof."

Bonnie gave her wings a shake, making them shudder as if trying to throw off a chill. "So you're willing to take chances with these girls but not with yourself? I guess it's okay if something happens to them, because they're not as smart as you are. I guess they're expendable."

Ashley folded her arms across her chest. "Well, I wouldn't put it that way."

Bonnie drilled her stare into Ashley. "Then how would you put it?"

Ashley stepped toward Bonnie, gazing down at her from her two-inch height advantage. "These girls would either be dead or on their way to prostitution by now if they weren't here. They have food and clothes, and their sacrifice will benefit the entire world."

"Sacrifice?" Bonnie waved her arms. "You call being imprisoned and forced to be a lab rat a sacrifice? The Nazis experimented on the Jews in the name of science. Oh, those wonderful sacrificial Jews. Wasn't it nice how they gave their lives for the benefit of mankind? And how about aborted babies? Isn't it sweet of them to lend their bodies to scientists for stem cell research? Some day all of humanity will give thanks for their sacrifice."

Bonnie scowled and turned her back on Ashley, folding her arms and huffing. "For being so smart, you sure are clueless, Ashley. My father's got the wool pulled over your eyes big time."

Ashley's voice lowered. "What do you mean by that?" She sounded more like a wounded puppy than an intimidating debater.

Bonnie turned toward her again. The pain in Ashley's expression settled Bonnie's rapid boil. "Listen. There's a lot going on here that doesn't make sense." She picked up Ashley's keys from the bed and jingled them. "Tell me. Why don't you have a key to the Omega door?"

163

Ashley blinked at the key ring, as if trying to focus through sleepy eyes. "I haven't had a need for it. Your father has the only one."

"But you have keys to everything else, right?"

Ashley squinted, pausing for a second. "Yeah, I guess so."

"Well, what could be in that cave that's such a secret?"

Ashley let out an impatient sigh. "It's a passage that used to lead outside, but after we brought all our equipment in here, part of it caved in during a minor earthquake. It's too dangerous to go through anymore. That's why we named it Omega, the last letter in the Greek alphabet. It's sort of like saying, 'If you try to go through there, you're finished.' So, to protect the girls, your father has a continuous audio stream running on a laptop computer. It plays random monster noises that he downloaded from the Internet. He just wants to keep the kids from ever trying to go in there."

Bonnie nodded. "I figured it was something like that, but why doesn't he want *you* to go in there? Maybe he's hiding something else."

Ashley pushed her hand through her tangled hair. "I can't imagine what." She pointed at Bonnie's hand. "I guess he doesn't want any extra keys left around for people to get hold of."

"Okay, okay," Bonnie said, tossing the keys to Ashley's bed. "I'm busted. At least you're right about that." She gestured toward the hall. "But what about these girls, and what about Derrick? Do you really think it's right to use human beings as guinea pigs against their will?"

Ashley shrugged. "I guess I saw them as willing participants. We give them whatever they want, within reason, of course, and they do what we ask."

164

"But that's just the point. You're treating them like animals. You feed them, keep them warm, and clean their cages. So now it's okay to ravage their bodies? Don't you see that they're real people, and they're scared? Just because nobody loves them, you think you can use them?" Bonnie glanced upward and whispered a silent prayer. *God give me the right words to say.* She took a deep breath before continuing. "Well, I know someone who loves them, and he doesn't look kindly on mistreating orphans."

Ashley's lips tightened into two pale lines. "Is this turning into a God-loves-everyone speech? Because if it is, I don't want to hear it. Daddy kept trying to tell me that, always singing Amazing Grace, but I asked him to quit a long time ago. If God were so amazing or so loving, Daddy wouldn't have suffered so much, and I wouldn't be such a Brainiac freak." She waved her arm toward the hall. "If God loved Pebbles, she wouldn't have been left to die on the beach, wandering in a dirty diaper and spitting sand from her bloody lips. And if God loved Stacey, she wouldn't have been accosted by a pervert who would have abused her and left her for the other street predators to finish off. In everyone else's eyes, these kids were worthless throwaways. Nobody really loved them, and they wouldn't have amounted to anything. But here, at least we're making them into something useful, something they can be proud of."

Bonnie set a hand on Ashley's shoulder. She tried to pull away, but Bonnie held firm. "Ashley, love isn't based on what people can give or how much they can do. I mean, everyone loves the rich and famous, right? But it's all fake. People just want to hang around them because they've got money. True love is treating bums and outcasts like they have diamonds in their pockets, even when there's nothing there but moths and holes."

165

Bonnie pointed toward Ashley's painting on the wall. "It sounds to me like your grandfather was pretty worthless not too long ago, at least in other people's eyes. But your painting proves you had different eyes. You had eyes of love that saw past his decaying body and into his heart. I'll bet you can do the same for girls like Karen and me." Bonnie pulled up her sleeve and exposed the soft underside of her arm.

Ashley stared at her skin. Slowly, with trembling fingers, she touched one of the white needle scars. Bonnie pressed her hand over Ashley's. When their eyes met, Bonnie whispered, "Don't you think these girls deserve our love, too, Ashley?"

Ashley's eyes grew wet, and she lowered her gaze. She sniffed hard and sat on her bed.

Bonnie sat next to her, laid an arm around her shoulders, and leaned her cheek on Ashley's tousled hair.

Ashley wept, halting and sniffing while she tried to talk. "You're ... you're right. Deep inside I knew it all along. But I kept telling myself that it would ... that it would all be over soon. We'd finish up and get these girls into good homes somehow."

Ashley slid both arms around Bonnie's neck. They held each other for a few quiet minutes, Ashley's gentle crying the only sound breaking the silence. Tears dampened Bonnie's nightgown. The warm wetness raised a memory, a song from years ago. She sang the chorus softly.

"I felt every teardrop when in darkness you cried, and I strove to remind you, that for those tears I died." She whispered, "Love opens our eyes, Ashley. It always leads us to the truth, even if it takes a long time."

Ashley looked up. Thin red lines bordered her narrowing pupils. "Truth? Are you sure you want the truth? If you ever heard one of Stacey's stories, you might change your mind."

"Believe me, I understand. I saw my own mother lying in a pool of blood." Bonnie's throat caught, forcing her to swallow. "Sometimes the truth is ugly; sometimes it hurts, but love helps us overcome evil in all of its deceptions and brutality."

Ashley blinked, and a new tear trickled down her cheek. "Yeah, I forgot about what happened to your mother. I can't understand how you're not boiling with rage at your father after all you've been through."

"Well, I don't trust him." Bonnie sniffed and wiped away a new tear of her own. "But I still love him. ... I mean ... I choose to love him, even though it isn't easy." She pressed her finger on the bedspread and drew a cross, staring at it a moment before looking at Ashley again. "Don't you see? Love is a decision we make, even toward people who don't deserve it. It's the only way we can hope to win the battle against Devin, Stacey's nightmares, or your own fears."

"Maybe you're right." Ashley wiped her sleeve across her cheek and looked toward the hall again, sighing. "Speaking of truth and fears, I have to figure out what Doc's up to. I'm not sure he's telling me everything. My grandfather's getting sicker, and Doc doesn't want to call a doctor." She turned back to Bonnie and grasped both of her hands. "But I do know one thing for sure."

Warmth in Ashley's fingers radiated into Bonnie's. Could she trust this new friend with the information from the journal? Maybe it could wait a little while longer. "One thing? What's that?"

Ashley tightened her grip. "I know you want your mother back. We need to get her out of that candlestone, and I'm not going to let you down."

167

11

OLD WINESKINS

After a few hours of sleep in a Missoula motel, Billy sat upright in bed. He had been dreaming about lightning—scattered, streaking bolts through an ink black sky. It was peaceful at first, like watching a distant storm through a bedroom window while waiting for sleep to carry him away. But as the dream continued, the storm approached, stalking him as he tried to escape through dark, borderless realms. White-hot bolts crashed all around, trapping him in a circular cage of fiery bars of pure light. One of the bars grew appendages and plunged its supercharged fingers into his chest. The energy numbed his abdomen and thrust an electric shock through every nerve, from his toes to the top of his head.

Billy slid out of bed, stretched his arms, and let out a big, blood-pumping yawn. Smacking his dry lips, he glanced at Walter, wrapped in his blanket like a cocooned caterpillar who never heard spring's reveille. Mom lay in the other bed, curled to the side and hugging the extra pillow. The professor slept on a rollaway cot next to the door, his pillow on the carpet and one bare foot sticking out from under his covers.

Billy rubbed his eyes and read the digits on the bedside clock—6:15. He scratched his head. It seemed a shame to wake everyone, but they had to get moving. Still, he could use the bathroom first and let them sleep for a few more minutes.

Billy trudged toward the glow of their bathroom nightlight, glancing at the professor's open suitcase on the floor nearby. The light streaming past the slightly ajar door cast its beam on the book that rested on top of Prof's clothes—Merlin's Diary.

The old book lay open to the first blank page, or at least what had been the first blank page. From his place in the shadows, Billy stared at the yellowed parchment. Something new was there. He knelt next to the suitcase and tried to read the elaborate script. "Mom! Professor! Walter!"

"What? What?" Mom lurched to a sitting position. Walter groaned, but the professor was already walking toward Billy, smoothing out his hair and tucking in his shirt—the same shirt he had worn yesterday. Kneeling, he reached around Billy to his suitcase and fished out his spectacles. He slipped them on while Mom scrambled to their side.

Billy tried to slow his breathing while he read out loud.

No one tears a piece from a new garment and puts it on an old garment; otherwise he will both tear the new, and the piece from the new will not match the old. And no one puts new wine into old wineskins; otherwise the new wine will burst the skins, and it will be spilled out, and the skins will be ruined. But new wine must be put into fresh wineskins. And no one, after drinking old wine wishes for new; for he says, "The old is good enough."

The professor rose, slowly taking off his glasses. "Very interesting." He stepped over to the bathroom and opened the door fully, allowing the light to pour over them. "It's from the Bible," he said. "A parable of Christ."

Kneeling, Mom set a hand on the page and ran her fingers across the words. "What does it mean?"

"I have my opinions. It's fascinating that the quote is from a modern translation that came about long after Merlin's day."

Walter's sleepy voice chimed in from across the motel room. "Yeah, Prof, but didn't the book say we would be able to read it in our own language?"

"Yes, Walter, you are correct. It's a curious phenomenon, however, that an old prophet would find a way to write new prose in a book fifteen hundred years after his day in a dialect to which he is unaccustomed. I suppose, though, if a floating hand is able to write cryptic warnings on a Babylonian palace wall, then most anything is possible."

171

Billy rubbed his sleepy eyes, then blinked. "Floating hand, Professor?"

"Yes. That story is also in the Bible." Professor Hamilton put his spectacles on again and reread the script. "It's a good thing Merlin has become familiar with our tongue. If he had written it in Latin, I would have to dust off an old textbook or two to translate it."

Mom rose to her feet. "So, what does it mean?"

"I am familiar with the traditional interpretations of the Scriptural passage, but I'm not sure how the text applies to our situation. Considering our hurry, I should like to ponder it while I prepare for departure. I will share my thoughts during the drive to the university."

Mom and the professor folded the rollaway while Walter sat at the edge of his bed, stretching and yawning. Billy refocused on the book. This was the first time it didn't communicate in cryptic poetry, yet this entry was every bit as mysterious. But was the page finished? It looked like there was plenty of room for more. Maybe this message continued on the next page.

The mystery of the unknown dragged Billy down, like a hundred-ton weight hanging from his neck. The next page, although never seen and without a voice, beckoned like the beautiful sirens of Homer's Odyssey. Part of Billy's brain absolutely demanded that he turn the page, while another part whispered, *No, Billy. Danger lies ahead.* The warnings, penned in Merlin's own hand, resurrected, but they were distant, quiet voices, not like the screaming banshees that cried out for a view of the next page. The very warning seemed part of the temptation. What would really happen if he violated its words? If he never tried it, he would never know. No one would. And wouldn't that be a tragedy, not gaining wisdom that begged to be learned?

Billy's fingers, stiff, yet trembling, lifted the page, even as the battle in his mind raged on. His hand worked as if separated from his mind's commands, moving where he begged it not to go.

He turned the page. He let out a long breath as though he had just fought a great battle, but even without reading the newly revealed words, he knew he had lost.

"William!" The professor's heavy footsteps stomped toward him. "William! The page wasn't full!"

Billy couldn't answer. He could barely breathe. It seemed that a clamp squeezed his throat shut, tightening and cutting off his air supply until his lungs burned, begging for relief.

172

The professor's warm breath glanced off the back of Billy's neck as he read the new page. "William, I fear that this is very bad news. What you have revealed is a dire prophecy, indeed."

"Yeah," Billy replied, his voice low and weak. "I kind of guessed that."

When Mom and Walter drew close, the professor read out loud.

> Of covenants broken, covenants lost,
> A promise made yet torn in two.
> Thou never learned salvation's cost
> And now bring forth thy vengeance due.
>
> Cruel yokes and whips designed for slaves;
> No, not for heirs nor sons by birth.
> They tear the backs of stiff-necked knaves
> Who think their power comes from earth.
>
> Yet hope remains, dispelling fears,
> A faithful heart, entrapped, alone,
> Who prays for thee unceasing tears
> And casts appeals before his throne.
>
> The soul set free must face the beast
> And break his chains to fears of earth,
> To free the faithful heart of love
> And prove the seeds of royal birth.

The professor picked up the diary, slapped it closed, and with a quick thrust, tucked it tightly under his arm, his face turning red. "I shall keep it by my side from now on." He closed his suitcase and carried it into the bathroom. "If you don't mind, I would like to go first. I am fast and tidy, and I would like to hasten outside to consider this matter alone." He shut the door, leaving the rest of them in darkness.

Walter bounded over his bed and flipped on the lights. Mom grasped Billy's wrist, pulled him to his feet, and wrapped an arm around his shoulder as he straightened. Of course, she was trying to offer comfort, but it didn't help. Once again he had lost a battle, this time with his own mind. He mentally pummeled himself with insults he wouldn't throw at a dog. He felt weak, helpless, and trapped, like a beast in a cage, proud and deplorable at the same time, and most of all, selfish beyond belief.

When the professor emerged from the bathroom, he gave Billy a smile and a pat on the back. He said nothing, yet the gestures felt like healing salve on a deep wound. Although the sting diminished, a heavy, ponderous weight remained. Something was still wrong, deep and unexplainable.

174

After the professor bundled up and went outside, the other three hurried through quick showers and revolving-door bathroom sharing before joining him.

Billy stepped into the cold, dark Montana morning, a suitcase in each gloved hand. The professor stood across the parking lot, gazing at the sky. With Walter following a few paces behind, Billy hurried to the professor, his teeth already chattering. "Brrrr! It's gotta be about two degrees out here."

The professor opened the rear door of their rented Jeep and took a suitcase from Billy. "It's four degrees, William, on the Fahrenheit scale, of course."

Billy set his suitcase inside. "Four degrees? Professor, is there anything you don't know?"

The professor pointed toward a bank sign across the street. "I was merely taking note of the local media report. It has been dropping ever since I came out."

The sign announced the temperature, a numeral four flashing once, then changing to a three. "My guess was pretty close."

"We're not here to audition for the Weather Channel," Walter said. "Let's just get our freezing fannies moving and find something hot to eat."

Billy jogged back to the motel and carried Excalibur out in a long florist box they had found next to a dumpster at the rental car depot. Mom followed, hustling through the crackling cold air.

"Walter's hungry, Mom." Billy poked Walter's lean stomach. "As usual."

She pointed down the street at a set of bright neon lights. "We can grab something at that fast-food place."

The professor hugged himself and bounced on his toes. "Just some hot tea for me, and I'll be fine."

After a quick and quiet breakfast of meat-filled biscuits and orange juice, they headed for the university. Mom followed the signs pointing to the campus while the professor sat silently in the front passenger seat. Billy sat with Walter in the back and kept his eye on his teacher. The old professor's gaze was locked straight ahead, his arm stiff against his side, binding Merlin's Diary in place.

Wanting to get a conversation started, Billy nudged Walter and whispered, "Ask the professor about what we read in the book this morning."

Walter squinted at him. "Why me?"

"Because you're not the one who blew it by turning the page too soon."

"So you're dodging guilt. I get that." Walter leaned forward. "Hey, Prof, so what's with all that stuff about old garments and new wineskins?"

The professor angled his head toward the boys, his eyebrows turned downward. "I'm afraid I cannot tell you Walter, nor anyone, for that matter, at least for now."

Billy cringed. The professor's guarded words brought an even heavier weight of guilt. The diary held a secret, an old secret, the key to his questions. And the only man who seemed able to reveal the answers had decided to clam up.

Mom stopped at a traffic light and sighed. "If it's just a Bible verse, Professor, why can't you tell us what you think?"

The professor laid the book on his lap and placed his palm on the cover. "While I was in the shower, it occurred to me that William's temptation was understandable. I had projected my own strength upon him, assuming he could exercise self-control according to my own inner constitution. Such an assumption, of course, is nonsense. William has much to learn, and I fear that most of it will come through trials and suffering, as it did for me in my younger years.

"In any case, when I was preparing to leave the water closet, I desired to read the new poem again, but I first turned to the Scripture on the page before, and the rest of that page had appeared."

He tucked the book under his arm again. "But I'm unwilling to tell you what it said. The text itself forbade me from even explaining it. It gave me leave to inform you of my warning, my gag order, if you will. I'm afraid that I am now the only one who may read the book, at least until it gives me permission to share it with others."

Billy's throat narrowed. He was the cause of the professor's inability to explain. Would the feelings of guilt never go away?

Walter moaned. "But Prof, we need that book. It helped us get Excalibur. Who knows what else it could tell us?"

"You are correct, Walter, but I did not say that no one could read it. I shall continue to observe any new text and act according to wisdom's counsel."

*   *   *   *   *   *

When they arrived on campus, Mom parked near the Skaggs Building, and they hurried toward the door, dodging plowed snow mounds and keeping their arms tucked close to their bodies while jogging headlong into a whipping wind. After they hustled through the entryway and crossed the mop-streaked terrazzo floor, they chose the stairs instead of the elevator and tiptoed up to the third floor.

At the top of the stairs, they stepped into a deserted hall. Unblemished vacuum cleaner imprints on the carpet proved that a janitor had recently prepared for the morning's new stampede. Billy prowled down the corridor, scanning the number plates on each door. The longer they kept their approach secret, the better, since they had no way of knowing who or what awaited them.

When he found Room 340, he stopped and pointed, keeping his voice low. "Here it is."

The others joined him. Walter leaned close and whispered, "The door's open a crack."

Billy's danger monitor sent a warning signal, not real strong, but enough to provide an eerie sense that something wasn't quite right. He handed the flower box to the professor. "Mom left her gun in the plane, so you'd better take Excalibur. I can use my own weapon better anyway."

He took the box but kept his arms extended toward Billy as he spoke in a whisper. "William, the sword *is* your weapon, now. It was bestowed to you as a gift from above. It was meant for you to wield in battle."

Billy slid his shoe across one of the vacuum marks. "Maybe, but it would be better if we both had something to fight with. I can't lend you my fire-breathing."

The professor bowed his head. "Nor can I lend you my faith."

Billy bit his tongue. Had the professor noticed that the sword never glowed in his hands? He shook off the thought and focused on the door. "Okay," he said, keeping his voice low. "I'm going in."

"Be on your guard, William. An open door indicates an occupied room. An ambush is not out of the question."

"Right," Walter whispered. "Get your fire stoked, Billy. Turn the dial past broil and go straight to nuclear holocaust."

Billy glanced through the window to the left of the door. No one stood in sight. When he pulled the door, it creaked on its hinges until it swung about halfway open. The reception area lights shone brightly, allowing a scan of the anteroom. He pushed his head inside and listened. Nothing. No sound, no movement, no sign of anyone in the office. He took two steps in and looked around before gesturing for the others to follow.

A long, waist-high desk with a curved front faced the door. To the right of the desk, the anteroom opened into a sitting area, complete with a gray loveseat, a small table for magazines, and three single chairs covered with gingham upholstery. A painting of a lunging grizzly bear hung above the loveseat, as if Billy and his company might be someone's unsuspecting prey.

To the left and behind the reception desk, offices lined a hallway that led to the rear section of the suite. Another hallway at the far wall passed behind a set of partitions and out of view. Faint sounds came from the distant hall—clinking glass and running water.

"Someone's back there," Billy said, motioning with his head. "You guys wait here. It might just be a secretary or something."

While the others took off their coats, Billy tiptoed down the hall, then followed the corridor to the right as it led him across the rear of the suite near the back exit. As he closed in on the source of the noise, his danger sense grew. He slowed, each stride a furtive, silent step.

When he reached a partially open door, he pushed it fully open, then retreated behind a partition several feet down the hall.

A gray-haired woman poked her head out, an empty coffee pot jiggling in her hand. "Is someone out there?"

Billy blew out a long sigh. So much fear over a harmless little old lady. He stepped out from behind the partition and gave her a polite nod. "I'm sorry I startled you, ma'am. I'm here to see Dr. Conner. Is he available?"

The woman, about a head shorter than Billy and wearing thick glasses, smiled. "Oh, no. He's not here right now." She walked back into the kitchen, still talking. "Let me get the coffee on, and I'll be right out."

When she disappeared, Billy called toward the front of the suite. "Come on around. I found a woman back here. I think she's the receptionist."

Walter showed up first, hustling around the corner. "Does she look like trouble? You never know about those clerical types. Their letter openers can be sharp."

Although his danger meter continued throbbing, Billy shook his head. "Don't be so paranoid. She seems friendly enough, kind of like an old librarian."

"Well, I knew a librarian who threw an eraser fifty feet and hit me right between the eyes."

"What made her mad? Were you burping at a hundred decibels?"

"Yeah. Maybe more."

Billy peeked into the kitchen. "I don't think she's hiding an assault eraser, but she said she'd be right out."

When Mom and the professor came around the corner, Billy wiped his brow to show his relief. "No worries. It's just an old—"

A sharp pain jolted his back. The woman's voice returned, this time gruff and sour. "You're feeling the barrel of a three-fifty-seven magnum, Dragon Boy, and I know how to use it. Don't give me one spark of that fire from hell or it'll be pouring out your backside."

THE VALLEY OF THE SHADOW OF DEATH

Ashley bent over a thick logbook at the main control panel, filling in the boxes with a sharp yellow pencil and whispering the data as she wrote. "Bonnie Silver—Age, fourteen years, one month. Height—five-foot-six. Weight—" *Hmmm. Never had a chance to weigh her. I'll just guess one-twenty.* She scratched the digits in the box and continued. "Blood type—A positive with dragon simplex allele and phototropic receptor 1-A." She looked up from the book and listened. The lab had been dead quiet in the early morning hours, giving her an opportunity to check her equipment. Now a faint bustle from the girls' hall floated in, a sure sign that they were beginning the morning routine.

Ashley sniffed the air and detected a hint of bacon. Karen's work. She'd planned to rise early and make breakfast, and Bonnie had volunteered to help, though she couldn't have slept much the night before, not with the greatest adventure of her life ahead. Ashley hadn't slept much herself, and she couldn't eat. No way. Her stomach had twisted into a double-knotted rope as doubts streamed into her mind. Would this work? The final step had never been accomplished. Pulling Bonnie's mom out of the candlestone and restoring her body was possible only in theory. And now to try it, Ashley would risk Bonnie's life. She would send her on a journey into a dark, mysterious oblivion that required her to trust a vastly complicated machine—a machine that a teenager had pieced together with her own hands.

Ashley closed the logbook and laid it on a worktable next to the panel. Mere moments separated Bonnie from either a grand reunion with her mother or perhaps death or eternal imprisonment, tormented forever by the enemy of all dragons. Devin would be sure to transform the crystal prism into a living hell if given a chance.

Tightening her jaw, Ashley stared at the girls' dorm area. Soon Bonnie would emerge from that door filled with hope, and Ashley would make sure that hope was realized, or die trying.

*   *   *   *   *   *

Billy leaped to the side and spun. He blew a jet of yellow flames toward the woman's hands and enveloped them in a rushing rage of fire. With a shriek, she fell backwards into the kitchen, firing a bullet into the ceiling before rolling on the floor, cursing like a sailor's parrot. The river of fire scorched the walls and carpet. Billy fell back against the corridor's wall and slid to the floor, wincing and holding a hand over his stinging mouth.

The professor, still carrying the flower box, dashed past the others into the kitchen. He threw the box on the floor and dove for the writhing woman, reaching for her thrashing hand. "William!" he shouted. "The gun is fused to her fingers. I can't remove it."

The woman spat at the professor and cursed. "Get off me you dragon lover, you friend of the devil. Let go of my hand so I can send you straight to hell."

Walter rushed to the professor's side and wrapped his fingers around the gun barrel. "I can't eject the ammo magazine," he grunted. "Her skin's melted over it." While shifting his body around in the tiny room, Walter pushed the door closed with his feet.

Another door at the end of the hallway opened. Two men slunk into the corridor, one dressed completely in black.

Billy scrambled to his feet, but before he could run, the man in black grabbed him and wrapped a fibrous gag around his mouth. The second man twisted Billy's arms and held them firmly behind his back.

Mom lunged toward them. The first man whipped out a long serrated dagger and shouted at her, "Don't move, or the mongrel's dead!" She froze in place just out of reach, her stare riveted on Billy and his captors.

With one hand, the man in black held the gag in place. With the other, he pressed the blade against Billy's throat. The cold, sharp steel pricked his skin, drawing a trickle of blood that oozed toward his chest. The coarse gag smashed his lips against his teeth and ripped at his tender skin. He took a breath and tried to spew fire, but the flame rebounded as if hitting a thermal shield. The smell of his own blood caught in his nose.

Intense heat parched his throat. He couldn't breathe fire; he could barely breathe at all.

* * * * *

A click and a slow creaking sound made Ashley turn. Bonnie stood with her back to the lab, apparently relocking the door, her enormous wings shielding most of her body. Ashley couldn't help staring as Bonnie gracefully twirled toward the lab. In her white flowing robe, and with her peaceful radiant face, she looked like a storybook angel, her dragon wings set perfectly behind her shining, blonde-streaked hair. Her eyes danced, and if a smile could sing, Bonnie's song would have melted the most cynical heart.

Ashley felt ragged and dirty in Bonnie's presence, as if a blanket of shame had fallen on her like a smothering cloud of soot. When Bonnie drew close, she touched Ashley's shoulder. "What's wrong? Is your grandfather still getting worse?"

Ashley turned back to the control panel, trying to hide emerging tears. "A bit worse. Doc called for a nurse to come in, but we'll have to send him to a hospital if he doesn't get better soon." She sniffed and gestured toward the boys' dorm. "But I can't worry about that right now. Your father will be leading Derrick out at any minute."

Bonnie laid Ashley's keys on the control panel. "Leading him out?"

"Yes. There's something I didn't tell you about him. He's—"

The boys' hall door opened with a loud click. Doc exited, leading Derrick by the hand. More than a head shorter than Doc, he looked thin and frail by comparison, though a bright smile radiated against his dark face.

Bonnie whispered, "Is that Derrick?"

Ashley nodded.

"But Karen said he's seventeen."

"He doesn't look it, does he?"

With unblinking eyes staring straight ahead, Derrick followed Doc's lead.

"Is he blind?" Bonnie asked.

"Uh-huh. He got some kind of disease that killed his optic nerves. His parents died trying to get to Florida from Haiti on an overcrowded boat. When it sank, he was rescued. The government worker on the case didn't have the heart to ship him back. Your father got word and sent for him."

Bonnie followed his progress, her mouth dropping open. "How does he know what to do?"

"He's highly intelligent and brave. Ever since we first transluminated him, he keeps begging to do it again." She turned to Bonnie, not caring any longer that her tears were evident. "When he's transformed into light energy, he says he can see."

"No wonder he wants to do it again."

"Come and meet him," Ashley said, holding out her hand. "He's very inspiring."

The two walked over to the anchor dome. Saying nothing, Doc stepped toward the control panel, leaving Derrick with Ashley and Bonnie. "Derrick," Ashley said, "I'd like for you to meet Bonnie, the girl I told you about."

Derrick extended his hand and angled his head slightly away from Bonnie. "I'm glad to meet you." His sweet voice sounded like a song, decorated with a hint of a French accent.

Bonnie grabbed his hand and shook it firmly. Derrick adjusted his head angle in her direction. "Is it permissible to touch your wings?"

"Sure." Bonnie guided his hand to her wing.

He ran his fingers along the outer rib for a moment, then pulled away. "May I have your hand again?"

When Bonnie slid her hand back into his, he gripped it firmly. "I will hold your hand again, and when I do, I will see your face." He drew back and felt his way to the anchor dome platform.

Ashley extended an arm toward one of the other glass cylinders. "Are you ready, Bonnie?"

She retied the sash on her robe, smiling and bouncing lightly on her toes. "All dressed and ready to go."

Ashley surveyed Bonnie from top to bottom. When she saw Bonnie's ring, she reached for her hand. "I noticed your ring when we met. Is it an heirloom?"

Bonnie looked at the ring. "Not really, but a good friend gave it to me. I never take it off."

"Well, if you don't want to lose it, you'd better give it to me. It'll just fall to the floor when you get transluminated."

Bonnie curled her fingers. "Then could you pick it up for me? I want to wear it until the last second."

Ashley shrugged. "Sure. No problem."

"Great." Bonnie resumed her bouncing. "Let's get going."

Ashley frowned, hoping to communicate the gravity of the hour, the enormous risk that the next few moments would bring. Bonnie's bouncy, in-place dance slowed, and her smile faded. Ashley nodded. Good. Maybe this immovable rock of faith was finally having doubts. "All right. Let's go."

As they walked together toward the diver's dome, Bonnie touched Ashley's arm. "Don't worry about me. I won't be alone."

They stopped at the foot of the dome platform. "Right," Ashley said. "I'll be here, and Derrick won't let you go."

"That's not what I mean." Bonnie stepped onto the platform. As the glass lowered, her serene face radiated perfect peace. She looked at Ashley once more and folded her hands at her waist. "I'm never alone, no matter where I go."

*   *   *   *   *   *

Billy wrestled against his captors, but they clamped him down. Mom inched toward them, her knees flexed, obviously ready to spring to his aid at the first opportunity. Billy eyed the closed kitchen door. What were the professor and Walter doing in there?

The second man bound Billy's wrists behind him with duct tape while the man in black kept the knife against Billy's throat. He pressed the blade deeper and barked at his partner. "Where's Gretchen?"

Billy stiffened. That voice. The man in black was the dark knight, Palin.

"I think she's in the kitchen with the old man," the second man replied.

"I'll take the mongrel to Flathead," Palin said. "Kill his friends, haul their bodies to the gorge, and dispose of them. Then get back here and clean up the mess." Still holding the knife at Billy's throat, Palin dragged him toward the door, speaking gruffly into his ear. "It's early, so there shouldn't be anyone around to see us, but if you try to attract attention, I'll slice your throat like a ripe tomato. I'm pretty good with a blade. Remember, Dragon Boy?"

The second man drew a gun from his coat, aimed it at Mom, and pushed the kitchen door open with his foot.

Something jerked the man into the room. Walter hurtled headfirst into the hall and sprawled onto the carpet. The door slammed behind him. Muffled grunts erupted. A gunshot sounded, then another. Billy tried to slow Palin's progress by dragging his heels on the carpet.

As Palin hauled him out of the office suite, Mom helped Walter to his feet. A bright light flashed into the hallway from under the kitchen door. The suite's exit door swung shut, blocking Billy's view. Mom cried out his name. He tried to answer, but the gag held firm. Every second drew him farther from the battle, the painful knife preventing any struggle. Had the professor used the sword? Did he transluminate everyone in the kitchen, including himself?

Without warning, Billy fell. His head struck the carpeted floor with a thud. Palin's body toppled over him, and the knife scraped his ear as it jerked away from his throat.

Pinned by Palin, Billy tried squirm away. Mom leaped on Palin's back and pounded him with her fists while Walter wrapped both arms around his legs. Palin threw Mom to the side and shook his legs, trying to dislodge Walter, but Walter hung on like a mass of super glue.

Billy broke free. Still on his back, he kicked Palin's head, but his off-balance blow was weak. Mom jumped up and took a step toward the two jerking, squirming bodies, ready to dive in again. Palin, still clutching the knife, raised his hand to strike Walter. Billy tried to shout, but the gag stifled his voice, turning his call into a loud grunt.

Mom lunged at the dagger. Clasping Palin's wrist with both hands, she pushed the blade away, keeping him from plunging it into Walter's back. "Walter!" she called. "Let go! He's got a knife!"

Walter scrambled to his feet and stomped Palin's clenched fist, but the dark knight held fast to his blade. Walter yanked Palin's hair with one hand and gouged his eyes with the other. Billy swung his leg, hoping to deliver a knockout blow, but his foot merely glanced off Palin's shoulder.

Palin grabbed Mom by the neck and threw her to the side again. He slammed his elbow into Walter's face and jumped to his feet. With quick hands, he jerked Billy up by his hair and pressed the dagger against his throat again. Palin glared at them, sweat and blood trickling from his face and dripping to the floor as he gasped for air. "Don't … move … a muscle … or he's dead."

Billy's two defenders froze while Palin caught his breath. "I don't know what you did in there to my partner, but I don't have the weapons to fight both of you right now." He took another deep breath and stumbled into the elevator car with Billy in tow. Mom crept down the hall after him. Walter slumped against the wall, his eyelids swelling and a splotch of red growing on the shoulder of his sweatshirt.

Billy tried to watch what would happen to his would-be rescuers, but the elevator doors slid closed, blocking his view.

When the elevator opened on the lower floor, Billy shuffled out, the knife still at his throat and his hands still bound. Palin half dragged him through the empty hall to the building's exit, then across the barren campus yard. When they reached the parking lot, Palin shoved him against a faded blue sedan. With the click of a button on his key fob, Palin popped the trunk open. He lowered the dagger from Billy's neck, heaved him inside, and slammed the trunk shut.

Billy tumbled face first into icy darkness and bumped his head. Twisting his body out of its pretzel shape, he managed to

189

roll to his back, but as he tried to catch his breath, he gagged on the terrible smell. The taunting voice of the dark knight penetrated the stillness. "You'd better not try any fire-breathing, boy. I put four plastic jugs of gasoline in there to keep you company."

* * * * * *

Ashley took her place at the master control panel while Doc positioned Derrick at the center of the anchor dome. Derrick smiled as the glass shield lowered. Ashley returned the smile, though he couldn't see hers. His courage was amazing.

Doc stepped to the panel next to the anchor dome, one with fewer controls and displays than on the master board. He flipped a switch, rotated two dials to their maximum settings, and hurried toward the safe on the wall.

Ashley stretched a padded headset over her ears and spoke into its attached microphone, a tiny transmitter on the end of a flexible stem. "Derrick, can you hear me?"

"Yes." Derrick's smile widened.

"Bonnie? How about you?"

Bonnie nodded, her eyes partially closed.

"Go ahead and answer. I want to make sure the sound works both ways."

"Yes," she replied softly. "I can hear you."

"Good. Okay, Derrick knows the drill, so I'm going to talk through this for your sake, Bonnie. I know I explained everything in detail last night, but it won't hurt to remind you as we go." She slid the magneto's power bar up a couple of notches. A low hum emanated from under the domes. "The vibration you're feeling is just the magneto that creates part of our power grid. The real action will start in a minute when Doc brings the candlestone."

Ashley turned the illumination dial at the upper left corner of the panel. "I'm dimming the lights now." Doc soft-stepped across the floor, opening the box as the huge room dimmed. "Bonnie," Ashley continued, unable to keep from smiling, "your father is bringing your mother to the pedestal. Are you ready to go in and see her?"

Bonnie flashed a smile of her own and a thumbs-up signal.

"Good. Let's do it." Ashley raised the panel's covering to block out the display lights, though she could still see over its top edge to monitor the domes. When Doc placed the candle-stone on the pedestal at the center of the room, Bonnie lifted her robe's hood and covered her hair, her lips moving. Ashley strained to hear. The whisper-soft words came to her ears like a lilting song from a faraway land.

"The Lord is my Shepherd; I shall not want."

Ashley turned up the volume and stared at the peaceful fig-ure inside the dome.

"He maketh me to lie down in green pastures. He leadeth me beside the still waters."

Ashley stayed quiet. The words sang to her heart like a sacred aria, a moving tribute of spirit, but she had to get back to work. With her hands shaking and her voice trembling, she slid the translumination bar up. "It ... It's time, Bonnie. I'm turning on the beam."

"He restoreth my soul. He leadeth me in the paths of righteousness for his name's sake."

Ashley brushed away a tear. "Five ... ahem ... five seconds, Bonnie. You'll see a flash, and ... and grab Derrick's hand when he comes through."

"Yea, though I walk through the valley of the shadow of death, I will fear no evil, for thou art with me; thy rod and thy staff they comfort me."

A blaze of sparkling light engulfed Bonnie's lower half. Her hood slipped down as the sparks advanced upward, consuming her body until her glowing face disappeared, swallowed in the blinding display.

*   *   *   *   *   *

Derrick's gentle voice filtered into Bonnie's perception. "Take my hand, Bonnie." In an odd vision, bursts of light flashed, and something tugged her. Was that his hand? Somehow she was able to will herself to return a firm grasp. Another voice entered, sizzling and warped amid a host of eerie, humming sounds.

"Attachment successful. She's going in."

Bonnie felt herself being painlessly stretched, her body unraveling like a spool of thread tumbling down in a rushing river of light, hurtling into a deep, dark canyon. As she fell, the outside noises faded in the distance. Although she couldn't feel the g-forces she had expected, she sensed speed and a rapid dimming of her strange new world.

She slammed into a dark pliable barrier and passed through what seemed like a supple membrane, as though her body were traveling through a wall of black Jell-O. The river of light she was riding vanished, somehow blocked by the viscous wall and diverted somewhere she couldn't see. Finally, she stopped in a totally dark realm, not bumping into anything solid, just emerging from the membrane and floating in absolute gloom.

She could still feel a slight pull from above, her attachment to Derrick and the outside world. She had a detached sense that she had to hold to it, though her hands no longer felt like hands at all. Every input seemed different—seeing, hearing, smelling, even her sense of being came to her through new impulses, more spiritual than earthly, as though she had passed from one life to another. But heaven could never feel like this. The whole place weighed down on her, a stifling, heavy burden of impending doom.

Trying to orient herself, she took in the dark surroundings. She could see her own form, a pulsing mass of disturbed light, but for some reason, her body had no illuminating effect on the surrounding blackness. But that didn't matter. In this tiny house of glass there probably wasn't anything to see, anyway.

Above, a faint trail of light, thin and taut, stretched into an empty expanse—her lifeline to Derrick—but there was nothing else anywhere, no sounds and no bright pulses besides her own. Her mother was supposed to appear somewhere as another mass of light, but since only a short time remained, she couldn't just sit and wait.

Trying to figure out how to move was a trick in itself. There was no ground, no walls, nothing she could use to propel her new body. In total blackness, how could she tell if she was moving even if she tried? With her hand still clutching Derrick's, if she pulled against the force he exerted, and if his pull increased, that would mean she was traveling somewhere.

Movement seemed an act of the will rather than physical flexing of muscles. Pushing her shimmering body was like resisting the darkness in front of her. The black space split apart and fled as she guided her mind into its void, searching through it like a beacon in a black fog.

After a few seconds, she sensed something, another light, just a glimmer, but it was definitely there. As she adjusted to her newly discovered locomotion, she figured out how to accelerate and turn as she guided herself toward the spark of energy. Soon, the other light grew, apparently moving toward her as well.

Was this her mother at last? Just a few more seconds and they would be together. Her own body brightened, pulsing more rapidly. The other light grew further, sparkling, radiant, vibrating with excitement. It took shape, a human form, without detail or sharp features, but definitely human. As it drew closer, the feminine shape of a woman became clear, sharpening with each step, a radiant torso, long gleaming arms and legs, and finally her mother's sweet, gentle face. The form communicated—an excited voice in her mind, no, a stream of ecstatic thoughts, calling to her. "Bonnie! At last, you're here!"

An arm of light stretched toward her. She tried to reach out her own arm to meet it, but a brilliant flash blocked her. A huge wall of radiance, more dazzling than any earthly blaze, encircled Bonnie, a ring of magnificent, dancing fire, white and shimmering.

Bonnie retreated to the center of the ring. She felt no fear, just surprise and amazement. The hedge of light seemed almost to laugh, not with sinister contempt, but with joy, like a proud father in the midst of a playful encounter with a child. Bonnie stared at the sight, awestruck wonder mixing with dazed disappointment. What was happening? Why was this thing stopping her from meeting her mother?

*　　*　　*　　*　　*　　*

Ashley pushed her microphone stem away from her lips and watched a digital timer on her panel. "Ninety seconds to go, Doc. I see data for two human images on B frequency very clearly."

"Have they seen each other?"

"I think so. They seem to be in the same phase, but there's been no attachment yet." She reached for the frequency dial on the upper right corner of the panel. "Let's check A to make sure Devin's still there."

Doc swiped her hand away. "No. We'll see him come into B if he makes a move."

Ashley rolled her hand into a loose fist. That was weird. Why so rough? Shaking off his odd behavior, she followed the numbers and graph lines as they flashed across the screen. The organic light level spiked. Blinking, she pointed. "What's that?"

Doc stared at the monitor. "It can't be."

"It is! It's another presence in B!"

"Impossible."

Ashley glared at him. "Impossible? Why is it impossible? It has to be Devin. You said we'd see him if he moved over."

Doc returned her combative stare. "I tell you, it's not possible."

Ashley stamped her foot. "There's something going on. What are you keeping from me?"

Doc broke away from the eye lock. "Well, it's too late for you to stop us now." He pointed at the glimmering gem on the pedestal. "Bonnie's mother isn't in the candlestone. She never was. Devin's been able to move to B all along, and he answers for Irene when we call to talk to her."

"What?" Ashley shot up from her seat. "You've been lying to me all this time? Why?"

"It was the only way. You wouldn't have helped me if you knew the truth."

Ashley's eyes burned. In her fury, the mass of dials and displays seemed to mix into a boiling soup. "But I can't—"

"No time to argue." He pushed her back to her seat. "Just listen. If Devin stays in the candlestone, your grandfather will die. If you want to save him and Bonnie, you'd better get back to work. I don't know what that third presence is, but let's hope it doesn't get in the way."

Ashley shook her head and drew in a deep breath, trying to concentrate on the data again. She managed a business-like tone but clipped her words to punctuate her anger. "The third one's different. Its phase isn't human. Its signal is much stronger. But there's been no attachment among the three."

"How's Derrick holding out?"

Ashley read the anchor meter. "Not good at all. He's stretching thin, like something's pulling harder than usual." She turned the output audio on and jerked the microphone up to her lips. "Derrick, hang on!"

Doc set a finger on the main display. "We're at minus twenty seconds. When does our restoration confidence go below fifty percent?"

Ashley glanced at him. "At plus fifteen, but we can't go past zero. We're only at eighty percent, even then."

"We'll go past it if we have to. Plus fifteen is our new drop dead point."

"But Derrick can't make that. Maybe plus five. He's stretching to the breaking point. He'll have to let go or one of them will be dismembered."

"No choice. Ten seconds to zero now."

"He's down to less than a millimeter. He'll never make it. We have to reverse."

"No, look! Attachment is close. He can do it."

"He's under a hundred microns!" Ashley said, fear pitching her voice higher. "We can't even measure his attachment anymore. If he lets go, Bonnie will be trapped. We have to get her out now!"

Doc shouted, "We're at zero." He raised his arm like a starter at a race. "Prepare to reverse at my command. Twelve seconds to the drop dead point."

Ashley's fingers flew across a separate portion of the panel, setting the dials based on what her darting eyes read on the displays. "I'm putting the reverse power on ninety-five. It has to go quick."

"Right. There's no choice. We're at plus eleven."

Ashley shouted, nearly jumping from her seat. "We have attachment!"

Doc lowered his arm. "Hit it!"

THE GATES OF HELL

Walter dashed down the stairs and raced toward the exit. With a shove, he banged the double doors open and bolted into the nearly empty parking lot. Swiveling his head, he searched the area. Billy's kidnapper stood behind a car and slammed its trunk closed.

Walter burst into a sprint. Keeping his stare riveted on the kidnapper, he leaped over a snow mound and hurdled a tipped-over garbage can. Just as Palin closed the car door, Walter lunged for the handle and grabbed hold, wrenching the door open a crack. He slid his hands inside and clutched the frame.

The car started and lurched forward. Walter maintained his death grip, his shoes dragging against the pavement as the car swerved back and forth. His tight fingers slipped on the frame. *I can't let go! Gotta hang on!*

With a tight donut turn, the car spun him away and sent him tumbling across the lot. Still turning, the car careened in his direction. Walter jerked upright and lunged to the side, barely avoiding the squealing tires as the car sped toward the lot's exit.

Lying on his stomach, Walter peered through the gray plume of exhaust and read the Montana license plate. The first digit on the sky blue background was a seven, followed by a dot and the characters "A1." The other three digits looked like either fives or sixes, but he wasn't sure. He rolled to a sitting position, spitting, coughing, and rubbing his stinging eyes. After gathering his wits, he scrambled to his feet and hustled toward the building.

When he jerked the outer door open, he nearly collided with Mrs. Bannister. Her eyes seemed wild with fear. "Did you see Billy? What happened?"

Breathless and weak, Walter bent over and propped himself on his knees. "I think that guy … threw him … in the trunk. Couldn't stop him. He got away. But I got part of the plate." He hooked his arm in hers and started toward the elevator. "Let's check on the professor and call the cops."

When they reached the office, they hobbled straight to the kitchen where they found the professor sitting on the floor against the back wall. His eyes were open, and he held Excalibur on his lap. The blade glowed, covering his thighs with iridescent white.

"Prof!" Walter slid on his knees to his teacher's side. "Are you okay?"

The professor's face contorted, and a tear streamed down his cheek. "I have been better, Walter, but it seems that I have been shot in the heel of my left foot. I regret that I was not able to come to William's aid."

Walter looked at the wounded foot. The pant leg had already been turned up, and a trickle of blood oozed through a hole in the sock's heel. The back third of his shoe had been ripped off, part of the leather still hanging on one side. Mrs. Bannister scooted close on her knees and began carefully untying the remaining laces.

Using his shoe, Walter nudged a handgun that lay on the kitchen floor. "What happened to the other guy and that old hag?"

"I am happy to report—" Professor Hamilton winced as the front of the shoe slipped off. "I am happy to report that Excalibur works quite well. The two fiends are now scattered light. It was quite a display, actually. Yet, although it seems I had no choice in the matter, I am distressed with having to dispatch two human beings. After I pulled the man inside, I confronted him face-to-face, so my integrity is intact. Yet, death always seems a tragedy to me, no matter how vile the victims." He sighed, shaking his head and speaking more softly. "Wasted lives, wasted souls."

Walter glanced at the walls and ceiling, trying to find any trace of sparkling debris. "Shouldn't it have zapped you, too? Isn't that what happened to Merlin?"

"Yes, Walter. One moment, please."

The professor turned to Mrs. Bannister as she tried to fashion his sock into a bandage. "I think the bleeding has subsided, Marilyn. The wound is painful, but the bullet passed through. I don't think it's dangerous."

He handed Walter the sword and lifted his arms. "If you wouldn't mind lending me assistance." Mrs. Bannister and Walter obliged, each putting a shoulder under one of his arms.

"Walter," the professor said, now standing with his weight on his good foot, "in my efforts to dispose of the two aggressors, I did not think about what the sword might do to me. I was, however, concerned about you. That's why I shoved you out of the room."

Walter grinned. "Yeah. I guessed that. Good call."

"As soon as I raised the sword, an extraordinary beam emanated from its point. Although it startled me, I believe it terrified the other chap even more. He stumbled and fired his weapon at me, missing with his first shot and striking my foot with his second. Then, in an amazing flash of light, the beam consumed him along with the—ahem—lady on the floor."

Walter dragged his shoe along the floor where the woman had fallen, pushing through the various items the bad guys had left behind—a watch, a bracelet, a set of keys, and a gray wig lying beside two guns and a brown jacket.

"I suspect," the professor continued, "that Excalibur's bearer has more control over its power than we expected. Bonnie was not affected when she used it, nor was I, and I was able to guide it toward my targets. It makes me wonder if Merlin intended to bring about his own disintegration."

Walter squinted. "Merlin zapped himself on purpose?"

Mrs. Bannister took a step forward and supported the professor as she pushed him along. "We can make our guesses later. Right now we have to call the police and an ambulance. Walter got part of the license plate. And you, Professor, have to go to the hospital."

The professor hobbled along with his two helpers toward the reception area. He grimaced at every step but managed to keep his voice calm. "I beg your pardon, Marilyn, but I think going to the hospital would not be wise. Our delay would be unpredictable, and my wound is not life threatening. I also think involving the police would hamper our efforts. We would not be able to answer their questions, and based on Devin's record of keeping his affairs untraceable, my guess is that the license plate would lead to a dead end even if we had the entire number. Since there are no bodies here to examine or collect, we have no real obligation to involve the authorities."

When they reached the chairs, Mrs. Bannister pulled the professor's arm from around her neck and slowly released him. She ran a hand through her tousled hair and took a deep breath. "But what about your foot? It needs treatment. And what about Billy? Who's going to find him?"

The professor lowered himself to the loveseat, letting out a lengthy sigh. He gazed up at her with sad eyes. "Trust me, Marilyn. This crude villain cannot harm your son. I am sure of that. You may wish to pray about a later battle, but for now, William is safe. As for me, I suggest we purchase a bandage and crutches, perhaps a topical antibiotic as well. More thorough treatment can wait." The professor pointed toward Walter. "Walter, however, may need attention."

Mrs. Bannister's eyes widened, and she reached for his shoulder. "Walter! You're bleeding!"

Walter wrinkled his nose and stepped back. "It's nothing. Just a scratch from that creep's knife."

She cupped his chin in her hand and tilted his face toward the light. "And your eyes, they're swollen half shut."

"Mrs. B," Walter said, pulling away, "I don't mean any disrespect, but Prof and I don't need a mother right now." He tightened his grip on Excalibur. "We need to go skewer a slayer."

203

She glanced at the professor, then at Walter. New determination flashed in her eyes. "You're right. Where do we start?"

The professor's gaze seemed far away, as though he were staring straight through the wall. "Walter, do you remember the assailant's words? We were listening from the kitchen. He said that he was going to take William somewhere."

"Yeah, I heard him. He said to Flathead."

The professor's eyes narrowed to slits. "Flathead? Are you sure?"

"Yeah. It was a weird name, so I picked up on it."

The professor lowered his gaze as if to study the gray carpet at his feet. "I perused our map of Montana during our flight. I'm sure there's a Flathead Lake, but I believe there is also Flathead County and Flathead Forest. I'm afraid with all those options, our search region is far too large." With a brighter expression he looked up and tried to stand. "I don't think we can risk asking questions around the campus. We'll just drive into Flathead County and ask in that area if anyone knows Dr. Conner. Perhaps someone will be able to provide inform—"

A loud ring interrupted. The professor bent forward to reach for his phone but lost his balance. Walter and Mrs. Bannister caught him, each holding an arm. He nodded toward his hip. "Walter, would you please answer my phone. It's on my belt."

Walter grabbed the phone and lifted it to his ear. "Hello."

"Walter? It's Dad. I was trying to call the professor."

"Yep, and I answered. What's up?"

"I got a postcard from Bonnie."

"From Bonnie? Cool! What's it say?"

"I think she might be in danger. She was at a convenience store and gave the postcard to the owner. The owner suspected trouble, so she sent the card by overnight express. Bonnie was traveling with a man, I assume Dr. Conner, and another teen-aged girl in a maroon, late-model SUV. The card says, 'My father's taking me to a place he said was about thirty minutes from here. He said it's a lab near Flathead Lake, and the lab must be a pretty big place, because people live there. I hope you can find it. I don't trust him. Something's definitely wrong.' And I have an address. Can you write it down?"

"Sure. Hold on." Walter held a pretend pencil and wrote in the air. "Hey, Prof, you got anything to write with?"

He shook his head. "Have your father send his information to my e-mail address. I can bring it up on my phone."

Walter nodded. "Hey, Dad. Send it to Prof's e-mail. We'll get it."

"Will do. What's going on there?"

"Here? Oh, not much. We've been reading prophetic poems in a diary written by Merlin, and we found a real fire-breathing dragon in a cave, and after we got waylaid by a couple of gun-toting goons and an ugly old witch, Billy got kidnapped at knifepoint and thrown into a trunk. The kidnapper sped off just before I could get to him, and he tried to squash my head with his tires, but he missed. I'm okay, and it didn't hurt much when he stabbed me. Oh yeah, the professor's been shot. Other than that, it's been pretty quiet. See ya later." Walter pressed the disconnect button and snapped the phone back on the professor's belt.

"Walter," Mrs. Bannister said, "shouldn't you explain the situation to your father a little better than that?"

He waved a hand. "Nah. It would take too long. He probably thinks I was kidding, anyway."

The professor pointed toward their coats piled on the end of the sofa. "What information is he sending, Walter?"

205

"An address." Walter picked up the professor's coat and helped him put it on as he related his father's story, including Bonnie's message on the card.

The professor raised a finger. "So Flathead Lake is our destination. That corroborates our earlier information."

Walter hurried to the door and held it open. "Ready when you are."

The professor tested his foot and grimaced. "I see now that my foot is too badly damaged for walking. If you will assist me to the car, I can retrieve my e-mail there. After we procure a pair of crutches, our first stop will be the convenience store. Perhaps our eyewitness will be able to tell us a bit more." He nodded toward the florist box. "Walter, please fetch that. We might have more transluminating to do."

* * * * * *

206 The magneto engines whined. Ashley half-sat and half-stood while watching the display, rocking her body and peeking around the light-deflecting hood every couple of seconds to see what was going on in the diver's dome.

Two of the glass cylinders remained empty, while the anchor dome filled with sparkling light. Ashley, her face hot and her fingers trembling, turned the transformation knob fully counter-clockwise.

Within seconds, the dancing light solidified, re-creating Derrick's slender body. He collapsed to his knees, his thin dark hands covering his weeping face. "She let go! I tried to hold on, but she let go!"

Ashley threw off the headphones, flipped a switch to raise the glass, and ran with Doc to Derrick. Doc took one of Derrick's hands while Ashley held the other as they led him down to floor level.

"Ashley, get back and monitor the activity. I'll take care of Derrick." He lifted the trembling youth, cradling him in both arms, and carried him to the dorm while Ashley stood alone in the midst of her trinity of glass domes. She gazed at the diver's platform, the last place she had seen Bonnie's shining face.

As she dragged her feet toward the platform, she let her shoulders slump. A million thoughts zipped in, clogging her brain. The thoughts hurt, each one like a pricking needle, reminding her of her vows. *I know you want your mother back. We need to get her out of that candlestone, and I'm not going to let you down.*

She sniffed, trying to keep the tears back, but they broke through. She brushed the first few away, then gave up and let them flow. When she reached the diver's platform, she stooped and pressed the button on the base. With a low hum, the glass slowly ascended, reminding her of Bonnie's request. She knelt and searched the platform. *Her ring should be around here some-where. But where? It couldn't have gone far.*

Doc's voice broke in. "Why aren't you at the panel?"

Ashley jumped up, ran back to the controls, and peered again at the displays through a glaze of tears. His footsteps pounded toward her. "What's going on?"

Ashley pressed her lips together and squeezed her eyes shut for a moment, suppressing an emerging sob. "Only—" She gulped and took a breath. "Only two presences. That third one is gone."

Doc shook a finger at the monitor. "You said there was an attachment. What happened?"

Ashley took another breath, finding strength in her anger. "There was." She flipped the history switch near the bottom of the panel. "I'll run the data back on the screen. You can

207

see for yourself." They watched the stream of numbers while Ashley pointed. "Look, there's Bonnie. She's at six point two, and there's Devin. He's at seven point five. Then, here's the third presence, ranging from three point eight all the way to seven point two."

Doc squinted at the monitor, glancing now and then at the settings on the panel. "How can that be? We're not showing any shadow effect in the other two."

"Some kind of multiple presentation, I guess, but it's clearly the same entity." She pressed a finger on the display. "Now here's the connection. Bonnie was moving up, and when she reached six point eight—"

Doc's voice deepened to a growl. "It wasn't Devin attaching to her. It was that other thing, whatever it was."

Ashley lowered her head. "Yeah. I see that now."

Doc glared at her. "Are you playing me for a fool?"

"What?" Ashley jerked her head up and met his angry eyes. "Me playing you? Look who's talking. You and your lies about Bonnie's mom. What really happened to her? And what was all that about my grandfather dying?"

Doc stepped away from the control panel and stuffed his hands into his pockets, taking a few steps in a small circle before looking at Ashley again. "You've been wondering why your grandfather's health has been leveling off," he said, sarcasm coating his words. "And now he's sick. Very sick. It seems that our model patient is deteriorating. Your wonderful photoreceptors don't work. They never have."

He waved an arm at the glass domes glowing faintly in the dim room. "The receptors I've been putting into your restoration engine are real ones. And all this time I've been using the candlestone and dragon's blood to restore your precious

208

Daddy. Didn't you notice that he stopped improving at the same time Devin took the candlestone to West Virginia?"

The two glared at each other. After a few seconds Doc's scowl faded, and he returned his hand to his pocket. "But now that the stone's back here, it doesn't work. I think it's because Devin's in there, somehow messing up the process. He's trying to force us to get him out. He knows I can't leave him there if I want our research to continue. That's why I needed Bonnie. No one else has been able to get him out."

Ashley gripped the sides of the control panel until her knuckles turned white. This creep had used his own daughter as a glorified guinea pig. He had put her in danger just so he could keep his precious research going. Not only that, he lied about why her grandfather was sick.

Her thoughts stretched back to months ago, before her grandfather's treatments had started. Day after day she had told Daddy how much she loved him, explaining her research and how it would help him recover. It didn't matter that he sometimes couldn't respond. She was willing to do whatever he needed. On his nurse's days off, she changed his soiled sheets, cleaned his feeding tube, and washed his body. And every day she begged God to heal him. But God never answered.

She pinched the bridge of her nose to hold back her tears. Letting Doc see her pain was out of the question. She steadied her voice, but a tight squeak slipped out. "Why didn't you just tell me the truth?"

Doc kicked a power cord out of his way and resumed a slow pace around the lab. "Oh, come now. Would you have helped me if you knew that I needed dragon's blood every time we treated your grandfather and every time we sent a diver into the stone?"

209

He made a full circuit before continuing his rant. "Devin agreed not to hurt Bonnie if I got him out of the stone, but would you help set a monster like Devin free, knowing that his lust for Bonnie's blood would never die? Yes, Daddy's dying, but are you willing to risk someone else's life to save him?"

He stopped and faced her, a strange expression emerging, as if a light had flashed on in his brain. "Maybe you were willing after all. You knew Devin was in the candlestone, and you were easy to convince that he was trapped in the A frequency. You noticed his frequency drift, but it didn't stop you from sending Bonnie in there, did it?"

Ashley hesitated. His questions stung, and new questions flowed in, overloading her brain. She took a deep breath. "Where have you been getting dragon's blood?"

Doc dug his hands back into his pockets. After a long moment, he sighed and nodded. "I guess you might as well know everything." He walked toward the back of the lab and gestured with his head. "Follow me. It's time to open the Omega door."

* * * * * *

Karen stepped out of the hall and motioned for the other girls. "Let's go," she whispered. "The coast is clear."

Bundled in heavy coats, thick pants, and high boots, the four girls stole through the lab. Karen picked up Pebbles, and Stacey and Rebecca crowded beside her. They skirted the central lab area, traveling the long way around the cavern's perimeter. When they reached the door to the Alpha exit tunnel, Karen turned the knob. "It's unlocked. Let's go." She tapped the other two girls with her free hand and pointed at a flashlight hanging on a hook. "Beck, you first, then Stacey. Pebbles and I'll bring up the rear. On tiptoes, now."

Beck grabbed the flashlight and snapped it on, then she and Stacey crept along the narrow corridor. Karen peeked out the door before closing it behind her. She blew out a long sigh. So far, so good. She shifted Pebbles in her arms, balancing her against her hip. Her knees weakened, ready to buckle. *I have to do it! I just have to! There's a bunch of stairs, but I've done it before.* She set her jaw, pressing her lips together. *Bonnie did her part. Now I've gotta do mine.*

*   *   *   *   *   *

As quickly as the shimmering hedge came, it disappeared. Bonnie felt her hand zipping back toward her like a retractable measuring tape. In a way, it was a relief to have her new body all in one place, but her returning hand brought with it a new mystery. It carried an odd sparkle, a dark red glow that seemed attached to her own white light. Her ring? Somehow it came through with her.

The other light, the one she thought was her mother, had fallen back, as though cowering in the distance. She knew who it was now. The glowing fence of light had touched her, and it seemed as though it had fed her information, a gentle stream of thoughts that flowed from mind to mind.

The first light was none other than Devin, the dragon slayer, the very one who had plunged his sword into her mother's belly and ripped her open, the same hateful maniac who would kill Bonnie if he had the chance. Somehow he had morphed his light energy to look like her mother, and now he was reshaping again, his light congealing into a radiant image of his human form.

As the slayer drew closer, his thoughts buzzed into her mind like irritating static. "You're trapped in here with me, demon witch, at least for now. You're doomed to hell where you belong."

Bonnie stayed quiet. She didn't know how to talk anyway, though changes in her thoughts seemed to alter the ripples in her light pulses. Might he be able to read her mind by watching the variations in her light patterns? Although his light had drawn a human shape, hers was still disorganized, more like a flashing blob than anything resembling a girl.

"I, on the other hand," Devin continued, "plan to escape very soon. The good doctor, you see, knows that all of his plans will crumble if he doesn't get me out of here. We got close this time. If not for that cursed phantom, I'd be out of here now."

The slayer moved even closer, but he stopped suddenly. He took another step only to rebound, as though Bonnie had a shield around her. He sent another stream of thoughts. "I suppose you want to know where your mother is, don't you?" The slayer's light drifted away. "Follow me, and I'll show you."

Bonnie's light pulsed like a frenzied strobe. She didn't need a low-life scoundrel like him pretending to help her.

Yet, if she could display a calm, trusting glow, maybe she'd be able to coax some information out of him, ask enough questions to get him to slip. Since she seemed to have a force field protecting her, it was worth a try.

Bonnie edged forward. It was much easier to move now without her link to Derrick. The slayer led her into the crystal's mysterious depths and halted at a place that seemed a shade brighter. Bonnie halted as well, staying out of his reach.

His glowing arm extended downward. Part of it disappeared into the blackness. As he drew his arm back into place, his scratchy static filled her head. "That, my dear, is a crack in the floor, a flaw in the candlestone's structure. That's where your mother went."

Bonnie sent out her reply, a thought stream of sorts. "Why should I believe you?"

"Oh, you can talk now. You're a fast learner." He laughed, sending a wave of ripples through his body of light. "You should believe me, because it's in my best interests to help you. This is an exit, the only exit. I use it to send encoded light to speak to your father. Normally, this stone doesn't allow any encoded light to escape. You see, encoded light, like your body and mine, passes through that black membrane you probably felt when you came in. It gets lodged in this inner core. Fractured light, on the other hand, passes around that membrane and gets arrested and assembled before going through the exit channel that's right below this crack.

"The doctor's messages are encoded, so they come into this core to me. I can read that light and send it back through, encoded with my response, by sending it through this crack. It goes straight to the exit, bypassing the arresting stage."

"If that's a way out, why haven't you gone through it?"

"Because the channel would put me out of phase too much. I couldn't be restored. The good doctor's little genius, Ashley, hasn't figured out why yet, but it seems that the encoding of a female is not disturbed when she passes through this part of the structure. She sent both male and female animals in here, and I put them through the channel. Every female survived, and every male was disintegrated. That's why they always use girls as their divers. If Derrick were ever to lose a diver, she could just go through this crack to get out again. Your mother was in here, but when we learned about the escape route, we were able to send her back out when Dr. Conner was ready with her cure."

Bonnie's light flashed like blinking neon. "I don't believe you. Ashley would have told me. I know she would have."

Devin's light rippled from the center in tight halos, like rings from a tiny splash in a pond. "Ashley didn't know. Brilliant or not, she's as easy to dupe as you are. Dr. Conner and I have been using her for our purposes, and I've been speaking to them in your mother's place ever since she left. Dr. Conner knew all along, but we had to keep Ashley in the dark. I don't think she would want to help us if she knew what we were really doing."

"No, she wouldn't. That much I do believe."

Devin's light flashed brightly, stripes of energy passing from his head to his toes. "Well, believe this, witch. I'm telling you this because I need you to dive back in here and get me out. Once you're out there, I'll tell you where to find your mother. She's alive and restored."

Bonnie moved closer to the crack, but she kept her distance from the slayer. As she approached, the floor's blackness changed. A slight gray streak appeared, a fault in one of the jewel's inner planes.

Devin's voice came across in softer tones. "The candlestone is still on the pedestal outside. If you decide to go into this channel, you'll go straight to the restoration process." Devin drifted away. "I'll move out of sight. Take your time. Your mother didn't take long to decide, though. She said she hates dark places."

A few seconds later, Devin was gone, his light vanishing more quickly than Bonnie thought possible. Did this place have secret passages or walls he could hide behind?

Bonnie edged toward the gray streak, close enough to get a glimpse into the jagged fissure. It opened into a chasm, and way below, at the bottom of a glassy gorge, a stream of soft, white light poured through. It looked like a gentle river flowing in a peaceful valley, but she couldn't see where it went.

Something from below pulled on her, like the candlestone's light-drawing power was somehow stronger in the lower area. If she went down, there would probably be no way to get back up. She replayed the slayer's explanation in her mind, piecing together the candlestone's flow channels, and imagining this stream of light as a passage to the outside.

Faint voices emerged from the fissure, mournful laments in unrecognizable words, as though ghosts whispered eternal chants from haunted halls. If only she could understand. Were they calling her? Was it a warning?

She turned toward the blackness, resting her shining body and allowing her rapidly pulsing energy to settle. She gazed at her light, a stark contrast to the black surroundings.

215

Months ago, when she was moving from foster home to foster home, she cried in her bed at night, worrying about what the next day would bring. Every night, darkness covered her with a blanket of sorrow, but morning always brought new hope with the rising sun. Light was sort of like truth. It always showed a liar for what he really was. And when someone gave a word of encouragement, it was like the sun rising, revealing that things weren't really as bad as they seemed.

She peeked again at the chasm and listened to the voices, soft and dreary, one or two counterpoint solos tangled in the melancholy chorus. As they droned on, a familiar call blended in, the call she had heard all the way back in West Virginia, her name floating into her mind the same way her mother used to call at the end of a summer day. She peered into the fissure again and called, "Mama? Mama, is that you?"

There was no answer. The sad drone played on.

Bonnie floated away. As the blackness swallowed the edges of her body, her light diminished. This became her new way to cry, letting the dark oppression creep into her dimming soul and lay her energy to waste, as though allowing a black predator to consume her bit by bit.

With her waning soul quaking, her pulsing light faded even further. As darkness gnawed at her sanity, she shivered. If she gave in to sadness now, how could she help her mother? Putting her sorrowful thoughts away, she lifted her soul in song, streaming the words into the darkness with trembling quivers of light.

> Whither shall I go from thy spirit? Or whither shall I flee from thy presence?

> If I ascend up into heaven, thou art there: If I make my bed in hell, behold, thou art there.

> If I take the wings of the morning, and dwell in the uttermost parts of the sea;

> Even there shall thy hand lead me, and thy right hand shall hold me.

> If I say, Surely the darkness shall cover me; even the night shall be light about me.

> Yea, the darkness hideth not from thee; but the night shineth as the day:

> The darkness and the light are both alike to thee.

With each uttered word, with each phrase of truth, Bonnie's light brightened, clearing her mind and refreshing her soul. When she finished, the darkness crawled away like a wounded shadow. She could see more clearly now, her body illuminating the maze of dark walls that bordered the gem's center. Then, as though whispered into her ear by a close friend, a stream of words flowed into her mind. *Everyone who is of the truth hears my voice. No lie is of the truth.*

The voice was soft, pure, and whisper-quiet.

After a few seconds, the slayer's words returned, his static-filled voice grinding into her mind like a power drill. *She said she hates dark places.*

When everything fell silent again, Bonnie sat motionless and pondered the voices. *She hates dark places? But that can't be true. Mama used to turn all the lights off just to tell me stories in the dark.*

She looked again into the fissure. The chasm floor below now seemed much brighter. A mass of ghostly phantoms swirled at the river's edge, their expressions clear—sadness, regret, remorse, the pain of lost opportunity, never to be found again. Were these human beings? Did each dim pulse in that forsaken chasm represent a soul trapped in a lost netherworld?

Bonnie's light flashed. That's what the slayer really wanted, for her to cast herself into that hell. But is that really what happened to her mother? Was she fooled by Devin? Was she one of those poor, tormented souls?

And now there seemed to be no way out. Even if Karen could dive back into the candlestone, Ashley said she would probably be out of phase. It took someone with dragon blood to search the depths of this dungeon, and there was only one person who could possibly do it.

She drifted away from the fissure, sat on the crystalline floor, and folded her hands. It was time to pray for Billy.

14

SEEING RED

As the car roared away, Billy slammed against the side of the trunk. At each careening turn, cold steel pinched his arms. He squirmed to his side and felt around with his fingers, searching for something sharp near his back, anything with a metal edge to cut the strangling tape around his wrists. But the tape tightened with every move, numbing his fingers. He was in a mess, and a familiar rage boiled in his belly.

Billy flopped to his stomach and rested his cheek against the rough, gas-scented carpet. He had to get a grip and relax, focus on any good news. Although his throat had been slit, he hadn't bled to death yet. And the gag felt like it was scratching his lips off, but it might be starting to slip.

He pressed his lips against the rag as hard as he could, making it inch downward. *Okay, it moves. That's even better news. It'll take a while to get it off, but it does move.*

While Billy worked on the gag, the car's engine settled into a high-pitched drone, and the road straightened, which meant that they were probably on a highway. If this ordeal lasted much longer, the exhaust of the gas fumes might knock him out. He had to escape before it was too late.

Once more twisting to his side, Billy pulled his knees to his chest, lowered his head, and rubbed the scratchy cloth against his jeans. Each fiber felt like sharp nails digging into his bleeding lips, but the gag kept sliding downward. Maybe soon he would be ready for Palin.

Billy continued struggling. It was odd that Palin hadn't already sliced him into a spiral ham. What could be the reason for tossing him into this icebox trunk instead? Was this slayer hauling him to where they kept Bonnie? That was some comfort, to be at her side even if it meant torture or death. Maybe by some twist of fate he could figure out a way to save her, to have just one second with his mouth free to send the slayers to a fiery hell, even if he died trying.

He blew out a pain-filled sigh. Dying bravely surely beat letting that maniac do whatever he wanted to Bonnie. That was a no-brainer. There was no one else like her, no one else he'd lay down his life for. Well, he would for Walter, but that was different. He and Walter would fight together, battling enemies with everything they had until they either conquered their foes or fell in combat.

But Bonnie was different, special, like … well, she was just special. In his mind he saw her staring at him with her trusting eyes, felt her gentle hand in his. On the mountain after their airplane crashed, she'd been braver than anyone he knew, stronger than he'd imagined possible, with her wings extended, more beautiful than …

Billy lay motionless. He couldn't think about her any longer, not if he wanted to survive. He had to work on that gag.

*   *   *   *   *   *

I'm cold," Pebbles said, her tiny voice muffled by the falling snow.

Karen stooped and grabbed a pair of purple mittens from the snow-covered ground, whispering as she tried to put them back on the little girl's hands. "Well, it's no wonder. Your hands are like ice." Her gloved fingers fumbled through the effort. Karen stripped off her gloves and set them on a five-foot-high boulder she had chosen to shelter the girls from the whistling wind and to screen them from view.

"When are we going inside, Red? This isn't fun anymore."

Karen slid the mittens in place. "We can't go back, Pebbles, not yet. We have to get to that house out near the highway. Remember? The old man with the friendly horse?"

Pebbles nodded, shivering, while Stacey and Beck looked on, also shivering in spite of their winter-ready clothes.

"We'd get lost if we tried to get there in this storm. If the snow doesn't let up soon, we'll go back to the stairs. I promise." Karen crouched and tightened Monique's hood, brushing away a little snowcap from the top. "Don't worry. I won't let you freeze." Karen grabbed her gloves and slowly put them back on, covering her stiffening fingers and sighing. *If I don't freeze first. We have a long way to go.*

A few minutes later, something roared in the distance. Karen lowered her hood and tilted her head to keep the wind out of her ears. "It's a car," she whispered. "Everyone duck and be quiet."

With the three younger girls safely hidden, Karen stood on tiptoes and peered over the boulder. A faded blue car, a late-model Grand Marquis, toiled up the snowy incline, sliding and spinning, but managing to navigate the final turn into

221

the narrow driveway toward the stones that bordered the lab's entrance.

The car zipped past their hiding place, less than a snowball's throw from the stairway door, and parked about thirty feet behind Doc's SUV. The driver jumped out and hurried to the rear of the car, brandishing a pistol.

Karen gasped and pushed the other girls' heads lower. Would he see their footprints? The snow had fallen heavily since they had come outside, but she couldn't tell if it had covered their tracks completely. The man paced behind the car as if he wasn't sure what to do. Finally, he stood next to the car's trunk and yelled, "I've got a gun, kid. Do you think your breath's quicker than my trigger finger? Maybe that gag's still on, and maybe it's not, but I'll bet a bullet would discourage you real quick, either way."

The man lifted a key fob and pointed the gun at the trunk. His arm shook, and he shifted his weight from side to side, shivering in the bitter breeze. After what seemed like a full minute, he lowered the gun and kicked the rear bumper. "Don't make a sound. If you try to escape, I'll blow your brains out. I'm not the one who wants to keep you alive, you know."

The man stalked toward the stairway door and jerked it open. After glaring back at the car for a brief moment, he disappeared into the mountain.

＊　　＊　　＊　　＊　　＊　　＊

Billy managed to slip the gag down enough to open his mouth. He positioned his head to blast Palin at the first sign of light, ready to fry that creep quicker than he could aim and fire. As he imagined the dark knight burning in agony, the satisfaction of sweet revenge swelled his chest. In his mental picture, Palin cooked down to a dirty pile of soot, and Billy kicked the remains and scattered them in the dust.

A hard lump grew in Billy's throat, but he swallowed it away. *It's okay. Palin deserves to die. He's a dragon slayer, and he wants to kill both Bonnie and me.*

Billy had heard Palin yelling about having a gun, but now there was no sound at all. Did he leave? Was he waiting for help?

With the tape still strangling his wrists, Billy could do little to improve his situation. The trunk was too dark for him to hunt for a latch, and so far he hadn't found anything sharp. He could feel a pair of gasoline containers at his feet, and his nose told him that at least one more sat near his head.

He needed a plan. He couldn't yell. Palin might be standing close by. For all Billy knew, Palin could pop open the trunk from well beyond the range of Billy's fiery breath and shoot him just for having the gag off.

Billy sighed. Merlin's book was right. He shouldn't have turned that page. It was all his own fault.

"Who's in the trunk?"

Billy blinked. A voice! It sounded like a girl, trembling and kind of squeaky. Since she didn't know who was in the trunk, she couldn't be with Palin. "Billy Bannister. Some goon stuffed me in here. Please help me get out."

"Hold on."

Something shuffled outside, then clicked. The voice returned. "The door's locked. I can't get to the trunk latch."

"Did you try all the doors?"

"Of course I did. I'm not a moron."

Billy wrestled again with the tape. So close, yet so far. Some girl must have wandered by and heard him struggling. Now she was in danger too. "You'd better get out of sight. The guy who kidnapped me will probably be back soon."

"Not a chance. I saw where he went. It'll be a while."

"Can you call the police?"

"No. But I do have an idea."

"Okay. Let's hear it."

"This is a Grand Marquis. It oughta have a trunk release on the inside. It's a T-shaped handle that glows in the dark, and it should be dangling from a pull wire near the lock."

Billy glanced around the dark trunk. "No. There's nothing glowing. I would've seen that by now."

"Then he might have cut it off to hide it. If he did, the bare wire might still be sticking out near the latch. If you can get hold of it and pull, the trunk should pop open easily."

"Easily. Yeah, right. My hands are tied behind my back."

"How about your feet? Can you maybe get it between your feet and yank on it?"

"I don't think so. I'll try to arch my back up there. My fingers are kind of numb, but maybe I can find it."

Billy twisted his body and pushed his backside toward the trunk latch, bracing his feet against the floor. His fingers were like icicles, and he could barely feel anything he touched. As he worked, the girl's voice returned again.

"By the way, my name's Karen."

Billy grunted. "Pleased ... to meet you."

"If that guy comes back, I'll tap the trunk and—"

"I think I got it." Billy squeezed a wire between his frozen fingers and pulled. A click sounded. The lid flew open, filling the trunk with daylight and falling snow. Billy boosted himself to the frame and sat with his back toward Karen. "Can you get me loose?"

Karen pulled off her gloves and started tearing away the strips of duct tape around Billy's wrists, stuffing the pieces into her coat pocket. "It's all twisted," she said, "but it's coming off." She glanced over her shoulder at the mountainside a couple of times. "He must have really worked you over. Your lips look like they lost a fight with an orbital sander."

"Yeah. The gag just about tore them off."

"And your neck. Did you cut yourself shaving with a buzz saw?"

"Never mind. Just get me loose before he comes back to finish me off."

When the final band of tape gave way. Billy yanked the gag down from his chin to his neck and climbed slowly out of the trunk. With his muscles cramping like knotted steel, he staggered and gripped his calf. He glanced up at the perky redhead's beaming face. "Can you help me walk? We have to get out of sight before Palin comes back."

"You bet." Karen closed the trunk, slid an arm around his waist, and helped him walk toward a boulder next to a clearing, following a line of footprints in the tire tracks. When they reached the other side of the boulder, they found three bundled girls, all younger than Karen, hiding there.

Billy jerked the gag the rest of the way off, leaned over, and rubbed his legs to massage away the tingles. He nodded at the girls. "Hello."

The oldest of the younger trio gave him a big smile. "Hello yourself." She glanced at Karen. "Who's your new friend?"

Karen grinned. "His name's Billy, uh, Bannister, I think he said."

"Right. I'm Billy Bannister." He straightened and looked at Karen. "You said your name's Karen, right?"

"Right, but you can call me Red if you want to." She pointed at the others in turn. "And that's Stacey, Rebecca, and Monique."

Billy tried to smile, but his cracked lips hurt too much. "The weather's pretty bad for playing outside. What are you doing out here?"

"Actually, we were just hiding. We're planning to—" Karen jerked her head around. "He's back!"

Billy signaled for the girls to crouch behind the boulder. He sneaked to the edge of their refuge and watched. Palin stepped from a mountainside doorway, carrying a shield and a pistol.

Karen leaned close to Billy and whispered, "What do you think he'll do when he finds out you're gone?"

"Not sure." Billy focused straight ahead. Karen's warm breath blew across his cheek, too close for comfort. He had to ignore her. Palin was in sight, that murderous demon who had nearly killed him once before. Rage boiled inside. A good fire brewed in his belly. It would be easy to fry that creep, but with Karen literally breathing down his neck, he hesitated. Was he ashamed of what he wanted to do or just nervous about the girls seeing it?

Like the warmth of Karen's breath, the professor's words blew across his mind. *A knight opposes his enemy face to face. A stab in the back is the way of the coward. If you must fight, attack your enemy head on. That is the way of valor.*

Billy replied in his mind. *But he's a slayer. It's okay to fry a creep like him. It's not cowardly.*

The professor's words responded like an echoing call. *Considering the words of this prophecy, we can assume that God has ordained that we carry out no surprise attacks. Do you understand?*

Billy understood. But he didn't care. Palin had sliced his throat, beat up his mom and Walter, and tossed him into a trunk like a bag of dirty laundry. Palin had tried to kill him and Bonnie once before. He was sure to try again. It was time to light this torch and let it blaze.

He waved a hand at Karen. "You might not want to watch. This won't be pretty." She stepped back but stayed close.

Palin extended a key fob. The lid jumped open a crack. He swung the shield in front, reached with his foot, and kicked the lid up the rest of the way.

Thrusting with his whole body, Billy launched a stream of fire. The river of flames roared from his mouth and landed in the trunk, engulfing the interior in a tidal wave of raging heat and consuming the plastic gasoline containers.

The fuel erupted in a tremendous ball of yellow and orange. Flames billowed into the sky. As the car's frame ripped apart, the flames blew over Palin like a wall of white-hot fury, knocking him flat. His shield kept his face and chest from taking the brunt of the onslaught, but the blaze covered his legs and gun arm, eating his limbs like a ravenous lion.

Within seconds, the fire died down. Palin lay on his back with his shield still on his chest. Billy jumped out and ran to him, sliding to his knees when he arrived. Using both arms, he heaped snow onto the smoldering body.

Palin threw off the shield, ripping away his scorched sleeve. Billy grabbed the gun from the ground, jumped to his feet, and aimed it at Palin. His mouth, once again torched by an unusually hot stream, felt like a nest of scorpions.

Propping himself on his elbows, Palin glared at Billy. With his body devastated, he couldn't hope to fight. His eyes pierced Billy's with cold malice, and his coarse voice spewed mocking venom. "You think you're a hero now, don't you, boy? You're no hero, oh no, not a hero. You're just like me, boy, just like me. Does a hero kill a man whose back is turned? Couldn't fight me face-to-face, could you? I tried to kill you when you were wounded back on the mountain, and now you cooked me like a goose when my back was turned. Yes, boy, you're just like me. You kill to get what you want."

Palin coughed. He tried to continue, but his voice trailed away. He slumped back, and his body shuddered.

Billy edged closer, still wary of Palin's devices. The dying man clenched his fist and spat his final pain-streaked words. "My master will live on. He's a true believer, not a hypocrite like you or me. He endured Arthur. He survived Napoleon and Hitler. He will outlive you as well." He released a rattling sigh, then fell limp.

Billy stooped next to Palin and touched his wet, blackened chest, now motionless. His enemy was gone. Yet he felt no joy, no joy at all. His belly gurgled and sent burning fluid into his throat. *What have I done? The professor warned me, but I didn't listen.* Tears flowed, dripping down his nose and falling onto the snow-swept ground.

Billy chided himself, mentally buffeting his body. How could he weep over this brutal man, this hate-filled maniac? Was it the words he had spoken? Did his speech stab him like poisoned darts, accusing him of the same heinous crimes that dressed this foul creature in his cruel raiment of blood? It couldn't be. There hadn't been any other way, had there?

Billy rose slowly and gazed for a moment at the blackened shell of a car. Leaning over, he dragged Palin's corpse toward the boulder but stopped short, not wanting the girls to see the grotesque, half-melted body. He shoved a pile of snow together

228

over Palin, then hurried around the boulder to the hiding place. The girls were gone.

He spotted them far away, running across a field and into a line of skinny, naked trees. "Wait!" Billy's voice died in the blanket of falling snow. He ran after them, his legs again cramping. Of course, he would eventually catch them. The youngest girl couldn't possibly outrun him in the snow. Even if Karen helped her, they couldn't stay ahead for long.

After an exhausting chase, he finally came within earshot of them. "Wait!"

"Stay away!" Karen screamed, running at the rear of the group while carrying Monique. She tripped and tumbled head-first into a snowdrift. Monique flew from her grasp and joined her in the powdery mound.

Billy dashed ahead and scooped Monique into his arms. She gasped and stared straight at him. Rather than trying to escape, she kept staring, her brown eyes reflecting Billy's war-torn face.

229

Karen pushed up on all fours. "Don't hurt her, you … you monster!" The other two girls scurried behind a tree and peered out from either side.

Billy set Monique down gently. "I'm not a monster," he said, touching the top of her head. "If you'll give me a minute, I'll explain."

Karen rose to her feet and brushed snow from her coat and pants. Monique ran to her side and latched on to her leg. The other two girls crept out from behind their tree and crowded around Karen.

With snow cascading in thick torrents, Karen crossed her arms in front. "Okay, let's hear it," she said, her expression a blend of fear and skepticism. "This oughta be good."

* * * * * *

When Bonnie finished a long session of prayer and singing, she gazed into the darkness. Her improving vision allowed a view of a collection of shadowy walls bending into myriad corridors and corners, like black halls in a blacker house. Every now and then, a faint glimmer of light appeared, perhaps some other being watching, maybe hiding in a faraway recess.

It probably wasn't Devin. He tended to come out boldly rather than hide around corners. Could it be that phantom, that strange picket fence of light that first kept her out of the slayer's clutches? Bonnie had told Ashley that she wouldn't be alone in the candlestone, so why couldn't God's spirit show up in a spectacular way like he did in the fiery furnace with Shadrach, Meshach, and Abed-nego?

Yet, that glimmer could be something else. Maybe her mother really was out there somewhere.

The glimmer appeared again. When Bonnie moved toward it, it disappeared. She kept going, trying to follow a faint trail of luminescence. As she turned a corner, something gleamed from around the next angle. "Who's there?"

A bright radiance flashed into Bonnie's hallway, blinding her for a moment. A voice rose from somewhere out of sight. "I am a friend. Draw no closer, child."

Bonnie halted. The voice sounded nothing like Devin's. "What's your name?"

A gentle laugh echoed in the darkness. "As I said, I am a friend. That is all you need to know about me. But I know who you are, Bonnie Silver, and I have watched you for a long time. You have an enemy here, and he can harm you, yes, kill you, should you let down your shield."

"My shield?"

"Yes, lass. And a strong one it is. It nearly withered away, but you built it up again. Despair is the way of destruction. It will consume your light like a raging cancer and cast you into eternal shadows."

Bonnie caught a new glimpse of her own light. It had changed quite a bit. Her human shape was now forming, arms and legs, even a hint of fingers at the end of her flowing robe. Yet, her form didn't matter. Only her quest did. "Do you know my mother? Is she here?"

It seemed that she felt a sigh, an old, tired sigh, emanating from her mysterious friend. "Quite a number have entered this prison, but Irene has not passed by my eyes."

Bonnie's light dimmed, and the edges turned ragged. Her mother wasn't here after all? "You called her Irene. So you do know her?"

"I know her well, perhaps better than you do."

231

"But how is that possible? If you're in here, and she never entered, how can you know her?"

"Although I knew Irene long before I entered this stone, I have seen her since that time. It took many years, but I have learned to see beyond these walls. We do not have vision, so to speak. Our minds adapt to other input. If you stay long enough, you will learn. Your shape will naturally conform in appearance to that of your earthly body as your agitation diminishes. You can even learn to change your shape. Your enemy has learned. That is why he has an advantage over you."

"But why won't you let me see you? Why won't you tell me who you are?"

"Because viewing me will lower your shield. When faith is made sight, it is no longer faith. We may lower our shields when the danger has passed, but the danger is ever lurking. I perceive even now that your defenses are lowering, so I must leave you."

Bonnie felt an evil presence, the eerie sense of a ghostly sentinel watching, stalking. As the light from the other hall faded, it spoke once more. "Sing, child! Sing! For psalms and hymns are your leather and mail."

Bonnie shuddered and immediately lifted her voice.

> If I say, Surely the darkness shall cover me; even the night shall be light about me.

> Yea, the darkness hideth not from thee; but the night shineth as the day:

> The darkness and the light are both alike to thee.

The eerie feeling, like tickling hairs on a cold neck, slowly faded. The light of her friend also disappeared, slipping away into an imperceptible hall.

*   *   *   *   *   *

When Billy finished his story, Karen kept her arms tightly crossed, though a hint of a grin emerged. "So, I'm supposed to believe that you're a human and dragon in one body?"

Billy pushed his boot across the deepening snow. "Well, yeah. I was hoping you'd believe me."

"And what's next?" she continued, her smile bursting forth. "A girl with dragon wings?"

"Yeah, in fact—" Billy stopped and read Karen's grin. "Hey! Do you know Bonnie?"

"Like a sister." Karen ran to Billy, hooked her arm in his, and began leading him in the direction they had come. "Let's get you to the lab. Bonnie told us to escape and call for help. We were trying to get to a farmhouse I know, 'cause we couldn't really do anything to help her. But with that flame thrower you've got, you can do some serious damage."

The other girls followed while Karen and Billy ran ahead through the drifting snow. "Where is Bonnie? Is she safe?"

"I can't say for sure. She went into the candlestone to get her mother out. That's the last I heard."

Billy stopped and clenched a fist. "That's what I was afraid of. Her mother's dead, and she doesn't know it."

"Dead?" Karen squinted. "What are you talking about?"

"Bonnie's father told her that her mother's still alive, but now we know that isn't true. We found her death certificate in the hospital's records."

"Well," Karen replied, looking back at the girls as they drew closer, "I don't know about any death certificate, but I saw Bonnie's mom in the lab with Dr. Conner. I heard she was in a coma and they were going to transluminate her to keep her from dying."

233

"Transluminate her? You know about all that stuff?"

"Yep." Karen grinned. "What else do you want to know?"

Billy couldn't help but laugh at this spirited girl. Her hood had fallen back, and as the snow settled on her head, it seemed that her fiery hair would melt it away. He sighed and blew a long stream of white into the sky. "I just want to know what's going on. Devin's probably in the candlestone, and I think Bonnie's father wants her to drag him out. It's gotta be a trap."

"Then all the more reason for you to get into the lab." Karen hooked his arm again and pulled him along. "The door to the stairway is framed by those rocks over there."

"No. Wait." Billy withdrew a mechanical pencil from the pocket on the side of his pant leg, along with a small tablet of paper. He scratched down the professor's phone number and began sketching his face. "How far is it to the farmhouse you're trying to find?"

"Pretty far." Karen pointed at a slope. "The end of this trail, then about a mile down the road. We could get there in about thirty minutes if the storm lets up. But I don't want to get lost in this weather, especially with Monique."

"Yeah, I'll bet." He tore off the front page of the tablet. "Here. It's a drawing and a phone number."

Karen took the paper and studied the drawing while Billy pointed at the trail. "Just follow the car tracks. They should still be visible, and they'll keep you on the path. When you get to the house, call that number and ask for the professor."

"The professor?" She pointed at the sketch. "Is he this freaky dude with the big eyebrows?"

Billy laughed. "Yeah, the freaky dude. Tell him everything that's going on, especially what you told me about Bonnie's mom. Just give him the address of the house. He'll find you. And tell him to get here on the double."

DADDY'S DREAM

How could you do such a thing?" Ashley stormed back from the cave room and stomped across the lab. She sat heavily at the master control panel, making her chair spin half way around to avoid looking at Doc. She crossed her arms in front and heaved an angry sigh. "It's despicable! It's criminal!"

Doc called from across the room as he approached. "And it was keeping your grandfather alive!"

Ashley didn't know what to say. The whole world was crashing down on her. All of her brilliant plans were falling apart. And they were good plans, plans that would have helped a lot of sick and elderly people.

But now she despised herself. She was really an evil, mad scientist, holding children captive as lab rats, performing dangerous experiments on them, disintegrating an angelic girl to get a devil out of a crystal chamber, and now … and now, this new revelation.

And all for what? Nothing worked. Her photoreceptors had failed, Bonnie was trapped with that demon, and her grandfather was dying. Ashley laid her arms on the panel, hid her face between them, and sobbed.

Doc's hand fell gently on her shoulder. She jumped to her feet. "Just … just stay away from me." She walked backwards toward the girls' dorm. "I'm going to get Karen. We have to get Bonnie out of there."

"Yes," Doc said, nodding slowly. "Bonnie and Devin have to come out. It's the only way for your grandfather to survive, the only way to keep our research going. I'm glad you finally understand."

Her blood boiling, Ashley exploded in rage. "No, don't you get it? We can't keep using people to get what we want. I'm not doing this for my grandfather. It's for Bonnie."

"Fine, fine." He waved her away. "Whatever. Go ahead and get Karen dressed. We'll use her one last time."

Ashley ran toward the dorm hall. She stretched her key coil, pushed the key into the lock, and turned it. Something felt different. There was no resistance, no opening click. Hadn't Bonnie locked it?

She opened the door and hurried down the hall toward Karen's room, still pondering Doc's words. *We'll use her one last time.* She paused in front of Karen's sign—Red and Pebbles. *Use her? No! That's not right!*

She swung the door open and leaned in. All was quiet. She stepped back into the hall and listened to the eerie silence. Where were all the usual little-girl noises? She bolted into the room and threw open Karen's closet door. Her coat was gone. She dashed to Stacey and Beck's room. It, too, was vacant.

She dashed down the hall again, ready to shout the terrible news to Doc, but as she passed by her own open door, a light inside made her stop. The lamp on her desk was on and pointed toward her bed. The bright light shone on a three-ring binder that lay on the neatly made spread.

She stepped inside. *Bonnie's journal?*

She sat on the bed, picked up the journal, and set it on her lap. A note taped to the front said, "The girls are okay. Trust me." The finger-worn binder flopped open to a hand-written title page decorated with squiggly doodles and a half-dozen or so smiley faces. In beautiful script, the title spelled out:

Silver Tokens
My Hopes, My Prayers, My Dreams

Ashley turned the pages, drinking in Bonnie's beautiful prose. Although a rush of thoughts shouted to sound an alarm, Bonnie's simple words held her in place—*trust me*. Ashley raced through Bonnie's flowery sonnets, exciting stories, and tender dedications, each garnished with a dash of spiritual insight.

When she reached the end, she found an entry with today's date. She read it more slowly, savoring each word.

> *Greater love hath no man than this, that a man lay down his life for his friends.*

> *Ashley, I know you will understand this verse, and I pray that the heart of its message will fill yours. Daddy's dream might yet be fulfilled, though perhaps in a way you do not expect. You might think no one understands you, but God knows everything about you. He knows who you really are.*

> *"Come now, and let us reason together," saith the LORD. "Though your sins be as scarlet, they shall be as*

237

white as snow; though they be red like crimson, they shall be as wool."

Red will be made white
Darkness shall become light
Faith will be made sight
Squire shall become knight

May God bless you as he speaks to your heart.

Ashley nodded. Bonnie was right. She did understand, perhaps at a deeper level than Bonnie could possibly have intended. Not only did she now understand the heart of Bonnie Silver, a heart of pure refined gold, she knew what it all meant to her own heart. She knew what she had to do.

There was no need to sound the alarm, no need to recapture the scarlet-haired symbol of her dark experiments. All remnants of her selfish desires had to be purged, even if it meant sacrificing herself to save Bonnie.

Ashley looked up, the eyes of her mind seeing through the ceiling and dozens of feet of earth. A feeling of peace descended on her like a dove flittering down to alight. Her thoughts drifted, and for a moment she focused on the invisible world outside. *It must be snowing up there.*

* * * * * *

Billy stepped cautiously down the dark stairway. Karen had told him to look for a flashlight on a hook just inside the door, but it wasn't there. Palin probably took it when he went to get his shield and hadn't put it back.

It was good to get out of the bitter wind and snow, but tip-toeing down a pitch-black staircase into the unknown wasn't much better. Every few seconds he blew a puff of fire to light his way, quickly memorizing the fifteen or so steps in front of him during the brief seconds the flame endured. Although the stairway was straight, every now and then a stair would be slanted or broken, and he needed the illumination to keep from stumbling on a misshapen board.

When he finally reached the bottom of the stairs, he followed the gently curving corridor. The narrow, level tunnel was easier on his legs, but darkness still ruled the stuffy cave. His puffs of fire revealed a rocky ceiling with sporadic cross-beams less than a foot above his head as well as close, wood-framed walls at each side.

A door at the end of a long straightaway appeared, and a faint light emanated from its borders. When he reached it, he stared at its dark panels. Would anyone be able to hear him if he opened it just a crack to peek in? His dragon senses whispered warnings of danger, feelings of stark dread that ran from his tingling toes to the hairs standing on his neck. The fire in his belly reheated, ready to spew something more substantial than a temporary flashlight.

Taking a deep breath, he set a hand on the cold doorknob. As he turned it and pushed, he listened, hoping the hinges would stay quiet. The door inched open in silence. From the other side, a low hum drifted through the gap. Billy pushed the door open wider, enough for him to poke his head through.

The huge room inside was dim with only a few blinking lights at the center. Near the lights, a man's shadow hunched in silence—watching, studying. A glow cast a white light into his face, but the angle and distance kept his features indistinct.

Billy nudged the door open far enough to squeeze himself through. He tiptoed forward. When he came within about ten feet of the man, he spotted a large metal box on the floor. He crouched behind it and peered over the rim. The man sat at some kind of control panel, watching a display that cast light over his face and revealed his identity—Dr. Conner.

He looked at something in front of the panel. Billy traced his line of sight to a pedestal in the middle of a bunch of equipment. A red laser beam shot directly into an object perched on top, a sparkling gem. It had to be the candlestone.

Dr. Conner adjusted a series of dials on the panel, then spoke into a microphone. "Devin? Conner here. Can you hear me?"

Static blended with a familiar voice that emanated from a speaker unseen. "My good doctor, it seems that you have failed again. Your daughter is trapped in here with me, and I am not able to approach her. There must be some kind of polarity factor that repels me."

Billy gritted his teeth. That voice belonged to Devin, hard-edged and grating.

"I know of no polarity issues in your energy matrices that would cause that," Dr. Conner replied with an air of scientific precision. "According to these readings, you should be perfectly matched. But now we have to get both of you out if we're going to make the crystal pure again. The candlestone is worthless to me in this state."

The voice returned. "We could get her to try the dive again. I could force her into the abyss where I dumped all the animals you left in here, and then your little genius, Ashley, can try to get her out that way. I have not yet exhausted my arsenal of ideas to make her go willingly."

"I'm not going to risk my daughter's life any further. I let her dive in because that's been tested so many times, but that exit channel has never been tried. I notice you've never volunteered to go through it."

A short pause ensued before Devin continued. "Do you have the mongrel?"

"The Bannister boy? Yes. Palin came down to get a shield from the weapons cache and went back topside to get him. They should both be here soon."

"Good. You can lock him up in my old stockade in the cave."

"That's what I was thinking. The chains and locks are still in working order."

"They'd better be," Devin bellowed. "That part of my fortress is crucial. I don't want it falling prey to your precious lab project." His voice settled, becoming slow and meditative. "With the mongrel out of the way, my colleagues and I can storm the mountain and find that cursed Clefspeare. He is the last one, the very last one."

"Yes." Dr. Conner coughed, covering his mouth with his fist. "The last one."

241

"But first thing's first," Devin continued. "We need a diver."

"I thought I would try Karen again. She's the most experienced. Maybe she can pull both of you out."

"She translates badly, always has. She comes in so out of phase, I couldn't even see her until her last dive. Your adjustments aren't working. I'm growing impatient with your constant tweaking. It's time to try someone different. Send in the mongrel."

"But the male chimp was a blithering idiot when he returned." Dr. Conner's voice gave away a hint of fear. "All the males lost more than half their brain function during restoration."

Devin shouted, loud static punctuating his words. "What do I care about his brain function? Just make sure he's in phase!"

The static died away. "If I can attach, it won't matter if he's as dumb as a salamander. You pull him out, and I'll hang on. I know what causes male brain damage, and it can't happen to me."

"Just be sure to bring Bonnie."

"Yes, yes. Don't worry. Just get moving."

"But we need a good anchor. Derrick is sick and exhausted. It would be too dangerous to let him—"

A female voice interrupted. "I'll do it." It came from the other side of the room. Billy squinted into the darkness to find the source.

Dr. Conner spun. "Ashley? What did you say?"

"I'll do it. I'll be the anchor."

*   *   *   *   *   *

242 Walter opened the driver's door for Mrs. Bannister, then got in the back. He leaned forward between Mrs. Bannister and the professor. "She wasn't much help, was she?"

The professor sighed. "Not much, Walter, but we do have a few clues. We know the lab is about thirty minutes away and that there were rumors of a secret construction project near Camp Misery." He unfolded a map and set a finger next to Flathead Lake. "We can drive into these mountains and ask the locals about the rumors. It might not take long to narrow down the possibilities."

"Maybe, but it'll be like finding a needle in a haystack."

The professor raised a finger. "Not exactly, Walter. You see, needles and hay have a similar appearance, making visual discernment difficult, while a laboratory in the mountains would have a unique—"

"Prof." Walter rolled his eyes. "It was just an expression."

The professor lowered his finger. "Sorry, Walter. My mind is in analytical mode. Even idioms are not spared." He turned to Mrs. Bannister and pointed at a road to the right. "Marilyn, proceed eastbound on highway eighty-three. We are looking for Echo Lake Road on the left. Obviously a secret lab will not be labeled, so we'll have to be on the lookout for a newly forged road, perhaps a crude path for construction vehicles or a foot trail with a security gate."

The professor's phone rang. He grabbed it from his belt and lifted it to his ear. "Charles Hamilton here. ... Yes. I am the professor. ... Yes, Karen. Go on." He snatched a pen from the dashboard and scribbled on the map. "Yes. We will find it. ... No, I'm not sure how far we are. Can you put the owner on the phone? ... Thank you."

As he paused, Walter and Mrs. Bannister glanced at each other, then back at the professor. Goose bumps popped up on Walter's arms. He leaned back, drumming the seat with his fingers. Finally, the professor continued. "Yes. We are on highway eighty-three. ... Very good. I believe we can be there in about twenty minutes if the snow doesn't delay us. ... Yes, it might help if you plow the road. Thank you."

The professor clipped the phone back in place and smiled, his wild white eyebrows lifting. "A young lady named Karen is at a farmhouse near Camp Misery. She said that William is free from his captor, and she will take us to him."

Walter pumped his fist. "All right!"

"Thank God!" Mrs. Bannister placed a trembling hand over her heart and heaved a sigh. "Which way?"

The professor snapped his arm forward. "Straight ahead, Marilyn, and hurry. William is not out of the woods, yet."

. . . . . .

Billy shrank deeper into the shadowy darkness while Ashley marched toward the panel, her hands behind her back. In her flowing gown, she swept across the floor like a gray ghost, holding something in her hidden hands.

Dr. Conner squinted at her. "You can't be the anchor. You've never been trained. It took Derrick three times before he could hang on to anything."

"He trained with monkeys," Ashley countered as she stepped into the control area. "They were scared and tried to pull away."

Dr. Conner felt Ashley's gown. "You're in an organic robe. Didn't you bring Karen?"

Ashley lowered her head. "No, I didn't."

Dr. Conner glared at her dark silhouette. "What's going on?"

Ashley kept her hands behind her back. "Nothing," she replied, gazing at the display. "What's going on here?"

Dr. Conner tilted his head and looked past her. Billy followed his line of sight to the back of the lab room where an open door led into a brightly lit hallway. Dr. Conner grabbed Ashley's shoulder. "Where are they?"

Ashley stiffened in his grasp, but her voice was casual, almost indifferent. "I honestly don't know. Long gone, from what I can tell. Their hats and coats are missing."

Dr. Conner glanced at his watch. "It can't be that long. It's been less than an hour since we went into the Omega door cave." He ran toward the exit, passing Billy's hiding place, and grabbed a coat from a hook on the wall. "Devin can wait. Those girls will freeze in this weather."

He pushed his arms through the coat sleeves and threw open the door. After fishing his keys from his pocket, he flicked on a tiny light hooked to the ring. "Maybe I can track them in the snow." As the door began to swing shut, he added, "The laser's still running, and the microphone's on. Just keep an eye on the data and report anything unusual."

When the door slammed, Billy pivoted toward Ashley as she stared into the chamber. The stately girl's gaze swept the shadowy cavern like a lighthouse beacon in the fog.

She placed a palm on her chest as though feeling for her own heartbeat or covering it to keep others from hearing it pound. She cleared her throat and spoke straight into the dim room, her voice haunting, yet sweet. "You can come out now."

Billy gulped. *Is she talking to me?* He tried to swallow again, but it felt like a grapefruit had suddenly lodged in his throat.

Her voice continued, this time louder and more fervent. "Billy Bannister, my name is Ashley. I'm a friend of Bonnie's. I know you're here. Come on out. You can trust me."

245

Billy stayed low and peeked around the edge of the box. Trusting her made no sense. It looked like she was working with that creep.

Ashley pulled her hands out from behind her back and held up a notebook. "This is Bonnie's journal, Billy. She says that dragons can sense certain presences. They can sense when another dragon is near, and they can sense danger." She turned directly toward Billy's hiding place. It seemed that she spoke right to him, her voice calling like an alluring echo in a faraway valley. "Do you sense danger, Billy Bannister? Am I a threat to you?"

Billy kept silent. Yes, Ashley was right about the sense of danger. It died when Dr. Conner shut the door. How did she know so much? Did Bonnie really write stuff about dragons in her journal? Even if she did, it still didn't explain how Ashley knew he was there.

He rose slowly, his gaze meeting hers through a curtain of shifting darkness. She walked toward him and held out the journal, her expression soft and warm. She placed the journal in Billy's hands. "We have work to do." Her gentle tone matched her kind face. "But there's something here you have to read first."

Yielding to Ashley's serious, formal manner, Billy reined in his suspicions and bowed his head. "If Bonnie wrote it, then I'm sure it's worth reading."

She set a hand on his shoulder, motioning upward with her head, her voice still quiet. "Did you see any girls up there, a redheaded teenager and three younger girls?"

The blinking lights reflected in her dark wide pupils. He nodded. "Yeah, I saw them. Karen, right?"

"Right." Ashley pressed closer, so close he could smell a hint of toothpaste on her breath. Her nearness brought a strange sensation, like she was drawing warmth from his body, or like she was trying to read his mind by extracting his thoughts through his skin.

Her voice grew a notch louder. "Were they okay?"

Billy pulled back a little to keep his own breath from singeing her lips. "Yeah, they were fine, heading to a farmhouse Karen knows. I don't know if Dr. Conner will follow them or not when he sees what happened up there."

Ashley released his shoulder and stepped back. "What happened? And how did you find your way down here?"

Billy shifted his weight from foot to foot. "Well, that's a long story, but here's the short version. Karen helped me escape from a car trunk and showed me the stairway entrance.

246

But the girls are all safe. I dispatched the guy who locked me in the trunk and brought me here."

Ashley blinked. "You killed him?"

Focusing on the floor, Billy nodded. When Ashley didn't say anything, he looked at her again. Sadness clouded her expression, and the corners of her lips wilted. She opened the notebook in Billy's hands, flipped a few pages, and tapped her finger on the words. "It starts here. You'll know when it's finished." With tears forming in her eyes, she pulled aside Billy's coat and fingered the hem of his shirt. "Is it cotton?"

"Yeah, I think so."

"Good. I already saw your jeans. They should work fine, but I'll get a robe and a cotton belt for you anyway. If you have any metal fasteners, they'll be gone when you're restored." She turned her gaze to the middle of the room and gestured toward the pedestal. "You were listening in on Doc's conversation. Do you understand what's going on?"

Billy took a step closer to the center. A familiar surge of nausea flooded his stomach. He nodded and waved a finger toward the candlestone. "I think I figured it out. I'm supposed to go inside that gem somehow and get Bonnie."

"That's right." She pointed toward the lit hallway. "That's the girls' dorm. Why don't you go there to read? I have to pay someone a visit. I'll be back in a few minutes."

Billy raised a hand. "Wait. How did Bonnie get in there? And how do I go in? Can Devin hurt her? And what was that about losing brain function?"

Ashley set a gentle hand on the side of Billy's head. "Hold your questions and be patient. I'll tell you a little at a time. Too much information can make your brain choke."

Ashley smiled again before turning away. She walked to a panel and turned off the laser. She then hurried on to a door that was similar to the one she had pointed out, a closed door on the opposite side of the huge room. She unlocked it, went inside, and shut it behind her.

With his finger lodged in the pages, Billy tucked the journal under his arm and marched straight to the light. After entering the hallway, he set the journal on the floor, pulled off his coat, and sat on the tile floor with his back against a side wall. He took a deep breath and settled down to read.

✵   ✵   ✵   ✵   ✵   ✵

Ashley knocked on the first door on the left. "Daddy? Are you there?"

No one answered. She tapped again, this time with a bit more force. "Daddy? It's Ashley."

Still no answer.

Ashley reached for the doorknob, turned it slowly, and swung the door open. As she stuck her head into the dim room, a push of warm, stuffy air fanned her face.

Next to a bed, a single lamp pitched a slender ray of light on a man's sleeping form, the dim yellow beam shining from a miserably inadequate bulb. A single fly buzzed around the lamp's black shade in lazy, elliptical orbits.

Ashley stepped inside and watched the fly for a moment. How had it found its way deep into the heart of this mountain in the dead of winter? For that matter, why would anyone choose to live in a dark cave, far from life and love?

Her eyes followed the light back to the bed and her peaceful grandfather. An open book rode the tide of his rhythmic wheezing, its pages lying on his thick belly.

Ashley knelt at his bedside and tenderly pushed a strand of hair from his forehead, then stroked his thin, silvery mane.

"Daddy," she whispered. "It's Ashley. Can you hear me?"

His open pajama top exposed a forest of white hair and a wide, red scar, evidence of his heart surgery years ago.

Ashley laid her head on his once strengthening chest, now sunken and so much weaker than just a few days ago. She began crying, her heart ripping open in despair. "Oh, Daddy! I'm so sorry! I … I tried to make the receptors work. I really tried. But I failed you. I'm so sorry!"

She listened to his labored heartbeats as she cried on and on, tears rolling down her cheeks and wetting his pajama top. It was all right. She would take care of his shirt for him, just like she had a hundred times before.

Only a few months earlier she'd thought she would never have to be his nurse again. Now she didn't care if she had to wash him or change his clothes. She just wanted her Daddy.

249

Her gaze lingered on the complimentary colors of injury and decay, the angry red scar and the mat of white hair as they rose and fell in time with his labored breaths.

Still on her knees, and with her head resting on his chest, she tried to speak again, anguish filling her squeaking, faltering voice. "Red … will be made whi … white … Red will be—" She squeezed her eyes shut and opened her mouth in a silent, spasmodic wail.

When she finally settled herself, something brushed against her hair. Was it that fly? She raised her hand to shoo it away, but her fingers swiped against flesh. A hand? She grabbed it eagerly and lifted her head. Her grandfather smiled and stroked her knuckles.

"Ashley," he said softly, "I'm sorry you have to see me like this."

Ashley kissed his hand. "Oh, Daddy!" New tears flooded her eyes, and her voice cracked. "It's ... it's all my fault. I couldn't get the photoreceptors to work, and now you're ... you're—"

"Dying?"

Keeping her stare on their clasped hands, she nodded.

"I know you wanted me to live so we could be together, Ashley. I wanted it, too. But I guess God has other ideas." He lifted himself higher on his pillow, and his voice deepened. "Don't worry about me. I'm ready to face my maker. Remember? Amazing grace, how sweet the sound, that saved a wretch like me."

She nodded again, her stare locked on their hands. "I remember."

He lifted her hand to his lips and kissed it softly. "Maybe someday you'll sing it with me. Even if it's in heaven."

Ashley gazed at his face. His eyes and gentle smile melted away her anguish. She wanted to sing with him, to join his happy bass and cry out, "I once was lost, but now am found; was blind, but now I see." But she couldn't. ... She couldn't.

A soft breeze whispered through her tangled, flyaway hair. Above, a ceiling fan lazily paddled through the room's thick warmth. She wanted to stay like this forever, to squeeze out every possible moment in his presence. But she didn't have much time left. Doc would be back soon, and she had to get some information, the story her grandfather had never been willing to tell before.

She gazed into his pale gray eyes and again pushed her fingers through his wispy hair. "Daddy, what really happened to my mom and dad? Something's come up, and I really need to know."

He looked at a wall for a moment before fixing his eyes on hers again. "I guess I'd better tell you before I die."

"Yes. Yes, please."

"Are you sure you can take a surprise, I mean, a real shock?"

Ashley wiped her wet cheeks with her free hand. "After what I've seen, I think I'm ready for anything."

To Summon a Dragon

Bonnie looked high above into the candlestone's upper walls—dark crystalline planes that created an angled, bending sky. A stream of white light poured into the gem's stratosphere like a perpetual shooting star, striking the inner core and streaming around its black skin. Then, like sparkling dew rolling off polished obsidian, it spilled into a channel that disappeared into a blazing horizon—a waterfall of dancing sparkles splashing into a distant river of light.

Through the dark hours, she had grown accustomed to her sunless, moonless prison, a domain where gloom held sway over the remnants of light that lived and moved within. The slayer lurked. She had seen his angry sparks, sometimes peering around hidden planes, sometimes slowly approaching, then backing away.

It didn't take long to figure out that her singing kept the slayer at bay. With each musical phrase, her shimmering light created a faint dome of luminescence that built her confidence and made the protective glow persist. Adding to her unearthly light, her ring's dark red radiance pulsed like a beating heart, resonating in time with her song.

During a quiet moment, as excited particles from the laboratory lights continued to flow, Bonnie once again sensed the slayer's growing presence, an increase in staccato flashes and fleeing shadows. She released a stream of song, but this time he didn't retreat.

He crept across the glass floor, as though testing his barriers, and stopped at a safe distance. "I have been speaking to your father." His static-crusted voice wasn't as irritating as usual. "It seems that your half-breed boyfriend is in hand. My old friend, Palin, was able to capture him, as I expected."

Bonnie ended her song. "Billy has nothing to do with this. Why don't you just leave him alone?"

"How little you know. Or should I say, how much you pretend not to know?" Devin drew closer, bending Bonnie's shield until it halted his progress. "The boy will dive in here to get you, and we will attach to him and ride out to freedom."

"Not if I can help it," Bonnie said, backing away. "You can't even come close to me anymore. I'll go with him alone, and we'll leave you behind."

Devin let out a spiteful snort. "Oh, really? Do you know where a diver enters? I'll see him first. He knows nothing about creating shields, so I'll be able to attach to him, and we'll leave you here in this cozy prison."

Bonnie's light pulsed rapidly. "He'll find a way. Even if you do go without me, he'll come back."

"Not so fast, my dear. There's something else you don't know, another reason why they always send females in here. The male animals they tested couldn't be restored properly.

They always lost brain function, making them simpletons, or worse." A flash of light erupted from one side of his electric body, like a long electrostatic finger. "I saved that part of the conversation for you. Listen."

The light sparked and flowed into Bonnie's mind.

"But the male chimp was a blithering idiot when he returned," her father said. "All the males lost more than half their brain function during restoration."

When the light blinked off, Devin's energy field throbbed, as if he were laughing with delight. "Your sweetheart will turn into a gentle rutabaga. He won't care about diving back in to fetch you out. He'll be dribbling from sippy cups and soiling baby diapers for the rest of his life."

As the vivid image the slayer painted penetrated Bonnie's mind, her light dissipated. The horrible vision lingered, and her protective dome faded.

255

Devin slithered closer. The words to her song flew from memory. She tried to battle, tried to think through the turmoil of doubts and fears that waged war with her courage. Could it be true? How could Devin conjure a recording like that?

Bonnie finally managed to hum. The familiar tune trickled out on trembling light waves. After a few seconds, the words flowed to mind, then into the glowing stream. "If I make my bed in hell, behold, thou art there. If I take—"

"Don't sing that blasted song again!" Devin shouted. "No ancient Bible ditty will do you any good in this hellhole." His light-filled body floated back and forth in Bonnie's field of vision, like a man pacing in anger. "God isn't here. I should know. I've been in this forsaken place for weeks, and there's nothing but gloom and despair. There is no salvation within these walls."

Devin paused, and his voice softened, flowing into her mind like a gentle shower, smooth, yet dripping with malevolence. "But you can still save your boyfriend and yourself if you're willing to make a deal."

Bonnie's light flashed. "I don't make deals with the devil."

Devin took a step back, but his voice remained calm. "Fair enough. I know you don't trust me, but you heard your father's unguarded words for yourself. It might help if I explain why he's correct. Males don't translate well. Rather than adapt to their transluminated state, they fight against it. It isn't an act of the will; it's just the way they're built. I can see it in their light patterns when they come in. They're twisted and shaky. They don't have enough time in here to settle down. When the system tries to restore them, it can't translate the agitated state of their minds, and their brains aren't reconstructed properly. A few have even died."

"So what about you? Won't you lose brain function if you leave?"

"I've adapted. I felt my brain fighting it at first, but over time I've gotten it under control. It took a few weeks, but now my light patterns are smooth and even, so I'm not in an agitated state. Your mongrel friend, however, will be fully agitated. I wager that he'll come in here ready for a fight. His heart is full of rage."

He paused again, and his light began swirling like a pinwheel in a soft breeze. A thin stream of light oozed from Bonnie's glow as if pulled by Devin's bright whirlpool. His soft voice continued, rising slightly with the victorious tone of discovery. "And you know about that rage, don't you? Perhaps better than I?"

Bonnie edged away. Devin knew. Somehow her thoughts had spilled into the open, and the truth was out. Billy was vulnerable. She redoubled the guard on her mind. "What kind of deal are you offering?"

Devin returned to his human form and grinned, the expression of a riverboat gambler gathering his winnings. "I can't get close to you because of all that infernal singing you do. Attachment is impossible unless you let your defenses down, so for your part, you'll have to stop singing. And for my part, I'll show Billy the secret to leaving with his brain intact."

He waited for a moment, his flashing lips stretching into a thin line. "You're a smart girl. That's why I've never been able to defeat you. I'm sure you'll figure out that you have to trust me on this one."

Bonnie's light sparked and sputtered. She glared at him, watchful of his mind-reading trick. What was he up to? Obviously he wanted to get out, and the key was through attachment. But couldn't he just try to attach to Billy like he had said? Why did he want to attach to her?

257

No, she didn't trust him, but she wanted to know his secret, the way to protect Billy's brain from damage. What could she do to discover it? Let him attach? No. The very thought sent bursts of shivering light across her body. Here she was, a glittering pebble in a twisting black kaleidoscope, confused in a surreal existence and having to deal with a silky-tongued liar. Maybe there was another way. Maybe she could find that friendly light again and ask him. He had helped her before.

"I'll think about it." She turned and hurried away.

* * * * * *

Billy leaned over the neat, flowing script, the shadow of his head dimming the page as he mentally prepared himself for the words in his lap. Of course, Bonnie was a gifted writer, possessing a dragon-inspired talent far beyond that of a normal girl, but Ashley's manner when she gave him the journal made him think this entry might be more than he could handle.

He focused on the top line. It was a prayer, and although he didn't know much about praying, he guessed he should read it with reverence.

My Prayer for Billy

Dearest Heavenly Father, my heart longs for your presence, for you to sit by my side and whisper in my ear. Grant me counsel, the deep wisdom that listens to my heart and understands my pain in the midst of my groanings.

I have a friend who stands as close as a brother, a brave soul. Yet, you know him better than I. He is Billy Bannister, the son of Clefspeare, a dragon. I have seen in him the heart of a warrior, a knight's squire who follows the code, ready to die if need be to slay the forces of evil and rescue vulnerable maidens, brokenhearted widows, and grieving orphans. He is gallant, loyal, and true, sacrificing his esteem, forfeiting his comfort, even spilling his blood. But, what color is his soul?

Tell me, Father, holy and true, I have borne in my heart this ache for so long! My dear friend has a desperate need, and I have seen it. How can I be his accuser, condemning the one who has gladly poured out his blood in my stead? But shall I deny my witness? There is a darkness, a gnawing void behind those eyes of steel. And even in those placid pools, I see turmoil, uncertainty, even pride. Oh, how can love and vexation so violently mix, a brew of man and beast stirred in a cauldron of scales and flesh?

Yes, there is violence, a rage that does not rest, for he battles in the fields of his mind, resolutely standing his ground, his faith in the old ways, the ways of the code, the ways of the dragon, the ways of his father. Yet, his father has left him an orphan, a squire without a knight, and the cruelty of his passing has never ceased to consume his standing as he guzzles from the old wineskins on which he relies.

It is not a slayer who haunts his thoughts and dreams. Dare I ask it? Shall I be so bold? Is it you, my father, the pursuer of men's hearts, who brings war to his battlefield? Are you the fire that will purge his pride, his reliance on things of this world, honorable deeds, yet filthy rags in your sight? Will you teach him what pleases you? Will you tell him about weapons from above, the sword of truth and the shield of faith? Will you give him new wineskins, pouring into his heart the wine from above, the blood of the sacred covenant? Will you make him a knight, dressed in holy raiment, fit to take a seat at your table?

I fear the battle, Lord, lest you slay him with penetrating light, driving your two-edged sword deep into his fragile bosom, and searching out the dark recesses of his heart. For who can stand when your word declares judgment? How will he survive unless someone takes him to wash in the river, the wellspring of eternal life?

259

Who am I? How can I take him to your fountain? You know him far better than I, yet I feel I know his heart as well as my own. From dragon to dragon, I feel when he is near, as though his heart pounds in my own breast. When he touches me, the heat of his passion and the fire of his breath spread warming flames all around this cold orphan's crying soul. Yet I am not his counselor, nor his judge. I stand as one who bears a gift but knows not how to give it, for though I am emboldened in my closet, in his presence I melt like wax.

Dear Father, I confess. I confess that I love him. Yet how little I understand these words. We are bound by prophecy, destined for oneness, and this virgin's heart quakes at the thought. My heart longs for his, yet I know we cannot be one until the sun chases away his shadows, for light and darkness can have no fellowship.

Oh, Father! Whisper now in my ear. Shall I tell him of your saving grace? If I do, will he respond to you or to his passions? Would my feminine voice distract him from hearing yours? Would my face be his vision, or would he see the face of Christ? Oh, Father! Should such a maiden take this duty, to tell a heroic soldier that his scarlet soul needs to be made white?

And now, Heavenly Father, I ask you to take my entreaty and use it as you will. Whether in a whisper, a shout, or a song, let my voice be yours. Let my words be your balm. Use them to soften his heart, that you may inscribe your name there with indelible blood. Enlighten his mind, that truth may reside there forever. Cleanse his soul with fire and water, burning away the old and washing away the scarlet stain, that your spirit may indwell, empower, and preserve. Whatever must be done, whatever pain you must bring to make red into white, I pray that you will make the mortal squire into a holy knight.

Billy closed the notebook and hugged it close to his chest. His body trembled, ten thousand pounds of pressure building up inside and ready to burst.

A tear made its way to his eyes, then another. He looked up and sniffed, trying to blink away the tears and focus on the blank wall across the corridor—focus on anything but his many failures. Through the blur, a vision of Bonnie coalesced on the wall, her wings spread in full flight. She begged him to take something from her hands, but her gift was fuzzy, unfocused. He leaned closer until the object sharpened into a magnificent sword, the one and only Excalibur. The image was the portrait he had worked on in his studio, now complete and brought to life, and Excalibur's shining blade pierced his heart.

What were the professor's words that day? *It was bestowed to you as a gift from above. It was meant for you to wield in battle.*

Billy had refused the sword. He had rejected a precious gift, a weapon of righteousness.

And now look at the mess everyone is in.

His inner rage was real, and Bonnie knew it well. Even Palin with his sneering accusation could see his private darkness. *You're just like me, boy.* Billy had killed his accuser. He had scrapped his training, the professor's words of wisdom he was supposed to lock tightly in his heart. He refused to oppose his enemy face-to-face.

Cries of *murderer* came from all around, like a lynch mob demanding his death. He tried to swat them away. Oh, how he longed for freedom, for innocence, the purity he had always seen in Bonnie. But she couldn't bestow her integrity. She couldn't let him borrow her virtue, not even a slice of the righteousness that had always kept her in lasting peace.

The vision of Bonnie's eyes pierced Billy's own. She whispered the words the professor had uttered not so long ago. "Nor can I lend you my faith."

Billy laid his head on Bonnie's journal and cried. Rage, hate, fear, loneliness, all dissolved into his tears and splashed onto the precious book. Lifting his head, he gasped for breath. "I … I don't know how to have faith! Help … Help me believe in you!" As his tears subsided, he turned his eyes upward.

Above the ceiling lay countless tons of earth and rock, unseen, yet waiting to fall on him and crush his body. He'd always imagined God as that crushing rock. But Bonnie had painted God with majestic words of love, more like the sun and sky—beautiful, limitless, and forever giving light and warmth.

As he took a deep breath and released it slowly, a few unbidden fiery sparks flew out. He tried to fashion a prayer in his

261

mind, but all the thees and thous refused to come together. Would God even listen to a dragon boy? Did he really care as much as Bonnie thought he did?

Billy looked straight up with unblinking eyes. "I don't have much faith," he said softly. "Maybe you can lend me a little of yours."

*   *   *   *   *   *

How will we know her?" Walter asked as the Jeep sped down the road through the heavily falling snowflakes.

The professor pulled his coat closed and zipped it. "Karen told me she has red hair and that she would keep her hood down so we could see it. She also has three younger girls with her. They should be easy to locate."

Mrs. Bannister pointed ahead. "That must be it." She slowed the Jeep, careful to avoid sliding on the thin sheet of white, and parked behind another SUV just beyond the farmhouse driveway. A plowed drift blocked the entrance, preventing them from getting closer to the house.

Walter jumped from the Jeep and hurdled the drift, while Mrs. Bannister helped the professor through the snow on his crutches. When Walter came within fifty feet of the doorstep, he spotted Karen on the wooden porch passing by a big barrel stuffed with firewood. Three smaller girls crowded close to the redhead, and a man walked beside her, gripping her shoulder and herding the girls toward the snow-covered road. Except for a rumbling tractor pulling a snowplow toward a distant barn, the place seemed deserted.

"Wait!" Walter held up a hand and sprinted toward them.

The man stopped, tilting his head and squinting. Walter skidded to a stop within reach. *Bonnie's father!*

Dr. Conner faced Walter and gave him an uneasy smile. "Well, if it isn't Walter Foley. It's a small world, isn't it?"

Walter glowered at him. "Too small, I think." He planted his fists on his hips and turned toward the redhead. "Are you Karen?"

Karen tightened her lips and nodded.

Dr. Conner pulled her closer. "And how could you possibly know Karen?"

Walter folded his arms across his chest. "Like you said, Dr. Conner. It's a small world."

The professor hobbled up beside Walter and grabbed Dr. Conner's wrist. "Unhand this girl."

Dr. Conner jerked away. "Why should I? This is my daughter." He waved toward the other three shivering girls. "They're all my daughters."

Mrs. Bannister brushed snow off the shortest one's head and knelt to rebutton her coat. "And they're all freezing!"

Thick puffs of white billowed through the falling snow as the professor spoke. "Whether or not they are really your daughters, Dr. Conner, is immaterial to me. The eldest called me with an urgent message, and I believe you are the cause of her distress."

"Ridiculous!" He pulled Karen's hood up over her soaked hair. "They were out playing in the snow and went too far. I just found them, and I'm taking them home."

The professor lifted his brow, his eyelids drooping just a shade. "Indeed. And you told us we could visit Bonnie anytime we wished. Your card, however, carried the address of some rather unsavory characters. They did not greet us well, so we decided to pay you a visit to recommend that you correct your business cards, lest other visitors find the same rude greeting."

He gestured toward their Jeep. "Shall we drive to your home and complete our visit? I'm certain Bonnie will be glad to see us."

Walter grinned. The professor's smooth sarcasm was biting, yet sprinkled with gentlemanly charm. There was no way Dr. Conner could refuse.

Dr. Conner let out a long sigh. "Okay, okay."

Mrs. Bannister hurried toward the Jeep. "The path is clear now. I'll drive as close as I can and pick everyone up."

The professor smiled down at the trembling redhead. "Karen, I am at your service. You may speak freely." He gestured with his head toward Dr. Conner. "You need not fear this man. I assure you that I will keep you from harm."

Karen cast a doubtful glance at the professor's crutches and smiled uneasily.

264   Dr. Conner's voice shook with anger. "How dare you talk to my daughter that way? I'm her protector, not you, old man!" He grabbed Karen's hand. "Forget what I said. They're coming with me, and you can just—"

"Dr. Conner!" The professor's eyes blazed. "I suggest you reconsider." When Mrs. Bannister pulled the Jeep close, the professor turned to Walter. "Please fetch the flower box."

"Sure, Prof." He hustled toward the Jeep while glancing back at the action.

The professor shifted on his crutches and faced Dr. Conner. "A father certainly has protection rights, as you suggest. All rights, however, are forfeited if a child is abused."

"Abused?" Dr. Conner's voice spiked. "I've never abused her, and she knows it."

Walter returned, carrying the flower box. The professor handed one of his crutches to him. While leaning on the other crutch, the professor opened the box and withdrew Excalibur.

At the moment he touched the hilt, the great sword began to glow. The professor dropped the other crutch and steadied himself on his good leg, holding Excalibur in ready stance with both hands. Dr. Conner took a step backwards, his eyes wide.

"Now," the professor said as the sword brightened, "I will ask her myself." He gazed at Karen and spoke tenderly. "Young lady, what is troubling you, and why did you call me? Do you wish to be free from this man?"

She jumped to the professor's side and grabbed him around the waist, shivering. Dr. Conner stepped toward them, but the professor blocked him with the sword. "I suggest you halt."

Dr. Conner stopped. Excalibur's spectacular glow reflected in his frightened eyes.

The professor continued. "It seems that the maiden has spoken quite clearly, even in silence. So now, if you will acquiesce, sir, and do what I ask, I will put the sword away."

Dr. Conner spun and ran, slipping once and stopping his fall with his hands on the ground. Both legs churning, he dashed toward his SUV.

Mrs. Bannister hopped out from behind the wheel and ushered the three younger girls toward the Jeep.

Walter grabbed the professor's crutch from the ground. "We can't let him get away." He tossed both crutches into the rear of the Jeep and hustled back to help the professor. He and Karen help the professor climb into the front seat, then both squeezed into the back with the three girls.

As Mrs. Bannister drove, Karen scooted behind her. "I know the way. Just stay on this road for a few minutes. I'll let you know where to turn." After a couple of miles of slipping and sliding, Karen pointed to the right. "Up that path. We'd better hurry. Doc might have gone in the back way."

265

Mrs. Bannister stepped on the gas. The Jeep managed the first part of the slope easily. "I hope we can make it up there."

"No problem," Karen said. "This Jeep has Quadra-Drive. I saw a Grand Marquis make it to the top. I'm sure we can."

"What will happen if he gets there before we do?" Mrs. Bannister asked.

Karen pulled her hood down and leaned forward, her teeth chattering. "Billy sneaked into the lab to try to find Bonnie. I don't know what Ashley would do, but if Doc catches him, there's sure to be trouble."

"Ashley?" Mrs. Bannister said. "Who's Ashley?"

"Doc calls her a lab assistant. but she really runs the place."

Walter shifted to the edge of his seat. "How did Billy escape from that creep, Palin?"

Karen sighed. "You'll find out." When they reached the mountaintop, she said, "Turn left here." She pointed toward an arch of rocks. "That's the lab entrance, but it's a long way down a bunch of stairs and then through an even longer tunnel. I'll show you the way, but the other girls shouldn't go. They're real tired."

The professor touched Mrs. Bannister's arm. "Marilyn, do you mind staying? I assure you that Walter and I can handle this. We will find your son and restore him to you."

As she drove into the makeshift driveway, Mrs. Bannister took a deep breath. "I do mind, but it's the best plan. The girls need to stay warm."

Walter spotted a burned-out car well ahead. "What's that?"

Karen shook her head sadly. "It used to be a Mercury Grand Marquis. Palin had Billy in the trunk with a bunch of gas cans. Billy set it on fire."

"And what happened to Palin?" the professor asked.

"He went up in flames. He's dead."

The professor's face paled. He leaned over the seat, speaking earnestly. "Tell me, did you see it? Did William intentionally kill the man?"

Karen nodded. "It was pretty scary. We girls all ran away."

The professor clutched the seat. "But was it in face-to-face combat?"

Karen shrank back, and her voice lowered to a whisper. "Not really. Billy had already escaped from the trunk, and we could've all sneaked into the woods. The guy's back was turned." Karen rolled a hand into a fist. "But he deserved it, right? Wouldn't he have killed Billy if he had the chance?"

"Oh, no doubt. That foul skunk would likely have killed all of you if he thought it would help him achieve his goals." The professor took a deep breath before continuing. "Yes, he deserved to die, but the issue is not one of justification. It is a matter of valor, the code of a knight, of facing an enemy head-on rather than sneaking up on his unguarded flank. It's also a matter of obeying a command, of heeding prophecy."

He set a trembling hand on Merlin's Diary situated on a box between him and the driver's seat. As the Jeep came to a stop next to the blackened car, he pulled the book onto his lap. "Marilyn, Walter, we must call for help."

"Call who?" Mrs. Bannister asked. "The police? Walter's Dad?"

"No." He opened the diary to the prayer on the first page. "I have the translation here on a card. Please grant me silence as I read." In a clear voice, the professor read the prayer. "God, my lord, do send my plea to dragons' ears both far and nigh. Send me help I ask on knee. Transluminate me lest I die."

When the professor fell silent, Walter pulled on the back of his teacher's seat. "What's wrong, Prof? Why did you call for a dragon?"

The professor ran his palm over the rough parchment. "It's part of what I could not reveal to you earlier, Walter. A conditional prophecy has been fulfilled, and it seems that we will soon see a veritable eruption of crises, too many for us to handle alone."

"But can Clefspeare get here in time to help?"

A faraway look took over the professor's expression. "I don't know, Walter. I just don't know. I merely followed the prophecy's suggestion." He turned a couple of pages and placed a finger on the top line of text. "I can read this one to you now. I have been given leave to reveal prophecies already set in motion." The professor cleared his throat.

The child of doubt, still chained, still torn
Must choose his fateful path;
To take revenge and valor scorn,
Or quell his heart of wrath?

And should he choose the wanton way,
Appeasing vengeance due,
He sets the course for Judgment Day
And brings the end in view.

Yet hope remains, a dragon's aid
May come to quench the fire.
A fervent summons rightly prayed
Will call them to the squire.

But make no haste to quote the prayer
For dragons here to fly,
For if the child acquits the slayer,
The dragons called shall die.

"That one's not too hard to figure out," Walter said. "I think I liked it better when it was confusing."

"What is that book?" Karen asked, leaning forward. "It sounds scary, like something real bad's going to happen."

"It is a very special diary," the professor replied, "an old, prophetic book. Its author uses a simple rhyme and meter scheme, but his prophecies are deep and mysterious. And, yes, I would say that the coming of Judgment Day is something about which we might all be alarmed. I don't think he's speaking of a literal end-of-the-world scenario, but even with poetic license, I'm sure it could be very bad, indeed."

Mrs. Bannister took a deep breath and regripped the steering wheel. "Well, you'd better get going. There's no telling if Billy's in trouble or not."

Without another word, the professor, Walter, and Karen opened the doors and exited the Jeep. Karen led the way toward the arch of stones, crunching through the deep snowdrifts. Walter held the box containing Excalibur under one arm and used the other to steady the professor as he hobbled on crutches along the slippery trail.

269

As they neared the entrance, the ground shuddered. Walter halted and stopped the professor at a clearing. "Prof, do you feel something?"

He nodded. "I believe I do."

The ground swayed, then rocked. Walter widened his stance and bent his knees, keeping a firm grip on the professor's arm.

The professor spoke in a hushed tone. "It's a tremor, Walter. A slight one, to be sure, but it could be a harbinger of events to come."

"A tremor?" Karen asked. "You mean, like an earthquake?"

"Yes. It seems that our local Judgment Day might already be dawning."

THROUGH A GLASS DARKLY

As Billy approached the candlestone, tingling weakness spread through his arms and legs. Even with stabbing pain shooting through his back and sickening gases churning his stomach, he allowed himself to be drawn to the gem's unearthly pull.

A thin swirl of barely visible light streamed into a dense grouping of the stone's minute facets. It looked like a tiny vacuum cleaner sucking in a trail of dancing pixies from all around the room. On the other side of the gem, a steady, dim beam poured out, as if someone inside the stone had strangled the pixies, flattened their corpses with a mallet, and squeezed their bodies into a shaft of dead light.

The nausea worsened, and a throbbing headache pounded his brain. Even with dozens of odd gadgets surrounding him in the cold shadows, he could focus on only one thought. Bonnie was in that stone, and he had to set her free, no matter how bad the pain. As sick as he felt while standing on the outside, there was no telling how much it would hurt to actually be inside that rock.

"Billy," Ashley called from the darkness on the other side of the room. A shaft of light from an open door provided a backdrop for her beckoning silhouette. "You need a robe. Come over here."

He hurried toward Ashley. With the hood of her robe raised and her face still in the shadows, she looked like a cowled monk.

She held out another robe. "Take this and pull it on over your clothes. It should protect you from the candlestone's effects." She unfolded the robe and held it by its shoulders. "And you'll have to swap your belt. The robe has its own sash, but I wrapped an extra cotton belt in it for your jeans. You'll lose your metal buckle during the process, and we don't want your pants falling off when you come back."

Billy replaced his belt and pulled the robe over his head, pushing his arms through the sleeves. The shoulders were comfortable, but with the hemline dropping to just above his knees, it wasn't a perfect fit.

Ashley smoothed out the wrinkles. "It'll have to do." She grabbed a cuff on one of Billy's sleeves and straightened it around his arm, then took his hand and drew it close. "This ring looks a lot like Bonnie's, except bigger and older."

"Yeah. We have matching rings, sort of a dragon friendship thing."

She rubbed the gem's surface with her thumb. "What kind of stone is it?"

"It's called a rubellite. It's a kind of tourmaline."

"A rubellite? Where do you find those?"

Billy curled his fingers and slowly pulled his hand away. "My dad brought it to me." He pointed toward the candlestone in the central lab area. "Shouldn't we get going?"

Ashley took a step toward the domes, but a sudden jolt threw her back. She took a long step to keep from falling and spread her hands, balancing with her knees bent. "Oh, no!"

Billy slapped his hand against the wall to brace himself. The lights swayed, and vibrations drilled into his feet. "What's going on?"

Ashley grabbed Billy around his waist and pulled him toward the doorframe. She sank to her knees, dragging him down with her. "It felt like an earthquake," she said as the two huddled under the frame. "It's happened once before."

Steady ripples ran through Billy's back as he leaned against the frame's side. A gentle tapping of grit sounded from the drop ceiling. "Could this place collapse?"

"It's not out of the question." After a few seconds of calm, she took Billy's hand and rose. "The tremor's over, but there's a chance another one will follow. We'll have to hurry."

"C'mon, then." With his hand still in Ashley's, he led the way toward the candlestone. "Let's get transluminated!"

273

* * * * * *

Bonnie cast a glance around a crystal wall and looked down one of the dark halls. She hoped for a trace of light, a friendly shadow of luminescence. In this murky house, it seemed that light itself was a shadow, shades of mortal essence cast by wandering phantoms.

In the distance, a trail of light disappeared around a corner. She hurried along the dark corridor, but there were dozens of corners, some leading to abrupt dead ends. After an unsuccessful foray into a narrow cubbyhole, she spied the light again near the end of a wide hallway. It turned out of view, its sparkling trail vanishing in a corridor on the right.

"Wait! Please, wait!" Bonnie's thought stream raced after the glimmer.

The glowing trail halted. Bonnie dashed ahead, her light flashing like a strobe. "May I talk to you again?"

"Come no closer, child."

Bonnie stopped just before reaching the turn. The glimmer spoke again, this time joyfully, like a delighted grandfather. "What do you seek, my frightened little lamb?"

She waited a second, allowing her light pulses to settle. "I seek advice. Devin wants to make a deal with me."

"I see." The voice was slow and deliberate, yet it still carried a hint of mirth. "Has that foul creature tried to twist your mind?"

"Well, I do feel sort of confused. Devin wants me to let my shield down so we can both attach to my friend Billy when he comes in here. He says that Billy will lose brain function, maybe even die, when he gets restored. Devin says he has a way to keep that from happening, and he'll tell us how it works if we cooperate and all go together."

A gentle laugh emerged. "And you believe him?"

"Well, yeah. Sort of. He played this recording of my father, and it sounded real."

"It was real, but that is not the issue."

The white glow that seeped from around the corner morphed into fiery red mist that rolled across the dark crystalline floor like bloody fog. A current of darkness flowed through Bonnie's mind, as though a breeze had channeled through the hall, carrying the voice like an echo riding the wind. "Devin petitions your fears. He bids them to come out and wrestle with your faith. The battle is already met in fields of darkness, where fears are born and faith is proven."

Feeling a strange uneasiness, Bonnie stepped back. "My fears? But if my father was telling the truth, aren't my fears valid?"

The fog congealed, then separated into tiny red mounds of luminescent goop, like pliable bubbles plucked from a lava lamp. With invisible legs, they moved toward Bonnie, each emitting sparks, electrically charged robots marching in rows, spitting and sizzling as they advanced.

Bonnie backed away again, first one step, then another. Finally, she stopped and let them surround her. With a loud buzz, they all popped and disappeared, their static charges dispersing into the darkness.

The voice returned. "You stepped back, child. Were your fears valid?"

"I was surprised. I didn't know what those things were."

"But then you stood your ground. Why?"

"I'm not sure. I just ..." Bonnie let her words trail off. Her troubled thoughts burst into confused sparks that caught the hall's dark current and blew away. Her friend's light glowed brighter, reverting to white and casting its effervescent shadow farther into her hallway. The winds of darkness died away, and Bonnie felt her own glow strengthening.

"What is the nature of faith, child?" the voice continued. "Why did you stand fast? Your answer will guide you through the battle."

As he spoke, the entire hallway filled with light. The laboratory appeared as if she were standing outside the candlestone. Ashley and Billy, each wearing a diver's robe, huddled as Ashley studied Billy's rubellite ring. Although their words failed to come through, their plans were clear. One of them was getting ready to dive into the candlestone, probably Billy.

Darkness clouded the lab, and the scene dissolved into an expanding sea of blackness. Bonnie was again in the dark hallway, back in her gloomy prison, listening to the friendly voice.

"Learn the secret of seeing beyond the walls of your existence. When we were on the outside, we saw everything as though we were looking through a glass darkly. We were restricted, earthly, blinded by the limitations of our eyes. Now we are no longer flesh and bone, and we are able to see with spiritual eyes."

"Well, thank you for the advice and for building that fence of light around me when I first came in here. If you hadn't protected me, Devin would have grabbed me. Who knows what he might have done?"

The voice laughed merrily and began fading. "But, dear child, it was not I who protected you."

The trail of light disappeared. His words were puzzling, yet enlightening, and he raised more questions than he answered.

What is faith? What did the marching red blobs mean? And who built that radiant wall of protection? Maybe she was right after all, and God had been there, just as she had sung so many times.

Then the vision of Billy and Ashley returned to mind. One of them could show up at any moment. Bonnie retreated down the corridor to try to find the candlestone's entry point. The number of turns seemed endless, and darkness draped the passages, but she wound through the maze with a new kind of ability. Was she using the spiritual eyes her mysterious friend had mentioned?

As she approached an area that reminded her of the entry point, a new, unnerving sensation arose. The whole dark world pitched and yawed like a ghost ship on a midnight sea. Then, after several seconds, it stopped.

New fears crawled into her mind, like a horde of dark soldiers creeping onto a battlefield. It was time to sing. A Bible verse swirled up from Bonnie's memory, and she composed a tune to go with it. "For now we see through a glass, darkly; but then face to face: now I know in part; but then shall I know even as also I am known. And now abideth faith, hope, love, these three; but the greatest of these is love."

✦   ✦   ✦   ✦   ✦   ✦

I put the flashlight there," Karen said, pointing at a hook. "but I told Billy about it, so he must have taken it."

The professor reached into his oversized inner coat pocket where he had packed Merlin's Diary and withdrew a penlight. He clicked a button on the end and cast a tiny beam into the steep black entryway. "That's better." He struggled to the edge of the stairwell and propped his crutches against the wall. "I'll have to do without these."

Walter held the sword's box in both arms. "We can carry them … somehow."

The professor pointed the beam at the walls on each side of the steps. "There's no handrail, so I'll need one of you to support me on the way down. Walter, can you carry the sword and the crutches? Excalibur is very heavy in the hands of one who is not meant to use it."

"You're telling me. And it's getting heavier by the minute." Walter tucked the box under one arm and picked up the crutches with his free hand. "But these are light. I can do it."

"Very well. You and Karen can take turns if you should tire."

The professor draped an arm over Karen's shoulders, and Walter trailed them by a couple of steps. Their progress was slow, and the gray daylight shining through the open entrance faded like the setting of the sun. As darkness folded in, the professor's flashlight seemed to brighten as its laser-like beam illuminated each stair.

"Hey, Prof," Walter said, his whisper magnified in the cold stillness, "does this remind you of anything?"

"Not exactly, Walter. I am not accustomed to tromping down a dark, endless stairway with a bullet hole in my heel."

"Not that. I mean, we've been out hunting for Billy before. Last time we had a crossbow. This time we have a sword. Don't you get a feeling like déjà vu?"

"Indeed, the parallels are striking. I do expect, however, that there will be a drastic change. It is time for someone else's light to grow while mine diminishes."

"What do you mean by that?"

The professor just sighed and said no more. Walter clutched the sword box to his chest and hung back an extra step. Prof had always kept a few secrets, revealing what he thought necessary at appropriate times. Walter knew better than to press for more information. The earlier tremor had shaken him, and thoughts of disasters and end-of-the-world catastrophes tapped at his brain like a deadly ghost tip-toeing just a few steps behind.

After negotiating at least a hundred stairs, Walter whispered, "Karen, let me know when you think we're about two-thirds of the way."

"Okay," she whispered back. "Why?"

"From there on, we'll have to keep our mouths shut. We might need the element of surprise."

The professor kept his face forward. "Walter is correct, Karen. Although Dr. Conner doesn't seem to be either in front of us or behind us, you said that there exists another entrance into the laboratory. Silence is advisable in case he is already there."

"Yeah, it exists, all right. It's a tunnel that comes out into the valley near Camp Misery. And it leads through a big cave near the lab."

"A tunnel?" Walter said. "Why don't you use that instead of this crazy stairway? Wouldn't it be easier?"

Karen looped her arm around the professor's waist and grunted, adding to the sound of boots clopping on creaking stair boards. She finally muttered, "You wouldn't believe me."

The professor stopped and pointed his beam at Karen's chin. "You need not fear ridicule. We have seen enough oddities and peculiar phenomena to keep us from doubting almost anything."

"Right." Walter propped the crutches against the wall and balanced the sword box on the step behind them. "Anything short of ten-foot bunnies dancing in purple top hats and carrying bazookas, and we'll probably believe you."

"No," Karen deadpanned, "they don't have bazookas. They carry missile launchers."

Walter laughed out loud, then clamped a hand over his mouth. When he regained control, he whispered, "Girl, I like your style."

Walter retrieved his load, and the three resumed their descent. "Truthfully," Karen continued, after another twenty steps, "Doc told us there's a monster in the cave, and I've heard it. It sounds like rumbling and growling, and sometimes like an old man with a terrible rattling wheeze, like someone dumped a bag of rocks down a garbage disposal."

Walter stayed quiet for a moment, hoping the professor would speak up. "So, Prof," Walter said in a whisper, "now we might have to deal with a monster. Do you want me to take it, or can you handle it yourself?"

Karen snapped back, her voice sarcastically sweet. "We're about two-thirds of the way, Walter, dear. I think it's time for you to shut up."

The professor stopped and turned, forcing the other two to halt. He shone the thin beam, first in Walter's face, then in Karen's. "Walter, Karen," the professor began, his voice spiked with agitation, "although it is time for silence, I must make an entreaty." He took a deep breath before continuing more calmly. "Let us proceed as a team. We might be called upon to sacrifice a great deal for one another. A house divided against itself cannot stand."

Walter and Karen faced each other, neither saying a word for a few seconds until Walter stripped off his glove and extended his hand. "Prof's right. I shouldn't tease like that. I believe you heard a monster. I just like to joke around a lot. Still friends?"

Karen pulled off her glove and grasped his hand. "Don't worry, friend." She then took Excalibur's box from him and tucked it under her arm, patting it with her free hand. "If any ten-foot bunnies come hopping around, I've got your back."

*   *   *   *   *   *

After explaining the translumination procedure to Billy, Ashley pointed at a digital display on the control panel, its large numerals easy to see from a distance. "The controls will be set on a timer to reverse automatically. Right now it's showing the time until we transluminate. Then it will reset and count down again. When that counter gets to zero, there's no choice, we have to come back, with or without Bonnie. I can't override it, because I'll be hanging on to you. Understand?"

Billy gave her a quick nod. "Got it."

"Now there's one more decision to make," Ashley said as she smoothed out Billy's sleeve again. "I said all of that assuming you want to be the diver."

Billy drew his arm back and readjusted the cuff. "Well, yeah. Don't you think so? I mean, I've faced Devin before. I know his tricks."

Ashley walked across the lab to the diver's dome. "Yes, that's true. But there's a problem." Once at the dome, she sat on the platform as the glass enclosure hung a few feet above her head. "We never properly restored any of the male chimps we tested, and we don't know why. It couldn't be a coincidence. The females all worked fine."

Billy stepped over to the platform and set a foot on it. "I overheard Dr. Conner talking about that." He sat next to her, glad that the robe was keeping his nausea at bay. He tried to read Ashley's eyes, shadowy, yet penetrating. "I'm not a chimp. And I'm not worried about what happens to me, as long as I get Bonnie out. I'm not afraid."

"Well … maybe you should be." Ashley rose and waved toward the candlestone. "I read about your fire breathing, but I don't think you'll be able to use it in there."

Billy checked the cotton belt on his jeans and stepped up to the platform. "I won't need it."

Ashley pulled on the loose ends of his sash, tightening it further. "So I can't talk you out of it? I could be the diver. I know I could do it."

Billy slid his ring up and down on his finger, then balled his hand into a fist. The slayer was crafty, brutal. How could he let anyone else face that monster? This was his fight and his fight alone. He had to make up for his failure against Palin. "Nope. I got this."

"Gotta love your attitude." Ashley pressed a button on the base of the platform, lowering the glass dome. As the bottom edge passed below Billy's chest, she called, "Just remember. Don't let go of my hand."

Billy gave a thumbs-up signal. When the glass clicked against the platform, his legs shook. Firming his lips, he steeled every limb. He had to dive in with confidence. Devin would detect any hint of fear, and that could lead to disaster.

❋   ❋   ❋   ❋   ❋   ❋

282

When the professor stopped abruptly, Walter crept up behind him. Ahead, light framed a door. "Looks like we reached the end," Walter whispered.

"It's the door to the lab," Karen said. "The Alpha entrance."

The professor clicked off his penlight. "Then alpha marks the beginning of our next adventure. I suggest we listen for a few moments to ascertain the possible dangers we might face inside."

Walter laid the crutches and box next to the wall, then blew softly on his cupped hands. "Good. I need a breather."

Karen sighed. "We were supposed to take turns. You only let me carry it for two minutes."

"So I like flower boxes," Walter said. "Can't a guy show a little culture?"

Karen let out a low groan, and the professor stifled a laugh. "Very well, Walter. Our signal to enter will be your readiness to continue. I see no reason to burst in hastily."

Karen placed her ear on the door. "I hear something. It might be the equipment engines." She pulled on Walter's sleeve. "Rest up quick."

Walter slid down the wall and plopped on the floor. "I'm resting as fast as I can."

*　　　*　　　*　　　*　　　*　　　*

Ashley quick-stepped toward the anchor dome. As she passed the pedestal, she noticed that the candlestone had moved slightly, shaken from its place by the recent tremor. She picked it up gently and held it in the palm of her hand, peering through its input facets. Why did it sap the power of a dragon? Why did it steal Billy's breath and rob Bonnie's strength to fly? And yet, it seemed to choose its victims. Very strange.

She set the gem back in place and jumped up to her dome platform, then bent over and pressed the button to lower the glass. She glanced at the starting timer on the control panel. Thirty seconds to go.

283

Ashley shivered, though it wasn't that cold. In the diver's dome, Billy closed his eyes, his face adorned with a peaceful smile. He was courageous, perhaps naïvely so. Yet, he seemed to exude confidence, and he would need it. Ashley sighed. So would she. If only she could borrow some of his moxie.

A loud slam disrupted the chamber's peaceful hum. Ashley spun in her dome. Someone had entered the lab area from the Omega entrance. "Ashley!" Doc shouted. "Are you in here?"

Ashley's throat twisted like a tourniquet. They were caught. Would he try to stop them? She couldn't even squeak a reply. Only twelve seconds to translumination.

Doc turned on the lights and dashed into the lab's central area, his eyes wild. "Ashley, the cave collapsed. I could barely crawl through. I can't find her anywhere. She's gone."

Doc's clothes were dirty, and blood smudged his face. Ashley glanced again at the timer and held up her hand with her fingers splayed. Five seconds.

Doc spun in a quick circle as if taking in the scene for the first time. "What?" he yelled, almost shrieking. "You're doing a dive?"

Ashley nodded, vibrations shooting through her feet and legs. As Doc ran toward the control panel, her vision blurred, scattering into chaotic shards of light. Even Dr. Conner's words stirred into the confusing mix as they died away in her new world of dazzling light. She could barely hear him say, "I'll put a stop to this!"

18

THE CHASM

Ashley had no choice. Even though Doc might try to stop her, she was already transluminated. She had to continue. But how? Everything felt weird—puzzling and confusing—yet so bright she could hardly take in all her surroundings.

She had to think, pause for a second and just think. She had to find the exit point. Where was it? The whole room swirled. She had to get a grip.

She tried to move. Her brain's normal motion signals transformed into light pulses, a new kind of command her transluminated body struggled to understand. After a few tries, she had some success. As she inched along in her dome, the flood of light in her strange world shifted. Finally, she found the exit point and poured her flashing body into the flexible tube, grasping the anchoring spurs as she slid through the glass. *Watch out, Billy! Here I come!*

*   *   *   *   *   *

A flood of light poured into Billy's brain, snapping him to attention. Everything was different—altered and distorted. The whole procedure was timed, including when he would be sucked into the stone, so he expected Ashley to come into his cylinder at any second. She had to get through to him and attach or else he'd be slurped down that photon straw without an anchor.

A burst of light poured out from the anchor tube. Ashley extended her hand and grabbed his, and not too soon. One second later, he was falling, zipping down a gushing waterfall of light. An avalanche of flashing strobes zoomed all around his body. As he rocketed downward at a million miles per hour, a tidal wave of agitated light stung his face like a swarm of angry gnats poking with hot needles.

After a few seconds, he slammed into a black, jelly-like membrane, and his body punched through, leaving the flood of light, gnats and all, behind. The breakneck plunge slowed to a gentle, drifting sensation.

Except for Ashley's pull from above, he floated freely. His body pulsed—a chaotic jumble of white flashes with a circle of red at one edge. He stared at the crimson glow. *My rubellite?*

He came to a stop in a chasm of utter darkness, a land of charcoal drawings on a black canvas. This had to be the place. Now it was time to find Bonnie.

* * * * * *

Bonnie searched the dark crystal skies for Billy's entrance. In view lay the entry stream, which had exploded into a raging river, but where might a diver push through to the inner core? As she watched, a glimmer of light appeared in the sky and floated in her direction. Could it be Billy?

A voice, soft and sweet, flowed from the light. It wasn't of the same quality she had been hearing from Devin or her mysterious friend. It sounded far away and choppy. "You can come out now."

Bonnie studied the light. Was that Ashley's voice?

"I know you're here. Come on out."

Bonnie's light flashed. It *was* Ashley's voice! She came instead of Billy.

The light grew and floated closer, extending a ragged arm in her direction.

"Come on out. You can trust me."

Ashley's voice still sounded far off and strange, but there was no mistaking it. And since she had been in the stone for only a few seconds, she had not yet taken on her normal shape.

Bonnie extended her hand. In her willingness to join her rescuer, her shield of light eroded. The two hands inched closer. When Bonnie noticed her shield weakening, she paused.

The voice spoke again. "Do you sense danger?" The words were still choppy, still far away, but still Ashley's.

"No. No, it's just—"

"Hold your questions and be patient. Too much information can make your brain choke."

It had to be Ashley! Bonnie thrust her hand forward. "C'mon! Let's get out of here before Devin shows up!"

When the lights touched, the two melded, and the connection burned like an electric shock. "I've got you now, witch!"

Bonnie screamed and jerked back, but Devin's grip clamped down like the jaws of a pit bull. "How ... how did you?" She couldn't continue. The slayer's electric vise scorched all her senses, sending shockwaves of intense pain throughout her body.

287

The indistinct form swirled, reshaping into Devin's persona, returning a sinister smile to his malevolent face. "It was child's play, my dear. Recording voices is quite simple once you've been in here long enough. Our friends outside were kind enough to leave the communication lines open, and I did a bit of eavesdropping."

Bonnie struggled, twisting and pulling with all her might. Sparks flew, but she couldn't shake loose.

Devin dragged her away, his spiteful voice ripping its coarse static into her mind. "Time for you to join the monkeys and the fools, little angel." He stopped at the edge of the chasm and dangled her over its narrow opening. "You were a force to be reckoned with. It's a shame you were on the wrong side."

Bonnie froze, not wanting to slip from his grasp. She peered below. The swirling ghosts gathered, like crocodiles swarming to meet a fallen victim. "Billy will come," she cried. "He'll take care of you."

"Oh, I know he'll come. And he'll be duped as easily as you were. You've given me a nice collection of sounds to work with." His raspy voice mutated into Bonnie's recent, excited call. "C'mon! Let's get out of here!"

The words and tone were hers. What would Billy do? This would all be new to him. Would he be fooled? She shook away her fears and shouted, "You won't get away with it!"

"Oh, yes. Yes, I will. I've been getting away with it for more than a thousand years."

"Not this time." Bonnie tried to sing. "If I say, Surely the darkness shall cover—"

"Too late, witch!" Devin released Bonnie. She plummeted through the blackness of the gem's dungeon. She tried to grab with her hands of light, but nothing held. The walls were pure, crystalline glass, and something from beneath pulled with relentless force. She plunged farther and farther into the pit as the slayer's scornful laughter faded into a rush of dark wind.

＊　　＊　　＊　　＊　　＊　　＊

Walter nudged the door open a crack and peeked into the huge room. Near the center, Dr. Conner pounded on a panel of some kind. Walter ducked back inside the tunnel. "Dr. Conner's in there. He's mad as a hornet."

The professor turned to Karen. "The sword, please."

Karen opened the box. The professor reached in and grasped Excalibur's hilt. Instantly the sword changed from a lifeless gray blade into a blazing white saber. He took one crutch and pressed it under his armpit before turning back to Walter. "The time has come. Wisdom and caution must unite with action and speed. Let's go!"

289

＊　　＊　　＊　　＊　　＊　　＊

Billy searched through the vast darkness. It was like floating in a windowless closet without a speck of light in the universe except his own, and even that bounced off the blanket of blackness without making a dent. A breeze blew through his body, dark streams crisscrossing his shining form.

At last he spotted another light. *Bonnie?*

"Careful, Billy."

What? The warning voice seemed to come from inside his head. *Who said that?*

"It's Ashley. We're connected, so I can talk to you. And I can hear some of your thoughts. Guard them well."

Hear my thoughts? How does that work?

"I don't know. It's sort of a mind meld, I guess. Don't worry. I haven't heard much, so I guess I can hear only your louder thoughts. You'd better get moving. I can't see what you see, but I'm going to stretch out as far as I can so you can go find out who that light is."

You might not have to stretch. It's coming this way.

The light closed in rapidly, the shapeless mass forming into a young female. The face, though non-distinct, radiated, and an excited voice came from its direction. "C'mon! Let's get out of here!"

It was Bonnie! The light extended an appendage. Billy reached toward it, his glowing red ring floating in the black surroundings. The approaching light drew closer and closer, filled with energy and flashing white, but no circle of red.

No ring?

Something jerked Billy backwards. "I heard that, Billy. I know Bonnie's ring went in there with her."

As he flew away from the imposter, its bright light flashed crimson, crisscrossed with pulsing yellow stripes.

Billy yelled to Ashley, his thoughts now loud streams of static words. "I know it's Devin, but I have to go back."

"No, you can't possibly fight him. He knows the ways of the candlestone better than you do. He's been here for weeks."

"I'm not looking for a fight," Billy said as he pulled against Ashley's pressure. "I'm looking for Bonnie. But if I have to fight him, I will. Face to face."

＊　　＊　　＊　　＊　　＊　　＊

Lying flat on the cavern's crystalline floor, Bonnie shivered, her glowing skin flickering in what felt like a chilling breeze. At least there was no pain, and the phantoms were nowhere in sight. Apparently the swirling forces had tossed her to the side.

She pushed herself upright. It wasn't as dark here. The river of light flowed through this area and gushed toward the candlestone's exit point, and it lent a shimmering glow to the chasm's lower chamber.

Another light approached, its gentle radiance strengthening as it drew closer. A second light appeared, then a third. Within seconds, six flashing phantoms—a group of men with hardened faces and bright, flowing hair—pressed around her and stared, almost as if they were sniffing, like a pack of dogs trying to detect who or what she was.

"It is not Devin," one of them said.

"Another ape?" a second one asked.

"Probably. It has arms and legs. Its features are not yet distinct."

A third voice joined in. "Well, I didn't expect that he'd just slip and fall down here."

"Perhaps not. If he ever does, it will be his last mistake."

The lights began drifting away, apparently no longer concerned about Bonnie's arrival.

"Wait," she called. "I'm not an ape. I'm human. My name is Bonnie Silver."

One of the lights turned back. "Have you a tale?"

"No. I don't have a tail. I'm human."

The light rejoined the others, and the group dispersed, floating away like clouds in the wind. They sang a moaning dirge, much like the one she had heard earlier.

The constant pull that carried them away tugged on her as well, a strange air current that tried to draw everything toward the exiting river. The phantoms floated in the current, resisting at the last moment before it would have plunged them into the river. They curved back to where they started, only to begin another circuit.

Bonnie moved as far away from the river as she could, inching along the glass floor, pushing against the force. She found a pocket of angled planes carved into a lower part of the chasm's cliff—a cave of sorts, a narrow opening in the wall, lower than the surrounding floor, a good place to hide in case other ghosts came sniffing by.

After burying herself in the cleft, Bonnie peered out at the slow waltz of swirling specters. She imagined men and apes, rats and rabbits, all meshed in a dizzying eternal torture. Would she be the next victim of the candlestone's version of hell, joining the everlasting lament in this turmoil of dark despair?

She tried to shake away the sorrow, the agony of hopelessness. A similar cycle of misery came to mind, being passed from foster home to foster home, unwanted, unloved, still aching over her mother's recent death. And now—

A sob rose into her throat. Her light dimmed in a shudder of weakening flickers. She cried out in her mind, her sorrows pouring forth as her world turned darker and darker.

Where are you, Mama?

Anguish lashed, the threat of being locked in a forsaken tomb for an eternity. What could she do but cry? Although no liquid tears fell, Bonnie wept. The cleansing flow of emotions helped her form a prayer in her mind—a prayer for her mother, for herself, and especially for Billy. Somehow he would make his way to her side. But how could he possibly find her in this hidden dungeon?

* * * * * *

The professor limped into the lab, one hand gripping a crutch and the other carrying the glowing Excalibur as Walter and Karen crept close behind.

Dr. Conner sat with his chin propped in his hand, studying the control panel, barely moving a muscle.

The professor whispered to Karen, "Does anyone else live here?"

"Uh-huh. Ashley's grandfather and a boy named Derrick."

"Can you take Walter to them?"

She glanced across to the other side of the lab. "Yeah. The boys' dorm door is open, and—Wow! The Omega door, too!"

Walter shielded his eyes from the laboratory lights. "Where's the Omega door?"

The professor raised a shushing finger to his lips. He handed the crutch to Walter and balanced his weight on his good foot. "Set this down. Go with Karen and close the door behind you. Find them and make sure they're safe. Lead them back, but don't come in unless I call."

"Gotcha, Prof."

"And go quickly. Don't worry about Dr. Conner seeing you. I'll handle him."

Walter and Karen dashed across the chamber, their shoes clattering on the stone floor. Dr. Conner jerked his head up and yelled, "Karen! What are you doing? Come back here!" In a flash of motion, he turned two dials on the panel and sprang from his chair.

The professor tightened his grip on the sword. "Halt!" The glowing blade shot a brilliant beam upward, ripping a hole in the ceiling as the laser stream pierced the darkness above.

The doctor spun, terror in his eyes. Walter and Karen disappeared into the hallway, and the door slammed with a loud clap. The professor eyed Dr. Conner and allowed the sword's beam to diminish, though its fiery glow continued to drape the blade like a shining scabbard. "Dr. Conner," the professor said,

293

his tone crisp and matter-of-fact, "would you be so kind as to tell me the whereabouts of Billy Bannister and Bonnie Silver?"

Dr. Conner stepped back against the control panel. A shroud of fear clouded his eyes and lined his smudged face. He pointed at the candlestone. "They're … they're in there." Wringing his hands, he continued. "Bonnie went … went into the candlestone, and she got trapped. Ashley and Billy went in to … to try to get her out, I'm sure. I think they're all in there now. I … I tried to reverse it, but it's on automatic. Ashley changed the override password, so I can't bring them back." He swallowed hard, and his voice strengthened. "We have to get them out, and fast!"

The professor lowered the sword. "Is there any immediate danger?"

"Yes. I came in through the back tunnel. A major support wall caved in, so this mountain's entire structure has been compromised. Another tremor could bring this whole place down on top of us."

"What would happen if we were to simply remove the stone and leave?"

"We can't. Ashley's anchoring. She's halfway in and halfway out. If we move the stone, we'll tear her body in two. And our equipment is the only way in the world to restore them. I could never rebuild it without her."

The ceiling panels rattled, and the lights flickered. The floor of the cave began vibrating, the intensity increasing. Dr. Conner ran to the pedestal and pinched the candlestone between his fingers. "I have to hold the stone in place."

Limping painfully toward the center of the chamber, the professor called through a growing din, "Walter! Karen! Come quickly!"

They scrambled out of the hallway, Karen pulling Derrick by the hand and Walter pushing Ashley's grandfather in a wheelchair. The floor bucked and swayed, and they careened back and forth like sailors on the deck of a wind-tossed ship.

Sand sprinkled the floor and bounced across the tile. Taps from above signaled pebbles dancing on the tops of the ceiling panels. The professor waved them forward. "You must evacuate immediately."

Walter hunched over to shield Ashley's grandfather. "You gotta be kidding me! I can't get this wheelchair up the stairs!"

A rush of rocks and sand ripped through a ceiling tile and buried a chair near a control panel. Dr. Conner crouched next to the central pedestal, still holding the candlestone in place.

"The Omega entrance." Dr. Conner nodded toward the door. "I cleared a path through the rubble. Try that."

"But what about the monster?" Karen shouted.

"There's no monster! Just go!"

Karen tugged on Walter's coat sleeve. "I know the way." She and Derrick seesawed over the teetering ground.

The professor pointed. "Walter! Follow her! Now!"

He grasped the wheelchair. "But what about you?"

"Go!"

*   *   *   *   *   *

Ashley's pull on Billy's arm lessened. As he floated back toward the slayer, he shouted his thoughts. "What have you done with Bonnie?"

"So," Devin said, his scratchy voice buzzing like a dentist's drill, "you've learned how to speak in here. Not bad."

Devin sprang toward Billy, but Billy backed away just in time to avoid his touch. The slayer laughed. "A little quicker now, I see. Well, you're obviously not much smarter than when you lost your battle with me on the mountain. All it took was a lock of hair to bring you stumbling up the slopes like an idiot to rescue your stupid girlfriend. What a surprise. She wasn't there. And now here you are again, swaggering in to fight me on my home turf. Didn't your old man teach you any better? Oh, yes. I forgot. He's a dragon, a stupid beast, just like all the others I've conquered over the years."

Billy ignored a dozen clever retorts that clamored in his head. "So is your sharp tongue your only sword now?"

Devin's light burst into radiant crimson. "You fool. You have no idea what I've learned in this cursed stone." A sphere of energy grew in the center of Devin's body like a cannonball of electrostatic fury. "I could have scattered you into a million lost electrons, mongrel. You're defenseless, without a weapon or even a song."

"A song?"

"Never mind." Devin's color slowly faded to white. "If you want to survive, you'd better cooperate with me. I'll bet they didn't tell you what happens to males when they're restored, did they?"

"I heard, and I don't care." Billy's own light changed to off-white. He couldn't let the slayer prod him into a fit of anger. He composed himself and continued in a calm voice. "Just tell me where Bonnie is."

"You'd better deal with me, kid. I'll tell you where she is, and I'll tell you how to save your brain if you'll let me attach and ride out of here with you."

"Is she alive?"

"She's alive."

Billy spoke in his mind. *Did you hear all of the conversation, Ashley? What should I do?*

"I didn't hear much. You don't have time to explain what's going on. Reversal is coming in about seventy seconds. You're on your own, and you have to act fast."

Devin's glow flashed, a rippling mass of humanoid light set against pure blackness. His blurry facial features gave no hint of an expression, nothing to help Billy decide how to deal with this liar. But the surrounding emptiness raised memories of his father's story. Shouldn't there be others trapped in the candlestone, Devin's fellow conspirators? If so, where were they? If they were partners in crime, why wasn't Devin with them now?

"Okay," Billy said. "Show me where Bonnie is first. If I see you're telling the truth, you can go with me."

Devin drifted away, a finger of light gesturing as his glow delved into the darkness. "Follow me."

Give me some slack, Ashley. I have to go somewhere. When Ashley's tension eased, Billy followed Devin's energy trail until he stopped. *Okay, Ashley. Be ready to yank me away if I call.*

"Just say the word."

"Do you see this little fault?" Devin said, his glowing finger pointing toward the floor.

"A fault? You mean, like a crack inside the stone?"

"Yes." He pushed his arm downward. It disappeared below the surface of the floor. "It leads to the candlestone's exit. Bonnie went down there to try to get out."

Ashley, did you catch that?

"All I heard was you saying something about a crack in the stone. I've mapped this entire matrix, and there is a crack leading from the inner core down into the exit channel. Doc told me that Devin said he couldn't use it to escape. But he might have been lying. We don't have much time, Billy. Less than forty seconds. You'd better hurry."

297

Got it. Billy addressed Devin again. "Why should I believe you?"

"You have no choice. I can't leave that way. Only females can. Pull me out, and not only will I save your worthless brain, I'll tell you how to get her out through the exit channel. You made the deal, Bannister. I showed you where she is, now it's your turn."

Billy crept toward the fault. Their two masses of light stood at the edge of the narrow chasm as they peered into the darkness. Below, the river of light exited, and radiant phantoms circled in a tight coil. "What are those?"

"Other souls like us who would like to escape. Bonnie is one of them, I'm sure."

"They look like sharks in a feeding tank, like they're angry."

"Perhaps they are. Some have been here for a very long time."

Billy eyed the phantoms. They had to be Devin's cronies from the rebellion against King Arthur. *Ashley, can you set up your system to restore from the exit channel?*

"Yes. But why?"

No time to explain. Just get ready to do it. Billy let go of her hand. The release made her snap back into the darkness.

"What?" Devin yelled. "What are you doing?"

"I'm keeping my word. I agreed that you could come with me." Billy looked down into the chasm, then back at Devin. "You're welcome to come along." Billy stepped into the crack and fell into darkness.

Catching the Light

Ashley, still clutching the anchor tube in the lab, rode on a heart-stopping updraft as her invention sucked her out of the candlestone. Her arm and torso battled against a surging current of raging light that tried to drag her back into the stone. When she released the anchor spurs, her body congealed. Seconds later, she floated in a bath of blazing light. As she tried to orient herself, a mosaic of flashing puzzle pieces came together to form the familiar laboratory.

Wrapping her arms around her restored body, she rubbed her chilled skin, bouncing while the glass cylinder rose exactly as programmed. Her vision quickly adjusted. Doc held the candlestone in place, and a strange old man leaned on a crutch while carrying a glowing sword. Whoever he was, questions had to wait.

Ashley jumped from the platform and lunged toward the pedestal. "I have to turn it!" She grabbed Doc's arm with a quick twist, forcing him to release the stone. Crouching, she

299

aligned the candlestone's exit beam with the tube leading to the diver's dome, but the gem wouldn't balance at that angle She glanced at Doc. "What were you doing to it?"

"Another tremor hit. I was holding it in place." Doc dropped to a knee beside her. "What are you planning?"

"Shhh! I'm thinking." Ashley rose, her hands on her hips. She surveyed her equipment, studying the connections. She would have to use the dome to restore everyone.

She lifted the candlestone from its pedestal and tiptoed to the diver's dome. After setting the flashing gem on the platform floor, she ran to the control panel. "Doc, they're coming out the exit channel. I'll have to shut off the anchor access tube and open the restore tube, but how am I going to get them through the restore tube so the computer can analyze them before the candlestone just sucks them back in?"

While Ashley adjusted the controls to set the proper parameters, Doc hustled to her. "You can bring an anchor person over from the restoration dome," he said, using his hands to sketch the process, "and have him pull exiting people through the tube."

Ashley studied a control display and whispered a calculation. "That's fifteen point seven from neutral." She flipped her hair back with a shake of her head. "Who could be the anchor? Karen's gone."

Doc squared his shoulders. "I'll do it."

"You?"

"Yes." His voice cracked as if painful words lodged in his throat. "I've got to do something to fix the mess I've made."

Ashley stared at him. She would probably never trust him again, but at this point there was no other choice. She let out a shallow sigh. "Okay. Then let's get going."

Ashley barked out instructions like a rapid-fire machine gun. "Since there's no Excalibur beam in the restoration dome, you'll have to get in the diver's dome with the candlestone. Remember to hang on to the tube, or you'll get sucked into the candlestone right after you get transluminated. Once you're a mass of light, I'll need you to go back and forth through the recovery tube a couple of times so I can read your light structure and quarantine your data in the computer. When you see something come out of the candlestone that's not normal light, try to grab it and escort it to the restoration dome.

"The photo analyzers in the tube will be able to read the person while it passes through, and I'll make sure the computer blocks your data out. Leave the person in the restoration dome and then go back through the tube to the diver's dome while I restore the person you brought over."

She took a deep breath and looked around at the dust and debris. "We'll have to work fast. Another tremor would give us serious problems, and we need to be ready when the first person comes out of the stone. I don't know how many are in there. I could catch only a few of Billy's thoughts, but I think we might get pretty busy."

Doc peered over her shoulder. "We didn't plan for an army. How are the photoreceptors holding out?"

Ashley brushed a thin layer of dust away from the panel's receptor meter. "Probably enough for several restorations, but I can't be sure."

"It'll have to do. Our source is gone." Doc ran toward the boys' dorm. "I'll get a robe."

Ashley blinked. Gone? How was that possible? Yet, it was too late to ask. As calculations clicked in her brain, she adjusted the controls on the board, tweaking dials and switches, then reading the meters and readjusting on the fly.

"Miss," someone with a gentle voice said, "may I be of any assistance?"

Ashley spun. An older man with wild white hair and a pain-pierced grimace hobbled toward her, the man with the crutch she had seen earlier. A layer of chalky dust coated his face, and he still carried a glowing sword. "Let me guess," she said, resuming her work. "You're the professor, right?"

He bowed his head. "Charles Hamilton, at your service. I inspected the rear exit, and there is no one in sight. It seems that my friend, Walter, and your relation, Karen, have safely guided a young man named Derrick and your grandfather through the first part of the passage."

Ashley breathed a relieved sigh. "Thank God!" As the professor joined her on the platform, she extended a hand. "I'm Ashley Stalworth. I read about you in Bonnie's journal, and yes, you can help." She flipped another series of switches and hustled toward the restoration dome. "Do you know about the candlestone?"

The professor followed her across the lab at half her speed. "I have heard of it. My students, Bonnie Silver and William Bannister, are inside it, if I am not mistaken."

"Billy, Bonnie, and quite a few others. If everything goes right, we'll be restoring people in this enclosure." She touched the glass on the cylinder, dropped to a crouch, and pressed a button on the low platform, making the shield slowly rise. "This switch raises and lowers the glass. When someone appears, I'll give a signal when restoration is complete. Your job is to raise the glass, get the person out, and close the cylinder again as quickly as possible. I could do it from the panel, but once people are being restored, my hands might be too busy, and I couldn't help anyone get out of the dome from there anyway."

The professor leaned on his crutch and laid Excalibur on the floor next to the restoration platform. "I believe I will be able to handle that task." After testing the switch, he straightened. "I am ready."

As soon as Ashley returned to the control panel, Doc dashed back into the lab, a white robe covering his dirty clothes. She pointed at the dome. "Go ahead, Doc. Get in position."

He hurried to the center of the lab, hopped up to the diver's platform, and straddled the candlestone.

"Okay," Ashley called. "I'm going to lower your glass and douse the lights. Let's get those people out of there."

The Omega door slammed, and Walter burst into the lab area. "Dr. Conner! Karen's hurt! It's really bad!"

*　　　*　　　*　　　*　　　*　　　*

Billy pulled himself off the chasm floor. Here at the bottom of the pit, the background brightened to a dull gray. The river of light emanated a halo that muted the darkness, its aura fading to black at the chasm's borders. The spiral of ghostly lights he had seen from above formed a tightening circle around him. When they drew too close for comfort, he lifted a hand. "Stop! Who are you?"

The radiant men slowed to a halt just out of Billy's reach. A buzz of chatter surrounded him, English-sounding phrases spoken with unfamiliar accents. Finally one of the specters stepped forward and bowed politely. "We are loyal knights of Arthur's court," he said, his voice carrying a traditional British accent. "My name is Barlow, Lord of Hickling Manor. And what type of beast might you be?"

Billy gave him a nod. "I am William, son of Jared. If you are of the king's court, Sir Barlow, you should know Jared's name."

"Yes." Barlow's glowing fingers rubbed his chin. "I remember Jared. He was appointed the king's adviser just before the rebellion. But that was centuries ago. How can someone who speaks the modern American tongue be the son of Jared? And you are new to the stone. Your indistinct form gives away your recent entry. Please, tell us your tale."

Billy's light sputtered and faded. As he had guessed, these were knights from the rebellion, but were they no longer Devin's allies? "Begging your pardon, Sir Barlow. I'm looking for a lost friend. Please allow me to find her. Then I will tell you my tale. And you can tell me how you know about American English and speak it so well."

The glowing sentry nodded. "Of course, William, but what is your hurry? We know of no way to safely leave this place. We have been here for hundreds of years, and the only entertainment we have is to tell each other tales. We have long since exhausted both true stories and absurd fables, though a traveler occasionally passes through and tells us of life on the outside. That's how we learned your language and some of your customs. We know about your sport utility vehicles and your widescreen televisions." He rubbed his middle section. "And your deep-dish pepperoni pizza."

Billy laughed in spite of his worry, but his amusement faded quickly. He glanced around for a sign of Bonnie's light before turning back to Barlow. "You said there's a traveler?"

"Yes, a mysterious fellow. Although we have never found a way out of this pit, he seems to come and go as he pleases and refuses to explain how. He gives no name, just a story or two."

304

He waved his arm with a friendly gesture. "Come now. Tell us your tale."

Billy glanced around again. He wasn't going to get any more information until he talked with Barlow for a while. "Okay. Let me start with a question." He pointed toward the cliff high above, still illuminated by Devin's glow. "When I was up there, I saw you circling. Were you hoping Devin would fall in?"

Barlow's light dimmed, then flashed bright green. "Do you know Devin? Because if he is your friend—"

A loud buzzing from the other phantoms interrupted. They turned several shades of crimson as they grumbled.

Billy held up his hands. "No, no. Devin's no friend of mine. But weren't you in league with Devin to overthrow the king?"

"Alas, it is true." Barlow's aura changed briefly to pale blue before shimmering back to white. "We have had centuries to unravel the plot in our minds. It seems that Devin and his foul scribe, Palin, hatched the scheme. They convinced us, fools that we were, to believe that an imposter had deposed our great king. They claimed that Merlin craved the throne, and that he used black arts to transform a dragon into Arthur's twin. Most of the knights scoffed, but I heard a strange tale from a certain wayfarer. He fancied seeing Merlin transforming dragons into humans on Bald Top in the middle of the night. He even claimed to see a man there who looked exactly like the king. Most said the wayfarer was a madman."

305

The other lights flashed as if to confirm Barlow's explanation. "I told the wayfarer," Barlow continued, "that no sane human would set foot on Bald Top, and King Arthur would never go there. Yes, Merlin is powerful, but changing dragons into humans? Ridiculous!

"But this traveler insisted on taking me to the scene. There was something in his wild eyes that spoke truth, so I went with him, his insanity taking me over, I suppose. Bald Top was a curious sight, indeed. I saw dragon tracks interspersed with human prints, a pile of discarded clothing, and Merlin's own saddlebag. I would have sworn it was witch's work. The human prints had no source but from whence the dragons stood. Yet with the old prophet's saddlebag there, could it be true? In my superstitious terror, I convinced my friends that Devin's story was the only explanation."

"How did you finally figure out Devin was lying?"

Barlow set his glowing hand on the shoulder of one of the knights. "The six of us you see before you now are loyal." He extended his fingers away from the circle toward the flowing currents of light where ghosts rode the eerie waves. "In conversing with those others, the traitors among us, we discovered their ruse. They could not hide their lies over all these years, and the mysterious traveler explained how the candlestone drew us all in, even as it hung around the neck of that fiend Devin. I only wish he had fallen down here instead of you. We would have cast him into the river, and he would have ridden out of this cursed stone and into oblivion."

Billy pointed toward the river's exit point. "So it *is* possible to get out this way?"

"Yes," Barlow replied. "I once captured a conspirator and threw him into the river. We were able to see his body fly apart once he got out in the open. He is now a twinkle in the twilight and will never deceive anyone again."

"That's weird. I wonder why the candlestone didn't just suck him back in again."

"A good question. We wondered about that as well." Barlow gave a heavy sigh, and his tone became melancholy. "So, to answer your question, William, yes, it is possible to leave, but it is better to be in here and still have hope than to die in eternal darkness, scattered into the heavens and yet separated from God forever."

* * * * * *

Walter gasped in time with his throbbing heart. "A boulder fell ... about twenty feet from the cave's exit. Karen pushed Derrick ... out of the way, and he ... he and the old guy are okay, but the boulder knocked her down. Her leg ... her leg's broken."

Dr. Conner jumped off the diver's platform and grabbed Walter's shoulders. "Is she bleeding? Was the bone sticking out?"

Walter coughed to clear the dust from his lungs, but his voice still cracked. "Yeah. It's sticking out. It's real bad."

Dr. Conner stripped the robe off and stuffed it into Walter's arms. "Ashley will tell you what to do." He ran to a cabinet near the cavern wall, withdrew a large bag with a red cross emblazoned on its side, and sprinted out the Omega door.

Clutching the wad of clothing, Walter stared into the dark lab. The silhouette of a girl hovered near the panel. He coughed again. "Ashley?"

"Yes. Put the robe on, whoever you are. I guess you'll have to go in. This operation is getting shakier every second."

Walter rested a hand on his knee and took in quick, deep breaths. "Go in? Where?"

"Come over here, Walter," the professor said, waving. He turned toward Ashley. "May I suggest, Miss Stalworth, that I be transluminated? I heard your instructions, and I assume I

307

shall not be crippled in there. I'm sure Walter can handle my duties."

Ashley let out a frustrated sigh. "That's fine. But we have to hurry."

When Walter arrived, the professor took the robe and pulled it on over his head. "Walter, look at the base of this platform, and you'll find a switch. Press once to raise the glass and again to lower it. When someone shows up in this restoration cylinder, Miss Stalworth will signal. Raise the glass, pull the person from the platform, and lower the glass again immediately. Got it?"

Walter nodded. "Got it."

"Be sure to wait for my signal," Ashley added. "If you do it too early, it could kill whoever's in there."

The professor limped over to another platform, set his healthy foot on it, and stepped up. When he straightened, the candlestone on the floor between his feet, he looked at Ashley. "I am ready."

She blew hair out of her eyes. "I'll lower your glass from here. Go back and forth through the tube twice. I want to be sure to map your matrix accurately. It won't take you long to figure out how to move. And don't forget to grab hold of the tube right at the start, or you'll get sucked in."

She pressed a button. The glass cylinder slowly descended. When the edge clicked shut, she turned a knob. "Here we go!"

*   *   *   *   *   *

Billy counted the six shining faces in the circle around him. "Listen, Sir Barlow, I'd love to sit and chat with you for a couple of centuries, but I'm looking for a friend of mine. Her name is Bonnie Silver. Have you seen her?"

"Bonnie Silver," Barlow repeated slowly. "The name … how do you say it? Ah, yes. The name rings a bell. I enjoy your American idioms, so I hope you don't mind if I practice."

One of the other knights moved forward, his voice deep, with a hint of an Irish brogue. "It's the talking she-ape we found. Silver is the name she used."

"Yes, yes," Barlow said. "Of course I remember her. I just wanted to test the idiom."

Billy's light blazed. "So she *is* in here? You saw her?"

"Only briefly," Barlow replied. "She said she had no tale, so we weren't interested."

"I wanted to talk to her," the other knight said. "The old traveler told us about your trained zoo apes, but he never said they could talk."

"Obviously, my dear Newman," Barlow said, his light flickering from top to bottom, "it was a lass, not an ape." He turned to Billy. "You see, William, they sent a number of apes and other animals in here, and now it seems that they're sending humans. Obviously I judged her too quickly, and I apologize for ignoring your friend."

Billy nodded. "It's okay, really, but do you have any idea where she is now?"

"No, William, but my men and I will help you search. She could not have gone far. There is really no place to go." Barlow faced the other knights. As he raised his hand, they lined up in a not-so-straight row. "Attention, fellow soldiers of the cross— Newman, Edward, Fiske, Standish, Woodrow. It seems that we finally have a fair damsel to rescue." He paused and whispered to Billy, "She is fair, isn't she?"

Billy suppressed a laugh. "Yes. Very fair, indeed."

"And this fair damsel," Barlow continued, "is lost in our eternal chasm. We must find her at all costs."

Billy copied the knight's oratory style. "And after we find her, we will leave this place once and for all."

A loud, frightened buzz in the specters' native language erupted. A number of them backed away, their lights flashing to gray, then yellow.

Barlow raised his hands. "No, my fellows. Not like what happened to Lester. Our friend, William, is saying we will leave this place in one piece." He turned to Billy again. "You did mean that, didn't you?"

"Yes. Everyone will be restored to their physical bodies."

"Let us begin the search," Barlow continued. "Fan out. If you find the damsel, bring her back here and call for the others."

Billy held up his glowing rubellite. "She should be wearing a reddish ring. If you find someone who doesn't have it and claims to be Bonnie, let me know. I'll be able to tell."

The knights dispersed, each searching a different section of the chasm's dark shadows. Billy followed Sir Barlow as he hunted in a particularly dark area. There were so many corners that carried hidden coves and short corridors, and they all needed to be explored. A fading glow could easily be overlooked in this land of flickering lights and wandering shadows.

After several minutes, one of the knights hustled to Barlow. "I have a report, sir."

Barlow faced him. "Proceed, Newman."

"We found another entity cowering in a crevice. I shouted questions at it but to no avail."

"One of the dumb animals," Sir Barlow said to Billy. "Most likely a chimp."

"Yes sir," Newman continued. "That makes three chimps, an overly excited dog, and a terrified rabbit. I wish to keep them corralled, sir, so that we are not wasting our time finding them repeatedly."

"I agree," Barlow said. "See to it."

Newman gave Barlow a slight bow. "May I have your assistance, sir? The rabbit is in my possession, and the chimps are currently teasing the dog, but I fear they will not tarry long."

Barlow turned to Billy. "By your leave, William?"

Billy nodded. "Sure. I think I know my way around now." When Barlow left, Billy continued his search, trying to feel his way with all his senses. Ever since he entered the pit, he had felt Bonnie's presence, though the perception seemed cold and weak. He used his awareness of her as a divining rod, trying to gauge his nearness to her hiding place. At times he felt warmer, but he still couldn't find a strong signal that would take him to her.

He had to hurry. Ashley might be ready to restore them at any minute. In this dark, confusing place, he couldn't afford to pass by even the smallest alcoves. There was no way he would ever leave without making sure Bonnie was safe.

311

* * * * * *

Bonnie peered out of her crystalline cleft as ghosts of light passed. Their stretching appendages of flashing energy poked around corners and sniffed under ledges. All across the expanse, their strange voices carried odd accents as their words echoed in the chasm, bouncing from plane to plane. "Boonnniiieee Siillvveerr!" The calls created an eerie, haunting harmony.

She squinted at the lights. Why were they calling her? She told them her name, but they thought she was an ape.

One of the phantoms drew close. She scooted farther into her cove and pressed her body against the back. As the phantom sniffed near the opening, it buzzed in a strange language, and flickers of its radiance spilled into her refuge.

Bonnie froze in place and tried to contain any hint of a glimmer. After a few seconds, the phantom left.

She shuddered. How long would this go on? Maybe time itself in this twisted stone was skewed. Had she been here for days? Weeks? Had her friends given her up for lost? Did anyone even care anymore?

As her faith sagged, her light dimmed, but she dared not sing. The weird predators had already come too close for comfort. She would meditate instead—on the past, her friends, and how they had never failed her before.

The professor was smart and brave and would try to figure out how to restore her if Ashley failed, that is, if he ever discovered her plight. But neither he nor Walter even knew about her dragon secrets. Although they were wonderful friends, how could they help?

Her only hope rested on Billy, but how could he outwit Devin? The evil slayer was crafty beyond belief. His trap had fooled her, even though she knew how evil he was and that he would try any trick to destroy her.

She shook her head hard. She had to have faith! Keep her mind focused on what was good!

An image of Billy's gentle eyes drifted into her thoughts, his words of comfort from not so long ago. "You can believe this," he had said, his ringed hand extended, "you can always trust me. This hand will never lead you astray." She had answered that she would never forget those words, and now, in the hour of her greatest loneliness, she took them again into her heart and reabsorbed each syllable. She repeated her answer out loud. "I do trust you." Her own words increased her faith, and with it, her shimmering light.

Another specter approached, pausing to investigate. Bonnie slid against the back wall again and tried to quell the pulsing of her newly energized glow. An appendage of light slipped into the narrow crevice, searching, probing. It stretched toward her until it nearly touched her light with a white finger circled in red.

She gasped. A red glow? Billy's ring! She lunged for the hand and grasped it with her own. A gush of warmth surged through her body. When Billy pulled her out of hiding and helped her stand at his side, other humanoid lights drew nearer. "Billy," she said, compressing his hand. "What are those? What's going on? How did you find me?"

"Shhh. No time. Ashley's probably waiting. We have to try to get out of here."

"But how?"

He pointed toward the chasm's light source. "Through the river. We know it leaves the candlestone, so if we just go with the flow, we should be able to get out."

Six other bodies of light had now gathered, listening intently. Billy introduced Bonnie to them and quickly explained their story, including the tale about Devin's treachery against King Arthur and how he had deceived these loyal knights.

When he finished, he took a deep breath. "My guess is that everything should be ready by now. The river's not flowing as heavily, so Ashley must have turned off the lights. That's a good enough signal for me. But there's a huge danger. If she can't restore us, we'll probably disintegrate right after we leave."

"Have no fear, William," Barlow said, stepping closer. "I volunteer to go first. If you see me disintegrate, then you will know it is unsafe for you. If I am restored, I will signal my safe arrival in your world."

Before Billy could protest, Barlow released himself into the ever-swirling current that drew all light toward the river. Bonnie followed Billy and the knights as they hurried toward the exiting stream to watch Barlow's progress.

He plunged into the river, a silent entry that raised a splash of static. Although he melded with the river's light, his shimmering form remained clear, like bubbling seltzer in a stagnant pool. He rushed forward in the flow, and his body hurtled toward the exit. With a flashing spew of sparks, the candlestone flung him out into the open air.

RESTORATION

Walter let a hand hover over the accordion-like hose that stretched between the domes. The professor had melted into a mass of sparkling light and now he was spreading through the semitransparent tube toward the restoration dome, or at least that's how Ashley explained it a moment ago.

Drying sweat cooled Walter's skin as he concentrated on his teacher's photo-gymnastics. The professor extended a limb into the diver's cylinder where the candlestone lay. "Prof's in the tube, and he's reaching back toward the candlestone."

"Good. I'm monitoring the activity in the exit chamber." Ashley blew dust from a screen. "I think something just came out. Do you see it?"

"Yep. A fizz of light. Prof's got a hold of it."

Ashley kept each hand on a dial and nudged a slider bar with an elbow, then flipped a switch on the side of the panel with her knee.

Pushing Excalibur to the side, Walter knelt beside the button at the base of the restoration dome. "What's going on over there? It looks like you're dancing with that machine."

"Just trust me. I know what I'm doing."

"Trust you? You sent Prof in there like an electric rescue dog, like he's Lightning Lassie or something. Do you really know how to bring him back to normal?"

"In theory." Ashley ran her finger across the display. "The process looks like it's working. I've got the new form isolated in the computer, and the professor is about to take it into the restoration dome." She looked up and pointed at the glass cylinder. "Get ready."

Walter set a finger on the switch. Within seconds, a stream of luminescence flowed from the connecting tube, filling the glass cylinder. The flashing light gathered into a translucent human form, a hefty, broad-shouldered male.

Ashley gasped. "It's already in human form. It's still light energy, but it's perfectly shaped."

"Yeah." Walter rubbed his sweaty palm on his jeans. "And it's sure nobody I know."

Ashley turned a knob on the panel. "The professor's out. I'm beginning the restoration."

The glow dispersed as the human form solidified into a mustachioed man. Dressed in black breeches and a flowing, long-sleeved shirt, he stared wide-eyed into the dimly lit room.

"Now, Walter," Ashley called. "The professor's out."

When Walter pressed the switch, the glass slowly lifted. The man waited until the shield rose above his eyes, then stepped down to floor level, his head erect. Walter hit the switch again and straightened to face the new arrival.

The man nodded. "I am Sir Winston Barlow, Lord of Hickling Manor, and I am a faithful servant of King Arthur."

Walter nodded in return. "Uh ... I'm Walter Foley."

"Master Foley, in the interest of avoiding catastrophe, I shall waive any further formalities." He glanced around the room. "Do you have light switches?"

Walter shrugged. "Ashley, where are the light switches?"

She waved an arm. "Over here."

The knight marched to the panel and gazed at the display of meters and blinking lights. Ashley set her finger on a dial. "I can control the lights from here by turning this knob."

"I must signal the remaining prisoners, my lady, including young Bannister." Sir Barlow placed his hand on Ashley's. "If I may?"

"My name is Ashley Stalworth." She slid her hand from under his. "And certainly you may."

Sir Barlow turned the dial. As the lights brightened, he laughed. "Ha! When Newman sees this, he will have to pay double. Torches in the ceiling, just as the old traveler said. Who would have believed it?"

With a few more quick twists, the lights flashed off and then on two more times before he restored the room to darkness. "That should do it. The others will be coming out momentarily."

"The others?" Ashley said. "How many?"

Barlow counted on his brawny fingers, mumbling a series of names. "Depending on how many attempt the escape, it could be twelve. Some could be rancorous, even violent."

"Twelve?" Ashley read a meter, her brow knitting. "There's no way the receptors can hold out for that many."

"There might be a thirteenth," Barlow added, "if the scoundrel follows us."

"The scoundrel? You mean Devin?"

"Yes." Sir Barlow fixed his gaze on her. "Are you in league with him?"

Ashley scowled. "Most definitely not!"

"In that case," Barlow said, bowing his head, "I am at your service."

"Good." Ashley pointed toward the recovery dome. "Go and help Walter. You'll find a sword over there. If some of our escapees get out of line, we can send them right back where they came from."

Barlow smiled, a set of yellow crooked teeth showing his delight. "Miss Stalworth, that would be my pleasure." He hustled over to Walter. "Where is the sword, lad?"

Walter nudged the sword with his foot. "Right here."

Barlow picked it up. A glow of faint light spread across the blade, illuminating his wide eyes. "Excalibur? The king's sword?" He set it on the floor. "I am not worthy!"

"It's either you or me, Sir Barlow. If we've got some mean ones coming, I'd rather you do the slicing and dicing."

Barlow retrieved the sword and raised its glowing blade, a proud smile spreading across his face. "Very well, Walter, my lad. The conspirators will not be armed, so I shall use the sword only if necessary. But if anyone gives us trouble, he will learn the meaning of slice and dice!"

*   *   *   *   *   *

Billy stared at the exiting stream of light. "That's the third time the river's gushed and then calmed down. It has to be Barlow's signal." He led Bonnie toward the river's edge, fighting the current's pull as they drew closer. "Are you ready?"

She grasped his hand. "We're going together, right?"

Billy gazed at her. She was becoming clearer, her blue eyes, her creamy smooth skin, and her facial features in shades of shifting light. "Uh … no. I think I should make sure everyone gets out."

"Even all the animals?"

"Yeah, I guess so. They probably don't want to be in here either."

She let go of his hand and retreated from the stream of light. "I'll help you gather them. I don't want to leave without you."

"No, the knights and I will get them." He grabbed her wrist and guided her back to the edge of the receding river. "I want you out of here now."

She resisted his pull, and her light flashed bright white. "Billy Bannister, I know you too well. What do you really have in mind?"

Billy dragged his glowing foot along the crystalline floor. "I'm not lying. I'll get the animals, but …"

"But what?"

He folded his arms across his chest. "I have to face him."

"Him? You mean Devin?"

"Yeah. I can't keep running from him. I can't keep ignoring the prophecies."

Bonnie's eyes lit up like two sapphires. "There are prophecies that say you have to face him?"

"Yeah, remember that old book the professor had? It's Merlin's Diary, and prophecies appear in it." Billy pressed his palms against his temples. "The words kept repeating in my head, almost like a bad song you can't get rid of. It was something about having to face the beast to break some chains. Don't you think it means I have to face him, once and for all?"

319

Bonnie lowered her gaze for several seconds, not making a sound. When she lifted her head again, her light shimmered like the sun on a wind-blown pond. "I think you're right. You do have to face him." Her flashing eyes suddenly dimmed, becoming gray and weak. "And I have to leave without you."

He pulled her toward the river again. "And we have to hustle. They're probably waiting."

"Okay, okay. I'll go." She touched him gently on the shoulder. "I don't know how to say this, but … try to be … well …"

"You want me to stay cool, right?"

Bonnie smiled and nodded. "And don't wait too long if Devin decides not to show his face."

"Don't worry." Billy shuddered, shaking off sparkles. "This place gives me the creeps."

Bonnie dipped her toe in the river's shallows. Just before the current swept her in, she held up her hand, displaying her glowing ring. Billy copied her gesture. Their palms faced each other, and the red glow from each ring bridged the gap between them, joining in a pulsing web of scarlet. The river then enveloped Bonnie and carried her away.

Billy watched helplessly as her body flew out of the candlestone. Her flashing light dangled in the air on the outside, her particles already beginning to separate. Her ring highlighted her groping hand as her fingers stretched for something to grasp. Again and again she clutched at empty air.

Billy whispered, "C'mon, Bonnie. Hang in there."

Her light vanished.

He blinked. Did she disperse? Was she sucked back into the candlestone? His legs dwindled into two spindly sparks, more like trembling, electric toothpicks than legs. He closed his eyes and balled his hands into flashing fists. *I gotta have faith!*

"Sir William," Newman said. "Will you go next?"

Billy shook his head. "The rest of the knights should go, but can you stay long enough to help me collect the animals and toss them into the river?"

"Certainly. The poor beasts cannot find their own way out. To leave them to their own devices would not be chivalrous. I know the places they usually congregate, so it won't take long to find them. We will all stay to help."

"Great. Thank you."

Newman lifted a small glowing animal. "This dog should go first. He refuses to leave my side, and I keep tripping on him."

Billy laughed. "Sir Newman, how can you trip over a body of light?" He took the dog from the knight and set him down. "Let's throw in the animals you've trapped, then we'll use the dog to hunt for the others together, okay?"

"My pleasure, William." Newman shouted into the cavern. "Men! Get ready for some chimp-tossing!"

321

＊　　　＊　　　＊　　　＊　　　＊　　　＊

Walter waited at the recovery dome, his hand poised over the platform button. Another body congealed under the glass. Its shape wasn't as distinct as Barlow's, but it was obviously human, with glittering arms and legs and strands of luminescence flowing from its head.

"Starting restoration," Ashley called. "Get ready."

The light solidified into a feminine shape, the strands falling on her shoulders as light brown tresses. A mass on her back morphed into folded wings. Within seconds, Bonnie materialized in a shining robe. She blinked and took in a deep breath.

Ashley's voice boomed across the lab. "Walter! Now!"

Walter slapped the switch, jumped to his feet, and bounced on his toes while waiting for the glass to rise. At his side, Sir Barlow set his feet and lifted Excalibur.

"You can lower your sword," Walter said. "She's a friend."

The knight relaxed his arm and rested Excalibur at his side.

Bonnie glanced around with glazed eyes, her arms and legs motionless. Walter leaped onto the platform, took her hand, and guided her to floor level.

"Walter?" she said dreamily. She clutched his arm as her legs wobbled. "What are you doing here?"

"Walter," Ashley called from the control panel. "She's disoriented. Her light waves were frazzled when she came out. We almost lost her."

Still holding her hand, Walter tapped the switch with his foot, sending the glass shield down again. "We're all here," he said to Bonnie. "I mean, the professor and me and Billy's mom." He pointed toward the glass cylinders. "The professor's the one who pulled you into that dome."

When Bonnie looked over her shoulder at the restoration process, she spied her uncovered wings and gasped.

Smiling, Walter waved a hand. "Don't worry. I've known about your wings for a long time."

"You've known?" Bonnie's wings trembled. "But how?"

Ashley interrupted. "We'll have time for explanations later. Right now Walter has a job to do."

Bonnie blinked. "Is that Ashley?"

"Right here, Bonnie," Ashley called, waving. "It's good to see you again. Sorry I can't come over there. I'm sort of busy."

"Ahem." Sir Barlow knelt in front of Bonnie. "Fair maiden, forgive me. I did not realize you were an angel. It is you who should bear the great sword." He extended Excalibur, hilt first.

Blinking, Bonnie reached for the sword and grasped the hilt with both hands. Its glow brightened to a fiery white blaze.

Barlow gasped, fell to his bottom, and slid away. "By all that is holy!"

"Oh, get up," Walter said, laughing and reaching a hand toward the frightened knight. "Bonnie's not an angel. She's a dragon."

"A dragon?" Barlow repeated as Walter hoisted him to his feet.

Ashley's voice boomed again out of the darkness. "Explain it later, Walter. Another one's coming."

As a new mass of light filtered into the dome, Walter jumped to his post. Barlow whispered to Bonnie, "Whatever you are, lass, be ready to strike. It might be one of the scoundrels."

Bonnie offered him the hilt. "I'd feel better if you were the one holding it. I was kind of in a stupor when I took it."

Barlow grasped the hilt and bowed his head. "If you so command, my lady. It will be my honor to bear it."

Walter dropped to his knees near the cylinder switch. "Whatever just came out of the stone is taking shape."

The light in the dome coalesced into a short, stooped form.

"An ape!" Barlow cried.

Ashley squinted at the hairy face. "That's Betsy. She was one of our first chimps to go in." Betsy pressed her nose against the glass. "She's ready, Walter. Get her out of there."

When Walter hit the button, Betsy scrambled down on all fours. Ashley clapped her hands. "C'mere, Betsy," The chimp dashed across the floor and jumped into her mistress's arms. Ashley let out a sigh. "If they send out all the animals, we're in for a long night."

❖   ❖   ❖   ❖   ❖   ❖

Billy wrestled a young chimp off his back and released him into the river. "Is that the last one, Sir Newman?"

"By my count, Sir William, yes."

"Then let's send your men. Who should go first?"

Newman looked his fellow knights over, each now standing at attention. "Since our leader is already out there, he can assemble the men when they arrive. I volunteer to go last. The next to go should be—"

Ploof!

Billy jerked his head around. "What was that?" The remnants of an electric splash rose from the river, leaving an effervescent fizz. Two seconds later, another splash plumed in a surge of spritzing static, then another.

"The conspirators!" Newman shouted.

"Get your men in there now!" Billy yelled. "We can't have them outnumbering our people in the lab!"

Newman waved his arms toward the river. "Edward, fly to the exit! Fiske, you follow him! Then Standish and Woodrow!"

The four phantoms dashed into the current, allowing it to hurl their bodies into the river. Their splashes combined with those of the remaining conspirators as they all flushed through the candlestone's wash.

Newman faced Billy and bowed. "You next, lad."

"No." Billy gave him a nod. "You go. I … I have something to do."

Newman straightened and folded his hands behind his back. "I am at your service, William. With that fiend lurking in the shadows, I stand as your ready guard."

"Thank you, but they need you out there." He gripped Newman's shoulder. "This is something I have to do alone."

Newman bowed. "Sir William, you are a brave knight indeed. I look forward to seeing you on the other side."

Without another word, Newman stepped toward the river. His body elongated as the current pulled him into its flow. His noble smile stretched with his thinning face, and he vanished into a vapor of streaming light.

Now alone in the chasm, Billy scanned the upper rim. *Where is he? He fooled me last time, so I guess my danger sensing doesn't work in here.*

When he turned to continue his search, a flashing storm of light blocked his path. "Going somewhere, mongrel?" An electric hand throttled his neck, jolting his body. "This party is just getting started."

* * * * * *

Get Bobo away from that machine!" Ashley yelled. "If she turns it on, this show's over for good!"

Bonnie flew across the lab and snatched Bobo into her arms. She carried the chimp through the air to the girls' dorm, slid her inside, and closed the door.

"Bonnie!" Ashley shouted. "Get Betsy, too. She's trying to fiddle with the lights. We need them to stay dim." She swatted the chimp's hairy hand away from the dial.

Airborne again, Bonnie zipped to the control panel, grabbed Betsy, and held the struggling ape away from the controls.

Ashley let out a relieved sigh, then immediately tensed. "Oh no! We have four, no, five in the diver's dome. There's no way the professor can grab them all before the candlestone reabsorbs them."

"Wait." Ashley's brow bent toward her nose. "The candlestone's not affecting them. Could it be because their light isn't agitated anymore?" She began shouting again. "Now there are six! Seven! What are we going to do? The receptors will never last!"

"I'll be back after I put Betsy away." Bonnie patted Ashley's hand. "If anyone can figure out what to do, you can."

"But how?" She blinked at the panel. "Now there are eight! No, nine!"

Bonnie zoomed toward the dorm with Betsy in her arms. As she flew past the domes, Sir Barlow wrestled for the sword with a larger chimp while a Scottish terrier nipped at Walter's socks as he knelt next to the restoration dome. She sighed. "Those two will just have to wait."

*　　　*　　　*　　　*　　　*　　　*

Waves of pain shot into Billy's body and rippled through his energy field. The stinging current drove into his brain, like hot needles zapping him again and again. The slayer's grip tightened around Billy's throat. Every light dimmed and spun. The slayer lifted him until his feet floated above the chasm floor.

"You have no idea who you're dealing with, Dragon Boy," the slayer growled. "I am the Minister of The New Table. I am Arthur's Bane. I am the Wandering Spirit who cannot die."

Billy could barely think. The slayer's words were surreal, a wave of strange ideas. The New Table? Arthur's bane? What was he talking about?

Devin's arm drew back. He threw a raging punch at Billy's face, like a blacksmith's mighty hammer crushing heated steel. Billy flew against one of the chasm's walls, splattering his body against the crystal and creating a splash of sizzling sparks.

The slayer stalked toward him again. His arms reached forward as if he were a demonic mantis. His evil voice sounded like an echo from the pit of hell. "It's time to end this for good, you whelp of a jackal!"

A blinding flash of light surged through the gap between the demon and his prey. In a split second, the light gathered into the tall stately form of a man, robed, with flowing silver hair. He spread his arms. Light beams shot from his hands and formed a glowing shield, an oblong bubble that enveloped Billy and his defender.

The slayer burst into enraged flames, and his fiery red finger shook with dripping sparks. "Begone, you old sorcerer. Your black magic won't keep me from slaying this foul son of the devil!"

Billy's ghostly friend replied in a soft but firm tone. "It is not young William who springs from Satan's loins, Devin. It is the liar who finds his home in the devil's house of worship. Darkness breeds there, and you are its offspring, the minister of the darkest of lies."

"Oh, so eloquent!" Devin sneered. "Is that what you've been doing for a thousand years, composing oral gems like that one? It makes me feel better knowing that you were in here conjuring trite little sayings while I was taking care of your dragon friends. Would you like an account of how many now remain in your draconic collection?"

The defender's voice remained calm. "I am aware of your deeds, but the prophecy is still intact."

"And so is mine." Devin's flame continued rippling across his radiant body. "Is your little lamb aware of the prophecies about me? I'll bet you haven't told him, have you?"

"No. He has seen enough of evil to know its character. A stinking pool need not be waded to learn that it is foul."

"Well, perhaps the mongrel would like to know more about my power in his world. Has he ever asked why I was able to become a school principal, how I could manipulate the Castlewood police, how I was able to stow away in his father's guarded airplane? Have you told him the truth about me?"

Billy pulled himself up to his knees. Devin's questions were his own questions—ones he had asked himself a hundred times.

"He will learn the truth," the defender replied. "But it will not come through your twisted words. I will not allow it." The silver-haired man lifted Billy to his feet and kept a hand on his back.

Billy stared into the face of his defender. "Professor?" he whispered. "How did you get in here?"

"It is time for you to go, brave lad."

"But it's not over. I have to face Devin."

"Not here and not now. You will face him, but you have not yet taken hold of your greatest weapons."

The defender lifted Billy into the air and threw him into the dark current. Billy sailed toward the stream of light, pulled through the swirling blackness without the strength to fight it. When he plunged into the river, light flashed all around. Millions of tiny sparks pecked at his body, and the pulsing lights dimmed to black.

* * * * * *

"Edward!" Sir Barlow cried as the glass rose. "You made it!" The knight, dressed in loose-fitting silk breeches and shirt, stepped down to the floor. "Yes," he replied breathlessly, "but our enemies might soon follow. I am the first, it seems, but the others are floating back in that glass case. I cannot tell who will be taken next."

Bonnie peered into the diver's dome. "What about Billy? Is he floating in there?"

Edward bowed toward her. "The lad is still in the stone, as far as I know. He is a valiant one, to be sure. My guess is that he wanted to oversee everyone's escape."

Ashley called from the control panel. "The receptors are dying! If the professor brings anyone else over, I won't be able to do another restoration. I might have to—"

A shout filled the lab. "She's gone!"

Ashley spun toward the voice. "Who's gone?"

Doc appeared in the dim light, leading Derrick and pushing Ashley's grandfather in his wheelchair.

"Daddy!" Ashley rushed toward them. Her grandfather's head lolled to one side, and he shivered violently, his eyes tightly shut and his hands clenched into fists. Bonnie followed close behind Ashley and took Derrick's hand from Doc.

Dirty tears streamed down Doc's earth-caked cheeks as he laid a trembling hand on Ashley's shoulder. "Karen's gone!"

COLLAPSE

Ashley enfolded her grandfather's stiff, wrinkled hands and held them against her cheeks. "He's freezing." She searched around his wheelchair. "Where's his blanket?"

"It was gone when I got there." Dr. Conner pointed toward the Omega door. "There's deep snow where the cave comes out into the valley, but I couldn't see any human tracks, just depressions and scratches in the snow. I saw blood next to the boulder that must have hit Karen, but there wasn't any trail." He took the medical bag from Derrick and set it on the floor. "It's like she just vanished into thin air. And the cave collapsed behind me on my way back here. There's no escaping that way now."

Ashley stroked Derrick's arm. "Did you hear anything? Can you even guess what happened?"

Derrick, his ebony skin streaked with tear tracks through gray dust, spoke slowly. "I heard weird noises, like wind … wind whipping a blanket on a clothes line." He wiped his face with his sleeve. "And there was a smell, a smell like plowed soil, and I felt a warm breeze for just a second or two."

Bonnie hugged Derrick and held his quivering face against her shoulder. Ashley grabbed the coat the professor had shed and laid it over her grandfather's shaking body, tucking it around his sides. "I ... I can't do much more for Daddy now, Doc. And I can't go looking for Karen." She waved an arm toward the diver's dome. "There are a bunch of people floating over there, and the professor left one in the restoration dome. I can't restore any of them until I get more photoreceptors. If we don't hurry, the people will disperse and die."

"But where can we get receptors?" Doc fumbled through his pocket and drew out his ring of keys. "You know our source is gone."

Bonnie extended her arms, exposing their scarred undersides. "Don't I have photoreceptors? Can't we use mine?"

"Yes," Ashley said, "you have them, but after getting transluminated and restored, your receptors could be weak or useless. Instead of letting the machine restore you, your receptors tried to do the work and drained themselves. And, besides, since you'll have a low receptor density right now, it would take a lot of blood. We need you to stay strong to help search for Karen from the air."

Walter stepped close to the wheelchair. "Search, smearch! If Bonnie's got photo-whatitz, then let's try to use them. Weak ones are better than none at all. Billy and Prof are going to die if we don't. And we'll find Karen one way or another."

Doc opened his medical bag and withdrew a syringe. "I promised myself I'd never draw another drop of Bonnie's blood, but I don't think we have any choice."

Letting out a deep sigh, Ashley rolled up a robe sleeve and extended her arm toward Doc. "Take them from me."

He stared at Ashley's bare forearm. "Take what from you? What are you talking about?"

She nodded toward her arm. "I have photoreceptors in my blood. We can use them in the engine."

Bonnie set a hand on Ashley's skin. "You have them? How?"

She jerked her arm back. "I can't explain now. We've wasted too much time already. Doc, just get the needle and do it!"

He rummaged through the medical bag and pulled out a plastic tube. "We'll have to attach you directly to the equipment to be sure we get enough."

Ashley marched toward a machine near the lab's edge while Doc followed. "Can you run the board? It's programmed to isolate the professor's coding and analyze only who he brings with him. The code loop has already worked several times, so just keep the system tuned where I have it, experimental project eleven B. If everything keeps working, we could have a big search party in just a few minutes." She wheeled a chair to the machine and held out her arm.

333

"I can run the board. Just be ready to answer any questions I have." Doc stooped and pushed one end of the plastic tube into an adapter on the machine. With a quick twist, he fastened a needle on the other end of the tube and pressed the point into the crook of Ashley's arm. A dark stream of red seeped through the plastic and ran toward a collection tank on the machine. Doc jumped up and hustled to the control panel.

"Everyone back to your posts!" Ashley called. "Doc, signal Walter when each restoration is complete. Barlow, have the sword ready. Bonnie, see if you can keep my grandfather warm."

"You were right," Doc said. "The system is showing functional receptors." He turned a dial clockwise. "Here we go!"

Leading Derrick by the hand, Bonnie pushed the wheelchair closer to the dome near Walter and Sir Barlow. Barlow called out, "I can already identify who is in there. It is one of the conspirators, Addison by name. He is not very bright." Barlow lifted Excalibur to an attack position.

The form in the recovery dome congealed, creating a thin, shaking little man dressed only in a gray, girded loincloth.

Walter dropped to his knees. "Is he ready?"

Doc waved a hand. "Yes, go ahead."

Walter hit the switch. As soon as the glass rose to chest level, Addison fell to his knees, his eyes wide. He pointed at Bonnie and squeaked, "An angel! Am I in heaven?"

Sir Barlow lunged with Excalibur. "Death to all who dare enter heaven naked!" Addison shrieked and dashed into the darkness. With a hearty laugh, Barlow returned to his post. "The fool never did learn to wear proper garments under his mail. Serves him right."

A sudden jolt knocked Walter to his bottom. "What was that?"

"Another tremor!" Ashley shouted.

The tile floor buckled and cracked, swallowing a loop of cables into a shallow depression. Dr. Conner gripped the sides of the control panel. "Will the equipment hold out?"

Ashley pressed a hand on the needle in her arm to keep it steady. "Your guess is as good as mine." She twisted toward the wheelchair. "Bonnie, does your professor know Morse code?"

"Probably."

"Go to the wall switches. We need to send him an SOS."

334

Three ceiling panels gave way. Rocks and dirt crashed into the anchor dome, shattering the glass and sending fragments crunching to the floor. Bonnie hopped over the shards and dashed to the wall near the Alpha door. "Ready!"

"Find the switch on the far left and flip it on," Ashley called.

"Got it!"

"Now you have control of the lights. Use the middle switch and flip it three times—quick, short bursts. Follow that with three longer ones." Ashley counted the flashes above her head. "Now repeat the short ones." She held the tube against her arm and stood. "Doc, turn on both generators. Local power is bound to go out."

He opened a small plastic flap over a red switch. "I already fired up the first one." He flicked the switch and closed the flap. "Second one's up."

Ashley leaned over the machine and yelled at Barlow. "We might need Edward to go with Bonnie to shore up the ceiling." She spun toward Bonnie. "Can you fly him up there?"

She nodded. "He's no bigger than Billy, and I've carried him—"

"Good. Be ready to do that. And leave the lights on. Everyone should be out of the stone by now." She turned to Doc. "Move slider C fourteen to max. That should speed up the restorations. We'll have to risk a power sag."

"To max? It'll drain the receptors."

"I'm mainlining the supply, Doc. They'll last."

He pushed the buffer control to the top. "But will you last?"

Excited shrieks erupted within the dorm halls. "It's the chimps," Ashley yelled amidst the growing clamor. "Local power must be out, or else the dorms are caving in."

335

"The professor's moving faster," Doc shouted back. "He must have gotten the signal. We have a new body in the dome. The professor's clear. Restoring now."

"It's Standish," Barlow said. "An excellent knight. A bit eccentric, however."

"Get him out, Walter," Doc called. "The professor's already waiting."

Walter slapped the switch, reached under the glass as it rose, and dragged Standish off the platform. As soon as the knight was clear, Walter hit the switch again.

Doc brushed dirt from one of the panel's meters. "Good job." He rotated a dial with one hand and wiped his forehead with the other. "Get ready. We'll have another one in a few seconds."

Loose dirt pelted the ceiling. Doc glanced up. "Bonnie, the panel above the dome is sagging. Start with that one."

"I'm on it." The shadow of enormous wings passed across the lab floor, and Bonnie scooped Edward up from behind.

"Aaaah!" The knight's legs flailed in the air as he flew through the lab.

* * * * * *

Bonnie zoomed to the outer wall and shot into the upper reaches of the cavern. She flew Edward over the ceiling, and landed with him on top of one of the horizontal beams that suspended the ceiling panels' support wires. Tiny stones and dirt pelted them as Bonnie examined the ceiling below while bracing herself against a vertical beam. Shafts of light illuminated the area, shining upward through gaps in the drop ceiling.

Bonnie pointed toward a spot several feet away. "That pile of rubble is right over the diver's dome. Let's try to move the bigger stones."

"Do you feel that?" Edward asked, holding out his hand.

Bonnie looked up. "Snow?" She held out her own hand. An icy flake settled on her palm. How could snow get in here? "Hang on. I'll be right back." She leaped into the dimness, dodging a protruding rock formation, and found a gaping hole in the ceiling. Shooting through the gap, she cleared the rim of a volcano-like cone and flew into the cold, snow-filled sky. After surveying the area, she made a sharp U-turn, zipped back through the gap, and landed softly next to Edward, who was busily clearing debris from the sagging panel.

"We'd better hurry," she said. "The mountain looks like its splitting open."

"Almost done, Miss." Edward lifted a cannonball-sized stone, slid across the snow-slicked beam, and heaved it toward the far side of the cavern. "That should do it."

"Are you ready to fly back down?"

337

"Not to insult your skills, m'lady, but if you don't mind, I will take a more direct route." Edward leaped toward a hole in the ceiling, caught the frame, and swung down to the floor, landing with a bend of his knees. Bonnie flew across the tops of the panels, then back down the side of the cavern and landed in a run at the edge of the lab.

Ashley sat beside the blood receptacle, gaunt and pale. Barlow stood next to five other men who were similarly clad in dark breeches and loose cotton shirts. Walter crouched at his post waiting for the next signal. Billy was nowhere in sight.

Bonnie's throat caught. He hadn't come out yet. But there was no time to worry about that. "We have a major problem," she said to Ashley. "The mountain's splitting apart at the top."

"Not good." Ashley yanked the needle from her arm and jumped to her feet. Applying pressure to her wound, she staggered toward the panel. "That must be Billy coming in now.

We should have enough receptors. Restore him and then the professor, and let's get out of here."

Dr. Conner moved out of the way as Ashley stepped up to control the panel. She pulled on her headphones, adjusted the microphone, and flipped a switch. Her voice boomed through hidden speakers. "Barlow, get your men and carry my grandfather up the stairs in the Alpha exit. Bonnie will show you the way. Walter, as soon as Billy appears, help him out quickly. He might not recognize you or even understand what's going on."

"But the other males are fine," Bonnie said, wiping sweat from her forehead. "Won't Billy be okay?"

Ashley took a deep breath. Her pale skin regained a hint of color. "I can't be sure, but I have a theory. I think the longer a male's been in the candlestone, the better for his brain." Her eyes refocused on the recovery cylinder. "But there's no time to explain any further. Just pray that he's all right."

A male body materialized in the dome, but he sat crumpled, his head between his knees and his arms draped over his legs.

Walter punched the switch. "It's Billy!" He gripped the lower rim of the glass to make it rise faster.

Bonnie jumped toward the dome, but Barlow pushed the wheelchair into her path and grasped her elbow. "Show me the way out, lass. The conspirators have fled to the shadows, and we will allow the cowards to perish in God's wrath, but we must save the old man and the blind youth."

Bonnie looked at his kind, serious face and the solemn expressions of his men as they stood close by. "Okay. Sure."

Dr. Conner dashed over and grabbed the wheelchair handles. "I'll take them, Bonnie. You go to Billy."

"Thank you." Bonnie flapped her wings and half walked, half flew to Billy. He lay motionless on the floor where Walter had set him.

Walter hit the switch again. "Now we just need to get Prof."

Ashley's voice boomed through the speakers again. "The professor's already grabbed someone else, and they're both passing through the tube."

"But there isn't anyone else," Walter said, "except—"

"Devin?" Bonnie knelt on the floor. She cradled Billy's head in her arms and used her wings to shield his body from the raining debris.

"It's not Devin," Ashley said, "but it's strange. The analyzer says it has the same data coding as the professor. Since I have the professor's coding blocked, the computer assumes it *is* the professor and won't complete the restoration. I'll have to turn off the block and let it analyze them together." She began typing madly on a keyboard, reprogramming the computer with her flying fingers. "I don't know if this will work, but here goes."

Dr. Conner burst back into the room. "The Alpha exit's caved in, too. The whole side of the mountain is giving way." Barlow and his men reentered, carrying Ashley's grandfather, wheelchair and all, and leading Derrick by the hand. Doc waved an arm. "Everyone to the center of the lab!"

While Barlow and his knights rushed toward the central pedestal with Derrick and the wheelchair, Bonnie dragged Billy's limp body. He felt like a thousand pound sack of sand. Carrying Edward had sapped her strength.

Barlow ran to her and lifted Billy over his shoulder. "I'll take him, Miss."

The crowd clustered around the pedestal while larger rocks crashed to the floor, piling in front of the Alpha exit and raising a thick wall of dust. Ceiling panels, along with their twisted frames and support beams, tumbled. Barlow deflected two panels with one of his massive arms, while Fiske, Standish, and Woodrow arched their bodies over Ashley's grandfather and Derrick. Edward and Newman stood like shade trees over Bonnie while she sat cross-legged on the floor. Barlow placed Billy in her arms. She laid her cheek against his and silently prayed.

Walter stayed at his post and kept his stare trained on the restoration dome. Ashley's voice crackled through the speakers. "They're both in there." Lights flickered and loud pops sounded all around. Ashley threw off the headphones and pushed three sliders fully to the right. "Power's failing on generator number one. Going max on restoration while the second generator lasts. Get ready, Walter. As soon as you can recognize him, count to three and pull him out." Ashley left the panel and joined the huddled group.

Walter set a hand over the switch. Bulbs exploded, and every surrounding light went black, but the dome still buzzed with activity and emanated a light of its own. One second later, the professor's familiar form appeared, standing erect on the platform. "No time to wait for that glass to rise." Walter grabbed Excalibur from the floor, counted to three, and swung the glowing sword. The blade smashed the cylinder and sent glass flying everywhere.

The professor brushed shards from his robe and stepped down to floor level. With sharp, piercing eyes, he turned slowly and gazed at the battered lab—ceiling debris on the cracked tiles, a mound of rocks blocking the Alpha door, and the huddled group in the center of the cavern. A mangled frame and a few panels remained in the ceiling above. The sword in Walter's hands and a row of LED's still flickering on the control panel provided only scant light in the dim room. The professor shone against the blackness as if somehow he had retained some of his transluminated form.

Everything fell silent except for a droning hum. He reached out a hand, and his voice echoed in the darkness. "The sword, please, Walter."

Walter flipped the sword around and extended the hilt. The professor grasped it and limped toward the central pedestal. He knelt at Bonnie's side and placed the sword in Billy's hands, wrapping his own fingers on top and elevating the blade. Still wearing the protective robe, Billy opened his eyes and tightened his grasp on the hilt.

"William," the professor said, softly, "what now is your weapon?"

Billy's eyes reflected the professor's shining face, enhanced by Excalibur's glow.

"Truth," he whispered, his voice rasping. He cleared his throat. "Truth is my sword."

The professor's voice erupted in deep, echoing tones as if Billy's answer strengthened him. "And what now is your defense?"

Color returned to Billy's face, and his jaw tightened. His voice surged with emotion. "Faith … faith is my shield."

Excalibur's glow exploded in dazzling brilliance, sending out a sparkling corona and bathing the lab in a spectacular halo. A dozen shafts of light shot out from the sword's tip, angling in all directions and then bouncing back, combining into one huge bolt of lightning that plunged into Billy's chest.

His body lurched, and his skin shimmered like the sun on a perfectly polished suit of armor, his entire frame flashing like a human strobe light. He let out a long, loud yell, a warrior's battle cry that echoed across the littered cavern floor.

341

As the professor released his grip, the bright light faded. Billy sat up, clutching the glowing sword. He took Bonnie's hand in his and stared at the union, fingers interlocked and two rings touching, creating a glow of their own.

He smiled at her and whispered, "I have work to do."

Bonnie squeezed his hand, then withdrew from their clutch, smiling in return. "Then you'd better get to it."

A strange noise buzzed across the chamber. The cap of the broken restoration dome, now dangling from a bent frame by a mangled wire, sent a feeble beam toward the platform below. A new phantom appeared in the ray, a radiant ghost with yellow-green eyes that glowed like copper laser beams shooting through a night sky.

The professor grasped Billy's hand and pulled him to his feet. "Your work is beginning, William. The captives await their final liberation."

Billy raised the flashing sword high as though it weighed no more than a child's toy. "First thing's first. Where's the candlestone?"

Ashley pointed. "In the diver's dome."

Billy shouted, "No more prisoners!"

He rushed to the diver's dome and smashed the glass cylinder with one blow of the sword. He swung again, this time driving the blade directly into the stone, slicing through it cleanly. A tiny explosion of sparks erupted, and the two halves fell dark.

Billy spun toward the apparition on the recovery platform. Devin's body, not yet fully restored, pulsed between light and darkness, between man and glowing beast as the restoration ray continued to bathe his phantom form.

Billy raced to the control panel and ripped the metal surface with the blade. A wave of sparks flew high into the air.

The hum died, and every blinking light faded to black, leaving Excalibur's glow and the slayer's throbbing body the only lights in the room.

Devin remained on the platform, a glowing mass of electric plasma that seemed to float in place. "Addison," he growled. "I know you're out there somewhere. Assemble our men."

The nearly naked Addison ran to Devin's side, trembling like a chilled pup, and four fierce-looking men followed him. Devin turned to the huddled group near the pedestal. "Conner, open the weapons cache for my soldiers. It's time to get rid of the mongrel blight."

Dr. Conner rose to his feet. "Mongrel blight?" He glanced at Bonnie, gave her a weak smile, then spun back toward Devin, his chest puffing out. "You blind fool!" He waved a hand at the group sitting around his feet. "Look at them. You call them mongrels, but their love for each other, their willingness to sacrifice their lives for their friends, shows they have more heart than you'll ever have—more heart, more faith, and more courage."

Bonnie stood and grasped her father's hand. He squeezed hers in return. As he kept his defiant glare trained on Devin, a tear streamed down his cheek. "Someone told me not too long ago that my plans could fail because love might turn on me and set all the captives free. She was right, and I'm one of those freed captives." He took a step forward, still clutching Bonnie's hand. "Get lost, *Sir* Devin. I'm not afraid of you anymore."

Devin flashed, and sparks flew from his hands and hair. "A bit late for that, you fool." He jumped from the platform and glided toward a closet door, his own light illuminating his path. When he set a hand on the doorknob, a stream of fire engulfed the surface. With a Herculean pull, he jerked the door

343

open, tearing it from its hinges. "Men," he said, motioning toward the inside, "arm yourselves."

Addison and the other four men hustled toward the closet. Barlow leaped to his feet and raced to head them off. Edward surged ahead and tackled Addison, knocking him into two of the other conspirators. Barlow's remaining knights charged. Devin thrashed Newman and Standish with his fiery arms, sending them flying.

Billy pulled the robe over his head, tossed it to the side, and dashed toward the fray, Excalibur sparkling in his hands.

"Mind the beam, William!" the professor shouted. "It will disintegrate your friends as well as your enemies!"

Walter grabbed a broken piece of metal and followed Billy. Dr. Conner pried off a nail-studded two-by-four from a fallen panel and sprinted toward the battle. With her strength renewed, Bonnie snatched up a board and exploded into the air. She swooped in front of Addison's right-hand man and bashed him across the face, then zoomed upward before he could retaliate.

Flying over Billy, she gave him a quick glance. He battled with the sword like a champion warrior. Whatever renewed his strength, she prayed for the same power. This battle might take a long time.

* * * * * *

Ashley took a step to join them, but the professor held her back. "You are too weak, child. See to your grandfather. Cover him."

"You're right. I am weak." Using her back as a shield, she wrapped her arms around her grandfather. The professor arched over Derrick and braced himself with a palm on the floor.

"Another tremor," he said softly, closing his eyes. "As you might have guessed, Ashley Stalworth, this is no normal earthquake." As the battle continued in front of the weapons room, his voice melted into a lilting song.

Tremors, O, tremors of the earth,
Come now with mercy
To those of royal birth.

Answer, O, answer to our cry,
Open now the chasm
To bring fire from the sky.

A strong jolt shook the lab. The twisted ceiling frame crashed to the floor, followed by a hail of rocks and dirt. Knights and conspirators tumbled to the ground. As Billy knocked a sword from Addison's hand, the jolt threw him to the gritty floor, jarring Excalibur from his grasp. Addison sprang toward him, but Billy planted his feet in the conspirator's chest and thrust him toward a pile of rocks.

A falling panel struck Bonnie on her back and drove her to the floor, sending her weapon flying into the tangled heap of rubble. She smacked her palms and knees on the dirty, debris-strewn tile and slid to a stop. The door to the dorm hall flew open, and a frightened chimp dashed out along with the Scottish terrier and a scampering rabbit.

Devin, his bright, sizzling body radiating sparks, charged Billy, reaching for him with fiery hands. Staring at his attacker, Billy groped for Excalibur at his side. Devin leaped toward him. Billy launched a stream of flames into the slayer's face. The force blew the glowing phantom backwards and slammed him into a wall on the far side of the cavern. He disappeared in the midst of falling dirt and rocks, but his glow continued, penetrating the flying, swirling dust. Seconds later, he stalked out of the gloom, larger and brighter than before.

Billy whispered, "Did he absorb my fire?" He grabbed Excalibur and jumped to his feet in a battle stance as he waited to see what the slayer would do.

Barlow bowled over one of the conspirators and burst into the weapons room. His arms bulging with swords and shields, he scrambled to his allies and handed out weapons and shields while the conspirators regrouped and drew back into the shadows.

Bonnie took wing again and soared into the air. A moment later, she fluttered down and called out, "The ceiling and the top of the mountain are completely gone! We're in the open!"

Ashley grabbed the wheelchair handles. "Let's get Daddy and Derrick out of here, even if we have to climb over the rubble to get to the valley."

The professor set a hand on Ashley's shoulder. "Perhaps that won't be necessary," he said, pointing toward the sky. "The summoned one has arrived."

Scorched Earth

Bonnie shot upward once more. Shielded by a blanket of dense clouds, the moon's white glow painted ghostly images throughout the sky. The thick falling snow framed a silhouette, a winged shadow approaching the toppled mountain. She brushed flecks of snow from her hair. A dragon? Billy's dad? Had he flown all this way? She flew back to the lab and perched on a stone protrusion, just out of reach of the battlers. Should she tell the others, or did the dragon want to surprise their enemies?

Below, a cry rang out. The conspirators charged. Addison's sword pierced Walter's shield, the point stopping within inches of his face. He jerked the shield back and wrenched the sword from his attacker's grip. Barlow stepped in and landed a bruising elbow on Addison's cheek, sending his smaller opponent crashing to the ground. Woodrow and Fiske stood abreast, crossed swords with two conspirators, and beat them back toward a wall.

Edward and Newman fought the two remaining traitors, raising their shields next to Dr. Conner and keeping him tucked between them. Newman parried a sword thrust, spun gracefully on his toe, and plunged his blade into his enemy's midsection. Edward faced the biggest of the evil knights. He ducked under a sweeping sword, twirled on his knees, and swiped across the conspirator's ankles. The burly man toppled to the ground like a felled redwood. Standish stayed back, guarding Derrick and the others with a raised sword and shield.

With Excalibur blazing in his grip, Billy faced Devin. The slayer brought his palms together and fashioned a ball of flames from his own light energy. The fireball shot from his hands and hurtled toward Billy like a crawling nest of electric scorpions. With a quick swing, Billy smacked the ball with his blade and sent it rocketing into the night. The fireball lit up the cloud-covered sky, illuminating the dragon's silhouette.

"A dragon!" Devin roared across the crater. "The time has come. My prophecy is now fulfilled."

The dragon swooped, then pulled up, its massive body blocking the veiled moon. With its wings extended, it glided in a wide circle as if surveying the battle scene. The two remaining conspirators scampered into a dark pocket.

Angling its wings, the dragon swooped again, this time straight toward Devin. As the dragon opened its mouth to shoot a barrage of flames, Billy raised his hands. "Dad! No!"

It was too late. A huge jet of yellow surged through the cloud of snow and plunged into Devin's chest. An explosion of fire erupted, sending a blazing plume all around.

Devin's arms flapped wildly in the midst of the inferno. The wall of fire expanded, and Devin's body grew with it, seeming to absorb the energy until his form swelled into a massive, glowing monster of light. Now three times his normal size, Devin's evil face reappeared, and his eyes radiated like demonic beacons in a human lighthouse.

The reenergized slayer created another fireball and flung it at Barlow. The spherical lightning rolled through the battle-field, knocking Barlow to the side and bowling over Edward and Newman. The two conspirators sprang from their hiding places and pounced toward the fallen knights, but Fiske and Walter held them at bay. Dr. Conner ripped off his shirt and smothered the flames on Newman's clothes.

Bonnie leaped from her perch to the ground and grabbed two heavy stones from the floor. She vaulted into the air again and hurled the stones at the conspirators. The first crashed into the larger man's head while the second glanced off the smaller man's hip. They ducked and retreated again to the shadows.

349

*   *   *   *   *   *

Away from the battle scene, Ashley caressed her grand-father's face. Even as the battle raged, the whole world seemed eerily quiet. Fear squelched her vision. Snow muffled every sound. Ashley felt alone in the world, just Daddy and her.

Ashley rubbed heat into his frigid hands, but the warmth quickly faded. She pressed her hand on his neck, feeling for a pulse. A weak, chaotic beat thrummed against her fingers, then stopped. Ashley gulped, but the unsteady rhythm started again, weaker than before.

"Ashley," someone whispered.

She turned. The professor sat close by. She had forgotten he was still there.

The kindly-faced gentleman scooted to her side. "Ashley, your grandfather is slipping away. You know that, don't you?"

She nodded, firming her lips to keep from crying.

He placed a tender hand on the side of her head. "He has made his peace with God. It's time for you to make your peace with your grandfather." He rose and limped away quietly.

Ashley lowered her lips next to her grandfather's ear, her voice quaking. "Da … daddy. I … I love you so much." She pushed her fingers through his wet hair and braced his head with her hand. "You're the best … the best daddy a girl could ever want." She sniffed and laid her hand over his heart. "I know now that you were right … about everything. I … I promise I'll believe … I mean, I'll try to believe. Bonnie'll be here to help me. … I'll try to make you proud of me again."

* * * * * *

Clefspeare spread his wings and swooped again, but Devin sidestepped, as agile in his new form as a leaping gazelle. His huge wings angling, Clefspeare made a wide turn around a distant mound of stones.

Billy tightened his grip on Excalibur. He couldn't let Devin feed off dragon fire and get stronger again. A quick kill was his only chance.

While the slayer kept his stare on the dragon, Billy sneaked up close. He lunged and sliced into his opponent's side. The blow felt strange, like he had cut into a squishy mix of electrified jelly and rocks.

Devin roared and smacked Billy away with the back of his hand. Billy flew a dozen feet and bulldozed into what remained of the back wall of the lab. When he dropped to the ground, Excalibur fell from his grasp.

Clefspeare approached again, his mouth opening once more to fire. The flames struck the ground in a ring around Devin and encircled him with bubbling red rocks. Clefspeare slammed into the slayer's huge electric body and flattened him against the melting ground before zooming back into the sky.

Ignoring the pain, Billy jumped up, snatched Excalibur, and ran toward the slayer. Devin leaped to his feet, hurdled the ring of lava, and charged Walter, who was once again battling the determined pair of conspirators. Billy shouted, "Walter, look out!"

Walter ducked just as the slayer swung a flaming arm. He plunged his sword into Devin's thigh, then pulled it out and jumped to the side. A fountain of sparks spewed from Devin's wound, but the loss of energy didn't seem to slow him down. The slayer roared and shot a bolt of lightning from his hand, zapping Walter on the shoulder and sending his sword clanking to the ground. Walter grabbed at his wound and dropped to his knees, his face twisting in pain.

Devin shot two more bolts. Walter rolled away. One bolt ripped the ground at his side. The second exploded at his ear.

Billy leaped in front of Walter, holding Excalibur high and bracing his legs. Devin launched another bolt. Billy parried with the sword, deflecting the bolt into the air. As he set his feet again, his heart pounded. He couldn't hold off a barrage of lightning for long.

A loud roar pierced the darkness. Clefspeare circled through the blanket of falling snow, and a second dark figure swooped in from behind. Billy dropped to his knees. "Two dragons?"

Devin grabbed Walter's sword, a mere toy in his huge, glowing hands. As Clefspeare hurtled downward, the slayer thrust the sword at him. With a great beat of his wings, Clefspeare dodged the slayer's lunge and surged back into the sky.

"Hartanna!" Clefspeare shouted. "The slayer is armed. Use the flank, as we did at Chalice Hill." The dragons thrashed

351

the air with their massive wings and disappeared high into the darkness.

Bonnie tugged on Edward's sleeve, her head tilted upward as she searched the sky. She gasped for breath. "Did he … did he say, Hartanna?"

Edward pulled his bloodstained sword out of his fallen opponent. His labored breaths came in short gasps. "I am not sure, Miss, but it did sound like Hartanna. The name is familiar to me, but I cannot place it."

Bonnie clasped her hands. "Hartanna was my mother's name."

Devin's sizzling head turned in all directions as he scanned the skies. "Where are you, you cursed demons? Come out and fight in the open!"

Billy gripped Walter's wrist and pulled him to his feet. Walter rotated his shoulder, grimacing. "Wow! That overgrown Roman candle really packs a wallop!"

"C'mon," Billy whispered. "Let's find another sword for you. Maybe we can strike low while the dragons strike high."

Billy found Edward, and they salvaged a sword and shield for Walter. The three allies, now armed but winded, charged the flaming giant.

Devin, still holding the sword as he watched the sky, jerked around. Edward vaulted into the air. As Devin sidestepped, Edward cut a deep gash in the slayer's arm that sent a shower of sparkling blood to the floor. Devin backhanded him, launching him toward a wall. Edward landed on his feet but toppled over and banged his head on a fallen boulder. He moved no more.

Billy clutched Walter's collar and held him back. "Let's see if we can wait for the dragons. We're no match for Devin until he's distracted."

Walter shook his head. "There's no use risking the dragons' lives. You have to attack now. I'll get Edward out of the way so you can turn that sword up to deep fat fry and send that critter to join the Northern Lights."

Billy tightened his grip on the glowing sword and took a deep breath. "Okay." He nodded toward a heap of stones. "Take a wide path around that pile, and drag Edward to Dr. Conner. I'll see what I can do."

With his head low and knees bent, Walter sneaked away. Billy raised the sword. The blade gleamed in the night with a steady, unchanged brightness. The professor never mentioned any special words to say. Maybe the beam would appear when he attacked.

The slayer spat a stream of electricity into the sky. "Death to Satan and his angels!" Two dragons hurtled toward him from opposite directions, one diving from a sharp angle, the other swooping low.

Clefspeare dodged the swinging sword, while Hartanna slammed into Devin's legs, sending him tumbling over her back. With a swipe of her tail, she smacked him against the mountainside. A curtain of rocks cascaded over his body in a rumbling landslide. A bright flash blew a thousand sparks into the air like the glowing ashes of a bonfire's blaze.

Billy sprinted to the pile of rocks heaped over Devin's body. Nothing moved. He hoisted Excalibur over his shoulder and retreated a few steps toward his companions.

The two dragons landed near the professor and Ashley. Bonnie flew over and joined them. Her feet settled softly in front of the great female dragon. She edged closer and gazed at the scaly, winged creature. "Mama? Is that you?"

Hartanna's coarse voice lowered to a dragon whisper. "Yes, I have been your mother. I am now Hartanna once again." The dragon sounded tired, yet sympathetic.

Bonnie blinked at her. "But are you my mother now?"

"For as long as I live." Hartanna extended her forelegs and let out a soothing rumble. "Come, dearest one. I have called your name for weeks, and at last you have arrived."

Bonnie threw herself into her mother's embrace and wrapped her arms around her as far as she could. Bonnie's entire body shook, trembling in rhythmic sobs. "Mama!" she cried. "I missed you so much!"

Hartanna rubbed Bonnie's shoulders with her forelegs. "And I missed you as well."

"But how did you become a dragon again?" Bonnie drew back and looked at Hartanna. "I thought you were dead."

354

"I was near death, a dragon's blink from eternity. But your father kept me alive, in a hospital for a while, at least that is what he told me. When he needed my blood for his experiments, he transported me to his lab. Some weeks after we arrived, he said I took a turn for the worse, and he thought I was dead. Then my body began a slow transformation. I grew in size, and dragon features replaced my human ones.

"While I was still small enough, he dragged me to the cave and chained me, fearing that I would become a powerful dragon again. Being kept in the dark and having my blood drained, I could not escape. I was given only the barest of lights, candles and fireflies, just enough to keep me breathing. I could barely speak. Groans became my prayers as I called for my daughter to come and find me."

The professor edged behind Bonnie. "And she was restored because of your faith, Miss Silver. The dragon shorn has new life."

When the professor spoke, Hartanna's eyes widened. She released Bonnie and took a step back. "Master Merlin!" She bowed low. "Your servant, Hartanna, awaits your bidding."

Clefspeare snorted a stream of hot gases. "I made the same mistake, Hartanna. This is Professor Charles Hamilton. He does resemble Merlin, to be sure."

The professor looked up at the male dragon. "And the mistake is yours again, Clefspeare, for Merlin has returned. The professor and Merlin are melded in this body. It is strange and unexpected, yet God's purpose will not be thwarted, as witnessed by your response to the summons."

"I did not wait for a summons. I left my cave soon after Billy did. It is a long journey from West Virginia, and I have only just now arrived."

"I am the one who responded," Hartanna said. "The quake shook loose my chains, and I received a sudden surge of strength. That is when I—"

An explosion rocked the mountain. Flaming, red boulders flew in all directions. The slayer emerged from the pile of rubble, huge and menacing, his glow pulsing. In a blind rage, he charged. Lightning bolts shot from his hands. One hit Ashley's arm, setting fire to her sleeve. Dr. Conner sprinted to her and batted the flames away.

Another bolt slammed into the ground near Billy's foot. Electricity surged through his toes and out the back, burning his heel. A third bolt struck Hartanna's flank. She roared, "Clefspeare, take flight. We must mount another attack."

The professor shouted, "No. He has mastered the lightning. If you fly, he will shoot you down. There is only one who can save us now."

Billy limped toward the slayer, his scorched shoe sticking to the stone floor like old chewing gum. *I hope he doesn't mean me. I don't think I can even save myself.*

Another bolt shot from the slayer's hand. It ripped into Dr. Conner's back and covered him with dancing arcs of electricity. He stiffened, then slumped to the ground.

"Daddy!" Bonnie ran to him, pivoted, and faced the approaching slayer, her wings spread to protect her father, Ashley, her grandfather, the professor, and Derrick.

Devin halted within reach of Bonnie, his two laser eyes focused on her. With one hand, he grabbed her around the waist and lifted her, crumpling her wings in his fingers. Billy hobbled forward and swung his sword against the slayer's leg with all his might. It cut halfway through, but the jolt of electricity shot Billy backwards, sending him skidding through the snow, the sword buzzing in his grip.

A sinister smile grew on Devin's electrified face. "My prophecy says that the mountains will glow with red when the host has ensnared the virgin bride, and darkness will envelop the skies." As he spoke, snow fell like furious clouds of freezing cotton. Lightning flashed red across the ink-black sky, and thunder boomed like a battalion of cannons.

Bonnie wiggled her arms free, then pounded her fists against the slayer's gripping fist. Flashing sparks shot across her skin and lit her face like an X-ray image. A moment later, she slumped over his fingers, her chest heaving.

The two dragons rose on their haunches, ready to attack. With his free hand, Devin sent a surge of lightning over their heads. "She's dead if you move. One squeeze, and your little princess bride will be no more."

Billy groped along the snow-covered floor and found his sword. After fumbling with the hilt, he struggled to his feet and stumbled toward the slayer, approaching him from behind. Excalibur, now dim and wet, felt cold and heavy in his grip. When he came within a few feet of striking distance, he regripped the sword and shouted, "Turn and face me, Devin!"

The slayer's head slowly rotated, and his yellow-green eyes blazed. "You have no weapons against me, you stupid child. Arthur and Merlin were powerless against me. Your father cowers in my presence. God Himself has blessed my might. Can't you see that a thousand years could not bring death to my door? Do you think your little blade can stop me now?" He waved his arms in the deepening gloom. "Look at the sky, fool. Darkness will overcome."

Billy raised his sword. Snow covered his hair. Cold wetness chilled his skin. His strength faltering and the sword seeming like an anchor, he clenched his teeth and looked at Bonnie. Seeing her trapped in the slayer's fist brought echoes of her prayer to mind. He spoke the words with a clear, loud voice. "Light and darkness can have no fellowship." He glared at the slayer. "God is light," he said, his voice booming, "and so am I!"

Excalibur's blade burst into glorious light. A blinding beam shot from its point and split the clouds. The moon shone through the hole, illuminating the entire mountain and casting a curtain of white light across the gaping cavern.

Strength surged through Billy's arms. He pulled Excalibur back and swung its beam through Devin's huge, electroplasmic head. The blade of light tore into his sparkling skull, slicing it from ear to ear. Devin's fingers flew open, and Bonnie's limp body plummeted into the snow.

Excalibur's wave of light enveloped the slayer's collapsing body and transformed him into a glowing mass of red sparks. The particles spun into a cyclonic whirlpool and zipped away into the darkness like a shimmering scarlet tornado.

The sword's beam died away. Billy dropped his weapon and shuffled to Bonnie. He scooped her into his arms and carried her to a mound of rocks where the professor and Ashley knelt next to Dr. Conner. Bonnie moaned as Billy gently lowered her and sat with her head resting on his chest.

Clefspeare blew rivers of fire across the ground and melted the snow. Hartanna beat her wings and scooted toward Bonnie. Her head drooped and her wings faltered as she skidded to her daughter's side. "Bonnie," Hartanna said weakly, "are you all right?"

Bonnie opened her eyes and grimaced. "I think so. I might have a broken wing. I'm not sure." Hartanna turned to Dr. Conner. "Matthew, are you hurt?"

There was no answer.

"Is he dead?" Hartanna asked.

Ashley nodded, sniffling, her contorted face fighting back a sob. "He ... he said, 'Tell Irene that ... that I'm sorry. I was a fool, just like she said so ... so many times.'"

"Perhaps I was too harsh." Hartanna let out a long sigh. "It is a sin to withhold forgiveness from a contrite soul. He who held me captive in darkness, clasped in cold cruel chains, taking my life's blood and with it all of my strength, I forgive with all of my heart."

Bonnie gazed at her dead father. Her lower lip quivered. Squeezing her eyes shut, she broke into tears and reached for Billy. He set a hand behind her head and held her close.

Walter shuffled into the circle, his good shoulder under Edward's arm as he helped him walk through the melting snow. "Our knights are all alive, but Addison is the only survivor of the conspirators. He'll freeze soon, though, if we don't—"

"Ahem," Sir Barlow interrupted, limping to join them. He held Excalibur over one of his broad shoulders. "I have supplied the scoundrel with a cape from one of the dead conspirators. No need to worry about him." He bowed and handed the sword to Billy. "I found this on the ground, Master William."

The professor rose and spread his arms, his own tears glistening in the bright moonlight. "We have witnessed a great tragedy." His voice sounded old as his trembling hands wiped moisture from his eyes. "A man has died, a father, a husband, a traitor reborn to become a defender of the innocent. His sacrifice will not soon be forgotten. Yet, we must move on. The schemes of the evil one have been thwarted, and there are now more dragons in our midst. There is reason to weep and reason to rejoice, but there is also much unfinished business."

359

"Yeah," Walter said. "Like, where's Karen?"

"And my mother," Billy added, shivering. "And where are the other girls?"

"Your mother and the girls are all together," Hartanna said. "Karen was unconscious, so I wrapped her in a blanket, carried her to your mother's vehicle, and left Karen in her care. I flew to Kalispell to find a hospital and then came back and led the way. I do not know her current condition."

Bonnie pulled away from Billy. "We have to go see her."

"Not until we examine your wing," Hartanna said. "We dragons have to tend our wings carefully."

The professor raised a hand to quiet the group. "The word of God has come to me, and I have already revealed the word to Ashley. She has accepted it, and I tell it now to the rest of you." Closing his eyes and lifting his hands toward the sky, the professor spoke in bright singsong.

> Robust and strong, a body's dream
> Can never last in earthly stream.
> In heaven's gates the faithful sing
> With youth forever in their wings.

As the professor looked at Billy, his eyes seemed older and wiser than ever before. "Billy Bannister. Come to me."

Billy rose and limped forward, dragging his injured foot, Excalibur again at his side. *It's Billy now? Not William?*

The professor continued, but his familiar accent vanished. "The hour has come, Billy. It is time for me to go. Raise the beam once again, and strike me with it."

HEAVEN'S GATES

Billy let Excalibur droop at his side. Had he heard the professor correctly? Strike him with it? "What are you talking
about, Prof?"

The professor's face tightened into a stern frown, and his
voice reverted to his usual, younger-sounding British accent.
"Listen to him, William. This is the word of truth. Do not
refuse a direct command." He pointed at the sword. "Excalibur
is not your source of strength. It is merely an extension of a
greater power. Will you trust that power to do good and not
evil in your hands?"

Billy's entire body trembled. His mentor had never steered
him wrong before, but a mistake now could cost the professor
his life. "If you say so." He lifted the sword again. The beam
burst forth through the tip in a rich shaft of ivory radiance,
reaching beyond the few remaining clouds. The professor took
a deep breath, closed his eyes, and folded his hands at his waist.

Billy flexed his arms and swung Excalibur's beam straight at him. The white laser passed through his tall frame, and a fountain of glittering light coated his body. Sparks jumped up, swirled in the sky, and hovered in a circling cloud of luminescence.

When Excalibur's beam faded, the professor wiped his brow, his lively voice returning. "Now that was quite an experience! I must say I never want to share my body with another mind, especially one as powerful as Merlin's. It's very confusing."

Bonnie pointed at the hovering haze of sparks. "Is that Merlin?"

The professor's wild hair blew around with the electrical swirl. "I do believe it is. He's waiting for the next step."

"The next step," Walter said. "What's that?"

The professor placed a hand on the wheelchair and turned toward Ashley. "It's time, Miss Stalworth. I don't know if your grandfather will be able to hear you, but do you have anything else you wish to say to him?"

Smiling weakly, Ashley shook her head. "We're both ready."

The professor took her grandfather's pale, limp hand and slid it under the coat that covered his body. As he set the hand in place, his brow arched. He reached farther and pulled a book from the inner pocket—Merlin's Diary.

The hovering cloud of energy swirled downward and enveloped the old book. In a burst of light, the book dissolved and melded with Merlin's glittering whirlpool. The cloud then descended on Ashley's grandfather, caught his body upward, and transformed it into its own shimmering swirl of light. The wheelchair sat empty on the ground with only the professor's coat hanging on the edge of the seat.

The new swirl settled around Ashley's head, bathing her face in dazzling glitter. She closed her eyes and smiled as if listening to a secret message. The swirl then followed Merlin's, and they made a quick circuit around the chamber before shooting into the sky like a pair of Roman candle bursts. When the glow faded in the distance, darkness descended once again on the cavern, leaving only Excalibur's corona lighting the area.

Billy set Excalibur's point on the ground. His foot ached, and stabbing pain ran up and down his spine. He arched his back, feeling it pop several times. "What just happened, Prof?"

"Merlin took Ashley's grandfather home." The professor retrieved his coat from the wheelchair and slipped it on. As he sighed, his breath poured out in a heavy stream of white. "This is the natural order of things. Life and death decisions are best left in God's hands."

Ashley stepped up to the professor and hooked her arm around his. "My grandfather spoke to me from that swirl of light. He said, 'I got my new body, Ashley. I can hardly wait to hear how well it can sing.'"

The professor patted the back of her hand. "An excellent farewell, to be sure."

Ashley crouched and set a hand on Derrick's shoulder. "Are you all right?"

"I am fine, and so is your grandfather. I heard him singing."

"Amazing Grace?"

He shook his head. "It was a new song, one I haven't heard before. If I can remember it, I'll sing it for you later."

"Yes, I hope you will." She kissed Derrick's forehead. "Thank you for loving him so well."

Bonnie sat cross-legged on the ground, her ragged, dirty robe covering her legs. Billy lowered himself slowly. Every muscle ached as he sat next to her. "This transluminating business really wears me out."

"How badly are you hurt?" Bonnie asked.

He raised a hand to his neck. "The cut isn't so bad. It's mostly my foot that hurts right now."

Ashley crouched at Billy's feet and began untying his mangled shoe. "Do you want me to have a look at it?"

Billy shook his head. "There are plenty of people here worse off than I am."

Walter plopped down on a stone next to Billy. "Yeah, my shoulder got zapped by that overgrown thunderstorm. I think everyone gave at least a little blood today."

Bonnie slid Ashley's sleeve up her arm. "Okay, sister, speaking of blood, what's the story with the photoreceptors?"

Ashley extended her arm and pulled Bonnie's next to hers. "I guess *sister* is right." She ran a finger across Bonnie's scars, then her own needle mark. "My grandfather told me that his daughter-in-law, my mother, was a dragon. I'll tell you the whole story later, but it seems that Devin killed my parents, and my grandfather altered my birth records to show that I was born to his son by a different woman. He decided the best place to hide me was right under Devin's nose, where he would least expect to find me, working with him and your dad."

When Ashley mentioned Dr. Conner, Bonnie's face turned downward. Ashley pulled her into her arms. "I'm so sorry about your father, Bonnie. I know how much pain he caused you, but at least he tried to defend us in the end."

Walter jumped to his feet and pointed at Ashley. "So you're a dragon, too? That's so cool! I have three dragons for friends!"

Ashley rose and joined him. "Anthrozils is what Doc called us. Fully human and fully dragon."

"Anthrozils?" Walter shook his head. "No way. *Dragons* sounds cooler."

A small shadow moved among the rocks by the old Alpha entrance. It scampered over a ridge that bordered the entire cavern like the rim of a coffee cup. Billy pointed toward another fleeing shadow. "Is that one of the chimps?"

Ashley scanned the ruined lab. "Could be. This is their home, so they'll come back when everything settles down. Maybe in the morning."

Billy pushed his sore heel back into his shoe and looked around the moon-bathed cavern. He spotted the professor near the old entrance to the boys' dorm examining a narrow gap in the cavern's wall. Billy rose to his feet and brushed away a trace of mud from his pant leg. "I'm sure we'll find the animals. I'll stay here and wait for the return of the chimps."

"Sounds like a horror movie," Walter said. "The sequel to Invasion of the Spider Monkeys."

Sir Barlow stepped forward. "I offer my services. My men require care, but I am relatively unharmed."

Clefspeare blew a fiery snort at an alcove in a stone wall. "I will keep this area warm for whoever wishes to stay, but I cannot provide food or medical care."

Ashley set a hand on one of the sheer walls. "It'll be tough scaling these hunks of granite. How're we going to get out of here?"

The professor edged his way into the gap in the wall. "We seem to have a new exit over here, but I have not decided on a Greek letter for its name."

Walter rubbed his belly. "How about *pi*? I could sure use some about now."

"Then *pi* it is." The professor leaned into the gap, his head disappearing from view. "It's a steep grade," he shouted, "but it seems that we can skirt the mountain and find where the Alpha entrance begins." He withdrew his head. "I can't be sure in this light."

Clefspeare unfurled his wings. "Whoever is not afraid to ride my back can take a shortcut to the top."

A new voice echoed across the cavern. "Hello down there!"

Billy swung his head upward. "Mom?"

Standing at the upper edge of the canyon, her hands on her hips, Mom scanned the scene, nodding once with each count of a loved one. "You guys really know how to throw a party, don't you?"

"Yeah," Walter said. "We gave Devin a going away party. It was a real blast!"

*   *   *   *   *   *

The dragons ferried Billy, Bonnie, Walter, the professor, Derrick, and the wounded knights to the top of the cliff where Billy's mother had parked the Jeep. Ashley and Barlow helped the chimps climb out the Pi entrance and up the steep slope. Rebecca emerged from the Jeep and played "monkey see, monkey do" with Betsy until the chimp tired of the game. When they all gathered, Billy hugged his mom and gave her a summary of what happened. Bonnie drew close and stood at Billy's side while he related the tale.

When Billy finished, the professor limped forward and braced himself on the Jeep's hood. "Marilyn, how is Karen?"

Mom smiled. "She's going to make it. The doctor seemed pessimistic at first, but that girl's got a fighting spirit in her. She lost a lot of blood, but she came through surgery fine." She pulled Rebecca close to her side and rubbed her shoulder. "I left Stacey and Pebbles with a security guard at the hospital, so I need to get back there soon."

"Yeah," Rebecca said. "We're going out to get the latest copy of Car and Driver so Karen'll have it when she wakes up."

366

Billy whispered into his mother's ear. "Remember what I told you about Sir Barlow?" He pointed at the knights as they sat or sprawled across the snow-covered grass.

She winked and cupped her hands around her mouth. "Which one of you is Sir Barlow?"

Sir Barlow rose, strode forward, and bowed low. "I am at your service, Madam."

She jerked her thumb toward the SUV. "I understand you've never ridden in a Jeep."

Sir Barlow stared at the vehicle, his eyes wide. "No. No, Madam. Indeed, none of us has."

"And have your men ever had a large pepperoni pizza?"

Barlow's smile grew so wide, his mustache lifted into his nose. He shouted at his knights. "Did you hear that, men? Pepperoni pizza!"

Mom motioned with her thumb again. "I can't fit all of your men, but if you'll come with me, we'll bring back enough pizza for everyone."

Walter pumped a fist. "Pizza! That's my kind of pi!"

Barlow climbed into the back of the Jeep while Billy nodded toward the cavern. "I forgot to mention. Dr. Conner's body is still down there."

Mom shook her head sadly as she looked at each bloody, dirty face and the torn shirts and jackets. She reached for Bonnie and hugged her close. "When I first saw Hartanna," Mom said, "she told me what she thought was happening, so I bought some first aid stuff on the way back. It's in the Jeep."

"Aw, we won't need it," Walter said, waving a hand. "What's a little blood?"

Mom pushed Bonnie out to arm's length and looked her over. "Bonnie will need it. She can't get treated at the hospital."

367

Hartanna doused Bonnie with a surge of warm breath. "I know how to treat her, but I will need human help."

Ashley ran her fingers across Bonnie's wounded wing. "I'm your girl. Just tell me what to do."

Mom dug for the keys in her coat pocket. "That's fine. I can't fit everyone in the Jeep anyway. I'll bring back food for those who are staying." She looked at Billy. "Are you coming?"

Billy scraped the toe of his shoe through the snow. "No, I'll stay here. There are quite a few dead bodies to take care of, including Palin's. And maybe Dad and I will get a chance to talk." He angled his head toward a boulder near the newly formed cliff. "He's over there keeping Derrick warm."

She nodded. "Then I think I can squeeze in one more. Professor? Ready for some pizza?"

"Yes," the professor replied. "Pizza sounds good. But could we have one with mushrooms instead of pepperoni?"

SONG OF THE BARD

Billy knelt in front of the fireplace in the crowded den and blew a stream of fire at the stack of kindling. Within seconds, the thin boards burst into flames. He plopped onto a green beanbag chair between two identical beanbags that held Bonnie and Walter.

Mom set two snack trays next to several empty glass bottles on the coffee table. "Anyone hungry?"

Walter's dad and the professor each filled a small plate with raw vegetables, crackers, cubes of cheddar cheese, and slices of meat. Walter lifted an entire tray, but a sharp look from his dad brought it back to the table. Walter settled for a heaping pile of meat, cheese, and chips, then slid back into his beanbag.

A loud clatter sounded at Walter's feet. Billy jumped up. "Walter, you kicked Excalibur."

Walter pulled his feet back. "Oops Sorry."

Billy retrieved the sword and leaned it against the sofa's end table. With his fingers on the hilt, Excalibur brightened the den, its silver blade reflecting every light in the room. Billy straightened the other items on the table, a clear plastic folder that held Bonnie's adoption papers, signed and sealed, and an ornate pen at its side. Next to the folder, Bonnie's journal lay open to the last chapter, her description of their latest adventures. Dirt smudged a few pages, literal evidence that it had been unearthed from the mountain quake it described.

Billy kicked Walter's socked feet. "Where's your mom?"

Walter kicked back, landing a blow on Billy's shin. "In the kitchen getting more food." Walter smirked. "Barlow and his knights act like they haven't eaten in over a thousand years."

"Yeah, well look whose plate's stacked higher than his nose." Billy kicked at Walter again, but Walter dodged. "What video did they decide on, Planet of the Apes or Braveheart?"

"You missed out on a good scrap while you were fetching the wood. Newman argued for the apes, but Barlow finally convinced the others to vote for Braveheart. Dad sent them down to the basement TV when Barlow got too loud with his color commentary."

Billy grabbed a poker and stirred the logs. The flames licked the firewood and blazed brightly. "Yeah, I'll bet he knows quite a bit about warfare."

Mr. Foley plowed a chip into a bowl of salsa. "Well, with you around, I guess I won't need to buy starter logs for a while."

"Yes," the professor added, taking a sip from a steaming cup. "I believe there could be many practical uses for young William's talents."

Walter grabbed a big handful of chips and winked at Billy. "And some not so practical."

"What?" Mom glared at Billy with a pretend scowl. "What are you up to, Mister?"

Billy raised his eyebrows innocently as he slid into his bean-bag. "Uh, fireworks, Mom. We were going to set off some fireworks. Right, Walter?"

"Yeah," Walter said, his mouthful of potato chips crumbling into his hand, "for the next celebration, when Ashley and Karen and the others come to stay."

Mrs. Foley walked in with a tray of buffalo wings and set it on the snack table. She took two wings, snuggled into her husband's lap, and handed one to him. "Carl, tell them what Fred said when you asked if Ashley could have a job."

The professor set his cup down. "Yes, Carl. Did he make her an offer?"

Mr. Foley chuckled. "Are you kidding? He offered her twice what I make. He took one look at Ashley's computer schematic, and he acted like a goof. He even danced a jig on top of his desk. And he sang a song that went something like, 'Watch out big boys, here comes Fred, the techno-mouse who's gonna roar!'"

371

Mrs. Foley stuffed a chicken wing into his mouth. Everyone laughed, even Mr. Foley as his face turned fire-alarm red.

The professor sat back and smiled as he sipped his tea. "So Miss Stalworth will build the next generation supercomputer."

Mr. Foley took a bite from his chicken wing. "Ashley *is* the next generation supercomputer. But, yeah, she's already got it all in her head. She could have made even more money in a bigger city, but she has certain people she wants to be close to." He winked at Bonnie.

Bonnie smiled. A thin chain now hung around her neck, a broken crystal dangling at the bottom—a fractured half of the candlestone. With the blinds closed, she had shed her backpack, but her wings stayed folded close to her body, a homemade bandage wrapping one of the outer mainstays. "Did Ashley say when she's coming?"

Mr. Foley nibbled a last bit of chicken and dropped the stripped wing on a plate at his side. "As soon as Karen's cleared to travel, probably next week. Fred was going to fly them here, but Ashley wants to drive."

The professor rose to his feet and limped to the center of the room. He set his cup on the coffee table and cleared his throat. "All is going well, my friends, and now that many secrets have been revealed, I must bring a few more items into the light."

"Like what, Prof?" Walter asked. "Is Billy going to translu-minate someone else?"

Billy kicked Walter again. "Just listen."

Smiling, Walter drew a halo over his head. "With angel ears."

The professor glared at the two boys before clearing his throat again. "As did Devin, I came to Castlewood in search of someone—he for a dragon, I for an heir. It is clear that we fulfilled our quest in the same person, William Bannister, for he and Bonnie are the keys to all the prophecies concerning the future of the dragon race."

Billy sneaked a look at Bonnie. Her eyes were focused on the floor, her cheeks turning red.

"You might have guessed by now that my appearance is remarkably similar to Merlin's. That's because I am his direct descendant. Also, because of my resemblance to an ancient sketch that the people of my order possess, I have actually been dubbed Merlin by the Steward of the Circle of Knights."

Walter wrinkled his nose. "The Circle of Knights?"

The professor placed his palm on his chest. "We are a pro-tectorate, six men of knightly ancestry who continue to meet without their king. One man, Sir Patrick, has been named steward until he passes away or is found unworthy, or until Arthur returns to take his place as the head of the Circle."

Walter's face brightened. "The return of the king to replace a steward? Sounds like Lord of the Rings, doesn't it? Like Aragorn returning to replace Denethor?"

"Not exactly, Walter. Yet, there are similarities. Although Aragorn is cast in the image of Arthur, our Sir Patrick is not the fool, Denethor, of Mr. Tolkien's wondrous epic. In any case, the return of Arthur has been awaited since long before Mr. Tolkien took up a pen, and the Circle will welcome the great event."

"What does this circle do?" Bonnie asked.

The professor shook his head. "I cannot say while all of you are present. I will tell William the details later."

Walter punched Billy's leg. "Why can you tell Billy and not the rest of us?"

"Because, he is the heir I have sought. We have believed that Arthur would return at our time of greatest need, and our peril is truly great. You see, we have an enemy, a group of seven called The New Table. They are a ticking time bomb, so to speak, that threatens not only England, but every man, woman, and child in the world. We believe that William is our only hope to defeat this menace."

The professor pulled Billy to his feet, then dropped to one knee before him, bowing his head. "I salute you, William, Guardian of the True Light. May your service be long and prosperous."

Billy blinked. "You think I'm Arthur?" He shook his head. "I'm no king."

The professor rose. "Arthur's rule and his return are symbolic of a deliverer, typifying the Christ. You will soon learn of your mission, and you must learn quickly. The date of destruction is set in stone, and it is fast approaching. Our enemies have not rested."

"Enemies?" Billy lifted a necklace of his own. The other half of the candlestone dangled at the bottom. "Didn't we get rid of Devin? The candlestone's powerless. What can they do?"

"Merlin told me of another vulnerability in dragons, and I can only assume from observing your behavior that you and Bonnie have both inherited it. Apparently, Devin knew of this weakness—although I call it a weakness only for lack of a better word—and he has used it to kill many dragons in the past. I will tell you about it in private when the time is right."

Billy tucked the gem behind his shirt. "But if Devin's gone, maybe the secret will die with him."

"Perhaps Devin is gone, but do you have his body? And what of Palin?"

Billy balled a hand into a fist. "Yeah, no one found Palin. There was too much rubble where I dragged him."

"And there are more like him. Although Devin was not one of the seven in The New Table, he was their assassin, the cruel mind who commanded their violent activities. The claws and tail contain the poison of this beast, and there is yet another enemy who influences their minds, more cruel and sinister than Devin, a creature whose name I will not utter here."

Billy took a deep breath and exhaled heavily. "So what do I have to do?"

The professor withdrew a folded sheet of paper from his pocket and handed it to Billy. "I request that you come with me to England to meet Patrick and take on your mission."

"England!" Walter said. "Cool!"

Billy unfolded the page, a printout of an airline reservation. He refolded it and looked at the professor. "How about Walter and Bonnie? Can they come, too?"

"We must first go alone and meet the Circle. After I explain your mission, it is essential that Bonnie come to help you. Her place in the prophecy is vital. Regarding Walter, I will have to ask Patrick if he will be allowed to join you."

"What about Barlow and his knights? Are they part of this mission? They can't live in the Foleys' basement forever." Billy smirked. "That Braveheart video won't last a thousand years."

The professor smiled and laid a hand on Billy's back. "William, with your addition, the Circle will possess seven members. There are no other seats available. But our order will require the services of brave soldiers. Again, these assignments will be up to you, but Barlow and company are courageous and loyal men, true, authentic knights. As Merlin, your trusted adviser, I will likely make application for them, and they will be tested to prove their worth."

375

"And what about the dragons?" Billy asked. "Clefspeare and Hartanna."

The professor withdrew his hand and stepped back. "I can tell you this, William. If not for dragons, you would never succeed in your mission. Their role could make all the difference."

The professor's eyes mellowed into two aging oracles, as if they had seen hundreds of battles, scores of earthquakes, and even the changing of the guard in heaven. "Merlin has left me with many of his thoughts, William, as though I have retained his memories and learned his prophecies. In the light of his remaining flame, I see villains, ambushes, and tortures. Great danger is in your path."

He pulled a handkerchief from his pocket and wiped his brow. "There is also another prophecy I can share with you now. It was in the diary, and Merlin has somehow burned it indelibly in my memory. I will sing it, but do not bother to ask its meaning. As yet, I have no idea. I assume, however, that its message will become clear and helpful as we journey into our new adventure."

After clearing his throat once more, he sang with a rich, sweet tenor, like a prophetic bard of old.

> With sword and stone, the holy knight,
> Darkness as his bane,
> Will gather warriors in the light,
> Cast in heaven's flame.
>
> He comes to save a remnant band,
> Searching with his maid,
> But in a sea of sadness finds
> His warriors lying splayed.
>
> A valley deep, a valley long,
> Lay angels dry and dead.
> Now who can wake their cold, stone hearts,
> Their bones on table spread?
>
> Like wine that flows in skins made new,
> The spirit pours out fresh.
> Can hymns of love bring forth the dead
> And give them hearts of flesh?
>
> O will you learn from words of faith
> That sing in psalms from heaven,
> To valley floors where terrors lurk
> In circles numbering seven?

Billy shook his head. This was just too much to take in all at once. He had already been through a bloody battle. The professor just piped this weird new song that made no sense at all. And now he was supposed to be a deliverer? "What's next, Prof?"

"Only to say whether or not you will go with me. I guarantee nothing save that your trials are not complete."

Billy unfolded the printed page and stared at it. The professor really meant for him to fly to England. He had never been so serious before, so solemn. Was he afraid? And that song. Scary stuff. He looked at his mother and took in her worried expression. What was she thinking? She was proud of him, but should he go halfway around the world chasing after the professor's dream? Yet, he couldn't ask her. That wouldn't be fair.

Walter's ever-present smile faded. With a tight jaw and clenched fist, he gave Billy a firm nod. Bonnie, on the other hand, beamed like the glory of the rising sun. Having faced her greatest fears, she came out of the darkness to find her mother, whom she had sought through pain and tears. Billy also found a beacon in the darkness—the light that radiated in Bonnie's spirit—and she had shown him the way to its source. Now that light burned within his own heart more fervently than any dragon's fire. What could he do but pour it forth, shining his light down whatever path he might be called?

Billy folded the page and slid it into his pocket. "I'll do it."

Bonnie and Walter jumped to their feet. Bonnie gave him a warm embrace. "Trust in the Lord with all your heart," she whispered as she drew away.

Walter clapped him on the back. "You'd better learn to speak their language before you go. You won't even be able to find a bathroom if you don't learn to say water closet."

Mom gave him a hug. "I'm sure the professor will help him with the culture, Walter. If the professor is any indication, Billy will be among the finest of gentlemen."

A door slammed. A line of men tromped into the room from the basement stairwell. With a bag of potato chips in one hand and the cat, Gandalf, cradled in his arm, Sir Barlow led the way. Newman followed, his face buried in a National Geographic magazine, and Edward marched behind him, playing a high note on a trumpet. The three others brought up the rear, each wearing seventies era leisure suits, Fiske in Creamsicle orange, Standish in Avocado green, and Woodrow in electric grape.

"Yes," Mr. Foley said, his head shaking. "Real gentlemen."

"We found a fascinating little room," Barlow said as he halted, "packed with boxes marked Goodwill. If these boxes are filled with goodwill, I thought, it should permissible to investigate their contents. I was surprised to see this assortment of oddities." He handed Gandalf to Billy. "Your cat, sir, has taken quite a liking to me. Perhaps he thinks I am his pajamas."

Billy took the purring cat. "You mean Gandalf thinks you're the cat's pajamas?"

Barlow wiggled his mustache, a crimson blush creeping into his cheeks. "That's what I said, isn't it?"